THE LIST KEEPERS

THE LIST KEEPERS

JUSTAR JOURNAL BOOK THREE

BRANDT LEGG

LAUGHING RAIN

The List Keepers (Justar Journal Book Three)
v2

Published in the United States of America by Laughing Rain

Cataloging-in-Publication data for this book is available from the
Library of Congress.
ISBN-13: 978-1-935070-16-0
ISBN-10: 1-935070-16-9

Cover designed by: Jarowe and Eleni Karoumpali

BrandtLegg.com

This book is dedicated to Teakki and Ro

CHAPTER ONE

Monday, July 11, 2101

The AOI Chief had issued the execution order twenty-four hours after Ander Terik's death had been broadcast around the world via the Field. If she could have, she would have issued a second one for Lance Miner, the PharmaForce CEO who'd killed Terik, but he had too many friends on the A-Council. For now, just the one for Miner's former protégé and her former AOI Pacyfik Region Head, Polis Drast, would have to do.

That didn't mean Miner was out of trouble. She'd launched two separate investigations, one into the entire Ander Terik affair, ending with his untidy death at the hands of the PharmaForce CEO, and another into the specific connections and relationships among Terik and Drast, and Drast and Miner. The latter had been the subject of a previous investigation, but in light of recent events, the Chief decided she was no longer satisfied with those earlier, benign results.

"I swear I will kill that woman!" Miner shouted to his assistant, Sarlo.

The Rocky Mountains, visible from the massive windows on the top floor of the Denver PharmaForce building, were bathed in alpenglow. The dramatic view calmed her in the face of the greatest tirade she'd ever seen from her boss. There would be a chance to help him see the strategic benefits present in this problem, but for now, silence seemed imperative, dutifully serving as a surrogate for the real focus of his rage.

"If I don't kill her, she'll wish I had once I finish with her. I'll take her career, her identity, I'll banish her to sewage monitor in Bangladesh! Damn her for sending investigators in here. My family *built* the Aylantik! I'm on the torgon Council!"

Miner would have been more than just "on" the Council. If it hadn't been for Drast's betrayal, he would have been its Chairman.

Sarlo had not berated him for leaving her behind when he went to meet Grandyn Happerman, aka Ander Terik. If she had been there, she liked to think that it would have gone differently. Perhaps Grandyn would have talked, or he would have been held, maybe even turned over to the AOI, but Miner had wanted it all for himself. The glory, the information, the power, he couldn't bear sharing it with the AOI, or even Sarlo. He also knew she'd never have approved of his tactics, which was absolutely true. She understood how he worked, and agreed with his motives, but it frustrated her that Miner didn't realize that he was at his best with her.

Sarlo knew his anger was reserved not only for the AOI Chief. He was equally furious at Drast, Blaze, and Chelle Andreas, all of whom he believed had elaborately orchestrated his public humiliation. Most of all, Miner was outraged at himself for falling into their web. He'd been so desperate to win, but, blinded by his competition with Deuce Lipton, he had missed the real enemy. In all the years he'd been fighting against the war, he had failed to realize that the rebels weren't just seeking to overthrow the Aylantik for the sake of power, or even simply to effect change. Now he knew that the revolution *mattered* to these people. They were discontented, they felt oppressed, they'd been wronged. And that realization, that he was fighting people fueled by passion, terrified him.

"They aren't ever going to stop . . . they'll keep coming until they win," he whispered.

Sarlo heard him and took the opening. "There are many ways to win," she said. "For them, and for us."

Grandyn Happerman, long at the center of the storm, was now dead, at least to those who had spent years relentlessly pursuing him. Fye looked at his serene, yet troubled face, even at "death," and smiled the beautiful smile of relief. The kind that comes only when the brutal weight of fear has been lifted.

"We're free," she said. "We're at least a little free." Fye patted her belly, four months pregnant with their child. "Grandyn Happerman is dead." She laughed with the words – simultaneously nervous and joyous.

The two of them were in a small safe house near Mount Shasta, in the California Area. They couldn't stay long but, for now, it gave them a rare sense of normalcy.

"For now," Grandyn replied. "But there are no secrets in the Aylantik. Deuce and Munna know I'm alive, Drast knows, Nelson and Chelle . . . that's a lot of people. The AOI will discover it soon enough. And then there's Blaze. He may already be peddling the information to the highest bidder."

"But there are secrets," she said.

"Sure, there are plenty of secrets, but none long kept. And a secret told changes to something else. It becomes a danger."

"There are secrets long kept," she said. "I'm one of them."

"The List Keepers?"

"Yes."

"But even the List Keepers are rumored to exist. People know about them, they just haven't proved it yet."

"List Keepers are more secret than that. Whether we exist or not isn't the real question. List Keepers are actually more secret than secrecy itself." She put her hand on her belly.

He looked at her. "Tell me."

"You know I want to, and I will, but I can't yet." Her lips pursed and her eyes darkened.

"Why not?" he asked, so tired of the mystery. "We're going to have a baby, we're in love, we're building a life together . . . and all that has to start with trust."

His hurt look tugged at Fye, but the loyalties to the List Keepers had been present since birth, bred into her. "I can't, but I will," she repeated, giving him a pleading look. "This is not something I can tell you, it's something I have to show you . . ." Her gaze was drawn to an open window and the trees that stood strong, as if guarding them. *Always the trees,* she thought.

"When?" Grandyn asked.

"We'll go there together."

"To the city?"

"Yes, as soon as I get approval."

"Approval? Is that going to be a problem?"

"No, you're Grandyn Happerman. They'd probably invite you even if you weren't with me."

"Do they know Grandyn Happerman isn't really dead?"

"The List Keepers know *everything*."

CHAPTER TWO

For eight days, Munna had held the INUs dark so that the *Justar Journal* could not be read. She and the prophecies remained on Runit Island, but they might as well have not existed.

Deuce had tried everything he knew to overcome her mysterious ability to block the prophecies. He even attempted to run the programs on systems in other parts of the world, but nothing worked. At one point he had her moved away from the books and temporarily held on his Seattle Office Campus, but it made no difference, so he returned her to Runit Island where he believed she'd be safer.

All during that time, the two last "chapters" of the prophecies continued to scramble. The digital characters rolled through a seemingly endless and completely random sequence as if looking for a code to lock into. Or, as Deuce had come to believe, they were acting as a reminder of what power lay behind the screens, and to the control Munna wielded.

Throughout those same days, Chelle had been negotiating and arguing with Deuce for Nelson's release. She had demanded that he share the *Justar Journal*.

"That's up to Munna now, isn't it?" Deuce responded in their latest volley, after Chelle had threatened to make his life difficult. She hadn't forgotten that Deuce was the wealthiest person on earth, with the second largest army, and now in possession of the prophecies, but Chelle was not without assets and leverage of her own. She had the ability to disrupt the world at any time with the spark of revolution or guerrilla attacks. And, although Chelle and Munna had never been close, after the events on Runit Island during the decoding and with Nelson's connection to Cope, Chelle might have a better chance of convincing Munna to release the INUs so they could start running the prophecies again.

"Do I need to remind you that I have intimate knowledge of the AOI?" Chelle said, speaking from an undisclosed location.

"You don't need to remind me that you have *intimate* knowledge of a great many things. You are well known for your *intimate* work," Deuce said sarcastically while staring at the stars on the ceiling of his private study. They made it seem as if he were viewing the night sky from one of his space stations.

"I can cause you many problems," she said, choosing to ignore his cheap shot.

"Your threats are amusing, Chelle." Deuce knew more about the inner workings of the AOI than she did. Plus, PAWN still relied on Deuce for a significant portion of its funding. "With the world so close to war, are you really willing to lose my backing?"

"If PAWN gets the prophecies, we can win the revolution *without* your help."

"Maybe, but what if the *Justar Journal* shows that I'm the only hope PAWN has to defeat the AOI?" Deuce asked.

"Then you'll not be able to avoid your destiny."

"Destiny?" His brown eyes hardened. He didn't want to continue trading barbs with her. Even if he didn't believe in destiny as a metaphysical concept, he knew his grandfather had been powerful enough and would have given enough forethought to Deuce's life so that his destiny might have been arranged. "Anyway, we're wasting our time arguing. You should be talking with Munna."

"She's still refusing to speak to me, but Nelson is working on it."

Deuce had also considered releasing Nelson, knowing he would be pushing his sister's agenda and trying to secure Munna's cooperation for PAWN, but the prophecies needed to be unlocked, whether it was to Deuce or to Chelle.

"I would never underestimate your brother."

Deuce had his own inroad to the old woman. Twain, whom Munna loved, and whom was now recovered enough to start spending time with her. Unfortunately, all he wanted to do was go back to the redwoods.

"Can I come to the island?" Chelle asked.

"Of course," Deuce said, not sure he would let her leave. "Although the AOI has agents everywhere. I would think that leaving the POP is too risky, even borderline crazy." POPs, or PAWN Operational Pods, normally located underground were the rebels greatest strategic asset. Hundreds of the facilities— containing weapons, communications and monitoring equipment and personnel— were concealed in critical areas around the globe.

"I know, that's what my generals say. But thank you for allowing it. I'll come as soon as it's safe." Her frustration had reached an insanity-inducing level. They had the prophecies, but couldn't read them. Drast was alive, but sentenced to die in a matter of days. The war she'd always fought for was possibly hours away, but her coalition was deteriorating. "Damn it Deuce, find a way to fix this," she barked, and ended the zoom.

Nelson had tried to reason with Munna every day since the show-down with Deuce started, but this was the first time she had cried.

"What is it?" he asked in his most tender voice. Nelson had not been pressing her too hard, only saying that the prophecies could save lives when tears began to stream from her eyes.

"Lives . . . too many will be lost. The war is coming . . . I have not stopped it."

"You mean you can still see the prophecies?"

She nodded slowly.

"How?"

She motioned to the two monitors, which remained lit as if that would answer his question. But all he saw was what had been there for more than a week: millions of ever-changing alphabet letters running across the screen appearing to be participants in a race for confusion.

"What?" he tried again, shaking his head at the AirViews.

"We've lost . . . we've lost, we've lost," she said in a voice so sad his own eyes watered.

"I'm sorry Munna. I don't understand."

"No one does," she whispered.

Across the short distance of water that separated Runit and Ryder Islands, Deuce secretly watched the conversation between Munna and Nelson. The revelation that she could still see the prophecies caught him by surprise, but her tears concerned him.

This woman was one hundred thirty-three. She had seen it all. Deuce couldn't imagine anything to make a person like that break down.

What are you seeing that is so upsetting? he wondered. *War? That can't really be so shocking to you. The miracle is that the war hasn't happened sooner.*

"You have to tell me," Nelson said. "Munna, please. Cope told me there were things worse than the Banoff. Is that what you saw?"

She stared blankly at the two scrambling AirViews and then to the other six dark ones. Nelson wondered if she was considering bringing them back to life.

"Show me," he said, gently touching her hand. She jolted and turned toward him.

"It's too late," she said in a voice filled with despair.

"The prophecies can change, right?" Nelson asked. "Tell me what you saw. We can change it."

"I saw the end," she said quietly. "The cruelty of it. I saw the end."

"But—"

"The end allows for no compromise. The only thing left at the end is the lonely truth."

CHAPTER THREE

The AOI Chief looked over another string of reports. "Grandyn Happerman is finally, really, completely dead," she said to an aide. "This time it was him."

Although she'd have felt much better with a body, there really was no room for any doubt. It was an embarrassing story, and she skimmed the final draft of what she would present to the Council on the matter.

Grandyn Happerman, son of two revolutionaries, Harper and Runit Happerman, had sought to avenge his parents' deaths, at the hands of the AOI, by infiltrating the agency and destroying it from within while aiding in the revolution to overthrow the Aylantik. His identity had been switched so completely in their internal systems that, without the aid of cosmetic surgery or any physical transformations beyond a haircut, he was able to become a fictitious person known as Ander Terik. Although Grandyn/Terik attended an AOI training academy, everything prior to that was a complete fabrication. Investigations were still underway as to how he had been able to change all the photographic, optic, fingerprint, and DNA identifications within the AOI and Aylantik systems and create the new Terik identity, but early indications pointed to a group the AOI knew almost nothing about: the List Keepers.

She paused at that point in her reading, anticipating the questions the Council would hurl at her about the List Keepers, none of which she could answer. At least, not yet. In that case, she would answer with more questions about Lance Miner's involvement, how he came to uncover Grandyn/Terik, and how the bigger and more disturbing investigations into Miner and Drast would, hopefully, bring many more answers.

"Grandyn Happerman is dead," she repeated. "That should be enough. Move on. Much more to do."

The aide looked unsure whether to continue questioning.

"Peace prevails, always," the Chief hissed under her breath.

"Won't they question you about not having Grandyn's body?" the aide asked.

"All Grandyn sightings ceased as soon as the death of Ander Terik was broadcast," she answered. "Lance Miner confirmed it before he killed him. We've back-traced several of Terik's movements. It *was* Grandyn. The rebels would not have risked so much to rescue him, if it had not been him. Even once they knew he was dead, they continued to be sure we did not get his body. His mind was too valuable."

"So the world thinks their beloved PharmaForce CEO killed Ander Terik, a rogue AOI agent . . ."

"Yes," the Chief said absently, as she scanned incoming reports. "They never knew who Grandyn Happerman was, so the rebels' plan to discredit Miner, and us, by broadcasting Terik's execution, didn't have the desired effect."

The aide smiled, knowing this was one of the good points.

"I go before the Council in an hour. I think we have everything."

"Will Miner be there?"

"No. It's a special committee."

"I'm sure they'll see it your way," the aide said.

"There is no other way to see it," she replied, not looking up, dismissing her aide with a flick of her hand.

The A-Council Special Committee consisted of three men and two women linked across a Field-View conference. After curt introductions, the questioning began. As expected, they asked about the List Keepers first, which the Chief deflected with the promise of details to follow, while shifting quickly to Miner.

"Miner may be connected to the secretive group, which is part of our wide-reaching investigation into his affairs."

"Why isn't Lance Miner a hero?" the Chairman asked. "He killed Grandyn Happerman, one of the five-most-wanted."

"The world may believe he's a hero because he stopped a turncoat AOI agent, but we know what really happened. So, Mr. Chairman, I'll tell you why Lance Miner is *no* hero. He didn't report the killing, and he isn't saying how he found out that Grandyn Happerman and Agent Ander Terik were one and the same. We still have unanswered questions about Miner's involvement with Drast, especially since Terik was also connected to Drast and visiting him in prison."

"He may have a reasonable explanation for all of that."

"Yes, and it may be a lie. And, as you are aware, Miner's Enforcers engaged our troops in the Amazon. The man is as big a threat as the rebels."

"Wait a minute. I'm not Miner's biggest fan, and I know he can be abrasive and unorthodox in his approach to world security matters, but he's more committed to peace than anyone I know," the Chairman said.

"He is also a descendent of the founders," another committee member added. "As well as head of the biggest and most important pharmaceuticals responsible for incredible advances in healthcare that has saved countless lives and continues to prolong the life expectancy of all of us."

A third member interjected, "And Lance is a member of this council. Your comments are out of line. Perhaps he is aggressive and ambitious, but, Chief, remember that you technically work for him. You should be careful."

"I'm doing my job," the Chief said, glaring into the screen. "If you are not happy with my performance, release me. Otherwise, Mr. Chairman, members of the committee, I expect to be free to run this agency as I see fit."

"You have a certain latitude," the Chairman replied, "but let me remind you that you have essentially only two duties. Keeping us happy, and keeping the peace."

The Chief nodded once. "The two are indelibly linked."

"There can be no war," the Chairman said sternly.

"If there is a war, I will stop it," the Chief said. "And by stop it, I mean win it."

"There can be *no* war," the Chairman repeated.

"Peace prevails, always," the Chief said, concluding the zoom.

CHAPTER FOUR

"What to do?" Blaze asked, mostly to himself, as his round table convened. "What to do?"

He'd been studying simulations and probability models all morning. The war seemed inevitable now, with a ninety-eight-point-seventy-six percent chance to begin within the next forty-eight hours. The scenarios had also changed. No longer was it most likely that PAWN would ignite the storm, but rather an unknown group the DesTIn artificial intelligence program labeled X08, but that Blaze suspected were the Trapciers. He simply wasn't sure and, therefore, even less certain whether or not to bring it up with the knights.

Morholt, a CHRUDE, studied him. "Blaze, the war began long ago. Violence is but a stage, part of the definition that satisfies politicians and military leaders, but the semantics of reality are often a very different thing from what we think we know."

"And which side are the CHRUDEs on?" Blaze asked.

Morholt looked to Bors, and then to the other CHRUDEs. "As always, we are on the side of logic."

Blaze laughed at this. Although the answer made him slightly uncomfortable, he hid it well. "And the Imps?" he asked, looking toward Galahad.

"War, Blaze, you must understand, is not of our making . . . it is the Traditionals who have wrought this barbarism," Galahad replied with a look of disappointment.

"So are you going to start the war?" Blaze asked.

"As I told you," Morholt said. "It has already begun."

"Yes, you did. I'll rephrase then. Are you going to begin the violent stage?"

"Galahad, perhaps you'd like to handle that one," Morholt said smoothly.

"So the Imps and CHRUDEs are working together?" Blaze asked rhetorically. "That brings me to my next conclusion . . . you are the Trapciers."

"Yes, on both counts," Galahad said. "As for your first question, we would rather not get into specifics as to when things will start."

The "smart" table ran through a series of view transformations, showing the implant process Imps go through and the technical make-up of CHRUDEs. As the topic shifted, so did its displays. The lighting in the room also adjusted accordingly.

"And what are your aims?" Blaze asked, trying to mask his urgent concern.

"We are looking for a correction," Galahad answered, moving his hand so that the giant, round table projected images in front of them. It was mostly Seeker footage, showing people shopping, watching sports, movies, touring the Field, attending parties, and working. "Do you realize that this is primitive behavior?"

"Of course I do," Blaze said, as the trivial habits and actions of society played out in front of them.

Pre-Banoff images of wars, genocide, oil drilling, mining, pollution, extinctions, mass production and consumerism, replaced the shoppers and watchers.

"A waste of time, and I'm not talking about hours, months, or even lifetimes," Galahad said. "Traditionals aren't even close to fulfilling their potential . . . humans have been acting like children for more than thirty thousand years."

"Agreed," Blaze said. "But *war*? Is that something enlightened entities such as yourselves would resort to in order to effect change?"

"War is merely a tool," Morholt said. "You have been playing the game yourself, Blaze."

True. Blaze had been working all the sides in the conflict, but his aims were far different from those he feared the Trapciers had. The Imps and the CHRUDEs didn't even like each other, but they possessed an arrogance of intelligence that Blaze understood very well.

The Trapciers had somehow appointed themselves rectifiers of millennia of human folly. CHRUDEs were one thing, because they had no access to a higher consciousness, but the Imps surely had loftier ideas. Oddly, at that moment, Blaze thought of a long-banned book, *Animal Farm* by George Seeker.

"What happens if you win?" Blaze asked, looking directly at Galahad.

"Change." The images above the tables instantly darkened and were replaced by abstract patterns of light and stars. "Things they can't even begin to imagine."

CHAPTER FIVE

Munna and Nelson strolled in the warm summer air, cooled by a northwesterly breeze coming in off the ocean. Worn stone paths snaked across the island, which had otherwise grown wild with blackberries and fern. Munna liked to get out of the building as much as possible, but even when she was walking the paths, all but the scrambling AirViews back inside the building remained blank.

"Munna, if the war is imminent, then you *must* open the *Justar Journal* for us," Nelson pleaded.

Deuce, still able to monitor them from any spot on the island, was silently pleading from his star room, while at the same time directing BLAXERs to pull out of the Amazon. He'd decided to leave only a small force in the jungle. All indications pointed to hostilities breaking out in the northern Pacyfik and Aylantik regions. Deuce feared they were only days away. Controlling events in peacetime was difficult enough, but with a world at war, anything might happen.

"Nelson, you need to understand what is at stake. You and your PAWN compatriots have, from the beginning, had a single goal, and that was to overthrow Aylantik. This has always been an empty endeavor." She stopped and looked at a flock of seagulls circling off the rocky coast. Nelson followed her gaze and worried they were mimic-drones, while Munna could tell they were simply seagulls.

"But you can't condone allowing Aylantik to stay in power? The AOI is a dark force in the world."

"Of course I don't approve of the AOI." She shook her carved cane. "But their time will pass . . . it already has passed. They are no longer in existence, don't you see? We just haven't caught up to that reality yet."

"I have a hard time with concepts like that," Nelson admitted.

"It's why I took you to live and learn with Cope. You need to understand how the universe works. Our perception is so limited."

"Your perception is excluded from that statement, I assume."

"Oh, I'm no higher being. I just work at looking a lot harder than most. Anyone could see what I see, do what I do, live as long as I do." She looked at him, her bright eyes showing excitement. "It's all there for everyone, it's all possible, but this war can destroy us."

"But we can win."

"I have told you, wars are *never* won. It is impossible!" She walked off to the ocean and stared out to the horizon. The sky was gray, and it met a calm gray sea at a place where it became difficult to tell the two apart. Only a tiny sailboat, far in the distance, gave any definition or perspective to the view.

"Please, Munna," he said joining her. "Tell me what you've seen."

"The Aylantik is nothing. The AOI doesn't matter. Your revolutionaries are pursuing the wrong cause. Your every premise is incorrect. This war isn't about who will rule the world, or who wronged whom. It is about the survival of the species. The planet will go on without humans."

He stared at her, speechless, because he believed her. In the years he'd known Munna, he'd developed an absolute awe toward her. She conveyed a presence of knowing beyond all doubt and wasted no words. Munna had an aura of wisdom so vast, one felt a connection to all knowledge when in her presence.

"How does it happen?"

"While we fight among ourselves, distracted by our greed and selfishness, confused by our fear and lust, the machines we created, to make our lazy lives simpler, will destroy us."

"What machines?"

"Do you recall a person who called you 'Baker-Boy'?"

He looked at her, momentarily surprised.

"Don't say the person's name," Munna warned quickly. "You must leave this island immediately and contact that person. Do it from a place where you cannot be monitored."

Nelson looked around as if to ask if they were being listened to right now.

She nodded. "Now go!"

"But I don't want to leave you here under house arrest," he said, then added, while still looking around, "under surveillance."

"Don't worry about me. Deuce only thinks he knows the right thing to do, but he is a Lipton, and I believe that, in the end, he will do the right thing. He will learn soon enough." She stopped to watch a seagull land nearby.

"How?"

"There are generally three ways to learn: from experience, from the elders, and from the children. Deuce is about to get a full dose of all three." She looked directly into an impossible-to-see nano-camera, recording them from twenty meters away, and smiled.

Deuce pushed back against his chair as if someone had thrown something at him. "How do you do it?" he whispered, almost expecting Munna to answer.

"Is it really possible that humans will be wiped out?" Nelson asked. "I mean, how can it all just end? We're too advanced to allow that to happen."

"Advanced? Don't you understand Nelson? We are lost. Our people, the human race, we are wandering aimlessly through the cosmos without a clue as to who we are, where we came from, or what we're supposed to be doing. We know *nothing*."

CHAPTER SIX

Zaverly, the olive-skinned beauty, had personally pleaded with Parker Randolph to be reassigned to the Oregon area. The tough and athletic TreeRunner had been a decorated and heroic fighter in one of the most active areas of the near-war era, in the section of the Amazon that had seen the majority of the action.

Parker was actually happy to move her into an area where most believed the war would start. Zaverly was considered one of the group's best candidates to lead the TreeRunners combat contribution to the PAWN army. Parker reviewed the file and noted that Zaverly had seen several people close to her killed, including a Grandyn stand-in, but she had recommendations from every superior she'd served under, and more commendations than any other living TreeRunner. It was an easy decision as Parker entered the approval into her INU, completely unaware that Zaverly blamed two people for the death of the man she loved and sought revenge with every breath she took.

She'd been a TreeRunner since the age of five, having grown up in the lush forests of the old Virginia Area of the Aylantik region. She'd landed in the Amazon because it was the most important front of the unfought war. For Zaverly, it hadn't just been the chance to work with Grandyn and build a force and strategy against the AOI, but to also defend the greatest forest on Earth, that drew her to volunteer for the assignment. The Amazon, and its outposts, had become a collection of Creatives, Rejectionists, PAWN rebels, and TreeRunners, and now the entire Amazon-zone had been infiltrated with AOI and private mercenaries working for Deuce Lipton and Lance Miner. She could have led her side to victory, if the higher-ups would have let her make the decisions, instead of forcing her to follow orders.

"It's a torgon chess match down here," she had told Beckett, the real name of the man she loved who had been killed posing as, and protecting, Grandyn. "They're all afraid to start the real fight so we're left to these skirmishes in the trees that just make us bleed to death slowly."

But now Beckett was dead, and she'd left the Amazon behind, a place she knew she would always miss.

The Amazon felt more like home to her than the Virginia Area forests where she had grown up. Something about the way the South American jungle was a world unto itself, the impenetrable nature of the thick lush foliage made her feel safe.

As a young TreeRunner, at age fourteen, she'd been on a clan week-out, a TreeRunner survival trip where groups of five Tree-Runners spent a week deep in the forest alone. They wound up not far from a major AOI base and training center. On their fourth night, they ran into a unit of twelve rookie AOI agents who were doing their own wilderness training.

The AOI agents had been drinking, which unleashed a violent rampage. They raped Zaverly and the two other girls, aged sixteen and eighteen, and beat one of the boys until he was barely conscious. Then, finally, they raped the second boy, aged thirteen. It took an extra day for the battered TreeRunners to make it back. The crimes were immediately reported, but nothing was ever done. The only person she hated more than the grunge who raped her, was Grandyn.

Zaverly landed in Willamette Mandated Forest with two things on her mind: how to kill Parker Randolph slowly, and how to kill Grandyn, the real Grandyn Happerman, painfully. But she knew it would take time, so she began to blend in with her new units and learn the forest.

These were Grandyn's forests. He'd grown up in them, but they were strangely similar to the Virginia Area forests, and it wouldn't take her long to know them by heart. Zaverly had a way of memorizing trees, noticing the subtlest parts of undergrowth, the contours of the land, and even the color and patterns of bark.

Based on her record in the Amazon, Parker made Zaverly a commander with twenty TreeRunners reporting to her. Once she learned the area, that number would triple. War was coming, and the rebels owned the forests. The AOI had proven they could make things as difficult as they had in the Amazon, but with a full uprising, they didn't have the resources to take all the forests in the world. If war broke out, it could last a very long time.

As a commander in Grandyn's home region, she believed the chances were high that she would get to meet him. It was a well-known secret among the TreeRunners that the real Grandyn was still alive. The AOI, Enforcers, BLAXERs, and PAWN had been looking for Grandyn for three years and he had so far escaped. But *she* would get him.

She looked into the darkest part of the forest, where the trees grew so close the sun hadn't found the ground there in decades. Then she whispered to the tree gods, "Grandyn may seem invincible to the rest of the world. No one else has been able to find him. He may have eluded the others . . . but Grandyn Happerman hasn't ever had me hunting him. Never before has he had to escape another TreeRunner."

CHAPTER SEVEN

Tuesday July 12

The Aylantik World Premier, a slim man who looked more like an accountant than a politician, addressed the world from the Aylantik capital about the Terik affair for a second time since the worldwide broadcast across the Field regarding the AOI agent's killing. He announced that a complete investigation into the matter had shown that terrorists had targeted PharmaForce, and the plot's mastermind had been the mentally unstable agent killed by Lance Miner. The company was one of a few entrusted with the health of the 2.9 million inhabitants of Nusun, and the Premier hailed Miner, the firm's CEO, as a hero.

"I continue to have complete faith in Lance Miner and Pharma-Force." Footage was shown of the damage to the PharmaForce building and the rebels who had been captured by Seeker cameras. "The AOI has the situation under control and expects more arrests in the coming days."

The head of the Aylantik Health-Circle also announced that they had ordered precautionary reviews for millions of citizens in the Pacyfik region immediately following the terror attacks on PharmaForce.

"For the past week, and for the next two weeks, our offices will be working twenty-four hours a day in order to see each patient to make sure their boosters are up to date." The Health-Circle head, a middle-aged woman in a black Tekfabrik suit, stared directly into the camera. "As of now, there is no evidence that these terrorists were successful in introducing any biological weapons into the water supplies, and no airborne viruses have been detected, but until the AOI apprehends all the perpetrators, we must remain diligent."

Following that, the AOI Pacyfik Region head, who looked too young for the job and with a physique better suited for construction work than heading a large military/police force, made a similar announcement. However, with the current difficulties and given the fact that the Pacyfik was notorious for trouble, his tough-guy, iron-fist persona could not have been a better choice to calm the worried population. He reported that there had been massive arrests made in large sweeps and raids in the Amazon Jungle, as well as in the Portland and Washington Areas.

"Even before the brave intervention of Mr. Miner and his corporate security force, we had made countless arrests and have weakened the vicious group considerably." He made no mention of the fact that Enforcers were more than just corporate security and that they, in fact, were the third largest army on Earth after the AOI and BLAXERS, and he definitely didn't say anything about the secret on-going *real* investigations by the AOI into Miner's affairs.

Miner watched with Sarlo in his Denver office. "Damn them, they're beating the drums of war," he said, as an android handed him a drink. It was a stressful day, so he allowed himself a Blue Hawaii, an odd cocktail he'd taken a liking to on a trip in the Hawaii Area a decade earlier. The drink consisted of rum, pineapple juice, Curaçao, sweet and sour mix, and vodka. Not much penetrated his agitated body, but this instantly warmed his tense voice.

"It appears they are readying the population for more violence. I suspect they will build up the 'terrorists,' and name the group with a scary sounding tag like 'bio-dags' or some such thing in the coming days." Sarlo took a glass of plain apple-juice from the android server. "They'll never call them something soft like 'PAWN.' It sounds too weak to be a threat worthy of the massive response we can expect the AOI to launch."

"Notice the Chief didn't come out and say anything nice about me," Miner said, sipping his drink. He smiled dryly, raised his glass, and winked at her. "She thinks I'm the damned enemy, Sarlo. We're going to have to get rid of her soon. She has too much power, and she'll use it against me and the Enforcers instead of PAWN. I told the Chairman this morning that the Chief is obsessed with bringing me down to the point of distraction. I said I'll cooperate with the ridiculous AOI investigations, but we need a new Chief." He drained his drink and pointed for another.

"What did he say?"

"Not much, but I think he got my point. The world is on the brink of the first war since the Banoff, and she's worried about the Aylantik's leading citizen."

Sarlo looked at a small AirView projecting from her INU. "Charlemagne is here," she said. "Are you ready to behave?"

"I don't have a choice," he said, accepting another Blue Hawaii. He stared into the swirling liquid for a moment, got up, and tossed it into the sink.

The Imp entered a few seconds later and slid across the room as his pencil-thin legs seemed to drift, never allowing his feet to touch the floor. His weak wave was welcome because Miner wasn't sure Charlemagne would be friendly after what happened with the other Imps in the Amazon city of Manaus.

"Charlemagne, so good to see you again," Miner said, ushering him to a seat. "Care for a drink?"

The Imp shook his head.

"Fine, good. Listen Charlemagne, thank you for coming. I need your help. I'm sure you know what I want." Miner produced his best-buddy-look. "Hell, man. Can't we put this thing back together again? I was out of line with Sidis. Tell me what you advise."

"I advise that you prepare for war," Charlemagne said, squinting as if in pain. "A war you will lose."

"Come on, this is what I'm talking about. I want the Imps to help me *avoid* this damned war. You know I don't want a war."

"Yes, I am aware of your position. But you do not understand our position."

"Our?"

"The Imps. I am speaking on behalf of the Imps." He had a slightly condescending tone. "You may not want war, but the Imps do."

"The Imps?" Miner roared. "The Imps *want* war?"

"Charlemagne," Sarlo said calmly, "why do the Imps want war?"

Miner was pacing, trying desperately to keep from saying all the things he'd like to say to this person he considered a freak at best and a creature at worst, but in either case, didn't care how smart an implant had made Charlemagne. Yet, there was no doubt in his mind that this vampire was inferior to the great Lance Miner.

"When I say we want war, what I mean is we, the Imps . . ." he looked over toward Miner, who was still silently fuming, before continuing. "We believe war is necessary, the only way to correct the mess Traditionals have made of . . . well, everything."

Sarlo failed to suppress a small laugh. "Yes, that's a valid point." She laughed more, and then, after receiving a stern look from Miner, regained her composure. "But isn't there another way? War is such an awful thing. I'm sure you'd agree. You once told me that your high level of intelligence allows you to see things that we Traditionals cannot." She paused long enough for both to look at her. She softened her eyes and delivered smoothly,

"Beautiful, spiritual things. If that's so, then how can you reconcile those truths with this call to violence?"

Sarlo glanced out the panoramic window as clouds billowed into magnificent ships and moved slowly across an azure sky.

"That's just the point. Precisely because we can see beyond this mundane, materialistic world you have created, we find war to be the only way, similar to how an illness can cleanse the system. A one-hundred-and-eighty-degree change is required, and it cannot occur by legislation, hope, or even consensus." Charlemagne gazed from Sarlo to Miner. "The needed change, an upheaval really, can happen only with force."

CHAPTER EIGHT

Polis Drast, or better known at Hilton Prison as inmate Evren, sat in the prison yard with his fellow inmate, Mite. He still wasn't used to his altered appearance, and although he looked like a tough cowboy from the Wyoming Area and his barracuda eyes remained blue, no one would have recognized him from his days as the AOI Pacyfik Head. Drast was also as cunning and fiendishly creative as ever.

It was the first time he'd been allowed to mix with other inmates since the day Terik had been killed, more than a week earlier. The isolation of the lockdown had been difficult, but a few guards he'd long ago "bought off" were helpful in keeping him informed of events on the outside. Unfortunately, nearly half the guards were androids and could not be bribed, manipulated or influenced. But he had a plan for that. Once the riots began, if all went well, the system that ran security for the AOI facilities and linked the AOI androids would crash, taking all those guards with it.

The Warden had officially notified Drast of his execution date, now only two days away. He didn't fear death and was determined to cheat the Chief and the grim reaper—who he thought might be one in the same—from their prize.

"So, Thursday you die?" Mite said.

Drast looked at the small Asian man who had been his closest confidant inside the AOI supermax. "I don't think so."

"Really?" Mite asked, intrigued. The micro-whistler-mimic in his mouth automatically translated his words into something far less controversial; the prison food and latest sports scores. Every word they uttered was being monitored. "Is the Chief or the World Premier going to issue a stay?" Mite continued. "Because otherwise you'd have to break out of here tomorrow, and all of our plans were obliterated when you decided to listen to Terik."

Mite, obviously still upset about aborting their long-planned prison uprising scheme in the final minutes based on some sketchy information from the dead AOI agent, made every word an accusation in his tone.

Drast eyes narrowed and cut into Mite. "Those plans didn't just fade away, they lie dormant . . . waiting."

"For what?" Mite momentarily lost his critical tone.

"My word."

"Okay, now you're talking," Mite said, smiling. "But even if you *can* get the word out, how has our network held up within the other institutions?"

"I'm not certain," Drast admitted, staring into the yard and watching a skirmish between two inmates. Fights were somewhat rare in AOI prisons because most violent offenders were simply put to death. They only detained smart criminals with possible information that might benefit the AOI.

"Is that your work?" Mite asked, motioning to the fight.

"Yes," Drast said, impressed that Mite figured it out. "Just a precursor to the riot which will occur tomorrow."

"And the other prisons?"

"I'm hopeful our people will find out in time. But even *some* success will lead to complete disarray within the institutions."

"Then it will happen tomorrow?"

"Yes. We're back on schedule," Drast said, wondering if Chelle would receive his thread.

His normal routes for getting information to her, Terik and a key guard, were both unavailable, so he had to resort to a less reliable guard and a far more convoluted route. In either case, the uprising would occur, and he might make an escape without her help. But those odds were less than fifty-fifty. Most of the prison personnel would have to be killed or captured, and then he'd have to get out of the prison and off the island. The actual odds were probably far worse than he believed, but Drast didn't care. He wasn't kidding himself. He'd be dead either way, so there was nothing to lose.

Mite studied him, knowing that Drast had to try, but he worried that the AOI was now on alert about the prisons, or at least Hilton. "Without the coordination, without the surprise, we have less of a chance."

They watched the guards break up the fight, which had grown to include four inmates. Threats were exchanged, promises made in raged shouts. Drast was happy with the result. It wasn't even his life that concerned him most. He always knew that he might not live through the revolution, but he worried about what Grandyn had told him.

If the war started from the prisons, they would lose. That would now be up to Chelle. If she could help him and, at the same time, hold PAWN back for another week or two, then it might be okay. After that, they could start the war in the Aylantik region, which offered their best strategic advantage -- surprise.

Aylantik region included the east coast of what was formerly known as the United States of America. It was the AOI's stronghold, both in popular support and numbers of agents. PAWN, striking at the heart of the empire, would shock the AOI. Drast didn't expect the prison uprising to be nearly as damaging to the AOI as originally planned because of the muted effects of the delay, but the influx of "talent" to the revolution would still be helpful.

"It is true, waiting has weakened us. We may lose, but the AOI has made a mistake with their prisons. They've created a recruitment center, a think tank and a breeding ground for all those who oppose them." Drast looked up at the guard towers and continued in a raspy whisper, as elusive and vaporous as the wind that came off the ocean in momentary gusts. "A government that uses prisons as a tool to control is destined to become imprisoned by its control."

CHAPTER NINE

Deuce met Nelson at the dock on Ryder Island. "I need to go to the mainland," Nelson said as he got out of the small boat, which had carried him from Runit Island.

"What for?" Deuce asked, implying in his tone that Nelson might not be permitted to leave.

"Revolution business." Nelson accepted Deuce's hand to help him onto the dock.

"I'm going to have to know more about this."

"Look Deuce, you and I have been in this together for three years, and we've known each other a while. After all that, and with everything that's happened, I'm still not sure I can trust you." He looked at the trillionaire as if inspecting a dog that might turn rabid. "But I think you know you can trust me."

Deuce patted Nelson's upper arms, and after a long pause, where he looked into Nelson's stony eyes, he nodded. "Okay." He handed him a pack of neuro-caps. "If you're caught, don't let them discover what you know."

Nelson stuffed a hand in his pants pocket and pulled out two more packs. "Shoot, Deuce, are you forgetting who my sister is?" He took Deuce's and shoved them all back into his pocket. "But I assure you my mind is too messy for the AOI to find anything useful, except maybe the best doughnut place in Portland."

Almost two hours later, Nelson was on the outskirts of Vancouver in British Columbia Area. He had donned Seeker-beating nano-tracers, microscopic decals affixed to the face, and had entered and left enough shops, hotel and office building lobbies, and at least one restaurant with a great dessert menu, that he now felt sure he had not been followed. He'd positioned himself in a small park surrounded by trees. The shade was both strategic and comfortable, as it was a hot summer day. He ate a chocolate éclair, procured at the place with the dessert menu, and then zoomed the man who had called him Baker-Boy.

"I see you got my message," Blaze said.

"I wonder if you called me Baker-Boy at our first meeting just so you would have a code name that only I knew, made all the better because not even I knew it until you used it."

"Nothing is ever an accident," Blaze said, "nonetheless, it fits you. Even more than it used to. I think you've grown two sizes, and no surprise. There's a little chocolate on your cheek." Blaze shook his head in disapproval.

"I went to a lot of trouble to find a safe place away from Deuce's monitoring *and* I'm at risk of detection by the AOI, so I'm really not in the mood for your insults."

Nelson was in an entirely different position from when they first met three years earlier at the Portland airport. That was before the books had been taken, before the Doneharvest, and before the *Justar Journal* had been found. Blaze seemed to have the world in his hands in those days, but not now.

"All right, Baker-Boy, I'll leave you alone. I just don't like to see such a bright and talented person turn into a . . . well, let's just say it's a good thing the AOI hasn't caught you because they'd have a hard time deciding whether to toss you in prison, or send you to Hop." Nelson thought of the mandated weight limits issued by the government under threat of being forcibly sent to a State run health and fitness facilities known as Hops, and decided, as he took another bite of his dessert, that that was reason enough to have a revolution.

Nelson decided Blaze had annoyed him just a little too much and ended the zoom. His INU lit up almost immediately as Blaze tried to reconnect, but Nelson ignored it. Instead he finished the éclair, lit a bac, then took a swig from his freshly filled flask. As the INU continued to blink, he inhaled the wonderful smoke and felt it expand in his battered lungs. Warm and harsh, the calming combination of sugar, tobacco and alcohol washed over him. After he lit a second bac, he answered the zoom.

"Damn it, Baker-Boy! This is no time to fool around."

"I quite agree," Nelson said, squinting at the hologram image of Blaze.

Blaze stared back. Nelson thought he could detect a hint of respect in his eyes, or it might have been resignation. Either way, he didn't expect any more comments about his weight.

"You are correct. Forgive me. Sometimes I . . . get the better of myself." Blaze tipped his head in a slight bow. "It was good of you to come. The revolution just got a whole lot more complicated, the world more dangerous, and I fear the future of our species is in jeopardy." Blaze flashed a quick, apologetic smile as if the statement he'd just made would have a damaging effect.

"Care to elaborate?"

"The Imps have decided to enter the fray."

Nelson raised his eyebrows. "On whose side?"

"Their own."

"What are they thinking?"

"That they can do a better job at directing humans through the evolution of higher thought and on to enlightenment, but I have my doubts."

"I should think so. Those freaks can barely function in society. People call them vampires for a reason you know."

"Yes, well, I do know. I created the technology that enables them to do all that they do. That allows them to exist really." He paused and brushed away Nelson's cloud of smoke, but because he was a hologram nothing happened. "It's actually a bit worse than just that."

Nelson reached for his flask, then stopped for fear of another lecture, but it already seemed quite horrible, and he didn't want to know what could possibly be worse. There were too many sides to the conflict, which could erupt at any moment, but at least those were expected to fall into two sides once the action started. However, the Imps would fight in entirely different ways, ones that were impossible to know, and maybe difficult to combat.

"Not many people know this, but I have created a kind of cross between an Imp and a human."

Nelson felt sick.

Blaze continued. "I call them Cloned Human Replacement Unit DesTIn Enabled, or CHRUDEs. They are virtually impossible to tell apart from regular humans, but, as you might have guessed from their name, they are the most advanced form of artificial intelligence ever devised."

"Damn you Blaze," Nelson said, shaking his head. "You could have helped save the world and instead you're destroying it."

"We used a CHRUDE to help Grandyn stay hidden," Blaze said, ignoring Nelson's comment. "No one could tell the difference. Not even Lance Miner."

"So that's why they think they killed Grandyn? They actually killed a CHRUDE?"

"Yeah."

"Then the technology is that good? I saw the footage on the Field. I assumed it was another Grandyn look alike."

"No, it was a CHRUDE."

Nelson realized that nothing would ever be the same again. He could be talking to someone and not even know if they were human or not. Frightening. "And they're super smart?"

"Smarter than Imps, maybe smarter than me," Blaze said, completely serious. "I created the technology, which has enabled CHRUDEs and Imps to think on such elaborate scales—"

"Elaborate? They think they can take over the world, or at least do a better job of running it."

"Who's to say they can't?" Blaze said. "Humans have had thousands of years and all we do is keep torging it up. But you're missing the point, and I would think you'd be especially good at getting this. They aren't doing it for greed, or revenge, or justice, or even fear. None of the reasons the various Traditionals are killing each other for."

"Then why?"

"They believe they can save us from ourselves." Blaze gave an ironic smile. "They think they can show us how to reach our souls."

"Machines are going to connect us with God?"

"Or destroy us trying."

CHAPTER TEN

The Health-Circle issued another warning, expanding the call for medical checks to the Aylantik region and parts of several other areas. They cited the threat from terrorists and the feared use of bio-weapons. Rumors circulated in the population centers of the Pacyfik that a dangerous terror group known as PAWN wanted to re-create the Banoff. The Health-Circle assured people that booster shots would be given to protect from any attempts to infect them.

Fye watched the reports on an AirView projecting between her and Grandyn. He was busy reading PAWN assessments of current troop levels of Enforcers, BLAXERs, and AOI amid increasing tensions.

"This is it," Fye said, her sandy blonde hair twirled on top of her head and held with a silver stick capped with a small piece of turquoise. The temperature outside hovered above thirty-eight degrees Celsius for the third day.

Grandyn glanced up from his AirView. "What is it?"

"The Health-Circle is giving everyone boosters."

"That's nothing new," he said.

"But you know those shots are not a cure . . . they're control."

"I do know. Chelle Andreas saved me from my last one."

Fye nodded, smiling and looked at her stomach with a knitted brow. She was quiet for a moment. "It's just that the Health-Circle follows a schedule. Most people wouldn't notice it, but the List Keepers track them, and there is a real pattern to what the AHC does. This one is out of place."

"The AOI knows we're about to go to war, and they're using the fear of the Banoff plague to turn the population against PAWN even before the masses know who or what PAWN really is."

"That may be part of it, but the AOI underestimates how many people in the general population already know about, and are sympathetic to, PAWN. There are more people who belong to PAWN living in plain sight than those that live in the POPs," she said, looking at Grandyn softly. "Unfortunately, you're not the only one who has had loved ones killed by the AOI, and every time someone disappears, is arrested, or executed, a PAWN representative shows up to recruit the family and friends. It's been going on for decades."

Grandyn thought of his parents, and of Vida. The pain of those losses were as much a part of him as his heart and lungs, to the point where he couldn't remember what it felt like not to know that searing ache. Trying to imagine himself without it was impossible.

Of course there were others, he shared responsibility for many. All those TreeRunners who had pretended to be him in exchange for an AOI death sentence. In his time as Terik, with the AOI, he'd seen tens of thousands of files showing victims of the Doneharvest, and there were even more prior to that in everyday enforcement activities. Peace and the utopian world came at an unimaginable cost . . . a dystopian regime.

"I know," he said quietly.

"You know about it from the AOI side, but the Health-Circle is worse because people *trust* them. Painting PAWN as a terrorist group and giving the world a villain to hate is only a side benefit.

The Aylantik's real objective is to make sure everyone gets their shots. The regular boosters allow the Health-Circle to have total control. PharmaForce has developed a series of additives that can be released in the water supplies or even into the air." She paused.

Grandyn could tell by Fye's voice, as it got slightly higher, and her expression, which looked like a friend had just slapped her for no reason, that what she was about to say was going to be awful. "What is it?" he asked, reaching for her hand as she still hesitated.

"With PharmaForce's additives and the Health-Circle's booster shots, they can kill any, or all of the population with almost no effort."

They stared at each other's horrified expressions. Fye felt like she was cutting into Grandyn's heart each time she told him something new about the atrocities of the Aylantik. Grandyn thought about their unborn child, wondering if he wanted to bring yet another victim into the world.

"What if we lose?" Grandyn asked.

"It doesn't mean they win. As soon as this thing starts, the Aylantik as we know it is through. The question is, will we get something worse?"

"Hard to imagine."

She nodded, but it wasn't hard for her. She'd seen List Keeper simulations which made the Aylantik look like sweethearts. "It's so easy for us to make a few missteps that lead to a hellish reality. There are three List Keepers whose sole work is to use super powerful INUs to trace human history, looking for just such missteps. They've shown that what one person chose to study in college led to war. All kinds of mundane decisions have created havoc, but it's usually which laws we pass, which leaders we follow, and the economic models we pursue."

"What decision led to the Aylantik?" he asked.

"The List Keepers have traced that to the failure of the military industrial complex, particularly the last twenty years of the twentieth century, and the first twenty of this one. Something as awful as the Banoff and the Aylantik, which arose from the ashes, doesn't just happen overnight. We have insane amounts of data on that. Corrupt politicians, weapon manufacturers, giant banks, oil companies, agribusiness, pharmaceuticals, and the super wealthy who controlled them."

"We need to show the people proof of what happened and who did it. Show them what the Aylantik really is, tell them that PAWN aren't the terrorists, AOI and Aylantik Health-Circle are the evil in the world."

"I hope we get the chance."

"How can we stop the shots?"

"They've already started. They've been going on for days."

"I know, but it will take time to give tens of millions of them. We need to shut them down."

"Now you know why the List Keepers have been opposed to war. When it starts, the Health-Circle can simply wipe out any part of the population they want and blame PAWN . . . and it's over."

CHAPTER ELEVEN

Nelson returned to the safety of Runit Island. With the war about to start, he wanted to be in a POP somewhere, but he could do the most good with Munna and Deuce. When he arrived, he found Twain in conversation with his father. While Munna slept, Twain had just tried to make the AirViews show the prophecies.

"Nelson, welcome back," Deuce said.

Nelson gave him a quick nod on his way to Twain. The two former students of Cope hugged and smiled.

"Thanks for all you did," Twain said as they broke apart.

"Want to talk about it?" Nelson asked.

Twain glanced at his father.

"Don't mind me," Deuce said. "Pretend I'm not here." Although he'd asked his son several times to tell him what happened in the redwoods, so far Twain had refused.

"It's not that I don't want to tell you, Dad. It's that you won't approve, and I know you won't want me to go back."

"Twain, you're thirty-two years old. I can't stop you from doing whatever you want. I wouldn't even think of it. However, your mother is a different matter, especially after the scare you gave her, but that's between you and her. You have to lead the life that makes you happy, that feels true."

"What happened to me in the redwoods . . . " he began, while looking out the window to the ocean. "I was trying to control my cells like she does." He motioned to the hall which led to the bedrooms where Munna was napping.

Deuce already wanted to ask several questions, but held back. He did catch Nelson's eye, and gave him a look that he hoped would convey his desire to talk with him later.

"UC had taught me how Munna did it, a kind of intense meditation. She's been doing it so long that she can do it almost anywhere, but when you're just starting out, you need to be in the most remote place you can find, so deep in nature that there isn't even a trace of human activity. Not even a trail. At that point, you have to forget the world. This is not an easy thing, and can take days, weeks, or even longer."

"Wait a minute." Deuce didn't want to interrupt but couldn't help himself. "If UC taught you how to do this, then that means he could do it?"

"Yes."

"But he died," Deuce said as if feeling the loss anew. "Cope let himself die when he could have saved himself? He could be here now helping me through this . . . he must have known the world is at stake . . . the *world*!"

"What happened is that UC didn't *want* to live any longer. He wanted to go on to the next phase," Twain said. "After this life is a whole other thing, and he said he needed to see it."

"What was the rush?"

"He made the decision to let his life run its natural course."

"Who is to say what is natural? Look at Munna. She isn't on any medications. She is living a natural life."

"But she is consciously keeping herself alive."

"So?"

"UC had other ideas," Twain said. "Munna sees it one way, UC saw it another. He told me that he was done with this life, this planet, this dimension . . . he left it to us to try and figure it out."

"Nice," Deuce said sarcastically. "Thanks a hell of a lot, Uncle Cope."

Twain closed his eyes for a moment, remembering the time he shared with UC in the redwoods.

"You were telling us what happened to you," Nelson said. "Mind if we go outside? It's a beautiful day, and I'd love to grab a smoke."

Twain shook his head. "Here's a guy who's got a conscious plan to embrace death."

"Hey, I'm just trying to make my way through the bad dream," Nelson said.

They all followed him outside where he lit a bac as soon as they hit sunshine, and a warm salty breeze took the smoke out to sea.

"Anyway, as I said, I was trying to control my cells," Twain continued. "But I made mistakes, and it's not the kind of thing you want to do wrong. I addressed the wrong cells and nearly killed myself."

Deuce looked as if he'd just seen a fatal car wreck. He couldn't imagine what his son had done to himself, how close he'd come to losing him. Twice Deuce started to say something, but both times the words abandoned him in a conundrum of emotions. It was low tide, and they stood among large rocks covered halfway up with barnacles, several orange and maroon starfish clung to the larger boulders.

It was Nelson who broke the spell of the moment. "And you want to go back there and try it again?" Nelson asked. "Or are you just planning on catching up to Cope?"

"I'm not sure what will happen."

Deuce regarded his son with frightened eyes. He'd always tried to protect Twain, as most fathers do. It overwhelmed him. Trying to fathom what Twain was attempting to do, the forces involved, the possibilities were stunning. He'd had glimpses of all that from his grandfather and Cope, but they were wise old men, and even Munna was seemingly some kind of a wizard, but *Twain*? This was his little boy. How could he let him play with the power of the universe, the darkness and mysteries of which Deuce himself still didn't understand?

The sun was hot through Nelson's fair, thinning hair. "Maybe you should take Munna," Nelson said. "She obviously knows what she's doing."

"Maybe you should stay here and help us undo what Munna has done," Deuce argued. "You're still a young man. You have plenty of time to think about adding decades onto your life."

Perhaps not, Nelson wanted to say, thinking about the Imps and CHRUDEs. The world might be a strangely different place very soon, but Nelson wasn't ready to talk about that yet. He'd been in touch with Chelle on the way back to the island, and she didn't want Deuce to know. Information was power, and the game grew more dangerous with each passing hour. Between Eysen, Inc. and the BLAXERs, the trillionaire probably had the best chance to stop the Imps, but Blaze knew that too, and he wasn't ready to bring Deuce into the latest threat.

"Dad, Munna doesn't want us to have the prophecies because she thinks they give us more power than we're ready for. She will—"

"I will." Munna emerged from the building and finished Twain's sentence. "I will tell you that we humans have always screwed up using technology and scientific discoveries for weapons instead of to advance us – *us* as in all people. So why would I help Twain learn something he is clearly not ready for?"

"Maybe so he doesn't kill himself next time?" Deuce said quietly.

"If that is his destiny—" she said.

"If that were his destiny, why did you save him?" Deuce asked.

"I wasn't saving Twain," Munna said, smiling. "I was saving you, Deuce."

CHAPTER TWELVE

Zaverly, stationed at a secret base in an Oregon Area forest, looked at the new orders that had filtered through on her INU and smiled. More TreeRunners would be coming her way. Her command would be expanding much quicker than she'd hoped. It seemed that Chelle Andreas, PAWN's strategic leader, had contacted Parker and asked that TreeRunners concentrate their numbers in three Areas: Oregon, Colorado, and Virginia.

The war was near, possibly hours away. The Health-Circle warnings and continued Doneharvest crackdown by the AOI had sent thousands of PAWN sleepers into the POPs and forests. The major cities were charged with tension as groups that had lain dormant for years, even decades, were suddenly called into action.

"Denver?" Zaverly asked her second in command, a woman ten years older, and a longtime PAWN member.

"Word is that there is some kind of new opposition group based there."

"New? Shouldn't we be concerned with the AOI?"

"I don't know. But aren't you from Virginia? They may transfer you back there."

"No. I'm staying here. Hoping to work with Grandyn."

"He died."

"Don't kid yourself," Zaverly said. "Grandyn is too important to get killed before the war starts. He's used doubles all over the world."

"I heard that too. It drove the AOI crazy. Great strategy."

"Yeah, it was," Zaverly said, but all she could think about was Beckett, and how she'd lost the love of her life just so Grandyn could sit safe somewhere like a coward.

"I understand the AOI Chief has ordered anyone associated with PAWN to be executed immediately upon arrest. They're claiming we're terrorists," the woman said. "They think people are gonna believe that we want to unleash another plague. Doesn't the Chief know how many people hate the AOI?"

"What about everyone who likes their comfortable life?"

"There are fewer of those than the Aylantik would like to think. Being truly happy is different from being comfortable. Most folks are just comfortable. They work and watch all that entertainment on the Field, eat artificially tasty food and sleep in climate controlled beds, but they don't know what real happiness feels like. They just know enough to grasp the fact that they don't have it."

"And this war is going to change all that?" Zaverly asked.

"Damn right. Shove those AOI grunges back into the swamps they crawled out of."

Zaverly thought of the AOI agents who had raped her. "I hope to send them somewhere worse than a swamp," she said, patting her lasershod. "I've got a long list of them who have seats waiting in hell with their names on them."

Fye received the priority flash, read the frightening contents, grabbed her pack, and yelled for Grandyn.

"What is it?"

"We've got to go." Her eyes revealed a controlled panic, which was new since she'd gotten pregnant. Before that, her confidence was unshakable.

"AOI?"

"They're sweeping the area. We've got less than ten minutes to get out ahead of them."

He grabbed his pack, which was always ready. They traveled light. One last glance around and they were out the back door. It was a well-rehearsed escape. They'd been running for years and knew the tempo of it, knew the ticking seconds of fear and what they meant. But the extra heartbeat inside Fye had changed things for both of them. Risking their own lives was one thing, but risking the baby's was another. They had never talked about it, but both felt the responsibility to make sure their baby grew up with two parents. It was a conversation they avoided because the promise could not be *kept*. With the pending war, the promise could not even be *made*.

The neighborhood had been chosen carefully. It didn't take long to make it into the woods. After another half hour, a clearing appeared where a Flo-wing waited. Once in the air, she told him the rest of it. "Blaze zoomed just before I got word of the AOI sweep."

"And?"

"The Imps and CHRUDEs are joining the war," she said.

"Whose side?" He could tell by her face it wasn't PAWN's.

"Their own. They think they can save the world by running it themselves, or some such thing."

"Damn it!" He dropped his face in his hands. "The List Keepers *have* to come in Fye. It's the only chance we have. The Imps will do so much damage, and we can't fight another front."

"The List Keepers don't have the numbers."

"I know, you've told me that, but they have the power."

"I also told you why they can't."

"Why, because the Health-Circle is going to kill everyone? Don't you think they're going to do that anyway?"

"They can't kill CHRUDEs, and the Imps are also smart enough to have avoided the boosters."

"Fye, you have to take me to see them."

Her eyes showed pain. "We're going now."

"We're going to the city?"

"Not yet. We have to go through the outsider first."

"The outsider?"

"Munna."

"Munna is a List Keeper?"

Fye nodded.

"Wow!" Grandyn said. "This is a strange torgon world."

"You have no idea," Fye said softly, almost to herself.

CHAPTER THIRTEEN

The AOI Chief had taken the zoom from Sidis, somewhat hesitantly at first, but after it ended she had the feeling it would prove to be one of the most important decisions of her professional life. She accessed the small file the AOI had on the secretive group known as the Trapciers, and reviewed what they had known before.

Trapciers were revolutionaries utilizing DesTIn technology to infiltrate corporations. Beyond that, there were few traces of their work, and the Chief didn't believe much of the intelligence, which pointed to Trapciers whenever a recent attack on a corporate INU network or major Field breach had occurred. But now, thanks to Sidis, she knew much more.

Trapciers were almost all Imps, and they had their tentacles into just about every major company, including those controlled by Deuce Lipton and Lance Miner. As Sidis put it, "We hold the Field in the palm of our hand, and we can crush it at any time by simply making a fist."

His bold assertions did not end there either. He dared her to have the AOI do anything about it, and most stunning of all was his claim that the Trapciers could ensure that the AOI won the impending war.

She summoned her top advisors and, while waiting for the meeting to convene, she reflected on the most chilling part of the zoom. When she had told Sidis that what the AOI preferred was to avoid the war altogether and asked if the Trapciers could help with that, he laughed.

"It is too late for that, my fine woman. *Far* too late." He had stretched the word, "far," so that it lasted almost three seconds.

She had asked him why.

"The war started so long ago that it's impossible to know when," he'd said. "It's all the same war, you know? Politicians and historians keep naming them something different, but there's only been one war. One very long war."

It was what he said next that disturbed her the most.

"You can accept our help now, or not. But either way, we are going to make sure that this war, this cruel, ten thousand year old conflict, finally ends."

That line would replay in her mind many times in the days ahead. The Chief met with her advisors and ordered internal security reviews. She wanted to make sure that the Trapciers were not inside the AOI systems. She also needed assessments on what damage could be done if the world's major corporations were compromised and, finally, what effect a total Field breach would have.

Many of these studies had been conducted in the past. Encryption and defensive measures were so sophisticated they were believed to be invincible, but Sidis had shown her enough evidence that she now knew that not to be true.

After his zoom with the Chief, Sidis met with the other top Imps, including Charlemagne and Galahad. The dim room contained more than two thousand floating AirViews, and seventeen Imps wandering around like digital ghosts on the dark side.

"The AOI will be conducting full internal audits of its own security as we speak," Sidis, the razor-thin de facto leader of the Imps, said while walking between a dozen nearly translucent screens blinking with images and long data streams.

"Isn't that risky for us?" Galahad asked.

"Yes, it is all risky, but I am confident they will not discover our presence. Our infiltration into the AOI system is untraceable, and remember, we have *people* inside." Sidis said the word "people" as if he were saying something disgusting, such as "disease-riddled rats." The Trapciers had recruited Traditionals into their ranks, mainly for access to the AOI, because Imps were not allowed to be agents and CHRUDEs were too new to have been placed yet.

"We have a dozen CHRUDEs in AOI training academies," Charlemagne said, "but the war may well be over before they are able to help us inside the AOI."

"I see the Reno Project is progressing well," Galahad remarked, looking into an AirView, which he spun, among the hundreds of others, into his orbit.

The Reno Project was a massive undertaking spread between two cavernous warehouses outside a city in the Nevada Area. The Imps had stolen Blaze's plans and were building an army of CHRUDEs.

"Yes, it is," Sidis said smugly. It had been his idea. "Blaze has unwittingly given us the tools in which to bypass his will."

"Blaze is not to be underestimated," Galahad reminded. "His brilliance is otherworldly."

"Only machines can obtain perfection in the present. One day, perhaps, owed to our efforts, Traditionals will find the perfection they are capable of. A unification of energies. But that time is ages away, and it depends on our actions during the next few days."

"Galahad is correct about Blaze Cortez," Charlemagne said. "He is capable of stopping us."

"Your enthusiasm for our cause has been questionable from the start," Sidis hissed.

"My observation of facts and declarations of danger should not be construed to mean that I am any less loyal to our objectives than you, Sidis. Your suspicions illustrate my point, which I have made repeatedly. We Imps are mostly human, and therefore share the same flaws as our stepbrothers, the Traditionals, which would seem to make CHRUDEs superior because they lack the baggage we still carry. But they also are without true emotions. Wonderful traits, such as empathy, cannot really be programmed."

"We may be flawed like Traditionals," Sidis said, "but because our thinking is free, we are able to see so much deeper. What do you think of me, Charlemagne, Galahad, all of you?" He waved his arm out to the others. "Do you imagine I wish to rule the world? I am doing this for the same reasons as you. The Traditionals are blind, and we can see the Traditionals are lost. We have been to where they need to go. We can show them. We can save them." He flashed at least two hundred AirViews with stars so that they made one huge screen displaying a ballet of light. "Don't you understand? We were created for this. The Traditionals have brought this to pass. They created the machines that will now re-create them."

CHAPTER FOURTEEN

The Flo-wing carrying Fye and Grandyn received permission to land on Runit Island where Munna was waiting for them. She embraced Fye as one would a long lost daughter, and Fye cried.

Deuce, Nelson, and Twain watched from a distance. Munna had asked for a "private portion of time."

"Now you have brought Grandyn back to me," Munna said to Fye as they ended their emotional reunion.

"Yes. We need to go to the city. It's time to talk to Nian," Fye said, wiping tears.

"I see," Munna said, nodding. "Do you understand what this means Fye?"

"I do."

"And you believe Grandyn is ready?" Munna asked deliberately.

"Yes."

"And you? Are you ready? Or is this about something else?" Munna motioned her carved walking stick towards Fye's belly.

"It's about the Imps," Grandyn broke in.

"Yes," Munna said, smiling. "I know about the Trapciers."

"The war is about to start, Munna. Please— "

Munna silenced Grandyn with a wave of her hand. "Sweet boy,

I have lived through the violence of war. It is different to read about war, to think, or dream about war, to endure the long quiet parts of it than it is to survive the bloody upheaval and all-ending maliciousness of war." Her steely smile revealed a strength far younger than her physical years.

Grandyn stared into her ancient eyes. He felt so old, filled with experience and tragic lessons of life and yet she'd been alive more than a century longer than he had. Inside her eyes, he saw the eyes of thousands, as if everyone to whom she'd ever taught something was looking back at him, begging patience.

Finally, she nodded. "TreeRunner, this is a time of dramatic change, and you too must change." She took his hands. His cold fingers felt the warmth of her soft palms worn smooth, like rocks tumbled forever in a river. "You cannot be both a List Keeper *and* a TreeRunner."

Her statement surprised him. He looked to Fye for help, but her expression told him this was up to him. Grandyn turned back to Munna. Her gentle, smiling face appearing like a dried mountain flower, at one with the wind.

"But my TreeRunner oath?"

"Becoming a List Keeper is not going to betray that oath. In many ways it will enhance it, but your ultimate loyalty can belong only to the List Keepers. Even today, even if you decide, I cannot make you one. You must go to the City for that. All I may do is give you permission to enter the City. But if, once you get there, you decide *not* to become a List Keeper, then you will never be allowed to leave the City . . . not ever." She let go of his hands.

Grandyn loved Fye, their child would be born in five months. She was a List Keeper, and they had somehow kept him alive for three years. He didn't need to think about it.

"I've decided. Yes."

"Welcome, Grandyn." Munna hugged him. "You will soon see everything differently." Then she added in the softest whisper, "You will see so much."

Fye hugged him as soon as Munna released him.

"When do we go to the City?" he asked.

"Tomorrow," Fye said, "and you'll finally understand—"

"We are being rude to our host," Munna said, motioning toward Deuce, Twain, and Nelson. Fye and Grandyn followed her over to them, seated in a partially open shelter, protecting them from the sun and increasing breeze. The chairs were Over-holds, which contoured to their bodies, could automatically convert to chaises, and apply gentle massage.

Grandyn still felt oddly shaken about his decision. Something in Munna's words made him sure, but uneasy.

"What was all that about?" Deuce asked.

"Deuce, you should know that not all secrets are bad," Munna replied.

"I was just hoping they were trying to talk you into letting the prophecies go," Deuce said.

Nelson recalled Munna saying a person could learn from three things -- experience, elders and children -- and that Deuce was about to get hit with all three. He figured Munna was the elder, and that she might consider Fye, Grandyn, and probably even Twain, the children, relative to her age. Twain had certainly been teaching his father about many things.

But what would the experience be? he wondered.

"Munna, according to UC," Twain began, "the *Justar Journal* was not left by accident. It was created to guide us."

There was a twinkle in her eye when she answered. "Cope knew things far beyond this life, even while he was here, and I'm sure he knows a great deal more now. But he never exactly understood how dangerous the *Justar Journal* could be. I do agree it can guide us, but only when we are ready."

"But why do *you* get to decide?" Deuce asked. "Why aren't we ready?"

"I am not deciding Deuce. You are. I shouldn't have to explain, but because you all continue to persist, I shall. Ready has more than one definition; receptive, able to comprehend, and it can also mean safe."

The word "safe" made Deuce suddenly shiver, and he looked out at the ocean toward the horizon, then all around up in the air. He had made sure they were safe in every possible way, but now he worried if it had been enough.

"UC also told me that Munna can control certain external things," Twain said, then looked at her. "But it's mostly our perceptions that you are changing."

"What's that mean?" Deuce asked, shaking off his concern.

"The INUs are still running the prophecies. The AirViews aren't really blank," Twain said. "Munna has merely made us believe they've stopped. It's a kind of mass hypnosis that we are choosing to believe."

Deuce looked at Munna. "Is this true?"

She only smiled.

Deuce ran to the building. The last two AirViews, which had been scrambling, were now blank. The others were active, showing scene after scene, and what he saw made him drop to his knees.

CHAPTER FIFTEEN

Blaze called a meeting of his knights with the full knowledge that they were each also members of the Trapciers and, whether it was out of respect or curiosity, they all showed up.

"Thank you for coming," Blaze said, as they were all seated around the large, clear table. "I've asked you here today in the hope that we may avoid an outcome which none of us could foresee and no one desires."

"War is inevitable," Morholt said.

"Of course it is," Blaze replied. "But the end, to which I refer, is not."

"What end?" Percival asked. "We have run all the scenarios and simulations. We know every outcome."

"You know what the programs show you," Blaze said. "I understand that those results give the CHRUDEs absolute confidence. But Imps, can you tell me that you've strayed so far from your human roots that you no longer count on the unpredictable nature of the universe? Have you forgotten that there are surprises waiting behind every cluster of atoms?"

"Yes, nothing is guaranteed," Galahad said. "But Blaze, you, more than any of us, should know it is about the odds. There is always a chance of something else occurring. Just as lightning might strike me as I walk across the street, but it isn't going to happen."

"You are building an army of CHRUDEs," he said, looking at Galahad. "This is insane. You will not be able to control the outcome. I am telling you it will not go as you plan."

"You will, as always, be well positioned Blaze. Just enjoy the profits."

"My knights should know that profits are just an image I use, they are not the breath that propels my life. In fact, you have a slight problem in your scheme. I own DuPont, the company that is the sole manufacturer and supplier of the chemicals necessary to make the skin for CHRUDEs. Without it they will fool no one. They will appear like a typical android."

"What do you think Blaze? Do you assume we are building them for infiltrators?" Galahad asked. "We have enough completed for that purpose already. Perhaps you imagine they are for fighting, and if that were the case, what would it matter how real their face and hands appeared, as long as they could spot a target and fire a weapon? But our army of CHRUDEs is not for use during the war."

He paused, flashing a sinister grin, giving Blaze time to figure it out. As soon as he saw Blaze's expression change, signaling he understood, Galahad continued.

"Yes, we aren't building them to fight, we are building them for replacements, for humans – *after* the war."

"You must stop this," Blaze said, appalled.

"But someone will need to do the work after the war, and we don't expect enough humans will survive."

"Don't you realize we could become extinct?"

"Of course. It is possible, but humans have had such a long run, too long really, and they have basically done nothing but use, pollute, and destroy," Galahad said. "We aren't doing this out of concern for this world. We're trying to begin the next phase. And, as you know, flesh can become extinct, but energy is eternal, so extinction wouldn't bother us at all. It might just speed things up."

Blaze shook his head. He'd created this mess, but now wasn't sure how it had happened or what to do about it. He considered killing everyone in the room, but he knew there were countless others, and at least with the knights he could have a dialogue.

Keep your friends close and your enemies closer, he thought. It was a grave and uncharacteristic miscalculation.

Lance Miner and Sarlo flew to an untraceable building in Toronto. The city, along the shores of Lake Ontario, had nearly tripled in size since the Banoff. The skyline was filled with twisting needles, towers shaped like giant ski jumps, sails, intertwined glass lattice, and staggered stacks of silver plates, all of which rose higher than the pre-Banoff CN Tower. It mesmerized Sarlo. Miner had chosen the location for the building to provide the best view of the city reflecting in the lake.

"We're down to hours now," Sarlo said.

Miner nodded, brooding. It was the reason he'd moved to the secret location. That, and the fact that he couldn't be sure the Chief wouldn't have him arrested at any moment. But all indications and every simulation showed the war would start in the next twenty-four hours.

Miner felt failure as never before. The crushing weight of his powerlessness pressed him heavy and low. He'd always been able to make things happen. His money, clout, and power were almost unequaled in the world. "I was this close," he said holding his thumb and forefinger a centimeter apart. "Damn Drast. If not for him we could have stopped this war."

"As it turns out, we were wrong. At least a little," Sarlo replied.

"Deuce was never the real enemy. He was nothing more than a rival." She was being generous and they both knew it. Sarlo had tried many times over the years to stop him from obsessing over Deuce, but they had both missed the mark on reform. "We had a chance with the Council when Drast was Pacyfik Region head, and plenty of other times over the years where we could have pushed reforms and loosened the chains."

"Maybe, but the rebels might have just come sooner." Miner paced and looked out across the water as if searching for something.

"You're probably right." She stared out at the lake and the colored lights beginning to reflect on its smooth surface.

"Our only chance now is if it's a quick war," he said. A signal went off on a circle of linked INUs on his desk. AirViews flashed to life. "Someone's gotten into the PharmaForce system!" he shouted. "Damn Blaze!"

"How do you know it's him?"

"They're in the Enforcers section. Who else would be looking for troop movements and our strategies on the eve of war?"

"The AOI, Deuce, PAWN?"

"They would all like the information, but Blaze is the one to profit from it. It's him, he's looking for last minute sales. I'm sure he'll offer me their information." He zoomed Blaze.

"What is it Lance?" Blaze answered, not bothering to look up from an array of AirViews in front of him. Miner thought he appeared haggard, and noticed the drink in his hand.

"You seem stressed, my friend. I should think you'd be happy. The war will be so good for your various shady businesses."

"I'm very busy Lance. If you have nothing important— "

"Okay, if you've run out of snappy comebacks and biting sarcasm, I'll get to the point. I want you *out* of my system."

Blaze pulled up another AirView and scanned it for a few seconds. "It's not me."

"Really? Then who?"

"Trapciers."

"Who?" Lance asked, expecting a figure to be quoted.

Blaze surprised him again by simply answering. "The Imps. I suspect you know some of them. They've organized. I think they plan on winning the war."

Sarlo, still staring out the window and listening, closed her eyes, telling herself to breathe slowly.

"Are they out of their minds?"

"No. But the rest of us might be if we give them this war."

"I've been saying that for decades. Blaze, we have to stop it."

"I know," Blaze answered empathetically, locking eyes with Miner for a split second. Blaze's hologram sat there looking at AirViews, but they were shielded by a privacy control that meant that Miner couldn't see the screens. Miner was so surprised by Blaze's apparent change in attitude toward the war that he didn't know what to say. He wasn't sure he should trust it. In fact, he knew he shouldn't, but somehow did.

Maybe it's just because I want so badly to believe I have a new ally, he thought.

While he wrestled with the situation, Sarlo took the initiative.

"Blaze, what are you going to do?"

"I'm working on a plan. Do not give them any help. Lock down your system, *hard.*"

Miner looked at Sarlo. Shutting down their system just as war was about to break out was insane, yet someone was *in* the system. It could easily be another trick by Blaze. Miner had been burned enough.

Sarlo could see his hesitation. She knew the history and understood. Miner was about to say no, about to tell Blaze to go to hell. She widened her eyes and nodded, mouthing the words. *Shut. It. Down.*

Right now he trusted Sarlo more than himself. Obviously she

had some instinct still operating. Her concerned face softened him for a moment, and for a second he thought about how beautiful she was. With one final, deep breath, hoping for some clarity, which did not come, he entered the code sequence and worldwide, all PharmaForce went dark.

CHAPTER SIXTEEN

By the time the others reached Deuce, the AirViews displaying the prophecies had gone blank again, all but the last two, which went on scrambling as if they had never stopped. Grandyn looked at Deuce, who was still on his knees, and swallowed hard when he saw his face. Grandyn had seen enough awful things the past three years to immediately recognize terror.

Munna arrived last, but she wasn't the one Deuce first looked at. It was Fye. "You must remain strong."

She looked momentarily confused. Tears welled in her eyes. "I'll try."

"I don't even know who they are," he said.

"Who?" Grandyn asked.

"The List Keepers."

"What did you see?" Nelson asked.

Now Deuce turned to Munna. "I saw the most awful thing I've ever seen," he said hoarsely. His eyes locked with Munna's. "I saw the end of the world."

"How?" Nelson asked.

"I don't know, but in the end there were just a few of those torgon vampires left, picking through the waste."

"The Imps?" Nelson asked.

Deuce nodded, still not entirely back in the present. "But I also saw hope, an underground city, a place of wonder . . . the List Keepers."

Munna smiled and patted his shoulders. "Get up now Deuce."

"You meant for me to see that, didn't you?" he asked her.

She stared deeply into his soul, but didn't answer his question. She simply said, "War destroys all."

"Deuce, you should know that the Imps have banded together," Grandyn said. "They call themselves the Trapciers."

"As usual, Blaze was the first to hear of the new threat to world stability," Nelson said. "The Imps, a faction that owes their existence to Blaze and has always been a peaceful group, has decided to take matters into their own hands."

"Why?" Deuce asked. "The Imps, although misunderstood, could always be counted on to provide services to those willing to pay their price, and almost always the corporate elite. I don't like them, but I've used them. PharmaForce employs hundreds of them."

"Not anymore," Nelson said. "They're fully independent, and on top of their connection to the Field and all networks on Earth, they have a new weapon. A super advanced type of android with the most sophisticated DesTIn brains ever."

"They're called CHRUDEs," Grandyn explained. "They are so human-like it's impossible to tell them apart. Blaze built one that looked like me and it fooled the AOI, Miner, and even Fye."

"They're frightening," Fye whispered.

"I was always afraid Blaze would push technology too far. He's abnormally brilliant, though too often he falls on the insane side of the genius," Deuce said. "But I thought he kept the loyalty of the Imps, especially his advisors. He calls them his knights of the round table. How did he lose control?"

"The Imps have glimpsed enlightenment," Munna said. "The Trapciers started out as a spiritual group. Those Imps seeking to grasp what they had seen . . . the workings of the universe, the secrets of life, the light of dawn."

"You know about the Imps?" Grandyn asked.

"Dear boy, how could I not know?"

"Blaze told me that the Imps had a tight bond with one another," Nelson said. "Because even with their differences, they had witnessed what others could not, and they paid a price others were unwilling to pay."

"The bloodshed will be devastating," Munna said. A tear ran down her cheek. "The Imps are an inspiring group. They show what is possible." She looked at Fye. "They are an example of where our thoughts can go and what is out there, but they have forgotten that this is an instinct, a subtle shift, a breath in the trees. Not a mechanical process. You two go to the City and speak with Nian. Tell him I will release the *Justar Journal* if they do not act."

Fye nodded, a promise in her eyes.

Munna smiled, and then excused herself for a nap.

Deuce's INU lit up and he urgently left for Ryder Island to attend to "matters."

Twain, Nelson, Grandyn, and Fye shared a meal sitting among the books. Nelson would remain with Munna, the others would leave in the morning, Grandyn and Fye to the List Keepers' City, and Twain to the redwoods. After they finished the warm food, something they rarely had time for anymore, they took a sunset walk along the shore.

Nelson turned to Twain, who had been quiet for some time. "When you were in the redwoods, almost dead, did you see anything?"

"Yes, Shakespeare's line from Hamlet. 'To die, to sleep - To sleep, perchance to dream - ay, there's the rub, For in that sleep of death what dreams may come . . .' And then I saw rivers of stars flowing through a purple land."

"What do you think it means?" Nelson asked.

"I think it was real," he said.

"Then where is such a place?" Grandyn asked.

"I don't know, but I'll bet Munna does."

Grandyn nodded, wondering what he was going to find tomorrow. Munna was the most extraordinary person he'd ever met, and now he'd learned she was a List Keeper. The secret group might be powerful enough to save the world from what was coming. And for some reason, he knew he held an unspoken hope that he might find his father at the ListKeepers' city.

The *Justar Journal* showed the war leading to the end of the world, but he didn't need prophecies to tell him it was going to be horrible. He'd been feeling it grow toward a finality his whole life, as if each day the pressure built exponentially from the prior day until everything was going to explode into oblivion.

"Are the prophecies really still on the AirViews?" Nelson asked, looking back to the building as the sky streaked orange and magenta.

"I think the last two AirViews are a distraction, or some other thing," Twain said. "Maybe she controls the atoms in the INUs to simply show blank, but the information is still there."

"She can control atoms?" Nelson asked, trying to sound casual.

"Same as cells," Twain said. "She's far beyond where we are."

"How do you think it's possible to see the future when it hasn't happened yet?" Grandyn asked.

"Time's a funny thing," Twain said, echoing his great-grandfather's favorite expression. "The future isn't really ahead of us, just like the past isn't really behind us. There isn't anything linear about time except our human definition of it. Time is all happening *now*."

Grandyn looked at Fye as if this was a crazy notion, but she nodded.

"You'll learn more in the City," she said, "still it might be easier to look at it this way. Seeing the future is possible because all outcomes are clear, like looking at a chess set and seeing all the potential moves, and where the next ones would lead, and so on." She looked at him to see if it had registered, before continuing. "If we slow down enough and focus our minds, or speed up our minds to see it all, to see every possible outcome the way computers do, those programs which run all the scenarios and predict all the outcomes, then we can see it too."

"So that's how the *Justar Journal* works?" he asked.

"No," she said empathetically. "That's how people like Blaze or the Imps see the future. The *Justar Journal* is something entirely different."

CHAPTER SEVENTEEN

Wednesday July 13

The announcement caught everyone by surprise. The Aylantik Health-Circle issued a brief statement at 09:00 Aylantik time.

"Bearing rights restrictions are hereby lifted until further notice."

"It has begun," Chelle said, when Nelson answered her zoom.

"Where?" he asked.

"I'm not certain, but we should know in a few minutes. The AHC just lifted bearing rights restrictions," Chelle said referring to the law that stated couples could have no more than two children.

"Torgon damn," he whispered. "They're expecting big losses."

"Looks that way."

"Polis's date is tomorrow. Is there a plan?"

"There is."

"I see it now," Nelson said. He'd gone to the Field to check the AHC announcement, and had seen that inmates were staging uprisings in at least five AOI prisons. "They're rioting."

Chelle smiled. She had teams ready to help evacuate up to thirty-seven of the supermax facilities.

"Are you watching this?" he asked, alarmed.

"No." She moved an AirView next to the ones where she was monitoring the prisons. "Whoa!"

"That's not us is it?" Nelson asked.

"No, but it sure looks real." The screens were showing purported PAWN attacks on AOI buildings in Denver, Washington, Portland, Dublin, Hamburg, and Shanghai. "Nelson, I'll get back to you. I've got to find out what's going on. Make sure Deuce is on this. See if he knows who's behind it."

"I will. And Chelle, be careful . . . we're at war."

Deuce's wife showed Nelson back to the study where the trillionaire was already fully engaged in the crisis. "Damn it," he said as Nelson entered. "It's started. We're not ready, and it's started."

Nelson wondered how Deuce could *not* be ready for a war that has been building for more than seventy years. "I just talked with Chelle and it's not PAWN hitting the AOI."

"That makes it even worse!" Deuce yelled. He had AirViews sliding in all directions, and it appeared that he was in the middle of at least three zooms. The BLAXERs were a massive power, with a major presence on five continents, and although outnumbered by the AOI, they were probably outfitted with better technology than the Aylantik.

"Are we safe?" Nelson shouted above the chaos.

"No one is safe!" And, as if to punctuate his point, one of the larger AirViews showed a seven square-kilometer section of New Delhi in the aftermath of a Sonic-bombing. Hills of dust and debris, most of it no bigger than the size of a square meter, was all that remained.

"Oh no! What happened there?"

"Nelson I can't talk right now!" Deuce's forehead trickled with sweat. His energy made Nelson panic.

Nelson watched in horror as a dozen AirViews showed additional Sonic-bomb attacks around the globe. Another screen displayed thousands dead from an apparent bio-attack in San Francisco, a rapidly moving virus was reported to be overwhelming Santa Fe, and more Sonic-bombs hit Istanbul, Barcelona, and Caracas.

Nelson couldn't believe what he was seeing. It looked as if they were trying to fight the entire war in a single day. He zoomed Chelle, but couldn't reach her. The world had erupted. Decades of pent up rage searching for an outlet, forcing the innocent to pay for the crimes of the corrupt elite.

Nelson was used to the instant coverage the Field provided, but usually he would have expected a little more censorship. Instead, everything was exposed, like a plane wreck when bleeding bodies and open luggage lay strewn across a field with mangled plane parts, a seat cushion, torn metal, a shoe, a disembodied head, part of a wing, underwear, a leg missing its body. It was all there, the truth of it.

The desperate, repulsive, cold reality of war hit him as if he'd never heard of it before, a sickness gnawing at his insides, and he suddenly knew why Cope Lipton had allowed himself to die.

"Go prepare the books!" Deuce yelled, breaking him from his tragedy-induced stupor.

"Where are we taking them?" Nelson asked from a fog, realizing that if the books had to be moved, none of them were safe there. Grandyn and Fye hadn't left yet. Twain probably wasn't gone either, and Munna might still be asleep. He looked at his INU. It was only 07:12 Pacyfik time.

"Someone will meet you there. Go!"

Two BLAXERs were at the building by the time Nelson got back to Runit Island. Grandyn and Fye were helping to load books into a kind of shipping container.

"Where have you been?" Grandyn asked.

Nelson crushed out his bac. "Watching the war."

"How bad?" Grandyn asked. The BLAXERs had already told them about the early attacks.

Nelson shook his head, not sure how to describe it, or where to begin. "Torgon horrific." He lit another bac. "It's like Deuce said yesterday. . . It looks like the beginning of the end of the world."

Fye and Grandyn made eye contact, both thinking of their unborn child.

"We have to go," Fye said.

"As soon as the books are safe," Grandyn insisted.

They heaved the books, no longer bundled. Some spines broke, covers bent, pages tore. The damage made Grandyn, raised in a library to revere books, crazy, but they had to move fast.

"Where are they going?" Nelson asked a BLAXER.

"Bottom of the ocean," he answered, as if he'd said "two doors down."

Nelson stopped and looked at Grandyn. They gazed at the shipping container and realized it was triple-hulled with giant seals.

"It's water-tight," Grandyn said.

"It better be," Nelson replied.

"Brilliant," Grandyn continued. "A great place to hide them. And look." He pointed above the container. The short distance to the ocean was completely tree-covered. "They won't even see it from the satellites."

"Twenty meters of Nano-camo is deployed at the end of the trees extending out over the water," a BLAXER said. "No one but us will know the books are down there."

"How deep?" Nelson asked, ferrying another stack.

"Two-hundred-sixty meters. But don't worry. This baby can handle five times that depth. They'll be safe for a thousand years."

"Let's hope it doesn't take that long," Nelson muttered.

CHAPTER EIGHTEEN

Munna came out as the last books were being loaded and walked into the container, looking at the books as if she were considering which one to check out on her library card. Or, Nelson thought, she might be thinking about being shut in with them. But she walked out a moment later, a faint smile on her lips.

"Deuce is clever. And a man of his word. I think these books, Runit's books," she said, looking at Grandyn, "shall be quite safe."

"The question is, will we?" Nelson said.

Munna looked at the five blank AirViews and the two still scrambling, then waved her carved walking stick as if it were a magic wand. The AirViews lit up and the prophecies came to life.

The *Justar Journal* flowed across the large displays too fast to follow, but once they got used to it, they could see things they recognized. And it was awful.

Buildings burning and disintegrating, screaming people falling or jumping to their deaths, bridges collapsing, entire neighborhoods reduced to powdery rubble in less than a minute, children fleeing from exploding schools, lasers cutting lines of people in half . . .

"The gruesome and bitter love letter from war," Munna said.

Back on the other island, in his study, Deuce saw the *Journal* open again. Every angle of Runit Island was monitored. He could see and record each moment of the prophecies and slow them down for further viewing at a later time.

If there is a later time, he thought, *or even time later.*

Twain walked into his father's study. "I'm leaving now," he said.

"You can't go," Deuce argued, forcing his eyes away from the AirViews. "The war has begun." He motioned around the room, every space filled with nightmarish images.

"I know," Twain replied, not looking at them, instead staring only at his father's face. "But I have to go. I can do the most good in the redwoods."

"That's true, I'm sure, but . . . I don't want you to try the cell controlling act again. I don't want you to die."

"I have to do what I think is right. I'm not saying that's it, but I just don't know yet. Once you've spent so much time alone in the wilderness, coming back here is difficult. Everything is confusing. Not complex, just confusing, as though purposely making it hard to understand, and we're constantly bombarded with negativity. I have to go."

Deuce nodded. His stare lingered on his son. "Traveling is not safe right now. Can't you wait a few days at least?"

"Look at it, Dad." He motioned to the AirViews without looking at them himself. "How is this going to improve in a few days?"

Deuce knew it wouldn't. He had seen the *Justar Journal* "pages" for this period. "Okay. But you'll have to go by boat. It's too dangerous to go into the air right now. I've got nothing fast enough on the island, but give me two hours and I'll have one here which can get you to the redwoods in four or five hours."

Twain agreed.

"They could use your help with the books," Deuce said. "They won't be safe here now."

"The books or Grandyn and Munna?"

"Neither." He got up and hugged Twain, squeezing him tight, so tight tears dropped from father and son.

By the time Twain reached the building on Runit Island, most of the books had been loaded. Nelson and Grandyn were lost in the prophecies. Fye and Munna were deep in hushed conversation, seemingly ignoring the AirViews. It took another twenty minutes for Twain to help the BLAZERs finish loading. Nelson came over when it was time to seal the container and stared at what he considered a collection of the greatest work humanity had produced.

"That's our record," he said to Twain. "That's everything we've ever done, and we're about to sink it to the bottom of the ocean."

"It'll be safe," Twain said. "That container is more sophisticated than it looks. My dad had it custom-designed and built. It's filled with nano-technology."

"Grandyn," Nelson called out. "A final look?"

It jarred Grandyn out of his trance. He'd been so wrapped up in the prophecies that he'd forgotten anyone else was even in the room. He stumbled over, stood in the entrance of the container, and thought of his father and what he had sacrificed to save the books. *Where are you, dad?*

Nelson came up beside him and put his arm around his shoulder. "Your dad wouldn't believe all that's happened since these books sat on the shelves of his library."

"I don't believe it myself," Grandyn said, silently wondering if he'd been brave enough, true enough.

"It's fitting that the books will be tucked beneath the waters of an island named after him," Nelson mused, taking a sip from his flask and offering it to Grandyn. "If your dad were here, he'd look at this container filled with the treasures of our history, about to be hidden, and he'd quote some long dead author like Andre Malraux, who wrote, 'Man is not what he thinks he is, he is what he hides.' Or he'd come up with something about buried treasure, but I can't think of anything that inspired at the moment . . . All I can think about is the *Justar Journal* and so much of the world suffering. I can't help but wonder if we'd never taken these books, where we'd be right now."

"Seal it up," Grandyn said, accepting the flask and raising it. "To Runit." He took a swig, then sent his dad a kiss through the ethers. Grandyn turned back to the prophecies, but found Fye staring back at him instead.

You okay? she mouthed.

He nodded and went to her, falling into her arms as if she were the only escape from a burning building. She held him. They held each other. Their embrace lasted until the container began to move. Some kind of motorized device carried it to the sea. From the open bay door, they all stood and watched as it moved like a slow train car until it reached the shore, where a small rig under the Nano-camo towed the container out and away from the rocks. Once it was beyond the shelf, another mechanism disconnected the lines and, after a series of whooshing sounds, it began to sink.

No one moved, or spoke, or breathed, until the last books from the last library in the world, sank beneath the ocean.

CHAPTER NINETEEN

Although he didn't know it, Drast had gotten his wish. All but two of the forty-eight AOI supermax prisons were experiencing massive riots. Due to the unrest and battles occurring across the globe, the AOI could not send any extra resources to aid the overwhelmed guards. The scene at Hilton Prison was particularly bad, as just thirty minutes before the riot, nine staffers were sent to Portland to assist with the strike against that city's AOI headquarters.

Drast, aka inmate Evren, waited in his cell. The door had been deactivated moments before the riot by a bought-and-paid-for guard, but it was too dangerous to go out into general population yet. Sixty-seven inmates and fourteen guards were already dead, fires were sweeping through the common areas, and at least two explosions had rocked the small island which housed the facility.

Drast was waiting for a specific explosion, one that Mite had arranged. It would bring down half the east wall, including two guard towers. As soon as it hit, there would be twelve minutes to make it to the outside. A Flo-wing would be there, hopefully. He'd heard rumors that the war had started, but he had no way to reach

Chelle, and rumors in prison are like drunks at a party. Everyone talks a lot, but you can't believe any of it. Not even the truth.

The screams were clear as people died. The stinging sound of lasershods and laserstiks, like ripping sheets, repeated again and again. They'd been smuggled in with other weapons by drones and a reprogrammed android guard. Mysteriously, he heard old-fashioned conventional gunfire. The loud, distinctive pops were unmistakable. The sounds of pounding, running feet and clanking metal were constant among the cries and shouts, interrupted by sporadic explosions.

They'd been most concerned about the micro-drones, swarm-drones, and mimic-drones, which all AOI facilities kept stockpiled and ready. The first wave of the riot was supposed to take them out, but from his tiny window, he could see that had not been fully successful. He watched, helpless, as two inmates he'd recruited were picked apart by laser-equipped swarm-drones. It took no more than ninety seconds for the drones to kill them with synchronized, needle-sized laser strikes. It was an awful way to die. Like getting pecked to death by tiny birds.

Smoke suddenly wafted through the vents. At first he feared it was a poison gas, but that would have been too easy. It was the toxic smoke of burning wires, synthetic fibers, and chemically coated materials used to build a supermax. Now he'd have to leave. The thick black clouds choking the air burned at his lungs. He hit the floor and crawled to the solid cell door. Panic seized him. The damned door wouldn't open. His side had no latch or knob, just a thin electronic panel to release the latch, but that should already have been done.

Drast couldn't see anymore, as the cell was completely engulfed. With only seconds of air left in his lungs, he got to his knees and groped for a comb. His eyes burned and he had lost orientation, but he found the comb and forced it into the seal between the door and the jam. It was enough to break the suction that had held it shut.

As the door burst open he fell into the corridor. Smoke poured out after him, but otherwise there was now better visibility. He choked and coughed, but he could breathe. Just as he was getting to his feet, two young inmates ran by, knocking him back down. His head hit the metal grated floor and a foot landed hard on his back. He pushed through the pain and followed them.

The smoke increased with each step. He stumbled past locked cells, most likely filled with suffocated inmates. He made it to the guard station ten paces behind the guys who'd stepped on him. Luckily, someone had already been there. The steel gates were blown open, and three dead guards lay scattered nearby. Minutes later he hit sunlight and fresh air, but the scene that greeted him was Armageddon.

He immediately raced toward the wall opposite the one to be blown, but fires, small explosions, and at least a hundred bodies slowed his progress. People were running everywhere, trying to find a way out of the yard. The two he'd followed had disappeared into the confusion. He spotted a group of his recruits, but before he made it to them, three fell, victims of snipers from the guard tower.

Drast hit the ground and rolled behind a concrete bench. He yelled to the surviving man, but his voice couldn't be heard above the clamor. He worried that Mite's explosion wouldn't happen and he'd be trapped.

The chaos had grown faster and more violently than he'd predicted, and if the war rumors were true, his Flo-wing might not even make it to the prison. If the war had started, getting off the island would be the least of his worries. There were eight well-guarded boats that the administration used to ferry staff and inmates, but surely those would be overwhelmed before he could reach them.

He had to believe that Chelle would find a way to rescue him. Yet even if she didn't, he knew one thing for sure. They were not going to be able to execute him tomorrow. That thought gave him a brief respite from the surging hostility going on all around him, but it was short-lived as he fully realized that this riot could swallow him up, and that he might not even be alive to see tomorrow.

CHAPTER TWENTY

The Chief had about four minutes warning, thanks to her alliance with the Trapciers. The Imps had cracked into the Enforcers system and discovered the planned attacks on the AOI.

"Miner believes you will arrest him and seize his assets," Sidis had told her. "Enforcers are about to launch attacks on as many as sixteen AOI buildings in various cities. We are still trying to find out which ones."

"Lance Miner has gone mad," the Chief had said.

"His plan is to make the attacks appear to have come from PAWN, thereby starting the war and taking the focus off him. The AOI will obviously suspend all investigations at the outbreak of war."

"Of course. But what must he be hiding to take such extreme measures?" She hadn't waited for an answer. "Keep me updated every ten minutes," she'd said as she signed off, then immediately contacted the A-Council Chairman. "Sir, we are minutes from coming under attack."

"Details," he'd demanded.

"Lance Miner is about to bomb our buildings in multiple cities and lay the blame on PAWN."

"Are you sure?"

"Evacuations have been ordered. We'll know in a couple of minutes."

And it all happened just as Sidis had said it would. The warning had not been in time to evacuate more than a handful of agents, and the AOI took heavy losses. Missing from the Imps' warning were the prison riots. Those uprisings seemed to catch everyone by surprise. Between the prisons and the AOI buildings, enough blood was shed and trouble started that the "end" had begun. After more than seven decades, the fragile peace collapsed into a boiling caldron of war.

The Chief immediately ordered AOI troops to seize Pharma-Force properties, including the critical drug manufacturing plants, and in a move which Sidis had secretly predicted, the Chief decided to use the initiation of war as an excuse to purge the enemy. She authorized retaliatory strikes against many cities with areas suspected to be sympathetic to PAWN. Districts known to contain large pockets of Creatives or Rejectionists were hit. Statements were issued that the terrorists group known as PAWN had begun attacking en-masse. The Chief also allowed the media unlimited coverage. When the Chairman questioned that decision, she blasted his naïveté.

"The population will be begging us to protect them," she said. "They will be so terrified that they will turn in their own mothers and children in order for us to make the world safe again. Anything for us to restore their beloved entertainment sites."

"You turned off the entertainment?"

"Of course. There is a war on. The people can't expect sports and celebrities to keep on pretending everything is wonderful."

"It appears you were right about Miner all along. I owe you an apology."

"Accepted," she said. "You've seen the initial reports. We have positively identified no fewer than eighty Enforcers personnel at the sites of some of the attacks against us."

"Yes. Any idea where Lance is?"

"We're working on it. We've got people going to every known address, but that will take a while, and I doubt we'll find him there."

"What about the prisons? Is he involved there too?"

"Perhaps. As you know, he has long ties with Polis Drast, who is in custody at one of the rioting facilities," the Chief said. "But it is too soon to confirm that connection. Sir, I must go."

"Of course," he said. "Please keep us posted."

The Chief could barely suppress a smile when she thought about how quickly things had turned around. If she could end the war soon enough, they might make her World Premier. All they wanted was peace, and they did everything to avoid it, such as letting people like Lance Miner and Deuce Lipton get away with anything, including building their own private armies. But now that the war had started, they would do anything to stop it, therefore allowing her to strike both Miner and Lipton, which is exactly what she had planned.

The Chief zoomed Deuce in order to give him one chance to comply. If he were willing to officially join forces with the AOI and go after PAWN and Enforcers, she would let him keep his army, his companies, and his fortune. But if not, she would go full force against the trillionaire. She would use his money to pay for everything.

He has no idea the power we wield, she thought as she waited for the zoom to connect.

Deuce, in the middle of his makeshift command center, looked at the INU, one of more than two hundred employed in his study, and hesitated.

He knew who it was, and he knew what she was going to say. He just wasn't sure exactly how he wanted to handle it. But what he needed more than anything, was time, so that would be his course of action. Do whatever he had to do to get more time for the picture to become clear, and, if possible, convince Munna to open the damned *Justar Journal*.

"Chief, I'm glad you zoomed," he began. "This sure looks like our worst nightmare scenario, doesn't it?"

"I can't imagine things being any uglier right now," she said. "But I think we will have much of this under control by the end of the day."

"I'm glad to hear it," he said, while secretly authorizing troop movements on other AirViews.

"But we could use your help," she said. "In fact, I must insist upon it."

"Of course. I'm happy to do whatever is needed in order to preserve Aylantik," Deuce replied, continuing to click commands onto AirViews as they spoke. One screen confirmed that the books were under water, another displayed more BLAXERs moving toward Ryder Island, and there were many showing AOI movements. He turned to face the Chief and said, "I'm with you. Just tell me what you want."

CHAPTER TWENTY-ONE

Toronto had so far been spared any attacks, but Miner and Sarlo were not celebrating. With his PharmaForce INU network offline, including the connection to his Enforcers, Miner was unable to figure out exactly what was happening. With the outbreak of war, he abandoned the idea of safeguarding his system and was trying to get it back up, but that would take at least another hour or two because of the increased satellite traffic. He and Sarlo were doing their best with zooms and flashes, but attempting to manage the crisis as it spun out of control, and with such limited tools, made Miner crazy.

"Hell, I feel like I'm digging my own grave with a torgon plantik spoon!"

"They set you up," Sarlo said. "Blaze must have known."

"It would appear so," Miner replied, watching thirty AirViews all showing battles or the aftermath of attacks. They were all Aylantik-sanctioned feeds on the Field that anyone in the world could see. Miner couldn't access the back-door, private, or government networks until he got his own system back online. "The AOI thinks *I* did this. As if I, who wanted peace more than anyone on the torgon planet, would start a war!"

"When we took our system down to protect it, they must have gotten it back up. Somehow shifted the protocols," Sarlo said. "I don't know, but we've got to regain control."

"*If* we can regain control of the system. They may have us locked out, and I don't know anyone other than Blaze who can help us with that. And since he's probably the one who sold us out in the first place—"

"There has to be another way. Who's using us? PAWN? Trapciers? Maybe even the AOI?"

"I don't know, but the Chief has shut me off the Digi-link!" Miner suddenly yelled, trying to open accounts on an AirView. The Digi-link acted as a central bank for the entire world. Without access to it, one was essentially without funds. "She can't stop InvisiLine." He allowed himself a hopeful laugh.

InvisiLine, a control currency and secret bank set up by his father years earlier to avoid just such an instance, was encrypted currency that could not be traced or blocked. Although the senior Miner put the InvisiLine in place in case of something more along the lines of a political enemy trying to cut off his funds, in recent years, with the worry that war could disrupt Digi-Link, Lance had stashed billions in InvisiLine.

"I'm going to win this Sarlo. Just watch me."

"The AOI has taken over four of our manufacturing facilities," she reported.

"I'm not surprised," he said. "At least she'll keep them safe from PAWN without our having to use our resources. We'll get them back when the time is right."

"In the meantime we have to regain control of the Enforcers or we're nothing but a couple of fugitives in an out-of-the-way, nondescript building."

"Don't worry Sarlo. I may have spent my life trying to avoid war, but that doesn't mean I'm a pacifist, or a man without a plan!" Miner had found a second wind, and he'd always liked challenges, even if this would be his last.

"I'm counting on it."

"Look at this, would you?" Miner pointed at his private INU. "Blaze Cortez returns to the scene of the crime." Miner maneuvered his fingers to accept the zoom and project Blaze's hologram into the room. As soon as it came through, Miner punched "Blaze" in the face. "You damned guttersnipe!"

"Lance, my, my, such violence from a guy who is afraid of war."

"Blaze, I swear I will find you before this is all over and show you what war feels like."

"Really?" Blaze flicked his long brown hair out of his face and mimed a kiss to Sarlo. "If you want to fight so badly, I'll arrange a meeting with you and Deuce because, contrary to your obviously erroneous and premature conclusions, I am not responsible for your problems, nor am I your enemy."

"Hell, Blaze. Even if I could believe you, even if I *wanted* to, I can't believe a thing you say."

"Why is that? Did you flip your pretty silver coin and it told you not to?"

"No. I can't believe you because all you do is lie. You've been selling secrets for so long that you've forgotten how to recognize the truth. Because you don't care if your information is true or not, so long as it fetches a good price." Miner glared at Blaze. "How does it feel to have sold your soul for a little gold?"

"You tell me."

"This zoom is finished."

"Lance, the only thing that's finished is you and your empire unless you listen to me."

"Ha!" Miner smiled angrily. "You must think—"

"Sarlo, please," Blaze began, looking lustfully at her "please, save him one last time. Tell him to listen to me before it's too late."

Sarlo closed her eyes, searching for an answer. Normally she knew when Miner was blowing too fast, but she thought Blaze was a snake. "We took our system down as you suggested, and in our absence the world went to war."

"Yes, most troubling," Blaze said.

"Most troubling, indeed," Sarlo replied. "*We* are getting the blame."

"Sarlo, we're wasting time," Miner said. "I'll have assassins find this weasel."

"Weasel? Is that the best you can do?" Blaze asked, then he winked at Sarlo.

"We can't seem to get our system back up," Sarlo said.

"Of course not," Blaze answered. "The Imps have it completely captured."

Miner shook his head.

"Can you get us back?" Sarlo asked.

"Your question insults me far more than your boss's school-yard name-calling does," Blaze replied, feigning a hurt expression at Sarlo. "Why would you ask such a thing when you know that I can?"

"Do it then," she said.

"After."

"After what?"

"Lance has a conversation with me without his rude slurs."

"Forget it," Miner said. "He's the devil."

"There he goes again."

Sarlo looked at the AirViews showing the latest news. Four more cities had Sonic-bomb attacks, and an unidentified rebel base had fallen to the AOI. She recognized it not as a rebel base, but actually as an Enforcers outpost in Mexico. Time was evaporating, and so were their chances to save Miner's empire. They had to trust the last person they should trust.

"Lance, we have nothing more to lose. Blaze is our best chance," she said.

Blaze wisely stayed quiet.

Miner looked at her as if she had just told him to jump from the roof.

"They are taking your assets and breaking up Enforcers. We must get back into the system."

Miner shook his head and took a deep breath. "Tell me what you have to say," he said to Blaze, tightening a fist in his pocket.

Blaze had to stop himself from saying, *"Now there's a good lad,"* and, in the seriousness of the situation, he even suppressed his near constant smile. Then he said the last thing either Sarlo or Miner expected to hear from Blaze Cortez.

"Lance, I need your help."

CHAPTER TWENTY-TWO

Deuce promised the Chief full cooperation. She didn't believe him, but without evidence she could not move against him. Although Deuce and Miner were rivals and they each had sizable private corporate armies, their level of power was not even in the same neighborhood.

Deuce, because of Eysen, Inc., StarFly, and all his other tech companies, as well as three generations of infiltrating the Aylantik government, including AOI systems, had no equal. Miner's power was almost all linked to the Aylantik through the Council, the Health-Circle, and the AOI. The Chief's main objective was to avoid, or at least delay, the need to take on the BLAXERs.

Deuce was confident that he had time, but he had seen the prophecies, and knew worse trouble lay ahead. *Too close ahead*, he thought, as he stared at the AirViews in his study, which were now showing the prophecies from the building on Runit Island. They were changing, and getting worse. He expected that his zoom with the Chief would have improved things, but so far it had not.

Looking at the eight books that made up the *Justar Journal*, Deuce tried to figure his next move. The eight books were now completely digitized in his system and feeding the interpretations of the prophecies, so the physical copies were no longer needed, but he couldn't bear to send them into the ocean depths. Just before slipping them into a small pack, he held them, hoping for a magical inspiration, or at least to feel some sense of their power.

Nothing. The books were just books. It was the order of the letters they contained that gave them strength.

The AirViews, with the live screens, showed more attacks on other cities. He turned back to the prophecies. The *Justar Journal* was rewriting again. He knew they were safe from the AOI, and that PAWN was still in a mostly defensive posture, so he expected improvements. Instead, the situation had deteriorated further. *What the hell is happening?* he wondered urgently. *I've got to talk to Munna.*

Then he saw something in the prophecies that made him grab his INUs and the pack with the books, and run from the room.

Deuce found his wife and daughter and scrambled them onto a boat. He kissed them both and told the captain to head out to sea. His wife pleaded with him to come, but knew he wouldn't. She'd learned a long time ago that Deuce had been born for greater things. His daughter knew it too, for she shared the same burden.

With great wealth comes great responsibility. If humanity survived and the Lipton legacy remained intact, she would one day carry on that mantle which, in Deuce's case, meant to help save the future.

Deuce watched their boat speeding away, while continually checking the sky for any threats. By the time he got to Runit Island, Twain, Grandyn, and the others were at the docks getting into two boats. They'd all seen the same thing in the prophecies that prompted him to evacuate his family. He'd assured his wife that he'd personally get Twain to safety.

"How long do we have?" Grandyn asked as soon as he saw Deuce.

He checked his Eysen INU. "Twelve minutes."

"Who is it?" Nelson asked.

"I don't know," Deuce said.

"Munna blanked the AirViews, but what about the INUs?" Fye said. "The BLAXERs took the INUs." She pointed at the two men who'd loaded the books and were now sprinting toward them.

Deuce jogged to meet them. They handed him the INUs from the building, which he inserted into a strap that went from his shoulder to his belt, filled with other Eysen INUs. It made him appear as an old-time bandit wearing lines of ammunition. He quickly gave the men orders, and they immediately began talking into their INUs, relaying the commands.

"We've got to go!" Deuce yelled.

Munna was the last to board the boat. She stood staring out at the spot where the books were sunk.

"Don't worry," Deuce said. "They've removed the Nano-camo, and if anyone bothers to check the satellite surveillance, it will show a large shipping container leaving this island the day before you arrived. It was unloaded last night in San Francisco and from there the trail will get lost. If anyone is still concerned with the books after the start of the revolution, they'll never think to look in the water off this tiny island. The books are gone . . . and they're safe."

"It's not the books I'm worried about," Munna said.

Deuce nodded. "In order to change it . . . we need to live."

"I've wondered many times over the past few years if you were up to this task, Spencer Lipton," Munna said. No one had called him by his given name for as long as he could remember. "You and your father were named after an old friend of mine. Of course, he was a friend of Booker's too. I hope you have more of him in you than just his name."

"Me too," Deuce said. He'd heard stories about his namesake, Spencer Copeland, but was surprised to learn that Munna had known him. Of course he then realized he shouldn't have been surprised at all.

She reached up and put her small, soft, pale, wrinkled hands on his brown cheeks and looked into his eyes. "You have no idea how hard this is going to be. You have to make every right decision. You must trust only the worthy, and know just when to let go."

Her eyes seemed to have all of the answers. At that moment, he felt that if he could just keep looking into them instead of all the AirViews, he would know how to do what had to be done.

"I'm drawing on everything I have," he said, staring into her unblinking eyes. "I can do this."

"I believe you."

He nodded, silently thanking her. Then, after another moment of absorbing the wisdom from her irises, he whispered, "We have to go."

Nelson had come back for Munna and witnessed the scene between her and Deuce. It was at that moment that he finally knew for sure that Deuce could be trusted. Chelle needed to know. He'd also heard Deuce's explanation about the books and passed it on to Grandyn. The two of them cared most about the remnants of the Portland Library, for different reasons that went beyond the prophecies.

Grandyn, Fye, and Twain were on a boat being piloted by one of the BLAXERs who'd helped load the books. The other BLAXER captained the second vessel with Deuce, Munna, and Nelson. These were small pleasure boats meant to ferry people between Runit and Ryder Islands. There were bigger boats at Ryder's dock, but they were easier targets and no faster.

The plan was to rendezvous with a quicker boat that Deuce had ordered earlier for Twain. In order to avoid the expected trouble on the islands, Deuce had it slightly rerouted, and they should catch up to it in about twenty minutes if all went well.

They were less than six hundred meters from, and still well within sight of, the shore of Runit Island, when the sky filled with soldiers parachuting onto both islands.

CHAPTER TWENTY-THREE

The main yard of Hilton Prison looked like an exaggerated war zone. Streaming smoke, bursting explosions, lasers flying, and people running everywhere. Amidst the chaos, Drast looked up and saw a friendly face he never expected, Osc.

"Evren, you made it out!" he shouted as he approached.

"I made it this far anyway."

"Follow me." Osc never stopped moving. He was in full riot gear; Tekfabrik and impenetrable materials. He tossed Drast a small gas mask.

Drast was never sure if Osc had known Terik's real identity as Grandyn back when he was getting him in to visit Drast. Osc and Terik had been friends in the AOI Academy, and that may have been the only reason he broke rules for him. If that was the case, then Osc wasn't a revolutionary, and would have no reason to help Drast.

He could be leading me straight back to a cell, straight to the executioner's chamber, Drast thought. *Surely he now knows that Terik was Grandyn, and that he could be implicated in the investigation.*

Drast was already following Osc. He didn't have time to think, and he sure didn't have many alternatives. "Where are we going?" Drast shouted as he put on the mask.

"To the real outside," Osc shouted back.

Drast tried to get his bearings, but everything seemed backwards or upside down. A stocky man ran into him. Drast recognized the inmate, but it wasn't one of his team. The guy hardly slowed, and before he was a meter away, his head was sliced off by a long-range laser, probably from one of the towers. Osc turned and suddenly grabbed Drast, shoving him into a wall.

"Damn it, that's my face you torg!"

"Shut up Drast. There's a troop of guards coming. If it doesn't look like I've got you in custody then we're both dead!" He loosely cuffed Drast's wrists behind his back. "If you twist your hands right you should be able to get out of them. Now come on, let's go. And don't look happy."

"That won't be hard," Drast said as Osc pulled him roughly around and began pushing him in the direction they'd been headed.

A few seconds later they passed the troop, who were brandishing laser-clubs, electro-pipes, and other lethal weapons, which they were using without the slightest provocation or hesitation on every inmate they saw. A few of them looked at Drast. They recognized Osc and knew why he was bothering with a single inmate. Everyone knew Evren was due to be executed in the morning and, riot or not, the AOI liked its executions to go off as planned. Drast was sure that at least a few of the passing grunges were wondering why wait, just do him now. But if they had those thoughts they would have had to have been fleeting, as the whole prison was in siege.

They pushed through a door using some kind of emergency key, as the power had been cut. Just as they got inside, Mite's wall blew. They were showered in glass, as the reinforced, bulletproof windows couldn't resist the power of the blast. Right after the explosion, an endless curtain of smoke rushed over them, and was sucked out of the building as the windows allowed mingling air.

"Are you all right?" Osc asked.

Drast was covered in blood, but didn't feel any serious injuries, just what felt like a hundred cuts. Osc dragged him to his feet. He'd been completely protected by his uniform, helmet, and shield. Drast's gas mask was cracked and useless, but without his hands he couldn't get it off. A maze of dark corridors of fire and dead bodies, none of which there was time to recognize, led them to a clear hallway and a door Drast had never seen.

"This is one of our fallbacks. All AOI prisons have tunnels, safe rooms, reinforced emergency areas, and "doomsday" exits in case of riots or attacks," Osc said as he ripped off Drast's broken mask and they forged ahead.

Drast suddenly thought of the other prisons probably rioting at this very moment. The uprisings had all been coordinated as best they could in order to tax the AOI and not give the agency a chance to respond at any single facility with extra forces. Now he worried they might all fail. He hadn't known about the secret tunnels, safe rooms, and the rest of it. The AOI could respond much better than he'd anticipated.

What if the whole war is like that? Drast thought. *What if we've actually underestimated them?*

He had to remind himself that he'd been head of the Pacyfik region. He knew about the AOI, knew things the Chief didn't know. "Has the war started?" he shouted to Osc.

"Did you see that yard back there?" Osc asked without expecting an answer. "There are at least two dozen cities that look just like it!"

Drast stopped. Most of his adult life had been working toward the revolution, and part of him had never believed it would actually come. There'd been times when he moved through his daily activities as a high-powered member of the Aylantik and found the world to be a wonderful place. They had created something truly remarkable. A peaceful planet where everyone was happy, healthy, and fed. The feat was unparalleled in all of human history. On those days, and in the quiet of most mornings, he questioned whether revolution was the correct course. Now, picturing those cities in flames and rubble, he second-guessed again.

What if the Aylantik and the AOI are the good guys? What if I'm the villain?

"Damn it, come on Evren!" Osc said, tugging him forcefully along. Seconds later, they burst back into the daylight. Two hundred meters ahead the ocean churned as if taking part in the uprising. The winds carried the smoke from the yard across their view, but there was no action here.

"What now?" Drast asked.

Osc pointed into the distance. "I do believe that's your ride."

Drast looked up and could just make out a black dot in the sky moving toward them.

"Come on," he said, pushing Drast down a sloping lawn that was more gravel than grass. Soon they reached a semi-level spot near the edge of the water. The Flo-wing was coming in fast. Drast glanced back at the prison. Smoke and flame obscured much of it now.

A minute later Osc pushed him into the craft as it hovered half a meter off the beach. To Drast's surprise, Osc climbed in after him. Three grunges were heading toward the Flo-wing, firing as they came. The pilot spun the ship around and returned fire with onboard laserstiks. The grunges fell. Drast didn't see it, but Osc handed his INU to the pilot who quickly slid a window open and dropped it into the ocean. AOI-issued INUs had tracking chips.

Osc popped the cuffs off Drast. "They know I helped you escape," he said. "You and I both know what would have happened to me if I stayed."

"Why did you help?" Drast asked, but before Osc could answer, they both caught a glimpse of the prison. From their bird's-eye view, it looked like a cataclysmic disaster in some corner of hell.

Most of the prison was on fire. Mite's explosion and several other smaller ones had reduced large sections to rubble, and bodies were everywhere. Most of the inmates who'd made it out were getting picked off by snipers in the towers. Drast hoped the other prisons were faring better. He was lucky to be alive. He would have been dead without Osc, and turned back to his savior and repeated. "Why?"

"Chelle Andreas is my mother."

CHAPTER TWENTY-FOUR

Runit was in the middle of his rehabilitation session when the android guard collapsed. Over the long time he had spent in captivity he had actually come to see these mechanized jailers almost as friends. They had nursed him back to life, always been respectful, and treated him with nothing but kindness. Sadly, beyond his memories, they were all he knew of the world.

He rushed to Simon's aid, but the android's human-like body appeared as if he'd had a heart attack and died instantly. Although Runit cared about Simon, he knew he was only an android and did not possess a heart, or blood for it to pump, or anything other than an elaborate set of electronics, programs, mini-hydraulics and all the related machinery that made Simon so efficient. The only other person available was, of course, also not a person. Still, Runit felt obligated to find Wendall, the other android, and see if he could help.

Due to the security zones Runit wasn't even sure he could reach Wendell. Runit was surprised to find all the doors and gates which had previously sectioned off areas within the small facility, normally only accessible to the androids, were now suddenly open. *What's going on?* He asked himself, as he passed through a section where he'd never been before.

When Runit finally reached Wendell, he was startled to find the second guard in the same state as the first. *Why did they shut down?* He quickly realized that there must've been some sort of major breakdown at the facility since the security and the guards had all gone out at the same moment. *Am I free? I may only have a limited amount of time.* He left Wendall and headed to the main entrance. *There's no one else on this island, so I am free, at least temporarily.*

He burst out into the damp day, half expecting AOI agents to be waiting, but there was nothing. Just the cold mist falling that seemed to continue for months during this time of year. *If I move fast enough I might be able to escape.* The androids had regularly taken him outside for exercise, but he had no real sense of the island that had been his home for more than three years. In fact, he wasn't even sure of its location. *Is it December?* Runit only loosely kept track of the months. But the chilly air, heavy with fog over a gray ocean suggested he was off the coast of either the north-eastern part of what used to be the United States or perhaps the former Pacific northwest, maybe Washington Area or into what had once been known as Canada. *They wanted me alive for a reason, they may have kept me close, for questioning or something*, he thought. *The Pacyfik region makes sense.* He'd been to Vancouver before in December, the weather had been the same.

The androids had told him once that this was a special kind of prison just for him, a former AOI base that had once been a coast guard outpost before the Banoff. He'd asked what made him deserve a "special prison," but the androids would say no more about it.

Now the same questions he'd been wrestling with since he'd remembered who he was, flooded his mind. *Why has no one ever come to question, interrogate, or even punished me further? Is Grandyn still alive? Did the revolution happened? Were Chelle and Nelson dead, or in prison somewhere else?*

Deuce immediately knew that the Chief had not violated their agreement. The paratroopers raining down on his islands weren't the glide-jumpers the AOI used. Grunges jumped with glide-wings and jet packs, but these were using more traditional chutes, albeit GPS-assisted, that could put them to within three square meters of their intended landing target. Deuce yelled to the captain. "Kill the motors! Deploy the tarps!"

Both boats instantly went silent and were individually covered with nano-camo tarps, rendering them invisible. Deuce worked an INU on his "gun belt," and from underneath the cover he moved small AirViews, which gave him full visuals of the islands and detailed looks into almost any spot he desired. Nelson and Munna watched the screens as images of the building that had contained the books flashed by.

Once all the soldiers had landed, Deuce began pushing virtual buttons, causing lasers to fire from concealed points across Ryder Island. A group of the seven paratroopers were taken down before they scattered. After that it was more difficult, but over the next five minutes he took out six more. Then they started to fire upon the boats.

"I thought they couldn't see us!" Nelson yelled as the water exploded three meters off their starboard side.

"Depends on what kind of equipment they have," he answered while pushing through AirViews, looking for something.

"Apparently they have the right kind," Nelson said ironically, stealing a sip from his flask. "Who are they?"

"My guess is Enforcers."

"Why would Lance Miner be attacking you?"

"Only one reason I can think of."

"What?"

"The prophecies."

Nelson shuddered, but it made sense. With the outbreak of war and his recent missteps, Miner was apparently on the outs with the AOI Chief. He had to make one last play for the prophecies. They were his best shot at redemption. Deuce confirmed Nelson's thoughts.

"The AOI has been seizing his assets, but the Enforcers are a *force* to reckon with. In many ways they're tougher than the AOI, and now that Miner has nothing to lose, it looks like he'll do anything to get the *Justar Journal*.

Nelson looked at Munna. She appeared to be meditating. Another munitions hit close enough that the boat rocked and listed. The other vessel, with Grandyn, Fye, and Twain, took in water, but was still seaworthy.

"Move off!" Deuce yelled at the captain, wanting to put some distance between the boats. "Let's not give them one easy target."

"Why haven't they hit us?" Nelson asked, knowing misses from that range were rare in the age of satellite-guided missiles.

"StarFly manufactures the system they're using. I've got a countermeasure code that buys us a few centimeters for every point seven meters they're covering."

"Impressive," Nelson said, but then he saw a dark green Flo-wing soaring toward them. "Deuce!" he yelled, pointing.

Deuce looked up from his AirViews and mouthed a curse word. He started pounding virtual keys like a crazed concert pianist. "Come on, come on!"

Nelson searched the waters for Grandyn's boat. It was at least five hundred meters away. The Flo-wing was coming fast from the opposite direction. *Maybe Grandyn will make it,* Nelson thought as he prepared for the impact of whatever the Flo-wing was going to fire. Deuce was completely focused on his screens and keys, and hadn't looked back at the Flo-wing as it bore down on them.

"Deuce!" Nelson yelled, certain it was now within striking distance.

Deuce waved him off.

"Damn it, Deuce!"

Deuce didn't flinch.

Munna's eyes were closed.

If the Flo-wing's glass hadn't been tinted, Nelson was sure he would have been able to see the pilot's expression. The kill in his sights.

Nelson thought of jumping overboard. "Deuce!"

"Hold on!" Deuce yelled sharply.

A second later, the explosion was the loudest thing Nelson had ever heard. It instantly deafened and blinded him, and then he was under water. Cold, dark water, crashing with debris and shrapnel. He fought the urge to breathe, the desperate need for air. It was impossible to tell which way to go as he spun.

Then he righted and saw light. Two or three meters, he could make it. He kicked and moved his arms, surprised but grateful that all his limbs seemed to be intact and functioning. Breaking the surface, Nelson gasped and gulped in air. Deuce came up seconds later and yelled something, but Nelson only heard a muffled sound that hurt his ears. Nelson waved. Deuce pointed at something. It was the boat! The boat was still in one piece. Capsized, but floating. They swam toward it.

Once they were close enough together, Deuce yelled again. Nelson couldn't understand what he was saying, but, reading lips, it was clear Deuce was asking the same thing Nelson was thinking.

Where was Munna?

They reached the overturned boat and found their answer. Clinging to the other side were Munna and the captain. She waved, smiling. The captain's leg was injured enough that he couldn't swim. Otherwise, they were all fine. Nelson's hearing had begun to come back to the level of the others, who all had echoing, ringing, and humming.

"What happened?" Nelson asked. He looked and saw Munna in the water and tried to reach her.

Grandyn's boat was racing toward them.

"Oh no!" Deuce yelled as another missile launched from the island. He crawled onto the bottom of their capsized boat and frantically pulled an INU from his belt. AirViews appeared around him while his fingers danced on virtual keys, hitting holographic points on a map.

The missile closed in fast. Nelson turned back to Deuce. The missile appeared to be heading straight for Grandyn's boat. Nelson wasn't sure exactly what Deuce was doing, but he didn't think there'd be enough time. Then he saw Munna. Her eyes were closed, she seemed calm.

How much longer can she last in this cold water? he wondered. *I'm shivering and I've got to weigh nearly three times what she does. And she's one hundred and thirty-three years old. We've got to get her warm and dry quickly.*

He moved next to her. The missile hit the water four meters from Grandyn's boat, causing it to rise out of the water, but it landed well and righted itself.

Deuce scanned back to the island, looking for another. "Looks like we have a minute," he said.

"Let's get her out of the water," Nelson said.

Grandyn's boat kept pushing toward them.

"Good idea. Munna?" Deuce asked, but she seemed lost in meditation.

A few seconds later, Grandyn's boat arrived.

"Is anyone hurt?" Fye asked.

"Munna, we're going to get you into the other boat."

She didn't respond. Nelson looked at Deuce.

"There's no time. Let's just do it."

Deuce, Grandyn, and Nelson managed to get her carefully into the other boat. They put her in the tiny cabin where Fye tended to her.

Grandyn and Deuce briefly discussed trying to flip the capsized boat, but they quickly abandoned the idea and all climbed aboard the surviving vessel. There was barely enough room, but everyone squeezed in. They headed into open waters as fast as the over-loaded craft could go. Two missiles came, but somehow Deuce was able to push them just far enough off course that they missed their targets.

"We should be out of their range now," Deuce announced.

"What about a second Flo-wing attack?" Grandyn asked.

"That's another story."

"How did we escape the last one?" Nelson repeated his earlier question.

"I shot it down," Deuce said.

"From where?"

"Satellite."

"Shoot," Nelson said. "That's damned impressive."

"Barely made it," Deuce said.

"Can you do it again?" Twain asked, pointing at an approaching Flo-wing.

CHAPTER TWENTY-FIVE

The Chief reviewed the latest reports from each region and was appalled to learn that the rebels had been using several decommissioned AOI bases. Several attacks had come from these Aylantik facilities. "PAWN and those other filthy insurgents are using our own assets to kill us," she growled. "We'll see how well they do dead." The Chief zoomed an urgent declaration to all regional heads. "Destroy all unused, abandoned former AOI bases immediately."

In Toronto, Miner and Sarlo played catch-up as the entire Pharma-Force system got back online, thanks to their deal with Blaze—actually more than a deal; it was an alliance. Blaze agreed to provide intelligence, information, and technical prowess, while Miner would give what Blaze needed most: a standing army. Enforcers were one of only four solider-based "militaries" in the world, the others being PAWN's coalition, Deuce's BLAXERs, and the AOI. Now that the war had started, the Enforcers were perhaps Miner's most valuable asset.

The first order, after they regained command and control capabilities for his elite mercenaries, was to take Ryder and Runit Islands and to capture Deuce Lipton, Nelson Wright, and Munna.

With the entry of the Trapciers, Blaze needed the prophecies. Although he had great respect for Deuce, he knew that he would never share them with him, and Blaze didn't trust anyone else to be able to handle the information and power contained in the prophecies. Not with the fate of humanity on the line.

"The Imps are super smart. They've tapped into the hidden universe," Blaze had explained to Miner and Sarlo. "That connection the rest of us usually miss, that gets lost in the buzz of everyday life, of survival, because when you get down to it, ever since the Stone Age, that's all we've been doing, surviving and propagating the species. In that way, we're no different from the rest of the animals."

"But we've explored the heavens, we've made incredible art, written and created. We're much more than just another animal," Sarlo had argued.

"Yes, those things occur when someone makes the connection to the infinite. Even an accidental brush against the universe produces genius. Some of the greatest people in history have had mere moments of touching the source. Where they reached into the stars and pulled out magnificence, enough to inspire the rest of us, to leave a mark of awe imprinted on the world."

"Can we get drunk and discuss philosophy later?" Miner had asked impatiently. "Our friends are busy taking over the world."

After that, Blaze brought them back online and Miner gave the order to attack Deuce. In between monitoring the action on the islands, Miner had moved to engage the AOI in four key areas. If the Chief was going to blame him for the violence, he was going to make her feel the reality she'd created. He'd also sent a secret message to the A-Council explaining the situation and, in a final act to thwart the Chief, he'd sent small groups of guerrillas to all forty-eight AOI prisons hoping to aid the escapes.

Blaze had promised to share the prophecies, and even though Miner didn't trust him, he had the advantage. It would be *his* team that recovered them, and if, somehow, Blaze did manage to get his hands on them first, Miner figured it was better to have him get them instead of Deuce, the AOI or, worst of all, the monsters, which is how he now referred to the Imps and CHRUDEs that made up the Trapciers.

Blaze was back in a zoom. "Damn it Lance. Your jerk-force has just blown the boat carrying Deuce out of the water."

Miner smiled. "Too bad. I certainly hope Deuce is dead."

"I don't care what happens to Deuce, but as I told you earlier, he most likely has the key to the prophecies on him. It does me no good at the bottom of the ocean. Your people are supposed to take him prisoner! He's a damned businessman! How hard could it be for a few hundred highly trained soldiers to grab an old lady, a writer, and a businessman?"

Miner would have liked to have the prophecies, but he'd managed his whole life without them and wasn't even sure they were real, or accurate enough to worry about. He was willing to take his chances with the forecasts made by the DesTIn programs and let his Enforcers overpower the AOI while they were fighting a multi-front war. Still, he needed to keep Blaze happy. At least for the moment.

The Chief was in the AOI war room in Washington. It had been constructed on her orders at the beginning of the Doneharvest, but had been used infrequently, whenever some serious crisis arose. Two years ago a major earthquake in the Chiantik region required the AOI to assist in disaster relief. The situation in the Amazon when Enforcers, BLAXERs, PAWN, and the AOI went to the brink had also required the war room.

Above the entrance to the underground command center the

words, "PEACE PREVAILS ALWAYS," etched in gold, seemed odd for a war room and now, more than ever, they were extremely out of place.

Giant AirViews filled the walls, enabling the Chief to see the entire world. Her seven top advisors were all present. Each sat in a hovering Tru-chair, floating through the room, working virtual keyboards, holographic maps, and interpreting up-to-the-second scenarios – their own kind of prophecies. The INUs were so advanced that their programs could predict events days and weeks ahead of time with alarming accuracy, and, like the *Justar Journal,* they would rewrite themselves as variables changed.

The head of each of the twenty-four regions was available on a live feed as they worked in their respective areas to abate crisis after crisis. Their images floated in a ring on the exterior wall just under an active map and real-time footage from every region.

The Chief barked orders and sought updates in a constant barrage of statistics, data, and requests for action and troops. The prisons had been a low priority in the early hours of the war, but now, as some of them had fallen, and with word that inmate Lex Evren, aka Polis Drast, had escaped, they were getting the Chief's glaring attention. Talking to the head of the Pacyfik, and the man in charge of AOI prisons, the Chief showed garbled footage of the Drast escape.

"He had inside help!"

"Even without that," the Pacyfik head said, "with the war and the prison uprisings, he may well have escaped anyway."

"Oh, I guess we should be glad it didn't rain today, or the wind didn't blow too hard," she said sarcastically. "These prisons are supposed to be *rocks!* Secure. Impenetrable. Escape-proof!"

"Yes, ma'am," the prison official said.

"You find me Drast," she snapped to both of them. "By the end of the day!"

They both answered in the affirmative, trying to figure out how it would be possible with their resources spread so thin and her deadline so close. In that same instant of their stuttered response, they also wondered what would happen if they failed.

"In the meantime," the Chief said coolly. "Any prison not brought under control within the next three hours, will be leveled."

"But Chief," The prison official began. "With the war on, aren't we going to need all the prison space we can get?"

She looked at him as if he were a total fool. "We aren't going to be taking any *prisoners*."

CHAPTER TWENTY-SIX

Drast studied Osc, certain he'd just been lied to, but unsure why. "Chelle doesn't have a son."

"She had me out of the system when she was seventeen. Before you knew her," Osc explained, removing the rest of his heavy riot gear.

"But I knew her through the years when you would have been growing up. She had no child." Drast looked out of the Flo-wing, wondering where they were taking him.

"I was raised by someone else," he said, averting his eyes.

"But why did she give you up?" Drast couldn't imagine Chelle doing such a thing.

Osc didn't immediately answer. He continued to stare at the ocean blurring by below them. Finally, he spoke, but still didn't look at Drast.

"My father had used his bearing rights. He was married. And my mother had sold hers."

"Sold hers?"

"Many wealthy couples want more than two children, and they hire brokers to secure the bearing rights of girls from poor families," Osc said, anger showing on his face, tensing as the words chopped out. "A broker had convinced her. Gave her money in exchange for her right to have a child."

Drast, of course, knew about the selling of bearing rights, but he had more questions. How long before she had gotten pregnant did she sell them? Why didn't the father try to buy the bearing rights back? What did she need and use the money for? But he didn't ask any of them. They were all about the past, which was obviously very difficult for Osc to discuss. Drast, a trained interrogator, could have verbally sliced and diced Osc and his story, but given the events of the last hour and his present location, he didn't think that wise. Instead, he asked a question much closer to the present time.

"If you're Chelle's son, why didn't you get word to me from her?"

"I haven't spoken to my mother since I entered the academy."

"Why?"

"It was too dangerous. The illegitimate son of one of PAWN's top leaders, deep undercover in the AOI to save the greatest traitor in the history of the Aylantik . . . can you imagine how much damage there would be, if I were caught?"

"But you were working with Grandyn." *This doesn't make sense, but why the elaborate lie?*

"I had no idea that Terik was Grandyn until Lance Miner killed him," Osc explained as the Flo-wing banked and descended until it flew about a meter above the water. "It was the most incredible coincidence that we were both in the Academy at the same time and became friends. I was always on the lookout for sympathizers to recruit. You know better than I do that there are only two types who enlist in the AOI. The ones in it for the honor, to protect the peace, preserve the Aylantik, and then those who just see it as a good career path. The latter, the people using it as a stepping stone, are often easily turned."

"Yes, I know that. I owe my survival to them. And to you." Drast tipped his head. "The Aylantik bureaucracy imagines everyone loves the world as it is, but the Chief understands that 'Peace prevails, always,' means peace at a price, and that price is usually paid by the 'commoners.'" Drast stared back at Osc. "You said protect the traitor."

"The day you were arrested, my mother asked me to join the AOI to find you. She always believed they hadn't killed you. But . . . if you *were* dead, I could still help the revolution from inside the AOI. And once I got in, I couldn't believe how many 'traitors' were working for the agency."

"That has always been our best hope for victory," Drast said. "I believe up to twelve percent of agents are sympathetic to the revolution."

"That's even higher than I thought."

Drast nodded and was quiet for a while. In spite of himself, he believed Osc. Chelle had sent her only son to find him, to save him. He looked back at Osc and could see his mother's eyes. The questions stacked up in his mind, but they would have to wait until he saw her again. He allowed himself to believe it was all true. It had been forever since he'd seen her, and now the war had begun. The war they'd tried for so long to start. They would fight side by side and love in the moments between.

A few minutes later, they landed on a remote beach north of Vancouver, in the country formerly known as Canada. The pilot gave them two codes, pointed at a trail, and told them a LEV would be waiting. They hiked up the hill on a narrow path through the trees. It was farther than they expected, however after almost ten minutes they came to a small parking area. No one was in the LEV, but Osc punched the code in the door and it opened. It had been preprogrammed, and took them on a winding drive through back roads for about thirty-five-minutes. They never saw another vehicle.

Eventually they were carried down a long, secluded driveway, stopping in front of a security gate. The LEV was scanned and the high metal panels slid back. The LEV continued for another few minutes until it reached a small house shrouded in trees. At the door, Osc used the second code and it instantly opened.

Inside they found food, water, blankets, cots, a lasershod, and an INU. Drast didn't need to ask where they were. He knew enough to recognize a PAWN safe house. He got cleaned up and scrubbed off the blood. His hopes of seeing Chelle that day were quickly dashed, and as soon as they opened an AirView from the INU, he knew why.

The war had begun with shocking intensity. Drast and Osc watched the coverage across the Field, which was all they had access to at the moment, in stunned silence. Even in his time with the AOI, Drast had not seen scenarios such as this, and he worried that Grandyn had been right about what would happen if the war began in the prisons. As near as he could tell, it had, or at least the start of the war and the prison uprisings had happened simultaneously.

As Drast watched parts of cities crumble and calls for citizens to report immediately to their Health-Circle stations, he thought it looked far less like a revolution and more of a sequel to the Banoff. There were hundreds of PAWN arrests and raids on homes of rebel sympathizers. The worst scenes showed POPs getting blown up.

"What is PAWN doing?" Drast asked. "The AOI is completely dominating."

"Remember, that's just what they're showing us," Osc said.

"They are showing us a lot," Drast said, fully aware of how the AOI's propaganda machine worked. "How can we reach Chelle?"

"I don't know," Osc replied.

"I can't sit in this tiny cabin in the woods while all of this is going on," Drast said.

"There really isn't a choice. We have to wait until PAWN contacts us."

Drast scoffed and shook his head. "Just look at this. If we wait too long there will be no PAWN left to contact us."

CHAPTER TWENTY-SEVEN

The panic on the tiny boat paralyzed them, and for an instant, as the Flo-wing zeroed in, no one knew what to do.

"Can you do it again Dad?" Twain repeated.

"I might not have to," Deuce said, nodding toward a second Flo-wing above the first one.

"Oh no, another one!" Nelson yelled, standing in a puddle of water from his dripping clothes, his shoes lost in the ocean.

"That one is mine," Deuce said triumphantly, and then, as if reacting to his words, it fired upon the first one. The strike hit perfectly, and the Enforcers' Flo-wing exploded and fell into the sea. Soon more Flo-wings appeared and began firing on the island. Even as their boat sped away, they could see BLAXERs landing and engaging the Enforcers.

"We'll be all right now," Deuce said. "We're less than ten minutes from our rendezvous with a much better boat."

Good to his word, they soon met up with another vessel. Surprisingly, it was as much plane as it was boat. This new craft docked next to them and they carefully climbed aboard. Munna had been concentrating on her self-healing methods, and was able to make the transfer without assistance. Only the BLAXER captain stayed on the smaller boat, then he sped away, back toward Ryder Island.

"I would hardly call this a boat," Nelson said as he marveled at the interior.

"It's called the 'Moon Shadow,'" Deuce replied. "We are almost completely invisible to AOI detection. And, because the Moon Shadow utilizes ADAM technology and relies mainly on solar, wind, and nano-energy sources, we can travel anywhere in the world as long as there is water."

"You mean it doesn't fly?" Nelson asked, because it looked like an arrowhead with wings.

"No, the shape is for speed. The Moon Shadow is very, *very* fast."

Fye had taken Munna to a bedroom to rest while her natural fiber clothes were dried in a solar dryer. A porter brought Nelson fresh clothes made of Tekfabrik. They would size, style, color adjust, and, just as Deuce's had, self-dry if they wound up in the water again. Nelson assumed that was extremely unlikely aboard a ship like the Moon Shadow.

Grandyn suddenly had renewed hope for their chances. With the fast evacuation from the island and the near misses, he'd been feeling defeated, even scared. *It's different having to worry about a child*, he thought, suddenly more connected with his own parents, but the Moon Shadow's interior exuded power and supremacy like nothing he'd experienced before.

The ship flew along at some unfathomable speed. The sides of the main cabin were covered with AirViews in place of windows. He'd later learn they would retract to reveal see-through walls. The horrors of the war were exposed, but so was a glimpse of Deuce's might and reach. BLAXERs were in transit to every hotspot in the world, and they watched it all happen live.

With everything relatively calm for the moment, Deuce finally took off his pack. Fortunately, its waterproof Tekfabrik covering had mostly protected the eight books. A little water had gotten in, but the only real damage was around the edges of the pages. They would dry out. He laid them open on a table. Grandyn took it as another display of Deuce's confidence. He was obviously not expecting an attack.

"Where are we going?" Grandyn asked.

"I was planning to drop you, Fye, and Twain off on the coast at the redwoods," Deuce said. "I'm not sure where Munna and Nelson want to go . . ." He turned toward Nelson. "But you're welcome to stay on the Moon Shadow. It's really the safest place right now."

"That's up to Munna," Nelson said. "Now that the uprising has begun, I don't know what she's going to do with the prophecies. You know she doesn't want them used for war."

"It's hardly her choice anymore."

"Really? You seem to forget how she blocked them back on Runit Island."

"No, I have not forgotten," Deuce said, lighting up more AirViews around the cabin, showing scenes from the fighting. "They're saying that PAWN is doing this."

"The people won't believe that," Nelson said.

"Why not?" Deuce asked. "You've been living in the revolution bubble for so long that you think everyone hates the Aylantik and welcomes a rebellion. Well Nelson, I'm here to tell you that's not the case. Look at what's happening out there: a peaceful world turned to cold, brutal, deadly, conflict. The population has no point of reference. No one alive remembers the last war."

"Except Munna," Nelson said.

The point hit Deuce, and he momentarily wavered, caught by the images of death and destruction, realizing that the only person in the world who had seen such a thing before was the one demanding the prophecies not be used as part of it.

"So she should want it ended as soon as possible, and the prophecies will do that."

"The *Justar Journal* is not for showing you how to win a war," Munna said, walking into the room and stomping her cane on the floor.

"Munna, how many need to die before you decide that we must end the war?"

She smiled at him, as one would to a child that did not understand what they were saying. Then she walked closer to him and looked up into his eyes. "The *Justar Journal* was *not* created to show you how to win a war."

"Then what good is it? What's it for?"

"How can you, someone who looks to the stars so constantly, not know what the *Justar* is for?" she asked, still not taking her eyes off his.

"If you know, tell me. Otherwise help me end this," he said, motioning his arm around at the vicious images. Then, with a cracking voice, he added, "Please, Munna. *Please*."

She shook her head. "But I will stay with you a while longer to see if one of us changes his mind."

They watched the news while Deuce directed the BLAZERs around the world and continued to monitor the AOI. Soon they were along a stunning stretch of coastline. Nelson recognized it as the area where they had pulled Twain out a few weeks earlier. It was part of a huge Earth Park. The Aylantik had combined and expanded eight former US State and National Parks into one super Earth Park that included all of the redwoods.

Goodbyes were said and a small launch, carrying Fye, Grandyn, and Twain, was sent to shore.

Just before they left the Moon Shadow, Deuce had connected Twain with his sister and mother. They had tried to talk him out of going back into the redwoods. Grandyn had watched as they cried, and it brought back memories of his own mother. The AOI had killed her thirteen years earlier . . . they had taken so much of his life, but he would not let them take any more. He and Fye were going to work their way to the List Keepers City, where he hoped to be able to convince them to use their power and resources to help PAWN win the revolution.

Grandyn had contacted Parker, the TreeRunners leader, and she'd arranged for Fye and himself to join a combat unit of the TreeRunners who could help them get through the area. Three or four hours after they'd left Twain in the redwoods, they met up with members of the TreeRunners. There were six of them, and Grandyn was disappointed that he didn't know any. The one in charge made introductions, and then told Grandyn, "We've got a POP about three kilometers from here where we can sleep tonight."

"Appreciate the help," Grandyn said. "This is a bit west of my old stomping grounds, but I suspect we'll get into familiar territory sometime tomorrow."

"Our orders are to get you as far as Mt. Shasta," the Tree-Runner said. "Our clan leader will be here in the morning. She'll have the latest information on what's going on out there. With all the fighting in the Oregon Area, we may have to lay low for a few days."

"We can fight if need be," Grandyn said, looking at Fye. "Who's your leader?" he asked, wondering if it might be one of his old clan mates.

"You probably don't know her. She just transferred into the area recently," the TreeRunner said. "Her name's Zaverly."

CHAPTER TWENTY-EIGHT

Runit scoured the shore for any kind of boat. After seeing nothing in the immediate vicinity, he ran back inside to get a jacket. Androids didn't need any heavy clothing and his outside time had been limited, so he only had a light coat. He also grabbed a couple long sleeve shirts and layered them under his parka. Back out in the weather, he returned to the main dock he'd seen earlier. Having never been there before today, he explored it as if searching for clues about his location and more important, a way off the island. *This modern structure clearly doesn't predate the Banoff. The AOI must have built it.* The sophisticated structure was wired with some sort of system that appeared to be able to handle automated vessels. *How often do they bring supplies. Maybe a supply boat will come soon.*

Runit looked out to the sea, straining to see through the thick fog. Nothing. Even on clear days he had never been able to see anything but ocean. Today, though, he was looking for AOI boats coming to kill him.

He jogged along the shore. Nearly five hours later he had completed the circumference. Portions had been too rocky or cliffs too sheer, forcing him away from the water's edge, he was nevertheless convinced that no seaworthy vessel of any kind existed on this desperate little slice of the world. The only other signs of civilization were a tidal energy generating station, which obviously provided power to the facility, and an ancient gun emplacements site that must have belonged to a long forgotten pre Banoff military—the guns were no longer there.

Exhausted and freezing, Runit stumbled back inside, half expecting the gates to be locked and the androids waiting. Yet, everything remained exactly how he had left it. *There must be a way*, he thought, as he began exploring all the off-limits areas of the facility. He found the android's office, equipped with charging stations, replacement parts, a small communication center, and after trying, found it too, was inoperable. There were two INUs, without access to the Field, he took them anyway. Nothing else useful.

Then he discovered the small kitchen area where they prepared his meals. Most of them had been pretty bleak, AOI rations for grunges working deep in the jungles, where food and supply chains didn't easily go. Frustration and discouragement overtook his tired mind, when he realized there must've been months of supplies of the terrible provisions.

He tried to recall if he'd ever seen a Flo-wing or a boat visit the island. He couldn't. "I'm still a librarian," he said out loud, falling back on his life's skills to sort out his plight. He counted up all the food as if it were books and did a calculation. "Damn it, ninety-eight days supplies." The thought of eating all that awful food before tasting freedom made him feel sick. "Think, Runit," he said. "The efficiency of the AOI. They might send a boat a week or two before the supplies run out." He sighed. "Either way, I've got three months. I've got to find another way."

Then he heard a paralyzing sound, like a dozen missiles flying toward his island. And that's just what it was, only worse.

Miner opened the connection and allowed Blaze's hologram to appear. "What happened?"

"We lost them for the moment," Miner admitted, shrugging at Sarlo.

Blaze wasn't surprised. Deuce was not an easy target. It was the reason he'd enlisted Miner's Enforcers in the first place. "Where is he now?"

"He's vanished into thin air," Miner said. "Before we could get backup to his islands to aid our jumpers, he'd gotten BLAXERs there and they outgunned and outnumbered our people."

"Anyone make it out alive?"

"No. In the interests of speed and surprise, we'd dropped them in without a retreat option until we could get reinforcements there . . . they ran out of time."

"Have you checked satellite tracking to see where Deuce went?" Blaze asked, but he already knew the answer.

"Deuce controls many of the satellites, and he's got some kind of stealth technology. I'm telling you he *vanished* out there."

"The Imps will find him."

"Can we use them to locate him?"

"They might be too smart for that, but you can try," Blaze said, looking at his reflection in a polished silver column and checking his hair. "I hope to implement a surprise for the Trapciers before they get that far, and when the time comes, I'll need a few thousand Enforcers to help pick up the pieces, but I'm not ready to talk about it."

"I assume the Imps have moved out of Denver?"

"Yes, and obviously the AOI is not pursuing them. It was a brilliant alliance they forged. Unless the Chief is smarter than we think."

"She's never impressed me," Miner said bitterly.

"He's biased," Sarlo said. "I don't think we should underestimate her. She seems to be doing a damn fine job executing the war so far. Especially when this is, allegedly, something the Chief never wanted." Sarlo gestured toward the AirViews, showing endless destruction and very little pushback from anyone. "And her two natural enemies are taking the blame. Publicly, PAWN is responsible for the trouble, and within the Council, Lance and Enforcers are the bad guys."

"It's just the first day, love," Blaze said. "We'll see how she's doing a week from now."

Sarlo looked back at the AirViews and shuddered, trying to imagine what horrors would come in the next week.

What will be left? she wondered. *And where the hell is PAWN?*

The Chief, Deuce Lipton, Lance Miner, and Blaze Cortez were all asking the same question. Thus far, Chelle and PAWN had been almost silent. All the parties were making the same assumption. That the war they'd been hoping for all those decades had caught them by surprise.

Blaze speculated that it might be some kind of strategy. Miner suggested perhaps PAWN had been overestimated, although Sarlo thought just the opposite. Deuce had been almost too busy to give it much thought, but after he'd regained control of his situation, worry about Chelle crept in. He'd never been entirely sure he trusted her, but he always thought her a dangerous foe, and one to be feared by all her adversaries.

They were all correct. Chelle had been surprised by the start of the war, but less about the timing and more about the AOI's rapid and lethal methods. Most of her day had been spent strategizing and making sure PAWN would be in a position to handle the AOI's tactics. She had also been worrying, mainly about Drast and Osc, but also about Nelson and Grandyn. Chelle was, above all, a warrior, and although the stress had torn at her unrelentingly for years, she used it to strengthen her focus. There were times when that technique wore thin, but there was no other choice.

She was also part of a strong team of revolutionaries who'd mostly hammered out their differences and were united in their opposition to Aylantik. However, they all knew their biggest threat might not be the AOI, but rather the Trapciers. Also, making the multifarious situation even more complex, were the List Keepers.

The Imps may have been a late surprise into the conflict, but PAWN understood that challenge, and knew whom they were dealing with. The List Keepers, a mysterious group that had longed vexed them, and were only now beginning to get attention from Deuce, Miner, and the AOI, had been an entity they'd been wrestling with for years. Yet even in all that time, they had only confirmed two members. Fye, who with her relationship with Grandyn, had direct influence and connection to the disposition of the *Justar Journal*, and Munna, who seemingly controlled the prophecies, making the List Keepers even more crucial to the fight.

Chelle believed them to be a friendly group who should side with PAWN. However, she had little to base those assumptions on, and now that the war had begun, anything was possible. *At least,* she thought, *with the outbreak of hostilities, we'll finally know where the List Keepers stand.* Chelle was also counting on Grandyn. If he was involved with Fye, he must know much more about the group, and he was as loyal to the revolution as anyone.

She concluded a Field-view, utilizing infinite-encryption that had linked representatives from the Creatives, the Rejectionists, as well as PAWN leaders from around the world. As expected, everyone had fallen in line and were fully committed to a unified front against Aylantik. That news was good, but there had already been heavy losses. The Chief was seemingly fighting the war solo, orchestrating all sides so that she could inflict huge casualties on PAWN and Enforcers. So far the BLAZERs had remained neutral, but all the INU and DesTIn generated simulations had shown Deuce's initial response. Chelle still expected him to join their side, although some of her peers weren't as convinced.

Finally alone, Chelle stared at more than forty AirViews floating in her private conference room. The constant images of the vicious blitzkrieg being pounded in unending furor by the AOI had left her traumatized. Still, she reviewed every strike and adjusted her plans accordingly. During the moments in between, Chelle searched for word of Osc and Drast. Communications in and from that quadrant of the Pacyfik, which included Hilton Prison, Portland, Ryder and Runit Islands, and a series of known PAWN strongholds and revolutionary sympathizers, had been sketchy all day.

Then, she spotted a report that stole her heart. The Flo-wing that had been sent to rescue them from Hilton Prison had been shot down. It had been a laser-blast strike. She knew that meant a fireball, which would result in almost no wreckage, and definitely no survivors. Chelle read the report three times, trying to wring a different meaning from the cold words.

How can I lose my son and Polis in one day? She couldn't believe it. *The cruelty of the stars could not waste such a harsh sentence on me. I've been tortured enough. I cannot give any more of a reaction to make this anything but a simple tragedy. I have no blood remaining, no tears available . . . I have been trampled and spent. Damn you! Torgon damn you!*

An aide found her a few minutes later, sitting silently, trembling.

"Chelle, are you all right?" she asked.

Chelle shook her head, but said, "Fine."

The aide looked around, unsure if that answer was adequate. Chelle's face seemed as if it had been deflated, and her scratchy voice didn't belong to the once beautiful woman, but when Chelle didn't say any more, the aide remembered she had news that might help.

"We've just received a signal from the Glade safe house. It's the closest to Hilton Prison. Someone is inside. They've used the INU."

It took a second for the words to register, but then Chelle

sprang back to life. She pulled up the details of the Glade safe house, then checked the report of the Flo-wing again and realized that it could have been shot down *after* it had dropped Osc and Drast to safety. There was no way to contact them directly yet, but they could be alive.

They are alive! I know it. She breathed oxygen into her lungs and felt her heart beat again.

CHAPTER TWENTY-NINE

Sidis marveled at the maps before him. Battles across the globe were shown above the outlines of cities, areas, and regions in three dimensional live views.

"They're actually hardly battles," he said to the other Imps and CHRUDEs that had gathered. "It is difficult to describe them as battles when no one is fighting back."

"The day has exceeded our expectations," Galahad said.

"Thanks to the ruthlessness of the AOI Chief. It turns out that woman is even more nasty than our models showed her to be."

"But tomorrow promises to be something different, when the shock wears off and PAWN, Enforcers, and BLAXERs are able to regroup and strike back."

"Yes, but that's precisely what we want them to do. Have you seen the latest DesTIn predictions? The war will last eight more days until both sides collapse. Then, in victory, our vision will begin, and we will have more than won. We will have accomplished what no one in world history has been able to achieve: the *end* of war. The Trapciers will be able to redirect the future of humanity and this planet. Imps and CHRUDEs will have saved the Traditionals and the world."

"It's her," Morholt said, allowing a holographic version of the Chief to enter.

"Still at work?" Sidis said. "It's been a long day."

"Yes," replied the Chief, looking around at the gathered misfits who always appeared to her as skeletons wearing clothes. The one called Percival actually looked more like a suit on a clothes hanger. Then there were the "healthy ones," who seemed like normal Traditionals, although she assumed they were some kind of elaborate android. She didn't really know who, or what they were, and that bothered her. The AOI was still well behind on understanding CHRUDE technology. Her typically stern face looked even more gray and chiseled. "It has been going well, but I'm concerned—"

"Concerned that PAWN has yet to react? That Miner has regained control of the Enforcers and that Deuce Lipton is not truly on our side?" Sidis said, finishing the Chief's statement, as if he'd read her mind. "Of course you are, and right you should be. Allow me to tell you what tomorrow will bring. Or, better yet, I will show you."

Sidis ran a simulation that had Enforcers pulling back and PAWN taking surgical strikes against AOI tech centers and troop-heavy bases.

"You believe Miner will back down?" she asked, surprised.

"He has to. Miner is an Aylantik loyalist. Although he'd like to see you fired, or more accurately, tortured and slowly killed, he has no desire to alienate his friends on the Council. He will seek to reconcile with them and to rejoin our alliance."

"Hard to believe, but plausible," she said. "And Deuce?"

"Deuce will eventually swing the other way. He is a problem because his BLAXERs are more numerous and better trained than Enforcers, but most troublesome is the fact that they are equipped with more superior weapons and technology than the AOI."

"Our assessment doesn't draw that conclusion," the Chief said.

"No, it wouldn't. You see Chief, in order for AOI assessments to present a true picture of the BLAXERs' capabilities, the basis and input data would have to be accurate, and they are not."

"Really?" the Chief asked indignantly.

"It's worse than that. Deuce Lipton controls a significant number of AOI suppliers."

"Impossible. We review ownership, conflicts of interest, affiliations, and connections quarterly, and maintain—"

"Tell it to the Council, Chief. I'm not here to judge you, just to prepare you. I'll flash you a list of the ownership, conflicts of interest, affiliations, and connections you missed. But don't punish yourself. We can deal with most of it."

"Most of *what*?"

"Deuce will have planted back-doors and the like," Sidis said. "When he turns from you, it will be easy to spot. It's while he is still an 'ally' that presents the greatest threat."

"I'll put a team on it," the Chief said.

"We're already working on a program."

"I'm also worried about a group called the List Keepers. We don't know enough about them, but there is increasing chatter through Seeker and Flash."

"Yes," Sidis said gravely, "we are also concerned. It is precisely because that chatter is so infinitesimal that tells us they are dangerous."

"Our records show mentions of them, like PAWN, all the way back to the Banoff. We have enormous amounts of data on PAWN, but with the List Keepers, the references and instances are very rare. Our conclusion is they are either very small, or very powerful."

"We believe they are actually both small *and* powerful. The List Keepers are a mystery we have been wrestling with for some time. They are the one factor that makes our forecast difficult. If we leave them out of a scenario, it is rendered accurate only to seventy-eight percent."

"And if you include them?"

"Because of the dearth of information about them, those results become inconclusive," Sidis said, deciding not to tell her that they had run two simulations which both showed the Aylantik falling because of the List Keepers.

Sidis and Galahad believed there was more information about the List Keepers within the Field than was visible, using typical data claiming techniques. "It's as if the Field is wrapped inside something much bigger than itself," Sidis had told Galahad, "and we can only scrape the data from the larger pool. From where it touches the Field." If that larger pool really existed, who created and controlled it was an extremely troubling matter because, they agreed, it could only be the List Keepers.

"The one person who may be able to unlock the List Keepers' secrets is Blaze Cortez," Sidis told the Chief.

"Ah, Blaze. Good. A man with a price. I'll track him down in the morning."

"Excellent. And Chief, you do know Blaze cannot be trusted?"

"Of course," she said in a clipped tone. "In my job, I know whom I can trust . . . no one."

CHAPTER THIRTY

On board the Moon Shadow, Deuce continued to monitor the war into the night. The AOI's assaults had been building in intensity with each passing hour. Like a volcano that builds pressure in an underground magma chamber for years until, one day, it blows a mountain apart. The Chief seemed to be counting on a short war, and wanted to take out as much opposition as possible. Deuce contacted the A-Council Chairman.

"Deuce, it's nearly midnight," the Chairman said, opening the voice-only zoom.

"Yes, I guess it is in your time zone. But I know you are usually up even later, and with the war, I assumed you might not sleep at all."

"All true. What can I do for you?"

The Chairman, also a wealthy man, owned multiple companies, including the largest manufacturer of LEVs, but even with a hundred billion-digis net worth, he didn't come close to Deuce's massive wealth.

"You can call off your dog."

"The Chief is just doing her job," the Chairman responded. "It's a difficult charge to keep the peace."

"Especially when you're starting a war."

"Deuce, come on, you know we're a peaceful government. That's the first item in the Constitution. The Aylantik has reigned over the longest period of peace in history."

"I know what the Aylantik has reigned over Chairman, but I'm telling you that the AOI started this war."

"PAWN started this. And perhaps Lance Miner got a little overzealous, but the AOI is only responding to the actions of others. The Chief will end this thing before it gets out of hand."

"Have you been watching the news? It's *already* out of hand. The Chief is using this as an excuse to wipe out dissidents on a massive scale."

"You know we have a no-tolerance policy for revolutionaries. This may seem harsh to some, but it has proven to be the secret to peace. Troublemakers have selfish agendas that are not for the better good."

Deuce knew the Chairman believed some of what he was saying. The Council members had been isolated in their cocoons of wealth and privilege for so long that they were completely out of touch with the reality of what the world was like for everyone else. True, they had created a utopian-appearing society, and maybe it couldn't have been done without their "no-tolerance" policy, but that same policy had directly led to the growth of PAWN and other revolutionary factions.

"Chairman, the Chief started this war. Do you want proof?"

"No, because even if what you say is true, it wouldn't matter now. This will turn out to be a good thing. In a few days it will all be over, and the world will be rid of PAWN, the Rejectionists, and all the other problems. Think of it as a cleansing. It'll guarantee us another fifty or a hundred years of peace and prosperity." The Chairman smiled perfectly. "Every so often a little revolution is a good thing. It allows us to exterminate all the rats, and rid the world of the disease and destruction those rodents carry."

"Okay Chairman." Deuce was at a loss. The man he'd been

hoping to reason with didn't understand how dangerous a position the world was in. He wished he could show him the *Justar Journal*, but that would be too risky. The Aylantik would simply use it to advance their own objectives. Deuce realized sadly that Munna thought the same thing of him. "We'll talk again in a few days. Perhaps then you'll understand that the Chief is leading us into an inferno that may be impossible to escape." He looked at a city, in what used to be known as Spain, burning on another AirView.

"Don't worry, Deuce. No flame burns forever."

After the zoom, Deuce checked in on Munna and Nelson and told them of his conversation with the Chairman.

"What if we can't stop it?" he asked Munna.

"It *must* stop," she said quietly.

"But what if it's not in time?"

"Time is a funny thing," she said, smiling slightly. "We are still just at the beginning of the end."

That didn't make Deuce feel any better. He believed Munna knew what was going to happen, or at least, what *could* happen, and she had the ability to show them what to do. He'd already decided not to fight her anymore about the prophecies, but somehow he needed to convince her to lead the people.

"The news is awful. It's as if the war has been going for a month," Nelson said. "The AOI is crushing everything. Can't you help?"

"I can do a lot, but if the Chief sees me as an enemy, I won't be able to do much except defend myself," Deuce said. "None of us were expecting this kind of annihilation, and the late entry of the Trapciers has changed things. They are mechanical, cold, calculating creatures. If I didn't know any better, I'd say the Chief was one of them."

The stealth luxury yacht flew through the water toward the south and into the open seas. There was a small Flo-wing on board in case of an emergency. Deuce's wife and daughter were secure on his safest island: a man-made, floating fortress constructed of the most advanced materials which rendered it virtually invisible while allowing it to feel like a well-stocked resort.

Deuce would stay as far away from it as possible so as not to lead any enemies to his sanctuary. The Chief would be working hard to track him. He'd already seen evidence inside the AOI system, and had been working to thwart those efforts. He worried about Twain, out there alone in the woods. He wanted him on the island with his wife, but he knew that Twain was not the same as the rest of them.

He turned back to Munna. "Please, tell me about the List Keepers . . . Who are they? What do they do? Where can I find them?"

"The List Keepers are our last chance," she said, staring out one of the abstract-shaped windows to the starry sky. Deuce had noticed Munna didn't look at the images of the war on the AirViews.

"That's why I need to talk to them."

"You want the *Justar Journal*, you want the List Keepers, you want to keep Twain away from the redwoods," Munna said, facing him and smiling. "You have so much already, do you really need more?" She turned back to the window. "Use what you have Deuce."

"Do you think the Enforcers came to the islands by accident?" Deuce asked, frustrated. "They were coming for the prophecies. They were coming for you and your secrets."

CHAPTER THIRTY-ONE

Fye and Grandyn stayed up talking well into the night. The POP was small, but they had a private room, and felt safe being deep in the forest.

"I wish we were already at the City," Grandyn said, as the low lights dimmed further. They lay close to each other. He could see her face. What they said about women's faces glowing when they were pregnant seemed extra-true with Fye. "If only we could get in a Flo-wing and fly there."

"You know it's way too dangerous right now."

"It's going to take forever to get there on foot."

"They said we'll meet up with Zaverly tomorrow. She's supposed to be a real hotshot TreeRunner commander," Fye said. "Maybe she can hook us up with an off-road vehicle, or at least a couple of AirSliders. Then we might make faster time to the City." An AirSlider was a jet-propelled scooter equipped with laser munitions. Grandyn had been trained on them extensively.

"I hope so, but we may see some fighting as we get closer to the edge of the forest. They say the AOI is sending scrap units of grunges into all the wilderness areas that are close to towns."

"I'm surprised they're using resources that way. It would seem smarter to protect the larger populations."

"When I was Terik, I saw AOI plans for just this scenario. They raid the forests looking for pockets of rebels on the move, hoping to hit them before they can strike the towns and take territory. The AOI is terrified that PAWN will capture a major town with access to weapons, communications, and transportation hubs."

"It's all so awful," Fye said.

"The List Keepers can stop this war, can't they?" Grandyn asked.

"I think they can," Fye said, "but I don't think they will."

"Why the hell not?" Grandyn asked angrily. "If they can stop it and they let all those innocent people die, they're no better than the AOI."

"You are forgetting *I* am a List Keeper. I am the 'they' you're talking about. And so are you."

"I can't be a List Keeper until they approve me in the City, but I'll tell you this. If the List Keepers won't do everything they can to help us stop the AOI, then I don't want to be one."

"One of the reasons the List Keepers have survived this long is that they know their purpose. They are the watchers, the keepers of information." She looked at him lovingly. "At great cost, the List Keepers will remain silent as the innocent fall . . . It isn't because we don't care, it's because we care more than anyone. We can't be concerned about saving a few when our mission is to save everyone."

"Why can't you do both?" he asked softly, his voice breaking.

"That isn't one of the choices. What if you were crossing a raging, flooded river with your parents and suddenly the three of you were overwhelmed and about to go under. You had a hold of your mother but your father was slipping. There was only a split second to decide whether to let him go, knowing he would drown, or hold onto him knowing that if you did, it would mean the three of you would die?"

"I'd find a way to save us all."

"There isn't one, and you only have a split second."

"The List Keepers have had at least seventy-five years, maybe a hundred."

"But that is only a split second."

"What does that mean?"

"Time's a funny thing, Grandyn," she said sweetly, as if patiently explaining something to a small child, but in no way sounding condescending. "When one is trying to save all of humanity, one hundred years is the blink of an eye."

He stared at her, and saw nothing but love in her returned gaze. He felt so angry and helpless. The world had seemed to worsen every day since his mother's death, and it kept getting worse, faster and faster. Now it was all coming apart. The last report they'd heard, before disappearing into the information void of the forests, was that more than a million people had died today. One single day.

"Why can't anyone get the Field in the forests?" he asked. "No communications, or monitoring systems, or satellite, or Field-based weapons, nothing works here."

Fye didn't answer.

"It's the List Keepers isn't it?" Grandyn asked. "When I was younger, I'd be camping in the woods with my TreeRunner clan and we would come up with these crazy theories as to why nothing got through in the wilderness areas. Aliens, Earth's magnetic field, secret government experiments, but we liked most of all to believe that nature just ruled supreme over technology. Then, in the past few years, I became convinced it was Deuce. But when Twain vanished, Deuce would have lifted the suppression if he were in control." He looked at her with his most serious expression. "Tell me the truth. I know it's the List Keepers, and I want to know why."

"It's not intentional. It's more of a byproduct."

"So I'm right?"

"Of course you're right." She closed her eyes for a moment. "You'll know when we get to the City. *If* we get there."

"What do you mean? Just tell me. Why so many secrets?"

"Grandyn, even if I were allowed to tell you, I couldn't explain it so you'd understand it. You have to see it."

"See the City?"

"Yes. And the List Keepers."

"But you're a List Keeper. I can see you. I understand you."

"There are different kinds of List Keepers. I'm not one of the special ones."

Her admission instantly softened him. "Baby, you're every kind of special." He took her hands. "I love you."

"I know. I love you too. It's just so hard not to be able to tell you what you want to know."

"The List Keepers can block all transmissions in or out of the forests around the world! They've been doing it for decades, even as the smartest scientists try to figure out what's going on, even when the AOI is desperate to know every move that every citizen makes and to root out the rebels hiding in the forests. Don't you see what kind of power that is? We *need* them. If they help, we might win this thing in a week."

She touched his hand. Her eyes filled until a single tear streamed down her cheek.

"Oh, Grandyn . . . there's no chance that this war will be over in a week."

CHAPTER THIRTY-TWO

Thursday, July 14

Drast woke in the safe house, completely disorientated. It was his first night away from prison in years. He lay in total silence, waiting for a guard to come around, waiting for the din of inmate noise. Then he remembered . . . he was free. Then something more entered his tense mind, further loosening the tightly wound defenses he'd built at Hilton Prison.

He was *alive*.

Today was to have been his "date with death." The execution had been scheduled and signed by the Chief and the warden. Looking at the sun trying to push in around the window shade, he smiled: executions were always at sunrise. He would have been dead by now. Instead, he was out, the war was on, and he was with Chelle's son, presumably heading toward her. It might take some time, but he could wait. Prison had taught him patience, but so had waiting a lifetime for the revolution.

Today was a good day to be alive.

The place was sparsely furnished, and what there was – a pine table, two spindly wooden chairs, and the cots they had slept on – looked to be more than one hundred years old.

Osc stirred as a stray stream of sunlight found him. "Are we still alive?" he mumbled.

"So far," Drast said. "Come on, get up. I'll buy you breakfast."

They'd found a small closet the night before with a two-week supply of provisions. Most of them were close to expiration dates, which didn't bode well for them because the freeze-dried foods were meant to last a decade.

"How long since anyone's been here?" Osc asked as they rummaged through the packages.

"Years," Drast said. "We're here only because some hack looked at a list and saw this was the closest safe house to the drop point. Here you go." Drast tossed a silver packet to Osc. "It says bacon and eggs. Told you I'd buy you breakfast."

"Thanks," Osc said. "It may be old, but I bet it beats prison food."

"Dirt beats prison food," Drast said with no trace of humor.

They ate in front of several AirViews showing war coverage. By the looks of things, the night had not seen any let up in the violence. The war had expanded to every continent, and had only increased in intensity. Sections of hundreds of cites had been destroyed, and homes of "rebel sympathizers" were raided with instant executions shown live on the Field.

"It's a shocking response," Drast said. "We never imagined this kind of Armageddon."

"Why are they doing it?"

"I think it's not *they*, it's just the Chief. Remember, the AOI's charge is peace at any price. I believe she's convinced that if they act swiftly to crush any possible opposition and portray PAWN as terrorists, peace can be restored in a few days."

The AirViews showed thousands of bodies lined up in the streets as the deadly virus, allegedly unleashed by PAWN, continued to spread rapidly. An announcer said the death toll, from just the outbreak, was estimated to be in the hundreds of thousands, and went on to report that the airborne pandemic, thought to be related to the Banoff plague, had an incubation period measured in minutes, and that after the initial onset of symptoms, a patient would die of seizures within a few hours.

"PAWN didn't do that," Osc said.

"Of course not. That kind of insanity and efficient killing could only have been ordered and carried out by the government."

"Health-Circle?"

"You got that right. The AHC is supposed to protect us from every kind of illness and ailment, and yet they have no cure for this. They aren't ready? Like hell they aren't. As soon as the specific portion of the population which the Aylantik *wants* removed is gone, the Health-Circle will miraculously save us. 'Just come in for your shots, folks. We'll keep everyone healthy and it won't hurt a bit.' Torgon bastards!"

The AirViews switched to more images of bombed-out cities, and lines of refugees made it appear as though the conflict was in its second month, not its second day.

"You can bet that some member of the Council owns the construction companies that will get the contracts to rebuild all of that," Drast said, motioning to the destruction. "But the Chief is playing a dangerous game. One wrong calculation and there won't be enough taxpayers left to pay for it all." He watched more bloody images appear. "We have to leave now."

"We're supposed to wait until they contact us. Someone will probably be here today."

Drast made an appalled face. "Look at it out there!" He pointed to the never-ending stream of utter chaos. "Do you really think PAWN gives a torg about us? Do you think *anyone* is coming?"

"My mother won't abandon us."

"She doesn't even know where we are. She's trying to save the torgon world. The Chief, that wretched woman, has decided to try to make Adolf Hitler look like a nice guy." Drast shook his head.

"How in the hell is Chelle supposed to fight back against that kind of callous evil?"

"She's not alone."

"Neither is the Chief." Drast scarfed down the last bit of his Styrofoam-tasting pancakes and sausage. "Chelle has enough to do just trying to avoid the complete annihilation of PAWN. We need to get to her."

"How do you suggest we do that?"

"If I can get to the real world, I can contact her. You stay if you want, but I'm going."

"I'll miss the great food, but I'm coming."

"Miss the food?" Drast asked. "You better bring it with you. Who knows what we're going to run into out there. I don't want to have to think about looking for a meal."

They loaded up half the food into the LEV, deciding to leave some of the stash for any future visitors. "Now we'll need to override the navigation program," Drast said.

"Not a problem," Osc replied. "We did a whole course at the academy on improvising technology."

"I know," Drast said, smiling. "I'm the one who added that to the curriculum."

Osc nodded. He kept forgetting Drast had been head of the Pacyfik AOI. He still thought of him as inmate Evren. A minute later, Osc had the LEV started.

"It's ready to program. What address should I put in?" When Drast gave him the information, Osc thought he was joking. "That's AOI headquarters in Vancouver. What do you have in mind? Surrendering?"

"One thing you should know," Drast said. "I never, ever surrender . . . *ever*."

"Then what's the plan?"

"I'll tell you on the way. Let's get moving. Every minute we waste is another thousand innocent people dead."

CHAPTER THIRTY-THREE

Chelle had slept less than two hours, but not all at once. She'd set her INU to wake her twenty minutes after it detected sleep. Some of the other PAWN leaders had slept even less.

Two of their top commanders were dead. More than twenty POPs had been located and destroyed. They had never lost a POP before yesterday, and they had no idea how the AOI was finding them. PAWN had hardly been able to do anything but duck and run. The overwhelming force that had come at them, around the world, was staggering. But they had resources and plans that had been in place for years, waiting to be implemented.

As the AOI continued to pound them from every direction, killing anyone who even might support them, PAWN was coming alive and surfacing from its underground existence.

Her first zoom that day was to the last person she wanted to speak with. He was the least likely to help PAWN, but the most likely to hurt the AOI, for the moment anyway.

"Lance, I thought we should talk," Chelle said as Miner accepted her voice-only zoom.

"Well, well, what a surprise you're still alive Chelle. I guess the Chief isn't quite as efficient as she seems."

"It's early in the day," Chelle said. "Neither you nor I is in a position to joke about being targets of the Chief."

"I wasn't joking. I really thought you were probably dead. But I must say, I'm happy you're still with us. You owe me a favor."

"Do I?'

"You recall the fires in the Amazon?"

"Oh, yes. Of course. Thank you again."

"Good. Then what I'd like you to do is kill the AOI Chief."

"Well I'd like to do that too."

"I thought you would."

"I mean I'd like to actually stick a knife in her heart and watch the life drain from her miserable face."

"In another life Chelle, we might have been close friends, you and I," Miner said. "I'd like to do it too, but there are reasons, I'm sure you can understand, that prevent anyone associated with the Enforcers or myself from doing such a thing."

"As I said, I'd be happy to, but I don't expect we'll get the chance."

"That's where you're wrong. See, even though I'm on the outs, so to speak, I am privy to all kinds of information which could assist you in an assassination of the Chief. In fact, in the next forty-eight hours, if she keeps this barbaric war going, I believe we'll have plenty of people inside the Aylantik who would be willing to help with such a mission."

"We'll see then," Chelle said. "But I was zooming to see if the Enforcers might assist PAWN in a counteroffensive against AOI positions."

"That's not an option, and you won't need me anyway if you just kill that woman," Miner responded, leaving no room for further negotiation, although Chelle tried.

After speaking with Miner, there were more zooms. Representatives of the Creatives wanted action. Their enclaves of writers, poets, artists, and musicians were getting leveled. They told Chelle, "If this continues at the current pace, the world won't have any Creatives left by next week. We're being punished because we backed PAWN. You have to come to our rescue now! PAWN needs to wake up and respond to this holocaust."

"The Aylantik has targeted you because you are freethinkers. It has very little to do with your support of PAWN. But we share an enemy, and we will do everything in our power to stop them. We will be retaliating today."

Next were the Rejectionists. They'd been immune to the brutal air and satellite campaign because of the remote locations of their outposts in the forests. Their largest presence, in the Amazon rainforest, was particularly hard to find, and even harder to reach, but the AOI had sent small parties of heavily armed grunges in, and they'd been doing serious damage. Chelle assured them PAWN would be working to slow the AOI in the coming hours.

In between everything, she checked the updates and continued to look for any sign of Osc and Drast. It wasn't looking good, and PAWN Flo-wings kept getting shot out of the sky. The only things in the air were the ever-present drones, squadrons of jet-packed grunges, and AOI planes. All commercial aviation had been suspended, and it made the search for her loved ones even more difficult. She knew that if PAWN were going to have a chance, they'd have to get a presence in the skies, and that depended on Deuce Lipton. Only he and Miner had enough air power to challenge the AOI, but Miner could handle only small regional operations, whereas Deuce had the capacity to challenge the AOI from space.

While she handled a situation with the Rejectionists, there was another zoom holding from a PAWN operative in Amsterdam. Almost twenty percent of that area's population was made up of either Creatives or PAWN loyalists, but before she could get to the zoom, the connection went dead.

In that instant, half of the city had been wiped off the map by a series of Sonic-bombs.

She wanted to cry, but tears weren't something she could afford to indulge in any longer. Instead, she zoomed Nelson, and was amazed when it actually connected.

"Thank goodness you're alive!" she said upon hearing his voice. The connection was weak, and she couldn't get a live picture even if she wanted one. "Are you seeing the nightmare?"

"Yeah, unfortunately, we are. It's sick. We need to get to the Chief."

"We're working on a lot of plans," Chelle said, not wanting to talk about Miner's proposition. Even with infinite-encryption, Chelle always worried someone could hear. "Has Munna let you see the *Justar Journal*?"

"Not really. Deuce has stopped pushing her about the prophecies. Now, he's trying to get her to reveal information on the List Keepers."

She told him about Osc and Drast. Nelson had met his nephew only twice, but he had a strong sense of family and had argued vehemently against sending him into the AOI undercover, but in the end it had been Osc's decision.

"Can you see if maybe something in the *Justar Journal* can help?" Chelle asked. "Or, maybe since you saved Deuce's son, he might return the favor if you ask."

"I'll do everything I can Chelle. I promise," Nelson said. "Don't worry, we'll find them."

"Thank you."

Nelson knew his sister well enough to know she could still run the war even with the personal stress she was dealing with, but PAWN had not been doing well so far. "What's the strategy for responding to the AOI?" he asked carefully.

"We've been fighting from the shadows for so long, that it's what we're best at. You'll start seeing us surface very soon."

"Good. Has everyone fallen in line?"

"All except Deuce."

"Don't worry, he'll end up with us," Nelson said. "And, in spite of the initial bombardment from AOI, I believe that once Deuce declares he's with us, and if we can get the List Keepers, we'll be able to beat Aylantik."

"Every time I hear about the List Keepers, I picture two old guys in a shack somewhere in the woods scribbling in an ancient ledger, counting leaves on a tree or something. We all think they are something, that maybe they can save us, but we don't know anything. Nelson, what if they're nothing?"

"They aren't 'nothing.' I think they are even more than we can imagine."

"How do you know that?"

"Because ever since my time with Cope Lipton, I've been wrestling with astonishing things, great mysteries, happenings I cannot explain."

"I know. I've read some of your recent work."

"That doesn't even scratch the surface. Much of what I saw isn't in my work, and I've not discussed it with you, or anyone. Yet even with all of that, there's one thing that's impressed me above all else."

"What?" Chelle asked, desperate for something powerful to cling to.

"Munna." Nelson knew his sister would be let down, that she was not the old woman's biggest fan, but he pushed on. "Think about it Chelle. She *controls* the prophecies. She knows the future without even looking at them. She is at least one hundred-thirty-three, and she got dunked in the ocean yesterday while we were under heavy attack and she wasn't even fazed. I'm still recovering myself. Of course, part of that could be I lost my bacs in the water." He chuckled. "But I mean it. She's like a woman out of a fantasy novel. Some old sorceress . . . and she's a List Keeper. What if there's a whole tribe of Munnas? What if they can do things with their minds like she controls her cells? What if they can control other people? I don't know, but I think if we get the List Keepers to help, we win."

"I think you need to write another novel and unload Gandalf and the dragons from your brain."

"I don't mind your ridicule because I know you love me, and I know you only half mean it anyway. But Chelle, consider it just for a moment. There is one common denominator between the pre-Banoff world and the Aylantik's entire rule, and also among Booker Lipton, Cope Lipton, Deuce Lipton, PAWN, the *Justar Journal,* and the List Keepers . . . It's Munna."

He looked across the large opulent room as Munna entered. She'd been in the private cabin that Deuce had given her, the nicest on the Moon Shadow. Munna smiled at him, as if agreeing with his assessment even though she couldn't have heard it.

"I'm telling you Chelle," he whispered. "If we are going to win, or even survive this, we *need* the List Keepers."

"And how are we supposed to get to them?"

"Grandyn is on his way right now. With any luck, we'll hear from him soon. I'm counting on a Happerman, one more time, to save the revolution."

CHAPTER THIRTY-FOUR

Grandyn and Fye left the POP at first light and headed due east. Their escorts could take them no further, but Grandyn knew the area.

"If all goes well, we should see Zaverly this afternoon around fifteen hundred near Ashland," Grandyn said, as they walked briskly through the woods. "It's sort of full circle. We'll be just a few kilometers from where my dad, Nelson, and I brought the books from the library. We hid them in a barn. I remember meeting Munna for the first time, and then . . ." He thought of the attack that had taken his father and wondered where he might have been all these years, could he really still be alive? How would he ever find him?

"I know," Fye said. "That same day you met Munna was also the first time I learned who you were. I knew you'd be important to the revolution, but I had no idea you'd be so important to me. Back then, you were just an assignment."

Grandyn flashed the Happerman smile and she laughed. For a moment, they were simply two people in love. The trees were temporarily shielding them from the war and disintegrating world.

He took her hand and they continued on in a happy silence until the reality of it all closed back in on them.

"Did you ever think the AOI would unleash such devastation?" Grandyn asked.

"Yes."

"Have you seen things? About the future, I mean. Did Munna show you?"

"I haven't myself, but I've been told."

"By Munna?"

"Some."

"Why won't she let us use the *Justar Journal*?"

"I don't know," Fye said. She wanted to stop and sit under a tree on a bed of pine needles and talk, but there wasn't time. They had so far to go, and they couldn't stop until they got to the City. "I thought Munna was going to let PAWN, or at least the TreeRunners, use the prophecies. But I think it has something to do with Deuce. Something he isn't doing, or something he shouldn't be doing."

Grandyn thought about that for a minute. He believed Fye knew much more than she was saying, and if she didn't, she was much smarter than he, so she ought to be able to figure it out, even if she didn't know. Grandyn didn't want to keep making her uncomfortable about what she wasn't allowed to talk about, but he needed to understand. The revolution had taken his family and many of his friends, and now, with a child on the way, he had to make it right.

"But you think we should be able to use the prophecies, right?" Grandyn asked.

Before she could answer, they heard someone call his name and quickly crouched behind a tree.

"Grandyn Happerman!" the man repeated.

Grandyn scanned the area and could see nothing.

"Oh TreeRunner, you've gotten old and careless."

Grandyn didn't say a word. Fye had to remind herself to breathe.

"I've been following you for almost a kilometer and I'm less than ten meters from you now. Pretty woman. I like her long hair, but didn't you fancy brunettes?"

Grandyn thought the voice sounded vaguely familiar, but it was echoing off the trees and he couldn't place it.

"I heard you were dead, TreeRunner. Glad that was bunk," the man said. "I guess I'll come out now, because you seem to have lost all your old skills. But I'm friendly, so don't shoot me or nothing."

A few seconds later, not much more than seven or eight meters in front of them, a man dropped out of a tree and landed with his hands up in the air.

"Grandyn, it's Wyle. Wyle Sunet."

Grandyn and Wyle had been members of the same TreeRunner clan, and had grown up together. Grandyn stood cautiously and peered around the tree.

"Wyle Sunet?" Grandyn shouted. He ran to him and they hugged each other. "Why the hell did you have to scare me like that?" Grandyn asked, irritated.

"Hey, if you're scared, don't sleep in the woods," Wyle said, repeating an old motto their clan leader used to say to them whenever they said they couldn't do something.

"I'm serious Wyle, these are different times!"

"Exactly," Wyle said. "That's why we can't be too serious."

Fye walked over and Grandyn introduced them.

"You're even prettier up close," Wyle said. "What are you doing with this clown?"

"I like to laugh."

"Oh, see Grandyn. She agrees with me. There's nothing humor can't make better."

Grandyn didn't agree. He might have a few years ago, but not anymore. He'd seen too much. Things he couldn't imagine ever being able to laugh about. But he was happy to see a friendly and familiar face. It brought back his years of innocence running through the forests of the Oregon mountains.

"I knew you weren't dead." Wyle said, breaking the silence, shaking his moppy, red hair.

"Not for lack of trying," Grandyn said.

Fye frowned.

"How have you been?" Grandyn asked.

"Good, all things considered. I guess it's been about five years since we moved away, when my dad got that job in San Diego. Hey, sorry about your dad. I loved Runit." Wyle put his fist on his heart and looked at Grandyn with sad eyes.

"Thanks, man. I miss him every minute."

Wyle nodded. "I got word of his death about the same time the AOI started killing TreeRunners. Of course, we went into hiding, but as the war got closer they asked for volunteers to come up here. I said, 'Hell yes, I'll go back home.' A group of us from Southern California Area worked our way up . . . I guess it's been about a month ago."

Grandyn decided not to tell him that his father might still be alive. "It's so good to see you. There aren't a lot of us left from the Portland Clan."

"I know. I kept hearing you were killed. It seemed every few weeks a new rumor of your death in some forest somewhere would surface. I never believed it. I don't know why, but I just didn't."

"I can't believe how good it is to see you," Grandyn said. "Fye, Wyle was like a brother when I was growing up."

"Yeah, there were like ten of us brothers, and three sisters, all TreeRunners. Remember Nester? I ran into her when we first got here."

"Seriously? I'd love to see her. How is she?"

"Great. They have her assigned to Zaverly Tandrum. She's in charge up here now. Answers directly to Parker."

"We're supposed to connect with Zaverly today. She's going to help us get south."

"It ain't gonna happen today, brother. Zaverly is in thick fighting north of Grants Pass. The AOI came in hard. I hear the grunges are going to be moving in deep down here in the next few hours." Three other TreeRunners, that Grandyn didn't know, joined them. "Have you seen any Grunges?"

"No. Luckily it's been pure nature all morning," Grandyn said.

"Without Zaverly's help," Fye began, "it'll take us more than a week to get there. I can't keep up this pace."

"Where you all heading?" Wyle asked.

"We've got a critical meeting southeast of here. Kind of top secret revolution stuff."

Wyle nodded knowingly. "We've got an extra unarmed AirSlider, fully charged."

"Really?" Grandyn said. "That would be great. We're already late, and Fye's pregnant so we can't push—"

"Hey, she's pregnant?" Wyle said, grinning. "Congratulations! Is it? I mean—"

"Yeah, I'm the father," Grandyn said.

"Wow! Another Happerman. Beautiful!" Wyle couldn't stop smiling and looking back and forth between them. "Here, take my AirSlider too. It's also not equipped with lasers, but it'll get you where you're going much faster."

"No, man, I couldn't," Grandyn said.

"With two of you on a board, you can only go half-speed, and it'll take you twice as long to get there," Wyle said. "I can ride with someone else until we meet up with another patrol on recon." He stared at Grandyn with a serious expression. "You can't be out here on foot right now."

Grandyn looked at Fye. She wanted him to take it. "Okay. You have no idea how big a deal this is."

"I'm sorry for shaking you up. I really didn't mean to scare you, I just wanted to see if you could spot me. Remember when we were kids? I never could find you when you hid in the trees."

"Yeah," Grandyn said. "Don't worry about it."

"This guy is a camouflage freak," Wyle said to Fye.

"I'll keep that in mind," she said.

"You should," Wyle said, "or you may not be able to find him one day. And you may need him to change a diaper or something."

Fye laughed, imagining that.

"What about weapons?" Wyle asked.

"We were at a POP last night. They armed us."

"Good. The AOI seems to be using a new tactic now that the war is on," Wyle said. "They used to send in full units to do big sweeps, but yesterday and today it's been two or three grunges alone. They're all over the place, and hard to spot."

"We'll be careful."

"You sure you can't wait for Zaverly?" Wyle asked. "She'll have a large force, and will be able to get you through anything."

"I wish we could, but we need to keep moving. If the fighting is that bad up there, she might still be days away," Grandyn said.

"And we can't risk not being able to make it through," Fye added.

"Okay," Wyle said. "Take these." He gave them extra charge sticks.

After a warm farewell, in which Wyle apologized again for scaring them, he sent them on their way.

"He's kind of a goofball," Fye said as they were on their own again. "But I like him." They were gliding right next to each other while Fye got used to the AirSlider she'd only ridden once before.

"He's a good guy," Grandyn said. "Lots of memories."

"You'll tell me all your old TreeRunner stories someday, right?"

"Any time you like. How about we trade stories . . . TreeRunners for List Keepers?"

Fye groaned. She had walked into that one. "As soon as we get to the City, it's a deal."

"I'm going to hold you to that."

She smiled. "When we get to the City, you won't have to wait for my stories. You're going to learn more than you ever imagined."

CHAPTER THIRTY-FIVE

Blaze had slept soundly. Years ago, he had invested heavily in research to alleviate the need for sleep, considering it a waste of valuable hours. But instead, he discovered that sleep was the time when one could most easily connect to an infinite pool of knowledge.

"Your mind works hardest while you sleep," he would tell subordinates. "Go to bed early."

And so, on the first night of the war, when most of the rest of the world was busy running, hiding, attacking, or dying, Blaze slept.

In the night, he'd dreamt of nothing but the List Keepers and the prophecies. Upon waking, he was not surprised to have a key insight. From that revelation, he extrapolated and soon sat stunned.

Blaze had a remarkable talent for assembling thousands of bits of information, shreds of data, and seemingly unrelated facts into a gigantic jigsaw puzzle that, when pieced together, revealed a picture of something no one else had seen. Just as a brilliant investigator pursues clues to solve a mystery and a painter creates a great painting from a few colors and inspired brush strokes,

Blaze, a master information artist, could find clarity where others saw only endless confusion.

He wished he could present his new understanding to the round table, but was glad it had now come only to him since the knights had betrayed their king. Like a palace coup, those he had trusted most were now his enemy. The trader of secrets now had one, that for the first time, he was not willing to sell. A secret so great that the future of humanity rode with it. What to *do* with such powerful information was another matter. Having always held them only until they could be sold off to the highest bidder or most strategic fit, Blaze had to do something different with this one. He had to use it for himself.

For someone so well connected, someone wealthy beyond reason, someone so highly intelligent, someone with whom the fate of the world rested, surprisingly, Blaze did not know what to do next. But a plan was formulating, and it began with one simple step.

He needed to reach the List Keepers. Only in the previous few days had he learned of the existence of a hidden community of them known as the "City." Blaze knew there were only three ways to discover the location of the City: get the prophecies, capture Munna, or find Fye and Grandyn. He intended to do all three.

Blaze made a series of zooms as the initial actions in his still-evolving plan. He'd need satellite data from Deuce Lipton. It would be an easy trade. Blaze had something Deuce needed.

"I've got an Eighty-seven Weighted Blue Diamond satellite that will do what you need," Deuce said. "I can give you the command codes if you really can do what you say."

"Why do you doubt me?" Blaze asked. "Have I ever *not* done what could not be done?"

"If you can stop the Imps from working with the AOI, I'll never doubt you again."

"Your greatest mistake was ever doubting me, but it's just one among so many that it's not worth harping on it," Blaze said. "But remember, this will not be permanent. I estimate that they will be thrown off-track for only twenty-four to forty-eight hours."

"In this war, that's an eternity." Deuce looked at the AirViews streaming coverage of the gruesome events around the globe. It continued to defy logic as the horrors were surpassed only by the death toll. "And I can spare the satellite for a couple of days."

"Excellent. I'll be back in touch as soon as my end is set up."

Blaze had always craved control, which may have been what drove him to search for, and broker, information. Information led to power. Secrets were illegal in the Aylantik. He always found that ironic. A regime, indeed an entire society, built upon one horrible secret – the Banoff – and they tried to eliminate secrets within that same society.

But there were small secrets and large secrets. Blaze didn't just have a talent for finding them, he also knew how to value them. Each had a price, depending on the damage or progress it could do.

The nature of the Aylantik system and the operations of their muscle, the AOI, are what actually created the climate and market that allowed someone like Blaze to flourish. Seeker and their other methods of constant monitoring had made most citizens oblivious to the complete lack of privacy. The AOI recorded and analyzed every step they took, every move on the Field, and every word they uttered. In that way, the secrets were all there just waiting to be mined. And the others, the really dangerous secrets that had been so carefully hidden they were concealed from all the tracking, those could command serious money.

To that end, when Blaze invented the Artificial Intelligence DesTIn technology that made both Imps and CHRUDEs possible, he installed a special feature. Originally, it had been designed to collect data, but now he had hopes he could modify it and use it to control the Trapciers, at least for a precious day or two.

Next, Blaze went to work on Lance Miner. He promised the pharmaceutical billionaire that he could slow the AOI's attacks and even give Miner advance warning, *if* Miner would deliver Munna.

"If I could get Munna, why wouldn't I keep her?" Miner asked.

"Because you wouldn't know what to do with her. She was only valuable to you before the war started. You wanted to use her to stop the rebels, but now that's not necessary, and the rebels aren't even your biggest problem," Blaze explained.

"You are correct about that," Miner said, looking across his desk at Sarlo as she manipulated INUs and watched AirViews to identify the Enforcers units closest to Deuce and Munna's last known location just off Ryder Island. He so enjoyed watching her work. "Munna is not my biggest problem any longer, nor is Chelle Andreas. But the Chief is." He paused when Sarlo turned to him, anticipating his next statement. "If I capture Munna, I will turn her over to you under one condition."

"Yes?" Blaze asked, already knowing Miner's demand.

"The Chief dies. I don't care how, or who, just make sure she is dead."

"Lance, she is one of the three most protected people on the planet. I have no army. Why do you think *I* can do it if Enforcers can't?"

"Enforcers can't, not because they aren't capable, but because it is not allowed. As for how *you* do it, that's *your* problem. But Blaze, I've always known you to be incredibly resourceful."

"Let me know when you have Munna then," Blaze said, ending the zoom. "It's too late to stop me now," he sang to himself as he pushed a button to file the image recording of the zoom.

He checked the news reports which showed more escalation.

The Chief's strategy was clear. She was coming on with everything they had at the start, hoping to end the war in days, hoping to end it before it had really begun. It was a good play, particularly for one charged with keeping the peace at any cost. If she could destroy enough of the opposition, and even any potential opposition, fast enough, she would scare anyone left into full Aylantik compliance.

But the Chief had never experienced a war that had exploded. She'd only lived through the long simmering "pre" war. She didn't know that once a volcano erupts, it cannot be stopped until the entire landscape has changed.

He turned on the first test and saw the data from his monitors come streaming in. Suddenly, the world of Trapciers secrets were added to his considerable stash of covert knowledge. Yet with all that he had gathered, he believed he'd finally come upon the holy grail of secrets. One that was priceless. And it was the one held by the List Keepers.

CHAPTER THIRTY-SIX

Munna set up seven AirViews in the large center deck of the Moon Shadow. When the windows were shaded, it looked more like they were in a skyscraper penthouse above Tokyo, with streamlined white and black furnishings. A wide chrome and teakwood spiral staircase led to the upper deck, and another went down into a larger lounge and the cabins. A galley was off the back of the center deck reception area, and the bridge was in front. Nelson, Deuce and Munna sat on white cloth, bench-style sofas, but because they were upholstered in Tekfabrik, the color, and even texture, could change on command. The same was true of the low-pile carpet, which was presently also white.

With the lights dimmed and windows shaded, Munna allowed the *Justar Journal* to tell its story. All seven AirViews came to life with swirling words, and then images.

Deuce didn't know why Munna had suddenly changed her mind, and he was afraid to ask. He didn't want to do anything that might make her reconsider. There was no way to know how long she would leave the *Justar Journal* open, so he sat attentively, barely breathing, with intense anticipation.

They knew the images on the seven AirViews had each originated from decoding the shifting text of the special books that had been found in the Portland Library, and that each made up one of the chapters of the *Justar Journal*. But up until now, they hadn't seen the final two chapters.

Deuce looked at the list in his INU. Although he'd already committed to memory what the first five were about, he was hoping to get some help with the missing two descriptions for the chapters hidden in *The Iliad*, by Homer, and *Rights of Man*, by Thomas Paine. So far, those two were showing only abstract images.

He reviewed the list of the books on a tiny AirView of his own. Below each author and title, he'd noted the corresponding "chapter" categories for the *Justar Journal*.

Meditations by Marcus Aurelius
Health and Birth
Spirituality and Death

Reflections of the Revolution in France, by Edmund Burke
War and Peace
Wealth and Power

Paradise Lost, by John Milton
Earth and Nature
Planets and Stars

The Federalist, by Alexander Hamilton, James Madison, and John Jay
Science and Technology
Art and Creativity

.   .   .

The Ingenious Gentleman Don Quixote of La Mancha, by Miguel de Cervantes Saavedra
   Time and Thoughts
   Dreams and Wishes

The Iliad, by Homer

Rights of Man, by Thomas Paine

He was about to ask Munna if she knew what the *Iliad* and *Rights of Man* chapters were about, when images suddenly changed across all AirViews. Health-Birth-Spirituality-Death had been showing victims of what Deuce had been calling the "new plague." Now it depicted that crisis worsening, with lines of people waiting to get into Health-Circle clinics, collapsing dead on the street. At the same time, War-Peace-Wealth-Power, which had shown cities crumbling under the unrelenting AOI air blitz, were now showing the first pause of the war.

"What's happening?" Nelson asked.

Deuce thought of Blaze and assumed he was going to be successful. "We might be making progress with the fighting, but obviously the new plague is out of control."

Earth-Nature-Planets-Stars changed from images of exploding mines on asteroids and water operations on Earth's moon, to satellite battles. It unnerved Deuce, the owner of StarFly and maker of the majority of the satellites in service. He'd known a space war was possible, but seeing it actually happen made him question many of the options he was currently considering.

Science-Technology-Art-Creativity shifted away from weapons factories, in high gear, to a meeting of Imps. Time-Thoughts-

Dreams-Wishes went from scenes of secret meetings of revolutionaries to a live image of Twain Lipton in the redwoods.

"What's going on?" Deuce exclaimed.

"We're seeing the future," Munna whispered.

The Iliad, which had been shuffling abstract images of lights
and color patterns, was now showing Munna sitting on the Moon
Shadow, and *Rights of Man* now had what they could only guess
was a basketball-sized Eysen INU.

"Why are they all displaying the future except the ones of you
and Twain?" Deuce asked, nodding at what they all could see. The
AirView showed Munna sitting exactly where she was presently,
on the Moon Shadow.

"Oh, Deuce, don't fall into that old way of thinking. They're all
showing a future. Time, remember, is not always what you think."

Nelson recalled many lectures Cope had given on the same
topic, but he still didn't get it. "Munna, the AirView is showing
precisely what you're doing, at this very moment," Nelson said
impatiently. "How can that be the future?"

"There are many ways to see the future. The present is the
future of a moment ago. Be assured, the *Justar Journal* speaks only
of the future. If we are seeing something, it is going to happen,
unless something else changes it. You all just witnessed a full
shift. All the AirViews were affected by something major that
happened to change our trajectory."

"Our trajectory?" Nelson asked.

Deuce was studying the footage of his son, meditating in the
redwoods, worrying what would happen if an AOI patrol
happened by and found him there, defenseless. Or worse, what if
Enforcers found him?

"Our trajectory, meaning the future direction of each of those
chapters of the human experience," Munna explained.

"So what are the last two?" he asked.

"I'm not certain, but one of them appears to be me." She smiled.

"Damn it, Munna!" Deuce snapped. "We've got hundreds of thousands being annihilated by either Sonic-bombs or plague. You talk about peace and love and whatever, but we have this, I don't know what it is, the *Justar Journal*, and it's our best chance to stop all of this death. Let me use it. I can do things, I can make big moves, but it could all be wrong unless you're willing to leave the AirViews on and let me watch them every time I do something. I'll know in minutes, maybe even seconds, if I was right or wrong. It's the safest way to navigate this torgon mess. I know what you've said, but I don't want to use it to win the war. I want to use it to *end* the war."

"The *Justar Journal* is not for war."

"Then what is it for!?" Deuce blasted.

"I've told you before. The *Justar Journal* is to help us find our way."

"Then why is it showing you and Twain right now? You say that's the future, but it sure looks like 'now' to me. Or, at least, it's extremely close to this exact moment in time."

Munna could see both Nelson and Deuce were impatient and confused. She knew they were scared. The world, as they had always known it, was disintegrating before their eyes.

Munna smiled and pointed back to the AirViews, then said softly, "Humans think because they invented clocks and calendars that they understand time, that they have somehow tamed it. Time is nothing like you imagine."

CHAPTER THIRTY-SEVEN

Grandyn and Fye followed the Rogue River, cruising several feet above the ground on their AirSliders, weaving through trees at maximum speed, when suddenly, Grandyn heard Fye scream. He turned just in time to see her tumbling down toward the water.

Grunges had appeared from nowhere and showered a barrage of laser strikes at them. Grandyn tried to get to her, but he was taking too much fire. She dropped almost eight meters before plunging into the white water.

Grandyn pulled a lasershod and blasted back, but trying to maintain balance while aiming his weapon proved impossible. The grunges' lasers sliced past him, and one caught his AirSlider. He dropped and swerved, nearly hitting a large cedar before regaining control. He tried to spot Fye in the river, looked along the bank, but couldn't find her. Circling back into their line of fire, Grandyn dropped a fist–sized spark-bomb. As soon as it hit, thousands of plate-sized sparks lit the area, blinding and inflicting serious burns to the surprised grunges.

Following the currents of the swift-moving river, Grandyn raced over the surface, searching for any trace of her. That close to the powerful surging, it was too loud to hear her as the water entered a narrow basalt canyon. There were no longer any banks, only steep, smooth, stone walls as the river churned and funneled into the chasm, roiling with swirling timbers, and exploding over rocks. Then, as he pushed the AirSlider to outrun the rapids, he saw her ahead.

"I'm coming!" he yelled, but she would never have heard him as she bobbed in and out of the thundering onslaught.

He got seven meters beyond her and hovered as close to the surface as he could while still holding the AirSlider steady. "Fye! I'm here!" he screamed above the roar.

She hadn't seen him. He couldn't tell if she was even conscious.

"Fye!"

She was only three meters away. He leaned down toward the water, so close that the violent flow soaked him and he almost slid off the AirSlider.

"Fye!"

She was coming backwards. He thrust his hand into the cold river just before she reached him. His fingers wrapped around her upper arm, but he couldn't keep his grip. He had to hold onto the AirSlider with his other hand. But she finally realized he was there.

Fye grabbed him, but it was too late. The force of the current took her. Their hands slipped apart and she went under the AirSlider. Grandyn recovered quickly and whipped back into the air, flying past her once again. This time she'd be ready for him.

He positioned himself just as before, but instead of holding on with his hand, he wrapped his legs around the base of the AirSlider, crossing them on the underside.

She looked up and saw him, her face was weary, but relieved as she raised her arms to him. Then, just before she got within reach, her face registered terror. "Grandyn!"

The laser just missed him, but it was enough to lose Fye again. He rolled the AirSlider and twisted it into a climb fifteen meters high, where he spotted the source of the laser strike; another grunge, who must have been part of the same unit of the two he'd blinded. Grandyn dove the AirSlider straight at the agent, who got off two strikes before Grandyn crashed into him. The grunge, unprepared for the impact, went into the river and was quickly lost in a foaming eddy. Grandyn righted his AirSlider centimeters before it would have splintered into the rocks and tore back down.

"Fye!" he shouted, as he flew over her head. Positioning above the water twelve meters ahead of her, Grandyn scanned the area for more grunges. All clear, but then he spotted something more terrifying than the AOI.

The river disappeared twenty meters beyond him. The raging waters were about to be sucked underground. Grandyn now realized exactly where they were.

The entire Rogue entered a maze of ancient subterranean lava tubes and didn't emerge for more than eighty meters. No one had ever lived through the underground flow. It was impossible to survive. If he missed her this time, there would not be another chance.

He wrapped his legs tight, flexed his fingers, and took a deep breath. "Focus TreeRunner," he told himself. "Focus."

The river was at its wildest now. Fye spun and fought to keep pointed toward him. At the same time, the suction of the lava tubes threatened to pull her under. She had to kick fast to remain buoyant.

"I'm going to get you!" he yelled as water spit all around him. With the booming, thrashing fury of the river funneling down, she could still not hear him, but she was ready.

At the last second, he had to move the AirSlider as the current took her a meter to his left, but he did it, and they managed to lock their hands around each other's wrists in a split second of triumph.

"It's pulling me!" she yelled, but he could hardly hear. As she went under the AirSlider, it rolled him over, and suddenly he was in the river.

"Torg!"

Miraculously, they still had each other. Grandyn saw a final hope and pulled his right hand away from her to grab an overhanging branch, part of a long-dead tree which had wedged itself between two massive stone slabs. As the lava tubes pulled at them, his hand slipped from the branch, but he caught another.

It broke.

His arm crashed through a third before squeezing hard around one almost too thick to grip. The branch was so smooth and slick that he didn't think he could hold on much longer. Fye was still on his left arm, but the pressure of the current and suction of the lava tubes were tremendous.

"Arrrrgh," he gritted. The roar of the water was explosive.

"Grandyn, let me go!" she screamed, but it sounded thin, buried by the rushing water.

"Never!"

"If you don't, we'll both go in! Please, Grandyn, save yourself!"

"Not. Letting. Go!"

"Help!" a voice suddenly shouted. The AOI grunge Grandyn had knocked in sailed quickly past, kicking and yelling for help. Seconds later he was sucked under and vanished into the lava tubes.

The raging turmoil had numbed his hearing, pummeled his thoughts. Grandyn's arms burned, but he couldn't think of anything other than holding on.

"Let me go!"

"No!"

"Hey! Hey!" someone shouted.

It took Grandyn a second to realize it wasn't Fye. The noise made it difficult to tell where it was coming from – the equivalent of a baby crying on a battlefield – but then he spotted the source.

Two hikers were yelling from the shore. "Hey! Grab this," one shouted, as they stood on a solid, level spot of prehistoric lava flow just ahead of the river's sink into the tubes. They held a long pole, actually a fallen sapling. "Can you get it?" They pushed it as close to Fye as they could without falling into the water themselves. Grandyn strained to hear above the pounding rapids.

Fye, barely cognizant, looked around, confused.

"Grab it!" Grandyn yelled. "Behind you!"

Another couple ran toward the two men with the pole. One of them held onto an oak tree while his female companion locked arms with the first two so they could stretch the sapling farther out.

Fye turned and saw the pole. She might be able to get it. She looked back at Grandyn, terrified. He knew she was scared. If she didn't catch their lifeline, letting go meant instant death. But he was about to lose his grip. Not much strength remained in his muscles.

"On three," he yelled, "grab that pole!"

She nodded, unsure.

"One. Two. Three!"

He let go.

She grasped wildly at the pole with both hands as the river pulled her away. The hikers painfully stretched and leaned an extra two centimeters, pushing the sapling at her. Miraculously, she caught it. The four hikers leveraged their legs and pulled with their combined power, that was almost not enough, against the force of the suction, but as they got her closer to shore she was able to get a foot onto a rock and push toward them. She landed in a pile with the first two hikers, crashing onto the rocky ground.

Grandyn hadn't seen her make it. The instant they separated, he used the momentum to propel himself around onto the wedged tree. It was so slimy and wet that he slipped back into the river, but slowly, he again made his way up the huge log until he was able to climb onto one of the rocks and make his way to the top of the cliff. From there, it took several more minutes before he could get down to Fye.

He fell breathlessly into her trembling arms. Cold, soaked, and shivering, but alive, they savored the embrace until he realized Fye was shaking too much. That's when he discovered their four rescuers were not just hikers.

CHAPTER THIRTY-EIGHT

Drast and Osc drove the LEV as far as they could. There were almost no other vehicles on the highway, but more drones than usual in the air. They'd taken the INU, and were concerned about how hard hit the area they were trying to get to had been. But there was nowhere else to go.

The few roads that existed toward the east led to thousands of kilometers of open country. To the north was the long route to Alaska, with good places to hide up there, but they weren't interested in hiding. To the west was the ocean, a great way to travel, but without a decent boat, or anything that floated, it was not an option. South was the only choice, and the way to Chelle and Drast's revolution strategies, as they had long prepared for rebel attacks in dozens of western cities in the Pacyfik region.

Prison had given him something that had been rare in his life as AOI Regional head; time to think and plan, and Drast had a list of ideas about how to win this war.

They cruised along as fast as the LEV was capable of going, which in that area was one hundred-thirty kilometers per hour. Osc knew there was a way to override the controls and force it to exceed the safe speed limit, but he would need a code breaker program, which he didn't have. There hadn't been any check-points, nor even low flyovers. They were feeling optimistic about their chances until, just outside Vancouver, the road became pitted with too many craters to proceed.

Drast suddenly thought of Runit since he knew he was being held on an island off the coast not far from there. *Could the librarian still be alive?* he wondered. The last report he had, prior to getting arrested, was that Runit was not doing well, he had still not come out of the coma at that point and the androids told Drast that his health had taken a turn for the worst. However, Drast had set things up so that the automation system would keep the prison running even in the event of Drast's imprisonment or death. He had chosen the site carefully, knowing neither the Chief nor PAWN would bother with the abandoned facility.

"Look at that," Osc said, bringing him back from the past.

Drast checked out Osc's window and saw the very clear foot-print of a Sonic-bomb, or probably several. He hadn't ever seen the aftermath in person. The ordnance had never been used on populated areas. Weapons manufacturers, in partnership with the AOI, developed the city-leveling explosive device sometime during the prior twenty years, but the images he'd seen yesterday and that morning on the Field, did not prepare him for the stark real-ity: kilometers of rubble, most pieces no bigger than a small refrigerator.

Total lifelessness.

"Why on earth would a peaceful government, with no external enemies, create such a weapon?" Osc asked.

Drast had seen the plans during his time in the AOI. As the fourth most senior official in the agency, after the Chief and the heads of the Aylantik and Chiantik regions, he'd sat in on many meetings devoted to reviewing strategies that would be used to beat back any uprisings.

"The world is large," Drast explained. "The Aylantik had held together a fragile peace for long enough to know that there were many diverse factions remaining in the world. And with each year, farther removed from the Banoff, it became more likely that one of those factions would revolt." He looked across at the massive damage to a once great city. "They did a good job of squashing every potential threat they saw, but as the Banoff faded beyond any living person's memory, the numbers grew too great. They needed weapons capable of . . . shock and awe."

He got out of the LEV and stared at the moonscape of destruction, wondering how many had died. How many of those that did had no idea that something like a revolutionary plot even existed, or a bomb so horrific?

Osc climbed out of the LEV. "What now?"

"We walk." He checked his lasershod. "The AOI has already done their best here. We shouldn't have any trouble."

Twenty-five minutes later, after walking along the shoulder of the damaged highway, they reached the bombed-out zone of the city. A warm breeze made the sun's glare even more intense as they picked their way through the wasteland. Much of it felt like walking on dark gray, gritty talcum powder. There were hundreds of bodies, but he knew that tens of thousands more lay buried under the rubble. There were no rescue efforts. Sonic-bombs left no survivors, and even if someone had miraculously lived, the people in parts of Vancouver that had been spared were too terrified to venture into what they were already calling a "dead zone."

But Drast and Osc saw no evidence that anyone had been issued a miracle.

As they stumbled through, mostly in silence, dusty and hot, Drast asked Osc about Chelle.

"Your mother is beautiful. Why didn't she find someone to marry who had bearing rights?"

"She didn't know anyone. You are aware that the Aylantik takes any illegal child born within the first six months of marriage."

Drast nodded. He felt bad about pressing Osc. It had to be

painful not to have been raised by his mother, especially one as dynamic as Chelle. He thought of Grandyn losing his mother, another strong woman, to the revolution. Drast knew Chelle didn't believe in abortion, especially the PharmaForce ones, as the only legal abortions were done with drugs. He wanted to ask who his father was and who had raised Osc, but he'd pried enough into the private and painful affairs of the man who had just saved his life.

"What if we can't get through?" Osc asked, worried they would both be dead by the end of the day. There was no fear of going to an AOI prison anymore. He could see what the AOI was doing with their problems. They were at the edge of the dead zone. Aside from a few crumbling buildings on the outlying section, a near perfect line delineated the safe area from the end of the world.

"Efficient, aren't they?" Drast mumbled. "We'll get through."

No explanation, no contingency plan, no plan at all. Osc wished they'd stayed back in the safe house. He didn't feel any better once they entered the "standing" city. The streets were deserted, and he half expected to see zombies crawling out of the storm drains. All day, he'd felt like he was in one of the end-of-the-world movies, and that was when they were in places where people weren't supposed to be, but Vancouver had a population of nearly nine hundred thousand. If even a third of them were killed in the Sonic-bombs, there should be more than half a million people wandering around, working, shopping, whatever.

But they were all hiding. He could feel their eyes upon him as they moved briskly through empty streets, past vacant shops and restaurants. Drast, on a mission, pushed ahead at nearly a jog, knowing exactly where he was headed.

After ten or twelve blocks, without seeing an AOI patrol, even in the air, Osc thought they might make it. Drast had stopped once to check the map on the INU, and after that they began to cut through alleys and narrower streets.

"We're getting closer," Drast said as he sped up.

Osc was amazed at how much stamina Drast possessed. He'd been a top performer with AOI fitness regimens, and he'd kept up his exercise in prison. Drast always knew he'd have to survive in the rough during the revolution.

They passed another abandoned LEV just as its windshield exploded. Drast dove into a doorway. Osc hit the pavement behind another LEV. More shots came, one only millimeters from Osc's head.

"There they are!" someone shouted.

Osc heard footsteps and knew he was about to be captured.

Damned Drast, he thought, *we never should have left the safe house.* Then he remembered everything they had seen. *No one is going to "capture" me . . . I'm a dead man.*

CHAPTER THIRTY-NINE

Blaze struggled for hours developing the system needed to listen to, and ultimately control, the Trapciers. There were constant interruptions and complications. The biggest was the continuous escalation of the war. He worked with two trusted assistants, a brilliant husband and wife team who had been with him for more than twenty years. Normally, their main objective was digging into corporate reporting and personnel to find useful and saleable information, but their real talent came after the acquisition of that data. They had a way of fitting it with other material and making it into a strategic package that buyers could not resist.

"I am amazed that the Chief is pushing this much," Blaze said to them.

"According to the war models we just ran through DesTIn, she has already surpassed a controllable level," the woman said.

"The Chief is taking a big chance. If PAWN begins to fight back, we could be looking at an extinction event," the man added.

"PAWN *is* going to fight back," Blaze said. "They are well hidden, and the Chief's 'carpet bombing' technique isn't getting to their core. She can't find them, and instead of helping, the Imps are advising her under their own agenda."

"Mis-advising her is more accurate," the woman mused.

"Yes," Blaze replied. "I need you two to develop a plan." He looked at them as he did when he was about to say something extremely important and equally confidential. "We need to assassinate the AOI Chief, and we need to do it in the next thirty-six hours."

They nodded, thinking it was an impossible task, but knowing Blaze knew even better than they that it was impossible. Long ago, they'd learned that there were ways, even if it was only a single obscure and very difficult path through to an insurmountable problem. Blaze had taught them that many times, and they had proven it back to themselves and him many more.

Instead of protesting or listing the obstacles, the two of them began imagining what they would need to achieve it. "Her schedule, her whereabouts?" the man asked.

"Lance Miner has promised that information."

The man's eyes widened. He knew Miner to be a staunch AOI ally, but war does funny things to alliances. The woman had followed the news more closely, and knew that the Chief was using Enforcers as a scapegoat.

"The Chief isn't just trying to restore peace," the woman said. "She's trying to exterminate all future opposition to the Aylantik, as well as consolidating her power within the government. She wants to be World Premier."

"She wants to be Dictator," Blaze corrected.

"We'll have a plan by the morning," the man said hopefully.

"I need it in six hours," Blaze pressed. "At least a preliminary draft. Our time window will be limited. I'll forward the information from Miner as soon as it comes in."

They weren't surprised.

It had been more difficult than he thought, but Blaze finally got the Trapciers monitoring set up through a filter program. The first problem had been that there were now close to fifty-five thousand Imps, far more than he'd thought. Blaze had overseen the making of a few dozen CHRUDEs, but the Imps had been secretly manufacturing CHRUDEs at an alarming rate. There were almost a thousand now, and they were able to crank out more than one hundred new ones each day. In another week they would run out of the DuPont chemical necessary for the skin, they'd still be able to use either what they were using for cyborg patches, or even the android coverings. The Imps didn't seem to care.

There was another scenario that troubled Blaze. The Imps might just get their buddies at the AOI to seize his DuPont factories. There wasn't much he could do to stop that. Blaze had to write a program to process all the information coming in from the more than fifty-six thousand Imp and CHRUDE sources. It had made him crazy at first, but it all seemed to be working now.

One of the first important pieces of information he gleaned was that the Imps, with the help of the AOI, had taken over the four main Cyborg creation facilities. Cyborgs, like Imps, were humans with "mechanical" parts, processors, and INU interfaces. They were far less sophisticated than Imps, or even CHRUDEs, mostly because they did not use the DesTIn program, but rather an outdated artificial intelligence developed by a mega pre-Banoff internet search company.

Even more alarming were the Trapciers. Again, with AOI backing, they had also taken over the company that manufactured eighty-one percent of the world's androids. They, like CHRUDEs, were entirely machines made to look human, but standard androids didn't fool anyone. It was easy to tell they were not human, and they didn't have the benefit of DesTIn. There was already a large android population doing menial jobs.

But, nonetheless, androids, cyborgs, and CHRUDEs could be dangerous. With some programming tweaks of the androids, the

Imps wouldn't even need the AOI. They'd have their own army. They were essentially replaceable soldiers.

The Aylantik estimated that android numbers had swelled to at least three hundred million, and according to what Blaze had picked up from his monitoring, the Trapciers planned to triple that number in the next three years. Stunning. Blaze had to do the calculations to see if it was even possible, and found that, figuring the time needed to build two more factories, it could be done using a fully-automated round-the-clock manufacturing plant.

What if they equipped them with DesTIn? he wondered. There would be almost one billion androids on the planet in less than three years. *What will they all be doing?* he asked himself.

But he knew the answer. He knew it because he had heard Galahad.

"It doesn't matter how many Traditionals we lose, we can make more," he had said, pointing to a CHRUDE. "The future of the human race isn't necessarily dependent on humans. Not when machines can think better and faster."

CHAPTER FORTY

Munna motioned her walking stick into the air. Nelson had been amazed she'd managed to keep hold of it during their plunge into the ocean, but everything about the old woman amazed him. As she moved the carved cane toward the AirViews, all but three went into abstract images.

"What are you doing?" Deuce asked.

"Focusing your attention," she said, smiling.

He saw that only the AirViews showing Twain, the war, and herself remained. Deuce desperately wanted to know how she did it, but for now he had to hold onto Twain's explanation that she was able to manipulate atoms as she did her own cells. It all seemed rather fantastic, but so did the ever changing prophecies and for that matter, the workings of the universe.

Even with all the research the Aylantik had done in space, and they'd done a lot, as had Deuce, the universe was still one massive mystery, made up almost entirely of things that can't be seen. Less than five percent of the known universe consisted of galaxies containing stars and planets. The remaining ninety-five percent is composed of indefinable substances known as dark matter and dark energy. He could still hear his grandfather's voice explaining it all to him. "The overwhelming majority of what's in the universe cannot be seen. We don't understand ninety-five percent of what exists, so don't ever think you truly know what you're talking about. Always look suspiciously on your own doubt, and remember that skeptics miss most of the possibilities."

"What is it you want me to see?" Deuce asked Munna.

"Why does the *Justar Journal* show us your son?" Munna countered, pointing her cane at him.

"Why does it show *you*?" Nelson asked.

"Both answers are the same," Munna said.

Deuce, beyond frustrated, tried and failed to contain himself. "Damn it, Munna. I'm not sure you're even in your right mind. Why do you allow this mass murder to continue? And make no mistake, you are as guilty as that poisonous woman leading the AOI. You have powers I don't begin to understand, but if we can see and change the future, then we *must*. Let me use the *Journal*."

"Poor Deuce," Munna said, smiling. "What would you do if the *Justar Journal* did not exist?"

"What are you talking about?"

Munna moved her cane and the AirViews showing the prophecies all went blank. "Surely a man of your means would act."

"Now you're making me question *my* sanity. Munna, please, I'm not asking much of you. Just turn on the *Journal* and leave it on."

"You don't listen very well."

"I know what you're trying to do. You want to give me some lesson in philosophy or quantum physics or something," Deuce said, exasperated. "But we could be in the final days of humanity. I don't have time for what you're peddling."

"If, as you suggest, we are near the end of humanity, then that is all you have time for. Don't you understand?"

"No. Apparently, I don't."

Nelson stirred from his silence and reached for a bac, forgetting they were ruined in the ocean. "Deuce, what Munna asked you earlier, 'What would you do if the *Journal* didn't exist?' Perhaps you should think about that and then do something."

"Look at this," Deuce said, pointing to another pattern of AirViews showing war news. "Do you think there's much room for error here? What if I send BLAZERs against the AOI and it results in escalation? What if I go against Enforcers and wipe out the only hope for a real alliance against the Chief? What if I do something that makes that evil woman spread more plague? My companies control satellites that the agriculture industry counts on. I could end up destroying the food supply. Technology that I own could be used to take down the safety infrastructure. Ships could sink, planes crash . . . Don't you see? One mistake and it could mean the end of us, of everything!"

"Munna, he's right," Nelson said. "The stakes are too high. We need to be careful. What is the harm in using the prophecies to make sure we don't screw this up worse than it already is?"

"It's beyond that," Deuce said. "It's about saving what's left of humanity."

"The *Justar Journal*. Is. Not. For. War." Munna said empathetically with a scolding look. "It is for the change."

"What *change*?" Deuce asked, raising his voice. "This change?" He pointed back to the war monitors. "Or whatever hellish world that comes after this?"

"That is up to you."

"Up to me?" Deuce paced around the grand room as the Moon Shadow continued speeding to an unknown destination. Nothing but a warm, blue day and open ocean were racing by on all sides. "It's up to you Munna. You're the one locking us away from the answers."

She shook her head slowly, studying the carvings on her cane.

"Tell us Munna," Nelson said, in a much calmer voice than Deuce had used. "If not to help us through this apocalypse," he motioned to the horrors on the war news AirViews, "please tell us specifically why the *Justar Journal* really exists?"

"It is to teach you how to survive this war, or something before the war, or after it. And by *survive*, I mean go to another step in human evolution. Do you think it is all about fancy clothes, the greatest camera, the newest Eysens, the most luxurious LEVs?" Munna paused, as if waiting for an answer or another question.

"Of course not!" Deuce said.

"We're not your run-of-the-mill idiots," Nelson added, annoyed.

"The *Justar Journal* shows my image, my good fellows," she continued, "because I am an example of the next step in human evolution. And it is showing Twain because he is demonstrating how to get there. All that war and destruction that you see, 'the end,' as you call it, is displayed because that is the current path. That is where we are going, and that is where we do not want to go."

Nelson, happy to still have a bit of elixir in his flask, took a swig. Deuce looked at his son, appearing so calm, so natural among the trees.

Munna began speaking again. "If we were all shown the choices of what life could be, and if we could see where the path we are on would lead us, I am certain we would all choose a different course. The *Justar Journal* gives us that, but it is not a map. It does not tell us how to get there, it is a view into where we are going. Indeed, where we *can* go."

"Are you telling me that I have to go into the redwoods, start meditating on how to rearrange my cells, and that will end the war? Are you saying I have to wait for all of us 'commoners' to meditate on our breathing to produce a massive raise in consciousness and *that* will end the war?" His voice was highly agitated. "Munna, we'll all be dead before I can even set foot on that mossy soil! Couldn't the *Journal* just show us?"

"If you use it as a map, it will not get you to where you *should* go, it will take you only to where you *want* to go. And you're not equipped to make that decision. If you were, you would already be where I am," Munna said, smiling.

"Well then, if you're equipped to decide then please, by all means, tell us what to do."

"End this war. Once and for all, end all war."

"That's all I want to do," Deuce said, more frustrated than he'd ever been. "I just want to end the war without ending the *world*."

CHAPTER FORTY-ONE

The woman and three men who had saved Grandyn looked at each other in a panic. "We've got to get her into dry clothes," the woman said, pointing toward Fye.

Grandyn was also shivering from the exertion and cold water, but he could see Fye was in real trouble. Her eyes were glazed, her lips blue over chattering teeth, and she couldn't complete a sentence. One of the men pulled a light jacket from his pack while the woman and Grandyn stripped Fye from her clothes. They got her into the dry jacket, and the woman stripped down and hugged her, naked, inside the jacket.

Grandyn knew from his TreeRunner training that the only way to save someone from hypothermia was with skin-on-skin body heat. He also knew that he was too wet and cold to do it. "Thank you," he panted. He wasn't even sure the woman heard him as she continued holding Fye in the sunlight, rubbing her back, frantically trying to generate heat from the friction.

"We've got to take her in," one of the men said to the others.

"No," one of them replied.

"Yes," the woman said firmly.

"What?" Grandyn demanded. "Take her where?" He was shivering uncontrollably.

"There's a doctor a few kilometers from here," the woman said.

Grandyn thought fast, looked around at the "hikers," and asked cautiously, "Is it a POP?"

The men looked at each other, surprised.

Grandyn looked at Fye, scared she was about to go into full shock. "Damn it, are you with PAWN?" Grandyn asked the woman.

She hesitated.-

"Answer me!"

"Who can you trust?" she finally whispered.

Grandyn had to ask the same question. He had nothing left to lose. "I'm Grandyn Happerman. If you're with PAWN, you are obliged to help me. If you're AOI, you're required to kill me, and right now I don't give a torg which one, but damn it, choose!"

They all looked at each other again. The name registered.

"Grandyn, we're also with the rebels, and we're honored to help you," the woman said. "There's a major PAWN facility about five kilometers from here." She continued to rub Fye.

"Thank you," Grandyn said.

"She won't make it on foot," the woman said gravely.

"We have to try," Grandyn replied.

One of the men stepped forward. "We've got an AirSlider. Pulled it off a grunge earlier."

"I'll take her on that," the woman said. "But we've got to hurry."

"I'll take her," Grandyn shot back.

"You'll never find it without one of us," the woman said.

Grandyn, knowing the AirSlider could hold only two and that time was limited, couldn't argue. But he also couldn't send Fye and their unborn child off with a stranger who could be anyone.

He suddenly remembered they were close to Crater Lake where one of PAWN's larger and oldest underground centers was located.

"Fye, listen to me. This woman . . ." he said, then paused to look at the woman.

"My name's Fuller," she said, getting dressed.

Grandyn memorized her face. She looked like she might have been of Asian descent; short, black, fine hair, shiny and silky even in the hardness of battle and trudging through the forest.

"Fye, Fuller is going to take you on the AirSlider to a PAWN facility," Grandyn said slowly, reassuringly. "I'll be right behind you on foot." He looked at the men, they nodded their agreement. "This isn't like the last POP, this is a command center. They'll have a doctor."

"A good doctor," Fuller added. "You're going to be fine." She held Fye close and wrapped her in another jacket while one of the men put the AirSlider next to them.

"No," Fye mouthed. "Don't—"

"You have to," Grandyn said, squeezing her hand. "I'll be right behind you."

Fuller pulled Fye over her. "Hold tight, honey. We'll be there in about five minutes."

Fye got out the word, "No," this time, but Grandyn signaled Fuller to take it up.

"Hold on, Fye. I'll be there before you even miss me."

He watched the AirSlider navigate the nearby trees, and it quickly disappeared into the forest. They could fly only about twenty-five meters above the ground, not high enough to avoid any AOI still in the area. Grandyn tried to suppress the thought that he might never see her again.

"Come on," he said to the men. "Which way?" He jogged in place to keep warm.

Two of the men froze and seemed to avoid eye contact.

"Which way?" Grandyn repeated, alarmed he might have been tricked. He looked back into the air in the direction that Fye had gone. "I'll go alone!" he shouted, and turned to run.

"No!" one of them shouted, his warning lost in a barrage of shots.

CHAPTER FORTY-TWO

Runit flashed back to the attack that had "killed" him the first time and knew he'd used up all of his luck. "The building is the target," he yelled, as if someone else was there. "Run!" Having no idea how long until impact, he tore through the familiar corridors until he reached the entrance. As he ran, he wondered what other parts of the island they would hit, the dock? The tidal energy power generating site? The antique gun emplacements? Maybe the . . . Even before he made it to the door, the first missile hit the building and ended his thoughts. Each of the next eleven came a tenth of a second apart. So that in less than a second and a half, Runit's tiny prison paradise was obliterated.

The Trapciers had helped the Chief develop and implement what many on the Council considered a risky war plan. Only the most prudent members, of the extremely conservative group, thought it was the correct course. Debate had raged for the past twenty-four hours among the billionaires as they too watched the AOI obliterate entire towns and reduce sections of cities to ruin. Some simply saw opportunity to profit from rebuilding the infrastructure. It was the rapidly spreading virus, which many were calling the new plague, that made the majority uneasy.

Flashbacks to the Banoff of their grandparents and great-grandparents' times, and the concern that it could quickly get out of control, grew. The Banoff was something this generation had chosen to forget. Just as the wealthy descendants of plantation owners wanted to forget slavery, they wanted to deny any connection to the past.

During the Council's latest Field-View, the hawkish minority had prevailed. They would give the Chief another forty-eight hours to prove her plan was working, that PAWN, along with any other opposition, was crushed, and to show them a clear path to end the war. The Chief's explanation, from the beginning, was that if they allowed PAWN or any of the rebel groups to get any traction, the war would be a long protracted one. Perhaps lasting a decade. The scenarios they'd run showed that there would be regular terrorist attacks, general insurgencies, and routine guerrilla fighting. No one wanted that. The Council knew that only peace could guarantee prosperity.

The Chairman spoke to the Chief. She was in the AOI War Room in Washington, where the golden words "PEACE PREVAILS ALWAYS" remained above the doors, even though anything but peace was prevailing across the land. The Chief had a bedroom suite at the back of the underground bunker, but had hardly used it. Instead, she'd been relying on stimulants. Pharma-Force made a great pill that could keep a person awake for stretches of up to fifty hours, and another pill that could put a person to sleep almost instantly for increments of twenty minutes at a time. A couple of hours earlier, she had taken three pills, which had given her an hour of sleep. Now she was back on the warpath.

"The Council is going to allow you a little more latitude with your plan," the Chairman said.

"That's a wise decision," the Chief replied in a monotone, not at all concerned with what the Council wanted. She was in charge now, whether they realized it yet or not. The Chief could have their companies seized, their neighborhoods destroyed, and no one could stop her because she was the AOI.

"Yes," the Chairman said, not liking her attitude. "Well, as I said, it's a *little* latitude. You've got forty-eight hours for the bombing and wiping out of all opposition. We certainly don't want any organization left that may start another war in a few years. This needs to be it. But the plague . . ." The Chairman hesitated. What he was about to say had not been authorized by the full Council. "The plague needs to be stopped immediately. I'll be talking to the AHC next and instructing them to assist you with reining that in."

"The Health-Circle is already under my jurisdiction," the Chief answered coolly. "The Constitution is clear. 'In the event of war, all government departments answer to the AOI Chief in order to provide a unified response, and to utilize all assets of the government.' So you'll have to defer to me on that."

The Chief's long history of control and being able to brush away uncomfortable – even abusive – situations began as a small child. She was the youngest of three children. Her Father, an important Aylantik government official, had received a waiver of the bearing rights restrictions, but her mother died giving birth. Growing up, her two brothers teased her mercilessly, and her father beat her.

She was not a woman to mess with. She had no sympathy for anyone, or anything, and would stop at nothing to suppress her feelings of shame and guilt. The Chief was determined to prove herself worthy of the task, worthy of anything. Peace would be returned at *any* price.

"Listen to me," the Chairman said sharply. "The Constitution doesn't mean a damned thing in how we run things. The AOI doesn't give a torg, you don't, and neither do I. The Constitution is just something nice for the kids to study in school and to make people feel that the government doesn't rule them, so don't quote the damned thing to me ever again. Do you understand?"

"I may be the only one who does." She felt strangely weak.

"Forty-eight hours on the war, and wrap up the plague right away. Are we clear?"

"Yes, sir," she said, looking over at the huge AirViews that filled the walls. The war played out like a collection of action movies. Her seven top advisors were busily working virtual keyboards as they hovered around the room on tru-chairs. A holographic map of the Chairman's hometown appeared and she zoomed in on his house. After a few moments, she could see him sitting at his desk. "We are very clear."

Once she finished with the Chairman, she took a zoom from Sidis. They spoke at least once an hour, and his input had proven to be startlingly accurate. The AOI's INUs were extremely sophisticated, and for years she'd relied on them to predict the outcome of events, but the Trapciers seemed to have an almost clairvoyant ability to know how a decision would affect the future. The Chief could give an order, recommended by the Imps, and seconds later the simulators would play out the results. Then, after actually implementing it, she watched in amazement as almost the exact results shown in the simulator were produced in real time.

Sidis gave her the latest objectives that the Trapciers had outlined. She reviewed them quickly and authorized the strikes.

In between all of that, she alternated between conversations with all twenty-four regional heads. Live feeds of their regions and direct links to their offices ringed the wall so she could take immediate action anywhere in the world. She asked the Pacyfik head, "Why haven't we found Drast?"

"As you know, the Flo-wing he escaped in was shot down."

"Did we recover a body?"

"No. Location and conditions did not permit."

"How did you get this job!?" she blasted.

"Chief, if he is still alive, we will find him."

"Your time is up," she said, punching buttons in the air. A woman walked into the Pacyfik Head's office a moment later. "The deputy head will relieve you of your duties," the Chief said, glaring at the man. "You are being reassigned to combat duty." She didn't wait for a response before moving on to another screen.

"Yes, ma'am?" the official in charge of AOI's prisons answered upon seeing the Chief appear.

"I see there are two uprisings still not contained," the Chief said.

"We expect to have them under control in the next few hours."

"Not good enough. You've got thirty minutes to evacuate your people before those facilities and all their inmates are turned to dust."

"But, Chief—"

"Twenty-nine minutes and forty-two seconds."

After dismissing the head of AOI prisons, the Chief reviewed the twenty-four regions again, and approved final attacks on cities in the countries long ago known as Australia, Czechoslovakia, India, Morocco, and Turkey. Everything was going well, although the outcome would be more assured if she knew Deuce Lipton's location and what he was doing.

She scanned a special AirView devoted to him, but it contained nothing new. Still, it had all been easier than expected, thanks to the last minute alliance with the Trapciers. Their talent for efficiently finding and utilizing essential data had made her look brilliant, with one success after another, and so far almost nothing from the stunned opposition.

She noted the time, and checked back with Sidis, but after their brief conversation, for the first time since the war had begun, she suddenly didn't feel invincible.

CHAPTER FORTY-THREE

Chelle wasn't surprised that her zoom to Deuce was accepted in voice-only mode. When she'd spoken to Nelson, it had been the same. Infinite encryption meant their conversation was safe from eavesdropping, but her hologram or someone else's might be able to see something that could reveal Deuce's whereabouts. Deuce answered his INU in his private cabin aboard the Moon Shadow.

"Thanks for taking the zoom," she said. "I have two urgent matters; one personal, and one revolution-related. Although, they both—"

"Sorry to hear about your son," Deuce said, not letting her finish. "I didn't know you had one." It was a lie. Deuce had discovered her dark secret in one of his overly thorough background checks several years earlier, when she had first surfaced as part of the team who got the books out of the Portland Library, but he had wanted to respect her privacy. "Nelson told me everything. Be assured, we're doing all we can to locate him. And Drast."

"Thank you Deuce. The two of them . . . I'm not sure how much more loss I can handle."

"Don't worry. If they're still alive, we'll get them." The fact that Osc was with Drast gave Deuce hope that her son might survive, and made him want to find them even more. Deuce also knew what it was like to have a son missing, and because Chelle's brother had saved his, he was determined to return the favor. He had satellites tracking everything that had happened in and around Hilton Prison since the PAWN Flo-wing had gone in.

"And the other matter . . . I feel so selfish talking about my loss when there are so many dying this very minute all around the world."

"PAWN needs to respond."

"We're working on it. They've buried a lot of our operatives."

"I know, but there will be a window opening in the next few hours. You need to be ready. The AOI will pause."

"Hard to believe. The Chief is following a merciless war plan that might have been written by Attila the Hun."

"Believe it. Be ready. It may only be a few hours. If we're lucky, we'll get a whole day. The Chief may be an icy despot, but it's the Trapciers driving this campaign, and they're more ruthless than old Attila ever was. They're ruled by cold, calculating, machines."

"But aren't the Imps in charge? They're much more human than machine," Chelle said, watching a section of Sydney, in what used to be known as Australia, getting leveled.

"The Imps have surrendered anything that blocks them from their objectives, which includes empathy, compassion, or the slightest regard for human – specifically Traditionals – life."

"What are their goals?"

"Oddly enough, it appears to be human enlightenment."

"Unbelievable," Chelle said. "They're just a bunch of demented freaks, and they're on the top of our target list."

"They are very difficult to find."

"I was hoping you could assist with that."

"Is that the second thing you needed my help with?"

"Not exactly, but as you know, it all kind of blurs together," Chelle said, her voice deepening. "Lance Miner has asked me a favor."

"Really? Are you two old chums?" Although, he couldn't see her, he peered into the Eysen INU as if he could see deception in her eyes. Or was it concern?

"He wants PAWN to assassinate the Chief," she said, ignoring Deuce's comment.

"Interesting. She has gotten under his skin. And of course, he can't do it himself. Hmm."

"Can you help?" Chelle pressed.

"That's a tricky one."

"Why? She's on the verge of destroying the world," Chelle said. "She should be put down like a rabid dog."

"Of course she should, but there's only one chance to get this right. It's why I want Munna to allow us to use the prophecies."

"She's a stubborn old woman. I wouldn't count on *her* changing at all. But you have the power, an army, technology, money, weapons, connections—"

"Yes, but if I misstep and the AOI turns on me, the results would be catastrophic. Not just for me, but for the world."

"Why?"

"Because when this war ends, there will be a vacuum, and something has to fill it, or there will be anarchy."

"Now I get it. You want to sit back and watch everyone else die and sacrifice and then step in at the end and rule what's left? Well torg that! The joke's on you, Deuce. There's probably not going to be anything left to rule!"

Deuce stared at the INU as if trying to see how it could have allowed such a ridiculous statement to be made. "I know you're exhausted and distraught over your son and Drast, so I'll ignore what you just said. But please, think about it later, and when you do, ask yourself how you could let such idiotic words slip from your lips." He paused for a minute, daring her to respond. When

she did not, he added, "I'll consider your request and be in touch."
He paused. "But you get PAWN ready to enter this thing in the
next sixty minutes. You'll see the pause when it happens, and
when it does, don't hold back. We may not get another chance."

The conversation between Munna and Nelson, which Deuce had
left in order to talk to Chelle, was still going on when he returned
to the main room of the Moon Shadow.

"The Aylantik has indeed done many good things," Munna was
saying as he walked in. "They've eliminated those silly lines on
the map that people used to define themselves like stick-on
nametags. 'I'm American,' or 'I'm Chinese,' or 'I'm Nigerian.'
None of it matters. We are *people*. They've eliminated religion, no
more tags. 'I'm Jewish,' or 'I'm Muslim,' 'I'm Christian,' whatever
. . . we are all *people*. They've encouraged the blending of cultures
and races. There isn't anymore 'I'm black,' 'I'm white,' 'I'm Asian,'
or 'Arab,' - nothing, because we're all *people*. One language, one
color, one home . . . Earth. And they have let us feel a long sense
of peace."

"Peace!" Deuce blasted. "There has been no peace."

"Of course not," Munna said. "But they allowed us to *feel* as if
there was. They let us breathe it in and walk as if it were there, so
it gave us something to look at."

"They killed any dissenters!" Deuce pointed at the AirViews.
"They are killing anyone who has even breathed the same air as
anyone who even dreamed of something different from what they
had to offer. Is that what you mean by breathing their peace?"

"They are wrong," Munna said, smiling. "The Aylantik has
always been wrong. But something good can come from something bad, and many very good things have come from their very
bad."

"One day I'll understand this?" Deuce asked with disdain.

"Yes." She smiled to herself. "I just hope you're alive when you do."

Deuce left them to their philosophical pursuits, confident that Nelson would be pushing for the release of her hold on the *Justar Journal's* promise of the prophecies. He had tried every conceivable way to break into them using the codes left in the books, but she possessed a magic key. He went on to pursue the course of action he would have followed if there had never been a *Justar Journal*.

The war escalated every few minutes to new levels of horror, and when he saw a shelter filled with hundreds of children reduced to rubble by a Sonic-bomb attack outside Cairo, he knew they had officially lost their status as a utopian society, and were now living in the worst dystopian world he could imagine. A place where truth had been manipulated so many times, there was no longer a point of reference for what it was when you heard it.

The school wasn't on the Aylantik news feeds. Only those desperate parents in the Egypt area would know of that atrocity, and even then, most of them were either already dead as well, or would be, when the next wave hit.

Even without Miner's request to Chelle and hers to him, Deuce knew the Chief had to die, and it had to be soon. He contacted Nolan and gave the order, but it had to come only after PAWN had come to life. It had to look like a PAWN mission. That might not be until tomorrow.

How many more will be dead by then?

But even if PAWN were up and running right now, they still needed the time to track the Chief and find a way into whatever bunker she'd barricaded herself in.

Meanwhile, Blaze was supposed to have the Trapciers down. It might be the only opening PAWN would get, unless it went well and the AOI showed some vulnerability. If that happened, Deuce had another move to make in the apocalyptic chess match, one that could mean either victory for the rebels, or death for Deuce.

CHAPTER FORTY-FOUR

Another laser pierced the side of the building where Osc was lying, but before he could be grateful of a second near-miss, six men descended on him. They searched and shoved him back to the ground. He felt the heat of the laser sight guide on his forehead. He closed his eyes and pictured his mother, thankful at least that Drast had gotten away. Knowing they were about to kill him, he was surprised that he almost felt relief. Life had been an exhausting obstacle course of disappointment and disillusionment. The stress and pressure had built and grown to where he almost welcomed death, as a fugitive sometimes wants to get caught, tired of running, hiding, fighting. A good long nap sounded so peaceful.

Then he heard Drast yelling.

The doorway Drast had dived into had actually been an archway that led to a courtyard with another exit. He called back to Osc and waited on the other side of the far wall, but there had been no response.

"Damn it," he'd said, knowing he'd have to go back. Even if Osc wasn't Chelle's son, he'd saved his life, and Drast never forgot a small favor, let alone something larger like his life. He'd counted to five, knowing that if Osc was not right behind him, something was wrong. Then he ran back into the courtyard.

He reached the archway, breathing heavily, sensing this was a suicide move. Anything could be out there, and none of it friendly. He peered around the archway, toward the alley he'd just made it through, and saw the crowd. There were now eight of them. From his vantage point, he could make out Osc's head lying on the road. He took the lasershod and aimed carefully. Drast, a champion marksman from his years growing up in the Wyoming Area wilderness, believed he could get three of them, but one of the survivors would surely kill Osc and come after him. No, he needed another strategy.

One of them pointed a weapon at Osc's forehead. Without really thinking, Drast ran into the alley with his hands up. "Wait, don't shoot!"

It had been a foolish thing to do, probably the worst lapse in judgment he'd ever made, but Drast couldn't abandon Osc. Even if he made it, Drast knew he'd never be able to look Chelle in the eyes knowing he'd run away and left Osc to die, and if he couldn't look into those beautiful eyes, he didn't need to live.

As he stepped out and saw the full view of the scene, he realized what was happening. The mob were rebels, or at least rebel sympathizers. They had attacked Osc because of his AOI uniform.

"We're not AOI!" Drast yelled, suddenly feeling the heat of several lasers on him. He knew plain old civilians would not have those advanced weapons. They had to be with PAWN. "We're PAWN."

"How do we know that?" one of them yelled.

"Look at me! I'm in a prison uniform, and he's not in a regular grunge uniform. Look closely. He's a prison guard. He helped me escape yesterday."

Several of them examined Osc. One of them lowered his weapon. Drast inched closer, all the time holding his weapon, by the barrel, high above his head.

"Please, I am a high-ranking PAWN leader," Drast said. "If you've got communications, call in. Check us out. Tell them you have Osc."

They looked at each other. One of them made some moves in the air and opened a small AirView. The others began looking nervously toward both ends of the alley, as if unsure who might be after these two important fugitives. The one who'd been working his INU shook his head.

The apparent leader, the only one who had spoken so far, said, "We can't get out." He stared at Drast, and then walked toward him. In one motion, the rebel pushed Drast hard enough to knock him down and took away his lasershod. With Drast recovering on the ground, the man inspected the weapon. "It's not AOI issue," he shouted back to the others, who still had lasers trained on Osc and Drast. "So maybe I believe you. It's a good story. What are you doing here? Why aren't you hiding somewhere instead?"

"We're on a mission. I broke out of prison in order to carry it out. Critical to the revolution."

"What is it?"

"I can't tell you."

"Torg man," the rebel said, surprised, pointing Drast's own weapon back at him. "You think you're in a position to decide what you can or cannot tell me?"

"Sorry, man. I don't know you. It is so classified that only three people in PAWN know about it, and I can't risk it getting out."

The man shook his head, appalled.

"If that means you have to kill me, then do it," Drast said, locked into a stare. "But know that you'll be killing more than just me. You'll be killing millions of *innocent* people."

The man licked his lips and his finger twitched lightly over the trigger. "How do I know?"

"You don't," Drast said, never releasing his gaze. "But millions of lives . . . is it worth the risk?"

The man stood there a moment, still staring, then turned. "Let him go."

One of them pulled Osc to his feet and pushed him toward Drast and the leader. Osc scrambled over to Drast and helped him up.

The rebel handed Drast back his lasershod, with one last look, then said, "Risk? What the torg does that word even mean anymore?"

"It means we stop the tyrants. It means we never stop fighting back," Drast said, making eye contact. "You did the right thing. Thank you."

The rebel barely smiled. "I don't know where you're heading, but I hope it's west. This quadrant, and the entire east side, is crawling with grunge patrols. So get out fast."

Drast nodded, and was about to ask if the rebels wanted to come with them, when the leader's head split open. Blood and flesh exploding, and he dropped to the road, dead.

Drast, only half a meter away, was hit with enough blood that for a moment he thought he'd also been shot. Osc shoved him down and they rolled toward the archway while trying to see where the shot had come from. By the time they got their bearings, all the rebels who had just released them were dead, and they were surrounded by ten AOI grunges.

CHAPTER FORTY-FIVE

Grandyn went into TreeRunner mode as dirt and leaves suddenly exploded around him. He focused through the blinding barrage of lasers and heavier blasts and found a low area at the base of large trees, well fed from the nearby river. Still soaking wet, he smeared black earth into his clothes, skin, and hair. Without a weapon, other than the knife strapped to his leg, he looked for anything else that might help.

In those precious moments concealed in the trees, he was also able to determine that it wasn't the "hikers" shooting him. It was AOI agents attacking both him and the rebels.

He found a large rock just as a grunge spotted his movements. Grandyn rolled and kicked and in an acrobatic move not used since his TreeRunner days before the war, he went up and came crashing down so fast that he crushed the unprepared grunge's skull.

He spun, and in less than a second had taken the man's weapons. He shot another grunge just as two of the rebels went down simultaneously. More lasers sliced through the air, cutting trees, tearing branches, and a minute later it was over. Five grunges were dead and two of the rebels. Only he and one other survived.

"Which way?" Grandyn demanded, as the man was still checking the bodies of his comrades.

"I'm not sure," the shaken rebel said.

Grandyn grabbed his shirt and shook him. "Damn it. We've got to move and you need to tell me where we're going."

"Okay, I just wanted to make sure—"

"No one survives lasers to the head or torso," Grandyn said. "I'm sorry, but war doesn't allow for proper mourning. The only way to avenge their deaths is to win. Now come on."

The man pointed in the direction the woman had left with Fye as they began to run. It was frustratingly slow for Grandyn, since he had to continually ease back his pace to allow the rebel to catch up, but there was nothing else he could do. The description of the entrance to the PAWN center, which the man gave him as they jogged through the trees was insanely intricate, and Grandyn believed what the woman had said; that he'd never find it alone. He just hoped they'd both make it there. Grunges could be anywhere, and although Grandyn ran silently, his companion absolutely did not. As they continued to climb in elevation, the trip grew even more sluggish. The rebel was not in bad shape, but the exertion at 1800 meters above sea level had him huffing and puffing. At least now, Grandyn was mostly dry.

Finally, after one two-minute rest and a very long sixty-five minutes after they began their journey, the rebel announced they were close. It took another eight minutes to navigate the labyrinth of traps and hidden entrances before they were at the final door. By then they were in a subchamber, four meters underground. The man's retina scan got him and Grandyn in, and the people inside were already expecting them.

Once they'd cleared the last of the entrance doors, Fuller, the woman who'd taken Fye, was waiting. "She's fine," were her first words to Grandyn.

"Take me to her."

"Of course, but you can't go into the medical wing like this." She motioned to his clothes and he looked down at the dirt and leaves plastered to his sweaty body.

"Take me to her," he repeated.

"Grandyn, they won't let you in. She's fine. Take ten minutes to clean up."

She started walking down the corridor. The walls were a silvery gray, with soft lighting. It appeared to be construction similar to the smaller POPs where the walls and rooms were built in modules and dropped in place before they were buried, but this one was much bigger, and more elaborate. As he followed her, he counted eighteen side corridors, and they were nowhere near the end of the main hall.

"You can shower in there," she said, pointing into a small room. "At the other side of that wall you'll find a rack of *clean* Tekfabrik jumpsuits."

Grandyn took one more look down the hall, wondering if he could find her by himself, imagining confronting armed guards. He ducked into the shower room, and less than five minutes later emerged looking like a new man. In the shower his mind had wandered from Fye to their baby, which Fuller had said nothing about. It was his first question when he found her waiting in the hall.

"I'm sorry, Grandyn . . . She lost the baby."

They'd murdered another Happerman. He wanted to cry. He wanted to collapse onto the hard floor. He wanted to kill every AOI agent in the world.

"Take me to her!"

When they arrived at the medical wing, there were no guards, nothing that would have stopped him from going inside. Twenty-eight beds lined the two sides of the long narrow space. Only a few were empty. An operating room was at the far end, and a smaller area off the entrance was filled with medical supplies on shelves and in cabinets.

Fuller took him to Fye and then left them alone. He stared for a moment, her face gaunt and pale. She looked empty.

Fye started to cry when she saw him, gently at first, but then, as he climbed in the bed and held her, she sobbed heavily. "We lost the baby," she whispered between the tears.

"I know. I know."

She held him tight. They lay together that way until her tears ran out. He'd been unable to cry. It was all he could do not to head back out into the forest and start hunting grunges.

"We can try again," she said softly.

"Yes, we will. I love you."

A few minutes later Fuller appeared. "We've informed upper-command that you're here. Chelle Andreas sends her regards, and has ordered an escort be provided whenever you're ready to leave. She'd send a Flo-wing, but the AOI is shooting everything out of the sky. She did authorize armed AirSliders for both of you.

"We need to go as soon as possible," Grandyn replied.

"The doctor would like her to stay put and rest for three days," Fuller said.

Grandyn looked at Fye.

"I'll be fine in a few hours," she argued.

The doctor was consulted and said she should not travel for at least thirty-six hours. He gave her something to make her sleep.

While Fye was out, Fuller took Grandyn on a tour of the underground center. It was expansive, one of PAWN's oldest and also one of the larger facilities.

"In the second part of the century, PAWN changed their tactics and opted for more numerous and much smaller POPs," Fuller explained.

Grandyn studied maps of the area and planned a route to their destination in the California mountains. He also watched the war updates. It was one brutal scene after another, but four hours into Fye's slumber, the news abruptly changed.

It appeared as if the AOI had stopped. There were no major bombings, and no new outbreaks reported. Were they waiting for something to happen? Were they trying to bait PAWN into coming out? The entire PAWN center was buzzing with questions.

Then, an hour later, an intercepted AOI communication changed everything.

"Get the doctor to give Fye a wakeup shot," Grandyn told Fuller. "We're leaving. Now."

She made no attempt to stop him.

When Fye woke, Grandyn explained the developments. She agreed that if they were going to have any chance at making it to the City, they would have to leave immediately.

CHAPTER FORTY-SIX

The Chief was furious. The Trapciers had been compromised. It had to have been either Blaze Cortez or Deuce Lipton behind the attack. Deuce had the technology to be able to change the program which controlled the INU-bio interface the Imps relied on to allow their human-thinking minds to mesh with the machine form, but Blaze, as the inventor of the entire DesTIn system, and so closely involved with the Imps, was even more likely to be the culprit.

Either way, it didn't matter at this point which one had done it. She had no proof, and no solid method of retaliation. The AOI didn't even know where either of them was and, without the Trapciers intel and analysis, she had bigger problems. Much bigger. Her war plan was suddenly in disarray.

She was actually correct in that both men were involved, although Deuce only indirectly, when he agreed to provide the satellite. When Blaze had first developed DesTIn, he'd installed a "back-door," through which he could extract information. Deuce's top engineers had, long ago, discovered the "flaw," and corrected it on all their installations. DesTIn was an indispensable program, and widely used. Deuce decided not to broadcast the presence of the issue, knowing that one day he might need some of the data Blaze would be able to collect. The Imps had never detected it.

Every Imp, CHRUDE, and even some high-end cyborgs were based on DesTIn, and therefore possessed the code. Blaze developed a new program that also allowed him to crash their systems, which were previously believed to be completely secure. The move effectively rendered all of the CHRUDEs useless, and turned Imps back into regular Traditionals, or, as he told an assistant, "The Imps are now like humans with a bad headache."

It was impossible to know how long it would last. It could be days, or as little as twelve hours. Blaze would have about a fifteen-minute warning before the Trapciers were up and running again. In the meantime, he had a second use for the satellite. He needed to find the "great TreeRunner," as he often called Grandyn. His hope was that he could locate Grandyn and Fye and then follow them straight to the List Keepers.

Earlier in the day, Blaze had written a DesTIn program to track Grandyn. It ran billions of variables and computed every possible route and destination. Utilizing unauthorized Seeker data and AOI military global overlays to formulate historical patterns and extrapolated data to applied radiuses. He caught a break by retroactively mapping movements along the coastlines from Deuce's Ryder Island, and eventually traced images that showed Grandyn, Fye, and Twain coming ashore in a small powerboat near the redwoods. From there, he tried to track Deuce's larger vessel, but it disappeared less than forty meters from the beach. Blaze, extremely impressed, shook his head.

"Deuce ought to be running the world," he said to himself. "I'd do a much better job, but he'd be good, too . . . and, at least people find him likeable."

As the program continued to search for Grandyn, the husband and wife team working on the Chief-assassination plan appeared at his office door. He'd moved his entire human team to this new location after the Imps' betrayal. The place was completely untraceable to him; a small building that, according to the signage on the blue-painted metal exterior, claimed to be a health research firm, but instead housed a "wizard's workshop" of AirViews, INUs strung together, and other gadgetry understood by no one but Blaze and a few assistants. The interior, comprising a series of glass rooms, contained a million kilometers of wires and tubes, half of which were part of his anti-monitoring, anti-detection defenses. The other half were used for the opposite purpose of monitoring and detecting *his* targets. Blaze liked the place, and although machines made him feel comfortable, the Imps weren't missed.

"We have an idea," the husband said. Miner had provided information on where the Chief was holed up. A special bunker had been constructed near Washington, DC, and not only was it ultra-secure, it would also enable her to survive down there for as long as a year. Supplies, communications, air, and water were all self-contained.

"It needs to be more than an idea," Blaze replied. "With all the special features and precautions she's got built into her subterranean world, you'll need help from Hades, the Greek god of the underworld."

"If she's really in the Washington bunker," the wife began, "we can destroy it by reprograming one of the AOI drones and dropping one of her own Sonic-bombs right on top of her."

Blaze smiled. "Poetic justice to be sure, but the only possibility would be to find a drone with a payload intended for a nearby city, somehow access and override the launch protocols, which are the most secure on earth, and of course, it could only be done in midflight, after which you'd then have to redirect the flight plan without detection, all that while avoiding Washington's entire conglomeration of air defenses."

"Correct," the husband said. "We think it can be done."

"Excellent," Blaze replied. "I always relish achieving the impossible. Show me."

The woman pulled up an AirView and began a simulation of the mission. "The bunker might survive," she said. "Sonic-bombs had been developed long before the bunker was built, so they may have factored that into construction design."

"If they could," Blaze said. "Look at what those bombs are doing around the world right now. It may not be *possible* to build something to withstand them."

"Yes," the man said. "That's why we like this idea. The bomb is intensely powerful, and because none of their enemies possess it, or anything close, they might have foregone the precaution."

"Your plan is ambitious, and according to your own scenarios, the odds of success are only fifty-four percent," Blaze said. "What is your backup?"

"We could use someone on the inside to get to her. We have assets," the man said.

Blaze, of course, knew this. He had long used and paid informants inside the AOI. The information was very valuable, particularly times and places of raids, suspects, and other activity that could save his clients' lives or property. But the likelihood of getting one of the moles into the Chief's bunker seemed extremely unlikely. The airstrike was a better plan.

"Stick to the bombing," Blaze said. "Make sure it works."

The Chief dusted off her original war plan, the one she'd spent years working on before the Imps handed her a foolproof version created by the highest forms of intelligence. The Trapciers' script, as they called it, had run trillions of scenarios and had taken into account every imaginable datapoint from air temperature, to the accuracy of lasershods when fired from every distance, to death rates, plague-spread paths, LEV speed, Seeker footage, and billions of other inputs. A few more days and it would have been over, but someone had to screw with her Imps.

"Damn them!"

She now saw her original plan as inept, but there were many salvageable aspects that could now be implemented. The Chief ordered the burning of all the forests in California, Oregon, and Washington Areas. At the same time, mass numbers of Breeze-Blowers were deployed. The dust-sized computers, equipped with video transmitters, which would blow along with the wind, would make hiding much more difficult for the rebels. But that was only the beginning.

In recent months, manufacturing had also been stepped up on swarm-drones, monitoring-mimic-drones, and neuron-mites. She may have lost her robotic brain trust, but that didn't mean she couldn't use machines to obliterate the enemy. Her final move was to order more plague.

"We'll see how the Council likes that," she said to herself. "I think all of Missouri Area is about to get sick. Oh, is that where the Chairman lives? How unfortunate."

CHAPTER FORTY-SEVEN

Lance toasted Sarlo. "The Trapciers are on the ropes and the Chief appears suddenly lost," he said cheerfully.

"I don't think I can celebrate after the endless deaths I've witnessed in this sadistic war," Sarlo said sadly. "And it's not going to stop. All this reprieve does is give PAWN a chance to blast the AOI back . . . and us. What damage are Enforcers going to do now that there's an opening?"

"We will return the peace," he said, ignoring her rhetorical question. She knew what Enforcers were about to do. "And I'm sure one of the assassins will succeed. The Chief can't survive this. I understand even the Council is worried that she's gone too far. And what do you think Deuce is thinking? He's also got to be trying to take her out. He can't sit by and watch as she destroys the whole world."

Looking at the AirViews, Sarlo said, "How are we ever going to recover?"

"We rebuilt after the Banoff. We'll do it again."

"The Banoff plague killed billions, but in five years. Even the Banoff war didn't do anything close to the kind of damage the Chief has done in the last two days."

"I hate the woman, but she isn't the only one to blame. The Trapciers, those filthy Imps, are using her to try to take over."

"I just don't believe it," Sarlo said, shaking her head.

"How can you say that? Look at what they're doing. We're Traditionals. They want to either kill us all or, at the very least, enslave us all."

"Why?"

"So they can rule the world," Miner said, looking out at the Toronto skyline.

"Then why not just eliminate us and make a billion androids?"

"That's probably just what they intend," Miner sneered. "This is only the beginning. A week from now, how many humans will be left? Then they'll need the AOI out of their way, and I bet the Imps will kill the Chief for us. But by then it won't matter anymore."

"I disagree," she said, taking a meal from a serving bot and then sending it to Miner.

"I know."

Miner wasn't used to her total opposition to any of his views. Sometimes she looked at an issue slightly differently. Her fresh perspective helped illuminate a point he might otherwise have missed, and her input ended up making his position stronger. But in this case, he believed her to be absolutely wrong. He wanted to change the subject.

"You know, if these damned List Keepers are really as great and powerful as some people seem to think, what the hell are they doing? Just watching the world die?"

"Maybe they don't exist," Sarlo said. "Or maybe they were all wiped out in one of the first waves of Sonic-bombs. If they were real, the Trapciers and the AOI would surely have seen them as a threat and taken them out early. I mean look at this bloodbath." She quickly enlarged several AirViews showing summaries of the AOI bombings. "These aren't all PAWN positions, or even people opposed to the Aylantik. Why is she hitting these places? How is the Chief choosing her targets?"

"It's those freaks you like so much," Miner snapped. "I'm telling you the Imps want to kill us all."

"Last week they were helping you."

"Were they? It's all part of their plan. I don't know why you don't realize what's going on. They're a lot smarter than the rest of us, and they have been directing the war. Why? How the hell should I know why or what, I just know they are!"

Sarlo turned to the live feeds from Enforcers. They had ten dedicated screens constantly rotating the increasing activities of Miner's private army. They had been doing a remarkable job of avoiding detection – a combination of tactics, training, technology, and luck.

"They still haven't found the Trapciers?"

"Not yet, but now that the Imps are down, we're going to have a big night. You heard the captain." Only minutes earlier, Miner had reviewed and approved plans with the captain of Enforcers. Guerilla attacks were scheduled for that night in forty-three locations. "If PAWN gets into it tonight, and with the Trapciers out of commission, I'm sure they will. It's going to be quite a different wake-up for the Chief in the morning."

"She's sure to be expecting it. She's been waiting for counter-attacks. Even without her Imp advisors, the Chief has certainly had a plan in place from the start, ready to deal with whatever Enforcers and PAWN throw at her. We need Deuce," Sarlo said, feeling the irony in her words, knowing they would taste extra bitter on Miner's lips. The man they had tried to destroy for years was the one most able to save them.

CHAPTER FORTY-EIGHT

Fye would not even consider staying at the Crater Lake PAWN center once they had intercepted AOI orders to torch all the forests in California, Oregon, and Washington Areas. The Chief had apparently grown impatient, and was desperate to flush out the rebels. Fye and Grandyn knew that with the forests in flames, they would never make it to the City buried deep within one of North America's largest wilderness areas. The doctor implored Fye not to go, but she could not be swayed.

"She could bleed," the doctor told Grandyn firmly. "If you're out in the woods and she starts losing blood, she'll be dead before you can get help."

"It's up to her," Grandyn said.

"I'd rather die trying," Fye replied.

Fuller begged Grandyn to help change Fye's mind, but he agreed with her.

"If there's one thing I've learned throughout the Doneharvest," Grandyn said, "it's that some things are bigger than we are . . . more important than a life." He suddenly choked up for a second, not meaning to think of the baby they'd lost. "My father spoke of duty and loyalty, not to governments or institutions, but to ideas and truth. We have to go."

"But where are you going?" Fuller asked.

"I would tell you if I could, but I can't. And we need to leave now." Grandyn was worried about Fye, but they had to get to the City, or, he believed, the world would end.

Fuller nodded. "Chelle Andreas authorized an escort. I'd like to be on it."

"As long as you're ready to go now," Grandyn said.

"Five minutes is the best I can do," Fuller replied. "It'll take me that long to get your AirSliders and round up a team."

"We'll meet you at the entrance," Grandyn said, knowing she didn't understand the stakes.

Grandyn checked the time. It had been seven minutes since Fuller went to put everything together. He would have left on foot, but knew Fye needed the AirSlider, and it would obviously save them days of travel time.

"There are reports of fires," Fuller said, running down the corridor toward them. "Sorry it took longer than I said, but I had to coordinate with PAWN Command." She could see the impatient look on Grandyn's face.

"Where are the fires?"

"They started in Washington Area. The Olympic mandated forest is burning."

Grandyn shook his head, imagining all the trees they would lose just because the Chief was scared. "We're not going that way."

"PAWN Command wants our route," Fuller said.

"They can't have it," Grandyn said.

Two men who'd been a few steps behind Fuller each carried a folded AirSlider. Fuller looked at them and then back to Grandyn.

"They want to protect you. Can you give us a little more detail?"

"No."

"North eastern California Area," Fye said.

Grandyn frowned.

Fuller brought up an AirView and spoke the information into her INU.

"Can we go?" Grandyn asked, reaching for the AirSliders.

Fuller nodded. "We'll get final orders in a few minutes."

"We need to *go*."

"Okay. We'll cross a highway in about ten minutes. We can pick up Command's flash then. She took an AirSlider from one of the men and handed it to Fye. "It's armed."

Grandyn took his. Another was handed to Fuller. Once outside, they found a team of five more PAWN members waiting. Each had an AirSlider. Grandyn was happy for the support, but worried about eight of them buzzing through the forest.

It didn't matter. They needed the protection. Grunges were everywhere. He'd learned that the hard way, and the fires were coming.

Near the empty highway, they stopped for the promised "quick check-in" with PAWN Command.

"Okay, we've been ordered to take you as far as the Siskiyou Pass," Fuller said. "And PAWN Command has coordinated with Parker. You probably know the TreeRunners are under PAWN Command, but you'll like this. TreeRunners will meet us below the pass and then take you south of Shasta. But from there, depending on fire activity, you'll have to meet up with another PAWN unit to go the rest of the way."

"Sounds good to me," Grandyn said. "Any help getting us to where we need to go will be appreciated." He thought of the grunges they'd met along the Rogue River, and how close they had come to dying. How much it had cost them. "The help means a lot." He bowed slightly to Fuller. "Sorry if I haven't thanked you properly. I know you lost friends because of us."

"It's not because of you. It's the damned grunges' fault."

Grandyn nodded.

"We owe you our lives," Fye added.

"Don't' worry about it. Just make sure you get where you're going and that you do what you have to do."

Fuller knew they were important, and that their mission must be a big deal because of how much help PAWN Command was giving them. Help was coming all the way from the top. Grandyn asked her for the names of the ones who had died saving them. He repeated them, along with their ID numbers, into his INU, and also added them to his long mental list, trying to memorize them.

"Who are we meeting from the TreeRunners?" Grandyn asked, hoping it was one of his old clan.

Fuller checked her INU. "Someone named Zaverly Tandrum."

CHAPTER FORTY-NINE

Every one of the ten AOI grunges surrounding Drast and Osc was aiming weapons. Drast felt the heat of so many lasers on him that it seemed he was being roasted for a meal as they were roughly searched and scanned.

"Torgon hell," one of the agents said. "We hit the jackpot today, boys!"

Two of them crowded in to see the results of the scan.

"Lex Evren, better known as public enemy number four, Polis Drast . . . and his traitor prison guard Osc Burg."

A few of them whooped.

Drast looked the men over.

"What's the order?" one of them asked.

"The guard is to be terminated, but we're to take Drast into custody. He's to be put on a secure flight to Washington, DC. Looks like the Chief wants to eat him alive or some such."

Several of them laughed.

Drast studied the faces of the ten men, looking for any opportunity.

"Who wants to do the guard?" the leader asked as he shoved Osc against the wall.

Another grunge volunteered. "I'll do it. I need the points."

"Wait!" Drast yelled.

They all turned to him. The leader looked incredulous. "Listen Drast, you may have been the head of the Pacyfik Region once, but that was a long time ago, and you don't give the orders anymore. So if you don't want to get shot next, you need to shut the torg up."

Drast's gaze went quickly from face to face.

The grunge who'd volunteered aimed a lasershod at Osc's head. "Guess you picked the wrong side," he said to Osc.

"Allies of innocence!" Drast yelled. "Allies of innocence!"

Lasers cut the air in a sudden burst of fireworks. Shouts and shots crossed in a blurred panicked scuffle. Two men hit the ground dead, the volunteer and the leader. Two more had dropped their weapons and had their hands held high.

Osc looked at Drast, confused.

While four grunges kept their weapons on the two holding up their hands, another approached Drast. "I'll need the word," he said quietly.

"Wolftrap," Drast replied.

The agent handed Drast a weapon.

Without any hesitation, Drast shot the two men holding up their hands. "Sorry if they were friends," Drast said to the man who'd handed him the lasershod. "We don't have the luxury of taking prisoners."

"We never got too close to any of the wolves," the man answered. "Still, we served with them for a while. We all covered each other . . . it was better you did it, instead of us."

"What's going on?" Osc asked, dazed.

"What's the Vancouver headquarters look like?" Drast asked, ignoring Osc.

"I think it's risky," the man who'd given him the weapon answered. "There have been a lot of transfers during the Doneharvest, even more yesterday. I don't think we have the numbers anymore."

"Too many wolves, for sure," another man said.

"Who are the wolves?" Osc asked.

Two of the surviving agents had taken defensive positions and were now covering both ends of the alley.

"Can we get in the air?" Drast asked.

"Negative."

"What about the water?" Drast asked.

The man looked at one of the other agents. "Possibly," he answered.

"Are we better taking you as a prisoner, or getting you a uniform?" the first agent asked, pointing to one of the bodies.

"Uniform. I'd draw too much attention as a prisoner."

"We need to move."

Drast started undressing one of the dead men. "You might want to switch out of that," Drast said to Osc. "Any regular AOI agent will know it's a prison guard uniform."

Osc picked the body closest to him in size, and started the process. "What's going on? Who are these guys?"

"There's an AOI inside the AOI," Drast said while getting dressed. "It's the Allies of Innocence. "It's kind of like PAWN, but it's made up entirely of AOI agents."

"Who are the wolves?"

"The wolves are the regular agents . . . the bad guys."

"And what do you call the good guys?" he asked as they finished dressing.

"We're known as the righteous warriors of hope and truth."

"Really?"

"No." He smiled. "We just call ourselves the 'Allies.'"

"Let's go," the unofficial leader said, as they moved out.

"Why wasn't I in the secret AOI?" Osc asked.

"You'll have to ask your mother that one. She may have thought it too risky for you, or maybe for the Allies. If anyone found out who you were, it would have blown the entire operation."

"How many Allies are there?"

"Thousands," Drast said.

Osc was impressed, but not entirely surprised. The AOI was not popular. They had filled the land with terror and tears. Peace came at a high price, and even among those supposedly loyal agents he'd known during his time in the AOI, many were discontented and remorseful about the brutal ways of the so-called "peacekeepers."

"Where are we heading?" Osc asked.

"We're heading to the Salish Sea," the unofficial leader explained. "Hopefully we can borrow a boat."

"And then?"

"Seattle," Drast said. "It'll be much quicker than trying to get there overland."

"What's in Seattle?" Osc asked.

"If all goes well and the stars are on our side, then we'll find something in Seattle that has eluded us for decades."

"What's that?"

"Victory."

CHAPTER FIFTY

The Chief watched the fires spread. Teams had started in Washington State Area and then moved into Oregon Area. Another crew worked California Area.

The strategy presented many risks, as scientists were still trying to reverse global warming. Beyond climate concerns, the massive fires could make it difficult for AOI bombing flights over large areas affected by smoke drift. There would also be collateral damage – loss of life and property within the massive fire zones – but she wasn't concerned about that. The fires would force PAWN out of their hiding places. Her best intelligence, and the Imps had agreed, showed the largest concentration of rebel bases to be within the zones she now targeted with fires.

It was late in the day in the Pacyfik region when Chelle ordered PAWN into the air. The pause, caused by the DesTIn crash, which in turn resulted in the Trapcier shutdown, provided the opportunity, but it was the fires that gave added urgency.

The Chief was correct; a large percentage of PAWN assets were in the fire zone. Nano-camo and other stealth methods had protected a small, but advanced fleet of PAWN fighter jets and bombers. They didn't have Sonic-bombs, but they would be able to cause substantial damage to AOI bases and infrastructure if they could stay in the air long enough. Chelle had been lobbying Deuce for help from space by way of his StarFly corporation, but so far he'd been resisting.

She couldn't wait any longer.

The fires surprised Miner. He saw it as a direct snub to the Council. And then he discovered that the center of a pandemic was now the area where the Council Chairman resided.

"She's making her move," Miner said to Sarlo.

"It's a *coup d'état*," Sarlo said, using the dead language phrase, as their Com language conveniently had no word to describe a military takeover of the government.

"I underestimated that dragon lady . . . both in her brilliance, and in her stupidity," Miner said, flipping his silver dollar. "Damn," he said quietly as it landed on tails.

Hidden in an air-conditioned warehouse on the outskirts of Prescott in the Arizona Area, Sidis, Charlemagne, and Galahad continued to monitor the war news even without the benefit of their implants, which had not been functioning for seventeen hours.

They were each in the throes of what could only be described as a migraine in hell. Pain tore at them, ravaging their nerves and clarity as their brains and nervous systems adjusted to no implants. The withdrawals had begun immediately after Blaze crashed the system, and the symptoms had continued to worsen as the hours passed. They had teams of people working to remove the bug Blaze had buried in each of them like a cancer. At that moment, writhing in pain, Sidis wanted to ditch all other efforts and concentrate on finding and painstakingly inflicting excruciating agony on Blaze Cortez and then killing him even more slowly, but Charlemagne persuaded him to keep focused on their original objective.

"The fires are a mistake," Galahad said.

"How the torg do you know?" Sidis asked. "I can't even think."

"The Chief is creating a giant choking obstacle in the middle of a key region. She thinks it will paralyze the rebels, but it will instead shut down the AOI across the critical western section of the continent."

"Many of the simulators agree with your assessment," Charlemagne said, looking at AirViews showing probability formulas run on non-DesTIn programs. "But she won't listen to us while we're unplugged."

"I wouldn't either," Sidis said. "I don't want to listen to anything right now. I don't even know why the torg we're involved."

Galahad shook his head. "You forget your connection. You must remember all that you have seen. Our mission is vital to the future of civilization. Work through the pain, ignore the void of knowledge, make power where there is none."

Fuller stopped again as they neared another stretch of civilization where she could get a connection. "The fires are now in California and Oregon, as well as Washington," she announced while pulling up an AirView so the others could see the report.

Grandyn looked at Fye. Their destination was still safe, but if they didn't move fast, the flames would close in from all sides and either block, or trap them.

"We can't stop anymore," Grandyn said.

"It isn't going to be just these," Fuller said. "They're still igniting all over the place. We'll be caught in a firestorm if we continue! We need to evacuate."

"You're free to go," Grandyn said. "I don't want to put any of you in more jeopardy than we already have."

"We'll go a little farther," Fuller said glancing at Fye, who was clearly weak and pale.

Grandyn also stared at Fye, concerned. "Are you . . . " he whispered.

"I'll be fine," she said, making her voice sound stronger than it was.

"Let's go," he said, squeezing the accelerator button. His AirSlider surged back into the air. Fye, Fuller, and the others followed. They were vigilantly watching for grunges as they navigated in and around the treetops.

A few hours later, while following a line of high tension power-lines up a ridge, Fuller was able to pick up another signal. She worked her INU while still soaring above the open range beneath the power lines. They were only about forty-five minutes from the Siskiyou Pass, and she provided their position to PAWN Command, who would relay their ETA to Zaverly. Once she'd completed the update, she flew up next to Grandyn and shouted across at him.

"PAWN is in the air!"

"They're fighting back?"

"It appears the war might finally be real."

"Hell yeah! More than a war, we got ourselves a revolution!"

Grandyn felt as if he'd been waiting for this moment since before he even knew PAWN existed. For more than three years he'd waited and worked for the revolution to begin, and now it had.

He could see smoke from distant fires as they raced toward them. Millions had died, proving they were on the right side, showing the Aylantik for what it was, the darkest side of evil ever to blight the Earth. Grandyn thought of his mother—she too had waited for this day—and his father. He smiled, knowing Runit would quote an author and knowing just the one, David Mitchell. His dad had always admired his book, *Cloud Atlas*. Grandyn recalled the exact words from the book, and his dad reciting them to him during one of the last times they were together.

"Fantasy. Lunacy. All revolutions are, until they happen, then they are historical inevitabilities."

CHAPTER FIFTY-ONE

Twain sat cross-legged in a grove of giants. Redwoods towered around him, reaching heights of more than one hundred meters. The setting sun struggled to filter its last rays of light to the soft forest floor where he sat, isolated and alone, no INUs or AirViews to distract him. The Field did not penetrate, and yet he knew what was to happen.

He'd been in a near trance for seven hours, preparing his body, concentrating on his cells and, during that intense meditation, he'd been interrupted three times by visions. The first told him that AOI squads were burning forests in the northern Pacyfik region, including ancient redwoods. The Chief obviously had no rational sense of the consequences of her actions.

The other two visions had to do with the end of the war. Neither was good. One showed a burnt, post-apocalyptic wasteland. There were only a few thousand survivors, wandering in search of food, or hiding, not sure what to do, where to go, or whom to trust. They wouldn't last long. The planet had been heavily damaged, and the new plague still lingered. Human extinction was only a few brutally unimaginable years away.

In the third vision, there had been hope. The planet, while in exceedingly desperate condition, was still habitable for human life. More than a billion had survived, which meant that more than a billion had not, but there was a sense of the third, and final chance for the species. The post-Banoff world had been the second opportunity to get it right, but the corruption built into that society made it a false premise. In his vision, he saw the start of the third attempt, a new direction, a very different approach. People shared and built a society on ideas instead of materialism.

He didn't know which vision would come true, and didn't know if he could do anything to influence the outcome. Still, it gave him insight into what Munna could do. He was only beginning to explore the things UC had taught him. Cope had said, "Anyone can do this. With enough patience and practice, everyone can find the way to the power."

He'd called this ability to tap into a universal energy, which connected everything, "the sway." It could allow them to slow the aging of our physical bodies as Munna had done, and through it, they could tap into the "ornament of time," as he called it. Twain had heard "time's a funny thing" his whole life, and now, through his experiences with UC, watching Munna, seeing the *Justar Journal,* and recently through his own meditations, he finally understood what it meant.

He wrote it down so he wouldn't lose the realization.

The ornament of time is a way of looking at life, the world, and the entire universe. It makes it easier for our minds to comprehend our connection to the other people and events that surround us. Speaking and thinking in terms of "one hundred years ago" is something we can understand; a linear look into the past, or our own age, or picturing the future as a date so many "years" ahead. But it is not much different from seeing the ocean as three meters deep because below that it is dark, or assuming that the stars visible in the night sky are all there is. Time is a funny thing because it is a pool we swim in, rather than a path we walk.

In that understanding, he realized the "future" could be wonderful. All that had to be done to make their third and "final" chance work, was to draw from the entire "pool." They could bring the best of every age, past-present-future, *and* use the wisdom and understanding to make it right this *time*.

He thought of Munna and the List Keepers. They were here for a reason. *If we made it to the third vision, they could show us where to go next. Lead the way*, he thought.

Two thousand kilometers away, on the deck of the Moon Shadow, Munna smiled. She could feel Twain. She felt many people, but some were stronger. UC, Twain's great-uncle, had been one of the strongest. With his passing, that connection had changed. It wasn't weaker, just different. But Twain, especially when in the redwoods, had a potent force within him.

Whenever someone first discovered the power, they projected a bright and vigorous energy. Munna knew that vital energy was needed now. Soon, she hoped, Grandyn would make it to the City and be another in the new generation of leaders and teachers.

In all history, this would be the most important test. If the war could be stopped soon enough, they still had a chance. Yet, in order to survive and change, it would take the complete focus of all who knew the secrets, understood the power, and could see into time.

Deuce looked over and, hoping for good news, asked, "What are you smiling about?"

"Twain."

"What about him?"

"He's alive and awake."

Deuce, deeply happy to hear this, had spent enough time with the old woman to know she wasn't just saying what she was saying. "Meaning?"

"He'll be there at the end."

"Are they going to burn the redwoods?"

She nodded. "They are going to try. They may succeed."

The way she looked at him, he had the feeling she was silently saying what she had verbalized several times since this had all started. "It depends on me?" Deuce asked.

Munna smiled. "Of course it does."

"Show me the *Justar Journal*."

She frowned.

"You knew my grandfather."

She nodded. "Quite well."

"I know he saw things in the future," Deuce said. "How did he do it? Did he have the *Justar Journal*, or was it Clastier's Papers? Or was it the same method that you use?"

"Clastier helped him the most, but he had many interesting friends who were into the mystical side of life." She smiled. "You don't need the *Justar Journal* to know what to do, Deuce. All you need is the quiet."

"We are in a war," he said, looking out to the horizon. The sun, low in the sky, had turned the ocean all shades of yellow and orange. "I don't know how to end it without joining it. I don't have the same kind of faith that you do."

She looked at him deeply, as a loving grandmother watches a young child write his first letters.

"I'm afraid if I don't fight back, I'll miss the chance to save us."

"Fear is a terrible place."

Deuce nodded. "I believe the world has to change, and *is* going to change. That you've shown the way to where we have to go. But the Chief is fighting for the old ways, and she's dictating the terms . . . it's all or nothing."

"Munna, I think I understand what Deuce is saying," Nelson interjected, "is that you know so much. I can see the wisdom in your eyes. And we just don't know what to do. Can't you give us a little help? Can't you tell us what we need to do?"

"We are not meant for war. We are not here to buy and accumulate things, not to fight or compete. Why is that so hard to see? Where has that ever gotten us? The truth is stronger than weapons, than things . . . than evil."

She looked at him. He saw sadness in her eyes.

"You've asked for my advice, here it is. This is the time, Deuce. You *have* to get it right."

"Get what right?"

She touched his hand. Her skin felt warm, although the evening was cool.

"We've lost before. It always seems to come back around, but it will be much harder to find another time. Getting it right may prove beyond *us*, if we let this chance slip away." She stared far beyond him as if studying the movements of the sea. "You are afraid of your own fear. That fear will pull you down, and it'll take the rest of us with you." She paused for a moment and looked back at him. "Your fear is based on something that doesn't really exist. You are locked in the Aylantik reality . . . Maybe you need to consider that reality isn't the rigid thing you believe it to be . . . Reality can bend."

CHAPTER FIFTY-TWO

Alone again in his private cabin, Deuce switched two AirViews to satellite mode. He brought the high-powered space cameras in close, so that the screen was filled with the fires. It seemed the flames covered most of the western portion of what used to be the United States. Smoke cut visibility, and flying had already become more difficult across the west. The massive cloud, like a dark storm, moved with the winds, and promised more blindness and mayhem as it spread east. But there were pockets, along the coast and south of the fires, where the skies remained clear, yet pierced with another kind of light.

The air battles had erupted over the Pacyfik and Aylantik regions.

PAWN fighters were unexpectedly superior to AOI planes, although that came as no surprise to Deuce, who had made sure it would be that way. For more than a decade, he'd held back technology and secretly controlled the companies that manufactured nearly every aspect of the electronic brains of the military planes. In addition, he had a monopoly on space navigation systems.

It wasn't as if the AOI was flying junk, but PAWN had better than a four percent advantage. Even that, however, might prove inadequate, because their planes were outnumbered by ninety-to-one.

It would have been worse, but for decades the AOI had not had a real enemy in the conventional sense of the word. With a single government ruling the entire planet, the AOI had not needed a massive air force. They'd had no trouble putting down any little flare-ups because compared to any small problem, the AOI always represented the overwhelming force. The AOI's miscalculation had been in assuming that PAWN, and their ragtag group of affiliated revolutionaries, didn't have any planes. The Chief had been trying to play catch-up, and in the three years since the Doneharvest had begun, they had almost doubled the size of the Aylantik Air Force.

PAWN had been adding planes as well, and because all military planes were autonomous drones, no pilots were needed. Base controllers were fairly simple to train. They'd been successful in recruiting a handful of civilian pilots. Passenger aircraft were capable of flying unmanned, but the law still required a pilot be onboard to oversee flight operations in case of a malfunction. Similarly, Flo-wings could be flown from ground control, but the crafts' flexible flying patterns made it complicated, so they were almost always piloted.

PAWN had focused on the air, especially under Chelle's leadership. Drast had told her years earlier that it would be the AOI's great weakness, especially if Deuce could be pulled into the war.

The sky battles exploded as stealth PAWN fighter jets ambushed entire AOI squadrons. AOI planes were also invisible to radar, but they could be seen by normal line of sight, and that proved a fatal flaw. In the first four hours, sixty-four planes had been shot down, and not a single one belonged to PAWN. The greatest victory came as Deuce was watching.

PAWN took out an AOI bomber that was about to drop a Sonic-bomb on Berkeley, a large city in the California Area. Since Sonic-bombs were detonated with sound waves following a lengthy sequence command, the ordnance would not explode on impact. Deuce cheered, but it was a muffled celebration, knowing the Chief would be going crazy, knowing her anger would lead to him. She wouldn't know where the attacks were coming from because the technology PAWN fighters were equipped with was so advanced. He used similar methods to keep the Moon Shadow untraceable.

It wouldn't take the Chief long to suspect one of Deuce's companies as the source of the elaborate cloaking defenses and sophisticated planes. She would be looking for blood, and would no longer give him the benefit of the doubt. In a matter of hours, he would be required to make the final decision.

If he entered the war on the side of PAWN, the world would never be the same again. Deuce Lipton had long since been suspected to be a rebel sympathizer, but actually putting the BLAXERs and all his wealth and power behind them, would prompt a total war. It would extend to every aspect of life, as the Chief would use every method she could to destroy him. The fragile threads of whatever fabric held this civilization together, would be lost forever.

Beyond that, no one could know what would happen. Even if Munna allowed full access to the prophecies, he wouldn't be able to find the answer in them because the *Justar Journal* would not write that chapter until he turned that "page," and by then it would be too late to go back.

"The point of no return," he whispered into the darkness, looking out to the dim light of the sea.

Deuce stood there a while, waiting for answers. Then, in what seemed the most natural thing to do, he asked his son, "Twain, what do you know? Can you help me? Can you hear me?" For reasons he didn't fully understand, he was surprised *not* to receive an answer from his son, even though a great distance separated them.

Other regions across what used to be Europe and Asia were

seeing air action as well. Mostly, PAWN was trying to intercept the bombers. The Chief had rallied late in the day, and was now sending Sonic-bombs down on seemingly random targets. PAWN, for the first time since the around-the-clock war had started days earlier, was finally able to fight back.

Even with their invisible technology, PAWN's planes weren't infallible. As soon as they fired a weapon, a heat signature would be traceable by any aircraft in the area. If they didn't get them all, there would be retaliation. The AOI had figured that out after taking poundings for hours.

Deuce watched as they took advantage of their superior numbers and increased the size of their squadrons to thirty-six planes. Anytime a PAWN drone took a shot, it would be quickly obliterated.

Deuce assumed PAWN Command would quickly change their tactics, and watched as they did just that. They went to an expensive alternative. Instead of using their best planes, they used older-generation fighters that were not equipped with any cloaking devices. Instead, an older plane would fly, concealed by several "invisible" planes, until the last second, when it shot out into an offensive dive and destroyed a bomber. The AOI retaliation caught only the "dispensable" aircraft. PAWN couldn't afford too many of these attacks, and reserved them only for bombers. A plane was worth the tens of thousands of lives it would save.

Deuce had to decide. Munna might talk in riddles, but one thing she said was clear. "The time is now." As he watched the war continue to explode across the world, he knew that by dawn he'd have to commit his BLAZERs fully or there might not be a later time to jump in.

It weighed heavily, however, as he knew Munna didn't want him to fight. He wished UC were still alive. He'd know what to do, but Deuce knew what he'd say. "Violence and hatred will never defeat violence and hatred." His grandfather had sent him a letter fifty years earlier that Cope gave Deuce before he died. Even then old Booker Lipton had warned against going to war.

But there is no other way, Deuce thought as he watched the world burning. *I'm already in it. We're only talking about degrees. Even with the wisest people I know advising against it, I can think of no other way to stop this nightmare. Munna's right, I am afraid. A couple more days of this and it will be beyond hope. I can't imagine how she thinks this will end otherwise.*

Runit woke amidst the rubble knowing he was somehow still alive because his head hurt too much to be dead. After checking for injuries, of which there were very few—a little blood, some bruises—he crawled from beneath the heavy beam which had most certainty saved him. The air pocket it created, as it wedged between a door jam and a slab of concrete, was still below almost three meters of debris. After the tedious process of moving enough to dig himself out, he surveyed the ruined landscape around him.

"Escaped the clutches of death again, old librarian," he said to himself in a raspy voice that didn't sound like his own. Then he thought of the famed pre-Banoff author George R. R. Martin who wrote in his book, *A Dance With Dragons,* "A reader lives a thousand lives before he dies . . . The man who never reads lives only one." *Perhaps I have died a thousand deaths,* he thought.

Then it occurred to him that the missiles had been aimed at an AOI facility. "What if PAWN is winning?" That idea buoyed him, as he tried to figure out how he could survive on the cold barren island for the next three months, maybe longer. For the rest of the day he scrounged for food, thirty-seven days of food remained intact. It had taken hours to round up the precious provisions, that he now considered incredibly delicious. He found a few extra articles of clothing and his old thin mattress. After deliberating if anywhere was safe, Runit dragged everything to the old gun emplacement on the cliff. It was a small fortress really. Grateful that the dock had not been bombed either, he would keep a daily vigil for PAWN rescue boats, or anything that could get him off the rock, as he now called it.

After a couple of days, he decided something else, something he'd always needed to do, something that he *had* to do before he died.

The Imps were also working, and although it was still light in the Arizona Area, the skies of Aylantik Region and all of old Europe were in darkness, except for the flying laser battles. They would work all night on patches to get around Blaze's backdoor. It was proving to be more difficult than they initially expected, partially because their greatest asset was the problem.

Without their super intelligence, in addition to the pain the Imps were experiencing, everything was a greater challenge. Still, they were making progress, and expected to be back online some-time the following day.

"When we get back to normal," Sidis said, "we are going to accelerate this damn war."

"That could be dangerous," Charlemagne cautioned.

"I certainly hope so," Sidis said, finally free from the explosive headaches. "But the longer it takes, the more likely Blaze or someone else will find another way to take us down."

Prior to the backdoor attack, Sidis and all the Imps had felt superior, invincible, but now they understood their great weak-ness. Imps, CHRUDEs, cyborgs, and androids could be brought down en masse. The machines were susceptible to viruses just like the humans.

"We must win before they can hurt us again."

CHAPTER FIFTY-THREE

Twenty minutes before their scheduled rendezvous with Zaverly, Grandyn heard the unmistakable sound of high-powered laser fire, a kind of *"ffttt, ffttt"* noise that he imagined a dagger would make stabbing in and out of his gut. He wrenched around as two of their escorts plummeted to the ground while their AirSliders crashed into the trees.

"Grunges!" he yelled to the others, pulling up on his own AirSlider.

Two of the surviving PAWN soldiers were already shooting back, but none of them could see the AOI anywhere.

Grandyn flew up next to Fye. "Stay close!" he yelled. "Let's get down that ridge!"

More lasers erupted out of the canopy. In the confusion, Fye had gone too high, and her AirSlider stalled. It dropped twenty meters before she managed to restart it. By then, Grandyn had dived in a dangerous maneuver, which could easily have ended in a crash. As it was, the two of them suddenly found themselves down in a large stand of fir trees, brushing by the needles.

"Let's land," Fye shouted.

Grandyn found a spot surrounded by bigger trees, on the edge of a steep drop-off. He came down harder than expected and his knee grazed the thick trunk of a ponderosa pine. There was a gash, but nothing that would slow him. He helped Fye off her AirSlider and they quickly found a hiding place in some underbrush, near the edge where there was still a good view. She looked awful.

"How are you?"

"Better than I look judging by your face," she replied.

"Good," he said. Then they heard a crash nearby, another PAWN casualty judging by the sound. "Wait here."

"Where are you going?"

He pulled out his lasershod. "Whoever that was may need help."

Fye looked at him. Her eyes said, *Don't go,* but she stayed quiet.

"Keep your weapon ready." And then he was gone. He'd left his AirSlider behind, preferring to move on foot. It always amazed her how silent he could be in the woods. TreeRunners had a reputation for sneaking noiselessly through the forests, but Grandyn's ability was more like magic.

Before Grandyn reached the fallen PAWN soldier, he spotted four grunges moving toward the injured man. He got as close as he dared and then sprang into a tree. After a few moments of observation, he leaped to another tree and fired two shots. Two grunges dropped. The two survivors returned fire, but by that time Grandyn was in the next tree, and seconds later he was beyond that. Grandyn came down behind them and shot as they turned. One of them fired as he fell to the ground, but the laser went wide, and took off a nearby tree limb.

With all four dead, he stripped them of their INUs and weapons. Three of them had shockers, hand-held laser-powered pulse bombs about the size of a hand grenade. Then he reached the PAWN soldier; he, too, was dead. Grandyn grabbed his INU, and also noted his name. He checked the area and found nothing else. He was about to head back to Fye when high-powered lasers shot at him from trees about one hundred meters away.

He scrambled over and discovered the location from where the attacks had originated. A group of six grunges were manning the powerful laser guns. Grandyn waited a minute to make sure there were no others and then, in quick succession, he tossed the shockers one after the other. There were no survivors.

When Grandyn reached Fye, she was asleep. He decided to let her rest a little longer and quietly grabbed his AirSlider, carrying it far enough away to be sure the takeoff wouldn't wake her. Soaring up in the trees, he tried to find Fuller and the other two PAWN soldiers, but no trace of them remained. After another wide circle, he headed back to Fye.

"We need to go," Grandyn said, waking her gently.

She smiled at seeing him. "Did you find anyone?"

"A bunch of grunges, and one of the PAWN guys. No one's left."

"Fuller?"

"We have to hope they made it, but it's time to get out of here."

He took the four INUs pulled from the dead grunges and tossed them over the cliff. He knew all AOI issued INUs had tracers. Someone would be looking soon, that is, unless the fires came first. They could see smoke rising in the distance. The setting sun was already draped over the trees in brown and orange haze that gave everything a surreal feel, like the strange lighting in an old futuristic science fiction movie.

They climbed on their AirSliders and went over the edge. The sloping cliff gave them good cover, and had just enough surface to allow them to skim along at full speed. Ten minutes later, they were back in the trees, cautiously winding their way up the Siskiyou Pass.

Grandyn looked longingly over at Mount Ashland. Years earlier, when the world still made sense, he'd come down from Portland with his clan of TreeRunners and they'd spent three weeks in the wilderness. Before the Banoff, it had been a ski area, but the mandated forest program and warmer winters had changed its status.

The Ashland TreeRunner clan had been an active one. He'd made good friends, but imagined that by now, most were dead. The AOI Chief's TreeRunner extermination program had been quite effective in the early days of the Doneharvest. Back then, no one knew how ruthless the Aylantik government could really be, and the Chief hadn't yet revealed her particular brand of evil.

He wondered if his parents had known what the world was going to become, and if they would have still brought him into it if they had. Grandyn didn't really understand his importance to the revolution. Aside from his rage against the AOI and his skills in the woods, he couldn't comprehend why he'd become so significant.

"Is there something about me?" he asked Fye as they hummed along, their AirSliders almost touching one another.

"What do you mean?"

"The List Keepers, you say they know everything. Do they know something about me? Aside from the fact that my mother discovered the truth about the Banoff and my father was the last librarian, and he saved the books."

"They know what I know," she said, wanting to hold him. "That you found the *Justar Journal* and figured out the code so we could read it. That you infiltrated the AOI for years and found Drast, and that you have frustrated and occupied the Chief while PAWN geared up for war and the List Keepers tried to avoid it. You're a hero, Grandyn. You've been saving the world, just like I said you would on the day we met."

"Did they know that? Before I did it?" he asked tentatively.

"I told you, they know everything." She smiled weakly. He worried she wouldn't be able to go on much farther, and the fires were growing ahead of them. Soon they'd meet Zaverly and be able to get war and fire updates, and most important, maybe Fye could rest a few hours. They were quiet for a while.

Fifteen minutes later, as they were heading down the pass, they saw a group of rebels. Grandyn sighed, relieved.

"Thank goodness," Fye said. "We've finally reached Zaverly."

CHAPTER FIFTY-FOUR

Chelle reviewed every report. She had dozens of open AirViews floating around the room, but there was still no sign of Osc and Drast. It would be days before they could get someone to the safe house, but she knew that if they had been there, they'd be long gone by now. Drast would never sit still, not when there was a world to conquer. They were a distraction, but she didn't allow it to divert too much of her attention. The best thing she could do for Osc, and any future he might hope to have, would be to defeat the AOI and bring down the Chief along with her Aylantik façade. Drast wouldn't want her to waste a minute on him. He'd happily trade himself for victory over the tyrants. He had said it many times.

Chelle got through to Deuce. His first question was about her son.

"Nothing," she said. "Thank you for asking."

"I've got a team on it. We're looking."

"I really appreciate it Deuce," she said, genuinely touched. "There is another son I'm worried about."

Deuce thought of Twain.

"Runit's son," she said. "Grandyn is trying to get to the List

Keepers. Obviously, I don't know exactly where that is, but I know the direction he is heading, and according to our sources, the AOI is about to firebomb the whole area."

Deuce closed his eyes. The decision was being made for him. "What do you want me to do?"

"Stop those planes."

"Can't PAWN?"

"We've got nothing close enough that can handle it," she said. "We're all over the populated targets."

Deuce had been watching, and knew PAWN's capabilities maybe better than she did. "What about rain?" he asked, knowing that only one person could move that much weather.

"Miner is my next zoom."

"Give me the coordinates and let me know what Miner says."

After the zoom, Deuce thought about trying to have another conversation with Munna, but he didn't want to confuse his mind even further with more of her philosophically circular words. Instead, he put on Billie Holiday. As he heard the first notes of the song, he smiled. *"Crazy, He Calls Me"* sounded better on vinyl, but most of his LPs had been left on Ryder Island.

Billie Holiday sang, *"I say I'll move the mountains. And I'll move the mountains."* Deuce thought about what he was about to do, wondered what it would mean. It felt as if he were moving mountains, even moving the entire Earth.

Lady Day's haunting voice broke through his thoughts again. *"I say I'll go through fire. And I'll go through fire. As he wants it, so it shall be. Crazy, he calls me."*

He thought about Grandyn. What would he find? Who were the List Keepers? Were they capable of saving what was left? Were they even real? He wasn't sure they were much more than a handful of old metaphysical devotees who, like his uncle Cope, sought to explore the deep powers of the mind and the quantum world. Munna and Fye were the only two people he'd ever met who admitted to being List Keepers. Even UC never made that claim, although Deuce now assumed he'd been one.

He'd heard bits and pieces about the List Keepers through the years, but nothing concrete. Munna's appearance was the first thing that substantiated any of the rumors. The group never seemed to matter, but the rumors were always intriguing; a secret organization that could control events, that monitored everything, even the AOI. How did they avoid detection? What was their objective?

Something about it nagged at him. He doubted they were any big deal, but at the same time, he believed they might be the thing that could make the difference, especially if his own actions screwed it all up.

He looked at reports on the search for Osc and Drast. No news. He checked the advancing plague. More dead, rapidly spreading. The fires, also spreading. The bombing, resumed. The INU-based simulations and predictions, extinction event likely.

He turned to the screen showing the *Justar Journal* monitors, still blank, except for Munna, Twain, and the war. He gazed at the live image of his son. "You're the future," he whispered.

There was another open link which verified that his wife and daughter were secure. Next he scanned the AirViews, checked the satellites, and took a deep breath.

Deuce rearranged the AirViews floating in his cabin, allowed his retina to be scanned, and began the sequence that would forever alter his life, the war, the world, and the outcome of everything.

CHAPTER FIFTY-FIVE

Runit realized his best chance of leaving the island before his rations ran out, was the crazy hope that whatever automated system that resupplied the facility would still show up. Yet, he knew this was nearly impossible. "Whatever knocked out the androids and the security systems, probably took out the AOI facilities management systems as well," he said to the ocean on the day that he got down to less than forty-five days of food left, and that after having only one meal a day since the missiles. "And if the regular system was still in place, why would it come to a bombed out prison?" He tried not dwell on it, but his practical mind thought he was a fool to have such hopes. "Maybe PAWN will win, maybe someone friendly will come."

He was hungry, and almost always cold. Runit might have gone insane if not for his "project." The librarian worked during every waking hour on what he considered the third most important thing he had done in his life—after being a good father, and saving the books—unsure if he would live long enough to complete it, and if somehow he did, would anyone ever know about it. And, all the while he watched the water, searching for anything. But even the skies were empty.

There must have been close to sixty rebels. Fye was relieved to see them, knowing a force that size would almost certainly be able to defeat any trouble standing between them and the City.

In the past few days, the TreeRunners had completely merged with PAWN, as had all other rebel factions. PAWN Command dictated every rebel response – defensive and offensive. As soon as Grandyn and Fye dismounted from their AirSliders and identified themselves, Zaverly came forward.

"We spotted you a few minutes ago," she said to Grandyn, ignoring Fye. "I've been waiting a long time to meet you." They shook hands.

He was about to introduce Fye, but another woman ran up at that very moment, shouting his name. He turned, letting go of Zaverly just in time to be nearly knocked over by a bear hug.

"It's so good to see you," the woman said. "I heard you were dead so many times!"

"Nester, I would never die without seeing you first," he said, hugging his childhood friend. "Fye, this is Nester. We grew up in the same clan."

Fye waved a hello.

"Hi," Nester said.

"Oh, and Zaverly, sorry. This is Fye, my fiancée."

Zaverly nodded and smiled at Fye. She could tell the woman was sick and needed medical attention, but she was more than delighted to have her along for the fun.

"Wyle said you were assigned to Zaverly," Grandyn said to Nester. "I hoped we'd see you."

"Damn, you look like your dad," she said, backing up and taking him in. "So sorry to hear about that. I loved him, you know?"

"I know," Grandyn said. "He always said you were the daughter he never had."

She hugged him again and then pulled back. "Sorry," she said to Zaverly. "We're very, very old friends."

"Apparently," Zaverly said, forcing a smile.

After a few more minutes of chatting and catching up, Grandyn asked if there was a place where Fye could sleep for a couple of hours before they moved on. There was a quick, makeshift, nano-camo made available.

"Okay," Fye agreed. "I'll rest for an hour, but no more."

She wanted to get to the City. Not just because of the implications for the war, but because they could take care of her, make her well again. She couldn't let Grandyn know how awful she felt, or he'd never agree to more travel. Even if she didn't make it, he had to, but she didn't know how to explain the location.

I'll think while I sleep, she thought, drifting off.

Grandyn let her sleep for two hours, but by then it was dark and the fires looked frightening. The window was closing. They had to leave.

While Fye had been out, Grandyn caught up with Nester and talked to other TreeRunners with whom he had friends in common. It was then that he learned that the bulk of the rebels would be heading back to Ashland.

"My dad might not be dead," Grandyn confided.

"What do you mean?"

"Last time I saw him he was breathing."

"Really?"

"Yeah, I mean he was really bad off, but--"

"Then where's he been?" she asked. "The Runit Happerman I knew would never stay away from his son if he could help it, if he had breath left in him."

"I know, they must have him in prison."

"Oh, Grandyn. I heard the Chief ordered all the prisoners killed and the prisons destroyed."

Grandyn looked down. "I know he's out there somewhere."

"I hope so," she said, but he could tell she didn't believe it.

"Anyway, I have to keep going, but one day, when this is all done, I will look for him . . . find him . . . or, at least, find out what happened."

Nester nodded, but changed the subject. "The fires are too close to risk us all going in. There won't be many grunges."

"So what is PAWN Command doing with us?" Grandyn asked.

"You know, we're spread mighty thin. They need us up north. Something about an AOI weapons depot near Medford," Nester said.

"We have to go south."

"I know. But don't worry, Zaverly says she had solid intel on the AOI locations for the next five hundred kilometers. And with the fires, the grunges aren't keeping too much of a presence in the woods except to burn them. They're using missiles now. The AOI is going to burn every tree on the planet. I can't believe they don't care about what that will do."

"It's not the AOI," Grandyn said. "It's the Chief, and she's made it quite clear she doesn't care about anything other than winning. Even if the world is in rubble, her damn peace will prevail always!"

"It's not over yet Grandyn. We're just starting to fight back. And you should have smooth sailing if you can sneak through the fires. Most of the grunges have pulled out and are keeping to the perimeters, waiting."

"Waiting?" Grandyn asked, afraid of an ambush.

"The Chief assumed all the TreeRunners and PAWN rebels who have been hiding will come streaming out of the woods like scared rabbits. She obviously doesn't know how many POPs there are, and if she does, she doesn't know they are built to withstand surface fires."

"Coming out of a POP into a burnt wasteland isn't exactly good cover," Grandyn said.

"Tomorrow's a new day. It might rain," Nester mused.

"I hope you're right. I guess we'll head out alone."

"No way," Nester said. "You're important enough to get a serious escort. Zaverly herself, and four of her most decorated soldiers are going with you. Don't worry, they won't let anything happen to you."

CHAPTER FIFTY-SIX

Miner looked at Sarlo when he saw who the zoom was from. She raised her eyebrows. Maybe Chelle had succeeded and the Chief was dead.

"Do you have good news for me?" Miner asked, as he opened the connection.

"Perhaps tomorrow," Chelle said, knowing exactly what he meant. "The Chief is very secure, very protected, and very paranoid; not an easy target."

"Yes," Miner said, disappointed. "That is why I gave the assignment to someone so capable." He was actually thinking of Blaze when he said that, but knew Chelle would assume he meant her.

He looked at the Toronto skyline reflecting on Lake Ontario, knowing it was one of the safe cities designated by AOI analysis that showed near zero rebel or dissenter presence. The CN Tower, once a dominant feature, was now one of many uniquely beautiful structures. A ring of needle-like buildings, spinning towers, round discs, and massive arches. Breathtaking.

"As you know, I'm more interested in succeeding with that task than you are, but I need a small favor," Chelle said, from underground in a heavily fortified PAWN facility.

"Then check back with me once you have a body to give me."

"It all goes toward the same goal," Chelle said. "It is very complicated to line everything up so that she can be eliminated. It will have a better chance of success if you can provide some very behind-the-scene assistance."

"If I wanted to do this myself, I would have," Miner replied.

At the same time, Sarlo got his attention and mouthed the words, *"Listen to her."*

"But tell me what you need," Miner said, before Chelle could respond to his last comment.

"I need rain."

"Again?" Miner was surprised. It wasn't an easy thing to do with the skies so restricted and dangerous, but it wouldn't be impossible, depending on where she needed it.

He looked at the AirView that showed the fire maps. Most of them were in the Pacyfik region in what used to be the western United States. Tough area.

"Between Mount Shasta, Lassen, and Yosemite in the California Area." Chelle didn't know exactly where Grandyn was.

"That's a stretch of almost five hundred kilometers," he said, checking the map. "That's a hell of a big storm."

"And I need it now."

"Impossible!" Miner scoffed.

"We could use the smoke," Sarlo whispered, but Chelle still heard her.

"The northern part of that range is the most important," Chelle said. "Whatever you can do."

"And what if you don't deliver your end? I've done this for nothing."

"If I don't succeed, you still will have saved some of our most pristine forests from destruction and infuriated the Chief. Not a bad night's work."

Sarlo nodded to Miner. He shook his head back. *"Do it,"* she mouthed.

"We might have a way," he said. "I'll see what I can do. But you better make me happy tomorrow."

"Tomorrow seems so far away, doesn't it?" Chelle said, watching the world fall apart on her AirViews.

Tomorrow, she thought. *What will be left by then?*

Blaze listened to a report from the husband and wife team working on the assassination. They might have been the only people in the world happy the Sonic-bombing had resumed.

"Our odds of success have increased to fifty-eight percent," the husband said. "There are predawn flights planned for targets in the Tennessee and Pennsylvania Areas, which would be within range of the Chief's bunker in Washington, DC."

"What about the launch protocols?" Blaze asked.

"We have them."

"Impressive," Blaze commended. "And altering the flight plan?"

"Working on it," the wife said.

"How are you going to avoid Washington's substantial air defenses?"

"We're trying to get something lined up, an authorization, it's still our biggest problem," the husband explained. "But we're confident."

"Air defenses are a big one," Blaze said. "Maybe we could give them something else to shoot at."

"Such as?" the husband asked.

"Steal a bunch of passenger planes. Someone did it a hundred years ago."

"Nine-eleven?"

"Exactly. The planes are all grounded. If you can get ten or so in the air above DC, you might give cover to your bomber."

The woman brought up AirViews showing the closest airports with grounded passenger fleets. They had plenty to choose from.

"I'm on it," the husband said.

"And do we know any more about the bunker?" Blaze asked.

"We need a direct hit if we have any chance of penetrating it," she said. "But even if the Chief survives, it will slow her, and the AOI Command and Control will be down for at least a week."

"Even if we fail, it might give us the break we need," Blaze said. "Draw up a plan to drop troops into DC after the bombing."

"Whose troops?" the wife asked.

"BLAXERs, PAWN, Enforcers," Blaze answered, "do them all. I'll convince someone to go in and mop up that mess."

Then Blaze dismissed them and jumped to his Grandyn-tracking efforts. He had it narrowed down to an area south of Mount Shasta in the California Area. His head throbbed when he saw that the AOI had spread fire across that entire sector.

Grandyn could be toast, he thought. *And worse, the Chief may have unknowingly destroyed her greatest threat.* "List Keepers . . . come out, come out, wherever you are," he sang at the AirViews of the fires.

Another assistant interrupted his musings and informed Blaze that the Imps were coming back to life. Blaze had been working all day to locate them through their processor chips, but there were so many, and they were spread out so much that it was proving to be a futile effort. He looked at the AirViews.

"They won't be anywhere near the fires. And Imps are not immune to plague, so they will be avoiding those areas like, well . . . the plague," he said with the slightest smile.

"Hmm." His assistant did not appreciate the humor. "That narrows it down to half the globe."

"Yes, I'm happy to help," Blaze said, annoyed. "I'm guessing Arizona, Oklahoma, or Venezuela. They've got the highest concentration of chips. We need to find them fast. Once they get fully back online, they'll figure out a way to erase the signal, and we may not find them again until they are ordering us to dig our own mass graves!"

The Imps were, in fact, working on the signal already. They knew Blaze had shut them down through the DesTIn system, and that he could reach each of them. Getting back online was secondary to making sure Blaze was blocked from all further contact.

Sidis said, "Monitoring and tracking, disabling and erasing all are within Blaze's capabilities."

"If he were as smart as he claims," Galahad said, "he would have installed a kill-switch and none of us would be here now to pick up the pieces."

"We're not back yet," Charlemagne said. "For all we know, he's infected our systems, and the CHRUDEs, with a slow-moving virus. We could be dead in hours."

No," Sidis said. "Blaze would not have risked that. He simply screwed up. He never thought the Imps would unite and move to take control."

Another Imp announced, "We're still at least six to eight hours away from one hundred percent."

"That's a lifetime," Sidis said. "Blaze could find us in that time, but if he doesn't, he's lost. They will all have lost. Now it's just a race. Our technology against theirs . . . Who do you think is going to win?"

Munna sat on the deck of the Moon Shadow, far enough out in the ocean that they were no longer at full speed. They were actually drifting slowly, and the stars were kissing a calm sea. It was as if she were floating among them.

She knew what Deuce had done. He'd made the wrong choice, but she wasn't surprised. Still, it might be okay. But *might* was an awfully weak word when one was talking about the end of all human life. It would decisively come down to what happened the next day, Friday.

She smiled and thought, *At least that. The day named for Venus, the goddess of love. We could use a little of that right now.*

Munna watched Grandyn in her mind. He concerned her even more than Deuce's mistake, more than the Imps, and more than the Chief.

"Grandyn must make it to the City," she whispered to the stars and to Venus.

Some two thousand kilometers to the north, Drast and Osc were sound asleep on a boat. Their plan was to slip into Seattle before first light, but Deuce didn't know anything about that. No one did. That's what Drast was counting on.

CHAPTER FIFTY-SEVEN

Grandyn, Fye, Zaverly, and the four PAWN soldiers moved at medium speed through the forest. Their AirSliders were equipped with night-vision shields, which telescoped out of the handle shaft. It allowed them to move without headlights, but it also meant they couldn't go at full speed. However, at medium, the AirSliders were extremely quiet, meaning they'd practically have to run over a grunge to get caught.

After about three hours, Zaverly signaled for everyone to stop. Grandyn was relieved because he was exhausted and needed a break, but Fye's condition really worried him. Even with her earlier nap, he knew she needed strict bed rest.

They found a small clearing and dismounted. Zaverly checked for a signal. Sometimes they were possible in clearings along high terrain, but she got nothing.

"Spread out, guard the perimeters," she said. The four soldiers walked slowly into the darkness.

Grandyn went to Fye. "How are you?" he asked.

"A little shaky, but I can keep going."

"We should be there in a few more hours," Grandyn said.

She nodded, downing big gulps of water.

"Grandyn Happerman, the real Grandyn Happerman, you are hereby charged with the murder of eight fellow TreeRunners," Zaverly said icily.

"What?" Grandyn said, swinging around just in time to meet the blow of one of her soldiers.

As he went down, he yelled, "Run, Fye! Run!"

She took off.

Grandyn tried to get up, but the soldier put a knee into his back. Grandyn struggled as the larger man pushed his face into the dirt. Two more punches convinced Grandyn to give up for the moment.

The soldier searched him for weapons, found Grandyn's laser-shod and a hunting knife, then kicked Grandyn hard in the ribs and stood up. A few seconds later, one of the other soldiers brought Fye back. Grandyn rolled over, but the razor-hot light of the laser trained on his face stopped him. He couldn't help Fye if he were dead.

"Sit," the man barked at Fye.

Fye sat down and looked over at Grandyn, his outline barely visible in the laser's glow.

"Grandyn Happerman, you've heard the charge. How do you plead?" Zaverly asked.

"What are you talking about?" Grandyn asked, panting, his voice strained, trying to move his head from the glare of the light. "How about lowering that thing to my chest so I can at least see my accuser."

She moved the beam down, centering it on his heart. "You've killed so many, I'll bet it's hard to remember them all."

"What? Are you with the AOI?" Grandyn groaned.

What can I do? He thought frantically. *What can I do? Even if I think of something, I can't leave Fye. I can't even see her.* Then he remembered his life's training. *Breathe, focus.*

"I'm a TreeRunner. A *true* TreeRunner," Zaverly said.

He didn't know what she meant. *What does this Zaverly freak think I did? How can I take out these three? Where is Fye? At least Fye is smarter than me, she's thinking too. Focus.*

"Tell me who you think I killed, Zaverly."

"Restrain her," Zaverly commanded. The man who brought Fye back quickly bound her legs and feet with zip-ties. "Now go. I don't want the perimeter compromised. He's got friends back there, and a stray band of grunges could be anywhere."

Grandyn heard the man run off. *So Zaverly doesn't know where all the grunges are,* he thought. *And she's worried about Nester. Would Nester be suspicious? Could she have followed us?* He had hope. *Focus. Think.*

"Yes, I'll tell you who you killed, because you, you torgon coward, you wouldn't know who, and how many lives you've ruined."

"Zaverly, you are a TreeRunner. You know the oath."

"How dare you speak of loyalty!" she snapped, her tone suddenly out of control. "I hadn't planned to kill your girl, but it might be a good idea . . . what do you think? Maybe then you'll understand."

"No," Grandyn said calmly. "Whatever this is, it's between you and me."

"I'm not so sure."

Grandyn wanted to ask her how anything could be more important than the war, than the plague, than the fires, than the end of the world, but he knew she was not a rational person. He wondered what Fye was thinking. He could hear the breathing of the man who had knocked him down. He was probably only a meter away, maybe less, but Grandyn couldn't see. The lasershod she'd pointed at him had a sight-light, which was bright enough to mess with his eyes.

"You've got the weapon, Zaverly," Grandyn said, trying to bring her back to him. "It sounds like you've been waiting for this for a long time. And since you haven't killed me yet, I'm guessing you want to make sure I know exactly what you think I did . . . so why don't you tell me?"

"I more than *think* you did it. I was there. I saw what you did," she said bitterly.

They didn't hear the jet. It was too far away. But because they were coming from behind Zaverly, Grandyn saw the missiles first. It gave him just enough time to brace for impact. He only hoped that Fye had also seen them. Less than half a second would decide if they lived or died.

The first missile hit less than fifty meters from where Grandyn sat. It exploded in a torrent of flames. Like a giant Molotov cocktail, the missile had been filled with a flammable liquid meant to spread fire fast. More missiles rained in, landing farther out in a grid designed to maximize the burn rate. But the impact of the first one gave Grandyn the chance he needed.

Because he'd been expecting it, he reacted faster than his adversaries. As the initial flash illuminated Fye's location, he dove toward her. He reached Fye before Zaverly had even jumped for cover. Grandyn grabbed Fye and rolled. The terrain worked in their favor as they went down a slight slope. Chaos ensued, with missiles bursting all around and flames ripping through the dry forest as if a lit match had been dropped in a haystack.

Grandyn lifted Fye's still bound body over his shoulder and ran into the smoky night. In less than ten meters, the tinder-scented fog enveloped them. There was enough light from the flames that he could easily find his way, but the smoke from the existing fires reduced visibility to about two or three meters. Both the smoke and the flames would make their getaway easier, unless it killed them first.

He laid her down gently and scavenged around for a rock. He could carry her for kilometers, if necessary, but if she could run, they would move much faster. Finally he found one small and jagged enough to break through the band on her legs.

"Who the hell is she?" Fye whispered.

"I have no idea why she's doing this."

"How long will it take her to find us?"

"She's not going to find us," Grandyn said, not really believing it. She was a TreeRunner, and one with a mission: to destroy him. He knew Zaverly was already looking for them.

"Can you run?" he asked while trying to cut the band binding her hands.

"I can try."

"Listen to me Fye. You're a List Keeper. I know you can heal yourself."

Fye started to cry.

"What?"

"I couldn't save the baby."

"Damn it, Fye. Don't punish yourself. It wasn't your fault."

"I tried . . . I should have been able."

Grandyn knew Zaverly might appear out of the fog at any moment. "Fye, you tried. That's enough. You're alive. I'm alive. We'll try again. We'll have as many kids as you want, but right now we have to move." He made it through the band and rubbed her freed wrists. "You need to heal yourself, or we won't make it. Can you do that for me?" He put his forehead against hers and cupped her cheeks in his hands. "We have to get to the City."

"Okay," she said, sniffling in an involuntary breath. "I'll try."

Then they heard the scream.

CHAPTER FIFTY-EIGHT

Friday, July 15

In the morning, the rain finally began. Miner had his people working all night. Although he hadn't pressed Chelle for details, he assumed the fires were threatening PAWN bases hidden in the north-central forests of the California Area. Either way, she would not have asked if it hadn't been an urgent need. But in the end, he didn't do it for her, he did it for Sarlo. Increasingly, he saw her as the calm he strived for but couldn't seem to reach. She made her decisions without the emotion that typically warped his deliberations.

The prior night, his disturbing dreams had returned. This time he was swallowed up by an unseen darkness and left out to die on a barren wasted plateau, high above a burnt forest. He woke with a painful whispered chant on his lips; "No flame burns forever."

Enforcers were making preparations for a ground war. For years the AOI had always assumed that Deuce and Miner were building up their private armies to fight each other in some strange and primitive contest, an act of corporate machismo, egos with nothing left to waste their billions on. The AOI had largely ignored them because both were prominent supporters of the

Aylantik, Miner on the A-Council, and Deuce well-vested in the Aylantik system as the world's wealthiest man. But the Chief and her predecessors had also believed that those corporate troops were essentially meaningless. There would never be a ground war involving humans. In the unlikely event that war ever broke out, the AOI knew the Aylantik's superior and automated weapons, coupled with their dominance in both control and surveillance, assured a quick victory.

But the AOI had been wrong. Deuce and Miner both knew something the AOI did not. Miner was preparing for what he called "Operation Retrograde." Deuce might have another name for it, and he was already prepared, because he was the one who brought Operation Retrograde into being.

"Do you really think he pushed the retrograde button?" Sarlo asked. She wanted to make sure they had the timing right.

"If he hasn't already done so, it will have to happen today," Miner said.

"Retrograde" was a scenario when the only four armies of the world, AOI, BLAXERs, Enforcers, and PAWN, would fight in old-style urban battles. They would seek and hold strategic cities and towns.

"I still don't know how he can do it," Sarlo said. "Surely the AOI planners would have detected the potential and corrected it?"

"Retrograde, as you know, is when Deuce cuts off all satellite transmissions. He thereby renders useless all the planes, including fighters and bombers, troop transports, and missile guidance systems. The result, a retrograde world in which we fight it out the old-fashioned way."

"I know, but how can he do it?" Sarlo asked. "How can the AOI not stop him?"

"For one thing, they don't know. I never told them. But even if I had, they couldn't stop it because it isn't just his company, Star-Fly, which makes most of the satellites. There are, of course, many that he doesn't manufacture, but most of those are operated by

Eysen INUs. So if we get down to the small number of super-sensitive satellites that he has no direct control over, we find his biggest advantage."

She nodded. "One of the things that has most scared you about him all these years."

"Right, the Searchers."

"But you've never proven they are more than telescopes."

"I have the report," Miner said gruffly as he pulled up an AirView. The report, as Sarlo knew well, predated both Lance and Deuce. It went back to the time of Doneharvest, not the recent AOI crackdown, but the original AOI Chief for whom the crackdown was named.

Doneharvest had never trusted Deuce's grandfather, Booker. He pried and pressed and bribed around every corner of the Lipton empire until he got lucky and found the right employee at the right time in a situation. The details were too old to recall, but Doneharvest had been able to extort the employee until he had enough to compile the report. Hours before Doneharvest was killed, by still unknown assassins who Lance believed worked for Booker, he gave the report to Lance's grandfather.

It showed that Booker's great space telescopes, which were capable of seeing ten times deeper into the universe than anything that had come before, including the Hubble or the Webb tele-scopes, were armed. Booker Lipton actually had the capability to take out any satellite in orbit. He could do it in seconds, and he could take them all down. Booker's telescopes could also be turned toward Earth, and they could see in amazing detail. The report was never made public, nor validated, but Doneharvest was dead practically before Miner's grandfather finished reading it.

"That report is ancient history," Sarlo said.

"Booker Lipton had Doneharvest killed, I have no doubt about that!" Miner rubbed his eyes. He hadn't slept much between getting the rain to the fires, readying Enforcers for a ground war, and surviving the damned nightmares. They had separate suites, extremely comfortable, on the same floor as the offices, both with fantastic views. But much of the night they worked, catching naps when they could.

"Decades have passed," Sarlo argued.

"Decades in which Deuce has single-mindedly obsessed over space. Most people would be happy with Eysen, Inc. and all the money in the world, but Deuce keeps pushing into space."

"So?"

"That's where his power is, his control . . . that's where the future is. By now Deuce can probably use those telescopes to read the date on my silver dollar while it's in my pocket and I'm inside a building!"

"The pictures of deep space he releases are incredible. It's impressive how he has kept increasing the range and clarity of the telescopes. But armed and spying on Earth? That seems hard to believe."

"You told me once never to underestimate Deuce, and yet here you are doing the same thing. You watch. Today we will lose the satellites."

"Is he ready for the AOI to turn on him?"

"Without satellites, they are just another army, one not well trained to fight his guerillas."

"Or ours."

"Right. But another point you and I disagree on is that the AOI isn't our biggest problem. It's the Trapciers."

CHAPTER FIFTY-NINE

After docking, Drast, Osc, and the four Allies easily navigated the streets of Seattle in their AOI uniforms. But their time was running out. The AOI bombing campaign had intensified, and the new plague was spreading. On the boat ride, Drast had shared some of the plan with Osc, and for the first time since the war began, he thought the good guys might have a chance.

"If we can just keep the wolves at bay," Drast had said.

The Allies had access to secret-screens within the AOI system, and Drast hungrily consumed the most useful data he'd seen since he'd been AOI head of the Pacyfik region. As they walked the short distance to their destination, they continued to peruse the updates. However, the news was not good. It showed a new threat, a group called the Trapciers, made up of Imps and incredibly advanced androids known as CHRUDEs.

"The Imps had been advising the Chief, but there are indications that they're now acting independently," one of the Allies told Drast. "And they aren't helping the rebels."

"There have just been three failed bombing missions," another said.

"Three?" Drast asked as they walked briskly. "Can the Imps interfere with those weapons systems?"

Nobody knew, but everyone agreed that three failures in three different regions was not a coincidence.

"On one hand," Drast began, "it exposes a potential vulnerability in the AOI. On the other, it demonstrates a dangerous power by someone. If it's Enforcers or the Trapciers, we're in for a much longer war than the world can endure."

They continued to debate the ramifications as reports of two more failures came in, closely followed by even stranger information. Twenty-eight AOI fighter drones had crashed in the past forty minutes.

"What the hell is going on?" Osc asked.

Drast stopped, looked up at the tall building in front of them, and said, "We're about to find out." The others followed him into the lobby of the Seattle headquarters of the AOI.

Inside the stark building, familiar clear walls with gold internal grids and visible Seeker cameras made this like every other AOI headquarter building. They all knew the protocol. FRIDG scans and surrendering weapons. Only two humans would be on duty, plus three androids. The walls were impenetrable, and lasers could kill any of them at any time.

Osc and Drast lingered by the door while the Allies stepped up to be scanned. After they were cleared through, one of them asked the guard if any other agents had arrived for the "Wolftrap" mission.

Unfortunately, the guard simply responded with an uninterested, "No." The thin hope that one of the security detail might have been an Ally, was gone. They'd have to wait to see if things went better upstairs.

The Ally told the guard that they were there to meet with a specific agent, whom he named. Then he went on to explain that Drast and Osc, although he used other names, were waiting for informants and would stay at the entrance.

This all seemed fine to the guard. Their story was probably helped by the fact that the agent they were there to meet was the number two man in Seattle. Drast and Osc waited nervously as the Allies disappeared behind the gold grid glass. They knew everything they said could be heard, so they kept the conversation to basic war news and occasionally looked out for the people for whom they were supposedly waiting.

All the while, Drast continued to ponder the failed bombings and crashed fighter drones. He'd narrowed it down to either very good news, or very bad.

The Trapciers might have hacked into the AOI system, Drast thought. *It's a tall order, but they have been working with the Chief. They could have found a crack. They have an almost infinite capacity for calculations and data manipulation. That would obviously be disastrous since the next natural step will be for them to use the AOI weapons for their own aims.*

He looked out to the street. The war had eliminated normal activity. Seattle's densely populated suburbs had been hit with two Sonic-bombs.

However, it's possible that Deuce Lipton has finally gotten off the fence. He may well have the technological means to wreak havoc with the AOI systems. Drast smiled. *If that's the case, and things go well upstairs, we might be able to win this thing fast.* After all the years and all the deaths, he hardly dared believe the end was in sight.

Twenty-five increasingly tense minutes passed before the Allies reappeared. With just one sentence, Drast knew they were good. "The sheep in wolves' clothing are torgon everywhere!"

Drast and Osc ran to the security gate and one of the Allies waved them through. The androids and human guards had been neutralized. Eighty-six "wolves," AOI agents loyal to the Chief, were being moved to the basement holding cells built to hold twenty-four. But they would jam them in and decide whether to kill them later. If PAWN and the Allies won, then one day they might put captured wolves on trial.

When they reached the upper floor, Osc was stunned to see

more than one hundred agents. "So you're saying the Allies outnumbered the wolves here?" Osc asked Drast.

"Not normally. There are close to five hundred out on assignments or patrols. Most of them are wolves. It was arranged that way."

"What happens when they come back in?"

"They'll be killed in the lobby, like the security risks they are."

Osc tried not to think about the lobby ambushes. It seemed so ruthless, but so did Drast's shooting those men in Vancouver who had surrendered with their arms in the air. But he respected Drast's will to win. The Aylantik had to go, and the AOI was the worst of it.

One of the Allies, who had come with them from Vancouver, told them that the takeover had been simple because Drast had planned it almost five years earlier. Osc was becoming more impressed with Drast by the minute.

"Five years ago?" he asked.

"I didn't know I'd be here," Drast said, "but I knew that whenever the revolution came, the only way we could win would be to take control of the AOI buildings, so I made sure it would be easy. All the AOI HQs have weapons checks. Meaning that even a few Allies could take over if they were armed. I made sure that all buildings in the Pacyfik region had a secret weapons locker on every floor, then worked it out so an Ally was in charge of each one. That's how we took the building so quickly."

Drast seemed pleased that it had gone smoothly. He'd waited so long to see his plans come to fruition, and there were many days, especially over the past two years, when he hadn't been sure they ever would.

"Seattle is a 'Key,' isn't it?" Osc asked. The AOI had headquarters in almost every major city in the world, but there were only a few hundred Key-headquarters. In the event of natural disasters or unrest, Keys were meant to provide agents with weapons, supplies, and intelligence for up to a thousand-kilometer radius.

"Damn right," Drast said, a bit of his old arrogance resurfacing as he assumed command of the facility. He'd single-handedly achieved the first major victory of the war. The rebels had secured a foremost tactical asset directly from the AOI.

A Key AOI building had months' worth of food and water and thousands of advanced weapons. The offices' INUs were also part of the emergency Scram network, a secret communications system that operated apart from the Field. Years earlier, Drast had done his best to make sure all the Key buildings in his region were staffed with as many Allies as he could get into them.

"The only weakness of Key buildings," Drast said to Osc, "is that they are still susceptible to Sonic-bombs, but those don't seem to be working so well right now." He smiled.

"How long until the Chief finds out we're here?" Osc asked.

"Hopefully, she won't find out until I tell her."

CHAPTER SIXTY

After narrowly escaping from Zaverly, Grandyn and Fye had heard one of her henchmen screaming, and listened while he burned to death. His shrieks of agony echoed in the haunted forest. They could almost see his flesh melting. The horror was made worse by the knowledge that they'd missed the same fate only by a breath, and it could still await them. Then, in the silent aftermath, they'd heard something even more terrifying - Zaverly's footsteps, coming fast.

Grandyn and Fye had run all night across a hellish landscape where fire fought the darkness and smoke filled their lungs. There had been too many close calls when lasers cut through the gray night. Zaverly, on an AirSlider, would normally have had the advantage, but her night vision had gone out, and the glitch slowed her enough to allow Grandyn and Fye to out-maneuver her on foot.

In the endless haze and choking air, it seemed that morning might come only in a burst of flames. Grandyn actually pictured an exploding sun burning everything he'd ever known. At times, between the near misses of Zaverly's lasershod, when the adrenaline wasn't pushing him on, he hoped for death. Some inner part of him imagining that dying would allow him to breathe fresh air again. Then training and something incomprehensible would thrust him forward.

At least Fye seemed to be improving. Grandyn marveled at her strength, and her ability which allowed her to heal herself even as they fled. They both needed rest. They'd been pushing so hard for so long, but Grandyn knew that getting through the night, even if they could avoid their pursuers, would be a miracle.

Then, in the endless hours before the sun was supposed to rise, it started to rain. *Heavily.* The monsoon helped save them from the flames, but the steam, the mud, and the cold rain presented new problems. They sloshed through the torrent until the sky, or what pretended to be a sky – a thing filled with smoke and steam, mist and fog, haze and clouds – began to lighten.

By the time the rain ended, they were exhausted. Dodging Zaverly and her single surviving henchman had been only one of their challenges, heaped on a pile of others. They'd had no food, no sleep, no visibility, no air, and were trying to get south in the face of a raging fire, only to find themselves lost in a forest that had suddenly become a muddy, flooding swamp filled with rushing gullies full of charred debris.

"Freeze!" a voice suddenly barked from out of nowhere.

They wanted to bolt, but they were drenched in the light of four AOI lasers.

We've escaped a lunatic TreeRunner and survived a night of the living dead only to lose it all to four grunges. Grandyn couldn't believe it. *What the hell are they even doing here?*

"Look, boys," one of the grunges said. "They sent us in here to scout for rebels, burnt out of their caves, and I told them it was a waste of time. But I was wrong."

Two of the other grunges laughed.

"All this trouble for two wet rats," one of them sneered.

Suddenly, one turned and fired. For a split second, both Grandyn and Fye thought the shot was meant for them, but it hit thirty meters to the left of Grandyn. The last of Zaverly's henchmen fell from a tree, dead.

"A friend of yours?" the first grunge asked.

Grandyn shook his head. The grunges had probably just saved their lives. He took it as a hopeful sign, but he glanced at Fye. She was faltering again. It had been too much; the night, the running, the almost dying too many times. He could tell by her face that she thought this was it. They were about to die.

"You dirt bags are with PAWN," the grunge said, as if it weren't a question.

Grandyn shook his head.

One of the other grunges was checking the henchman's body. They were all looking around as if there might be more stragglers.

"Can't you talk, maggot?" the grunge asked.

"We're not with PAWN," Grandyn said. "What's PAWN?"

The grunge laughed. "'What's PAWN?' That's funny. I guess that makes you a Creative, or maybe a Rejectionist. Being out here, perhaps you're a TreeRunner. I don't really give a torg. I just want to know where you came from, and where the rest of your litter is."

Ffttt, ffttt, ffttt. Three lasers dropped three grunges. Before the fourth one, who was returning from the henchman's body, could figure out where they had come from, another *ffttt* came from the mist, and he was also dead.

Grandyn was about to run, but Fye collapsed. Zaverly dropped a few meters in front of him. The grunges' lasers' light on his chest was quickly replaced by hers.

"Grandyn, how nice to see you," she said with a faux smile. "Don't *ever* run from me again."

"Let us go," Grandyn demanded.

"I see Fye hasn't fared so well in the night, but don't worry. She'll feel better once I kill you."

"But you just saved us," Fye said weakly from the ground.

"Yes. I've saved Grandyn Happerman, many times . . . too many. But that was the last one."

"I don't understand," Grandyn said, still trying to figure out why this deranged TreeRunner wanted to kill him.

"I know you're used to everyone saving you. Big important Grandyn has to be saved. So what? So he can save us all? Well you haven't done a very good job, have you Grandyn?" She said his name as if it were a sound one would make before vomiting. "Have you seen the world lately? It's on fire. It's *dying*. Millions are dead, but for three years the rebels pinned their hopes on you . . . *You*! And you've done nothing except get good torgon people killed."

"Listen to me, Zaverly—"

"No! You listen to me. You are not important here. You don't even look like a hero. You look like a failure. Like a scared loser running away from everyone. You've been running for three years, Grandyn. What are you afraid of? Are you afraid to die? I hope you're afraid to die."

Grandyn looked over at Fye. She still wasn't moving.

"Oh, don't worry about your girlfriend. I'm not going to kill her yet. I'm hoping she'll wake up. I want her to see you die. I want her to know what it's like to lose someone she loves. Does she love you?"

"She's just in our unit. I hardly know her."

"Ha! A coward *and* a liar. I'm not surprised. You've lied and hidden and run so long, you probably don't even know what it's like to be real anymore."

"Why do you hate me?" He kept trying to find a way out, but the heat from the laser on his chest told him to keep talking. Time was his only hope, and Zaverly sure seemed to want to talk.

"I loved you once," she said. "But, of course, it wasn't *actually* you. *He* was a good man, courageous and strong. *He* didn't hide behind others."

Grandyn began to get the picture. She must have been in love with one of the Grandyn doubles that the TreeRunners had dropped in forests around the world to confuse and distract the AOI.

"I didn't order those men to be used. I didn't want that at all."

"Shut up Grandyn! You lie too easily. 'You didn't want them to do that.' Even if I believed you, and I don't, it wouldn't matter because here we are. And you're still alive."

"Zaverly, we're on the same side. Turn your anger on the real people who murdered the man you loved: the AOI. They're killing all of us."

"The man I loved, he had a name. Do you even know any of the names of the people who died for you?"

"Yes, I do."

"Then name them. And if you name the man I'm talking about, I will let you go. How's that Grandyn Happerman? Prove to me that you are more than a leech."

Grandyn began quietly and slowly reciting the names of every person he knew who had died to protect him. It was a long list, and his ability to recall them was impressive. Zaverly kept count. The numbers shocked even her. She began to wonder if he was making them up. Once he said the sixtieth, she stopped him.

"How does that make you feel? That all those people are dead only because of you?"

"It makes me sick. They keep me awake at night, and it makes me want to kill every grunge in the world, slowly, one at a time." He glared at her as if she were keeping him from this task. Then his expression turned softer. "I'm not done. I'd like to name them all."

She gave a nod and looked over at Fye, still crumpled on the ground. "Do it. You still haven't named anyone I know, and I *know* quite a few who died for you." She shook her head in disgust.

He went on naming names. He reached one hundred before he said anyone she recognized. Several were from the unit in the Amazon where she had been stationed. He got to the ones who'd saved him and Fye from the Rogue River, then after a few more, the name "Beckett Connors" rolled off his dry lips. She held up a hand and stopped him.

"So you do know that you killed him. Another victim of your crimes," she said angrily, as if hearing Grandyn uttering the name of her loved one was too much. Her eyes flashed with tears and vengeance. "You took him from me!"

He thought she was about to pull the trigger. Glancing at Fye, Grandyn tried to remember any details he'd read in the reports he'd requested from Parker. Every time someone pretending to be him died, he'd get their dossier and read about them, find out what had happened, try to keep it all straight until one day he might be able to help their families. To do something to appease his guilt. The chaotic world had not allowed that yet, but try as he did, Grandyn could not recall anything about Beckett. There had been so many, and now he was exhausted and worried about Fye.

I have to get her help, he thought. *She might already be dead.* He swallowed hard at that possibility.

"I'm sorry Beckett died pretending to be me," he said. "I'm sure he was brave and true—"

"He was," Zaverly said, "and so much more."

"Ask Parker. I begged her not to let people pretend to be me. It was *her* program. I tried to stop it."

"You weren't worth it," she said, spitting on Fye.

Fye suddenly came to life, flinging a fist-sized rock. It caught Zaverly in the chest, and she stumbled backwards. It gave Grandyn just enough of an opening to lunge.

Grandyn and Zaverly struggled and rolled. Zaverly was a fit TreeRunner. Fye had used up her strength, and collapsed back to the ground. The eerie light, coupled with the drifting smoke and her weak condition, made her think it was all a bad dream. Seconds later, she heard the lasershod, *ffttt, ffttt,* and knew that one of them was dead.

CHAPTER SIXTY-ONE

Deuce woke from a fitful sleep. He'd sealed his fate with his decision hours earlier in the night to shut down satellite access around the world, including the ones the AOI used to guide its weapons, and which provided the backbone of the mass surveillance systems. For him and his empire, the ramifications would be far-reaching and long-lasting, of that he was certain. What remained unclear was the effectiveness of the most difficult decision of his life.

The Chief would know that Deuce had chosen sides. She would not be surprised. No one would be surprised. But the Chief would retaliate, swiftly, and with all the brutality she could muster. Now he would find out if his defenses were up to the test. However, it wasn't the Lipton empire that mattered most to him. It was the future of humanity.

"I did it to stop the slaughter," Deuce told Munna, "or at least slow it."

The Moon Shadow was farther south, and a tropical breeze warmed the early morning air. They sipped juice and watched the horizon turn from pink to blue.

"I know your intentions were good," she said, "but good intentions are often a mistake in disguise."

"Will you let me see the *Justar Journal?*" he asked, afraid she might say yes. Seeing what would happen as a result of his decision worried him almost as much as watching what was now happening while he did nothing.

Blame and guilt make a toxic potion that can transform a hero into a coward, he thought.

Munna nodded. He turned to go down below deck, but suddenly, she opened four AirViews. The first was *Reflections of the Revolution in France,* by Edmund Burke. It showed the war moving into orbit. The AOI had even destroyed Deuce's moon base, and satellites exploded in mass numbers, causing an almost impenetrable debris field around the earth. Space travel would become very difficult, but as Deuce watched, he realized it wouldn't matter.

The earth was in ruins. The Imps and the AOI had battled so efficiently against each other and the rebels, that the result was complete devastation. At the same time, in the distraction of war, the new plague had ravished the surviving population as it tore around the globe unchecked.

The Marcus Aurelius *Meditations* AirView showed the details and the dying, while the John Milton *Paradise Lost* AirView had a view of earth as a wasted, toxic mess. The forests had all burned, and the oceans were a brown and black stew of death. It was an unrecognizable place.

Deuce shuddered. "I did this?" he asked. "Were my mistakes too great?"

Munna looked into the highest part of the sky, where the indigo still clung to a faint star. "It is more than a mistake for us to fight one another. That was never—"

"I thought I would be battling a normal AOI, not one led by some new version of Hitler." Deuce was distraught. "And I never counted on the Imps trying to take over the world."

"Sometimes we see things one way, but something entirely different is occurring."

"I guess so," Deuce said, dejected and unsure of what to do. "Can we fix it? Is there anything I can do?"

She pointed to the still blank AirView, *Rights of Man*, by Thomas Paine. "It shows nothing can be done."

Deuce let out a long sigh. He thought of his children and his wife. A lump formed in his throat. *How could this be the end?*

"But it can change," Munna said, so quietly that in his despair he didn't hear her.

"What?"

"It can change," she said, raising her voice. "The *Justar Journal* is always being written and rewritten. We must keep an eye on the *Rights of Man*, for how that goes will tell us if the future is to be livable." Munna stared at him, her eyes filled with consequence, and then she repeated, "It can change."

CHAPTER SIXTY-TWO

Blaze Cortez yelled every obscenity he knew, including ones from three of the old, dead languages. He tried to reach Deuce, with no luck. The assassination attempt on the Chief had failed.

The husband and wife team had just reported in. The level of their frustration could not be measured. "We *had* her!" the husband had yelled.

Everything had gone perfectly. They would never know now if the Chief's bunker could have withstood the Sonic-bomb, because four minutes before the bomber dropped its payload, the satellite guiding it went dark, and the bomber's failsafe system immediately locked the weapons and automatically sent the large drone back to its base.

Blaze sat contemplating the irony of Deuce's move. If he'd waited, even five minutes, the Chief might be dead. The war could have been ended. It certainly would have become a more sensible war. Blaze almost smiled at his own oxymoron.

A sensible war, he thought. Blaze had recently acquired several large construction equipment manufacturers and other companies that would profit immensely from the rebuilding which would inevitably follow war. He believed that to be wise, but that was before the Chief had destroyed a substantial portion of civilization in a matter of days.

The assassination wasn't the only loss when the satellites went down. Blaze had closed in on Grandyn. It had been the artificial rainstorm that had been the final variable in his search. He finally had the TreeRunner, and was going to be able to follow him straight to the List Keepers. But now Grandyn would slip through his fingers again. If Blaze could reach Deuce, right after he chewed him out, he'd ask him if he had any BLAXERs close enough to get in there and track Grandyn the rest of the way. But if he couldn't contact Deuce soon, that option would evaporate like the steam from the fires.

Out of desperation, Blaze had authorized the backup plan, although he didn't think it had much chance of success. They had two operatives inside the bunker. If they could get word to them, and there was an opportunity, they would move on the Chief. But as Blaze told his team, "The bunker is very large, with multiple levels. It's not exactly a big open party inside."

Unbeknownst to Blaze, Nolan, one of Deuce's top BLAXERs, also had an agent inside. But he was different. He was willing to die. He'd been given the green light.

"Kill the Chief, by *any* means necessary."

The Imps, now fully operational again, took the satellite shutdown as a gift and seized the opportunity to attack the AOI. Imps had never meant the Trapciers-AOI alliances to be permanent, at least as far as Sidis was concerned. The AOI was just another piece of the human mess that the Traditionals needed to surrender.

The Imps' plan had been to go after the AOI in a few more days, but without satellites, the AOI was a much easier target. They used androids to bomb AOI targets, and used digital viruses to corrupt AOI weapons so they could be used against Aylantik assets.

There were many systems of communication and monitoring that were not completely reliant on satellites. Seeker and the Field being the two largest systems that would survive, albeit with some loss of functionality, could still be used. The Trapciers had established other methods, and would have the advantage. Or, at least until the AOI could open up space again.

The Trapciers had a three-phase plan to take control of the world. Phase One had been to use the AOI to radically reduce the human population and decimate the rebel opposition. Phase Two was to use the BLAXERS, Enforcers, and PAWN to weaken each other further. And Phase Three was to turn on the Chief and attack the AOI. It was all meant to cause chaos and put the Trapciers in control.

"Conducting Phases Two and Three simultaneously will be taxing," Galahad said. "We have only so many androids running our programs."

"The AOI is weak without satellites," Sidis countered. "The BLAXERS and Enforcers are not prepared for what this war has brought, and PAWN is overwhelmed. The world will be on its knees in less than two days."

"The world appears to be *past* its knees," Charlemagne added. "I think the world is lying on the ground grasping its chest."

"Just wait," Sidis smirked. "Even while we were down, our factories were churning out androids. I've also just received a bit of encouraging news from the Einstein group. We may have figured out a way to use the satellites without the AOI, StarFly, or even Deuce Lipton knowing about it."

While all sides worked on trying to control, restore, or keep the satellites dark, the Trapciers suddenly seemed to have the advantage. Through their vast network of machines, in a world run by machines, they were quickly able to multiply the bedlam. By hacking and corrupting, they were able to trick and manipulate

PAWN into battles with Enforcers and the BLAXERs, and likewise with the BLAXERs and Enforcers. The Trapciers had them all blindly fighting each other.

Sidis watched it unfold on dozens of AirViews and smiled. Many monitors showed the fires and the new plague spreading even faster. Others were filled with "accidental" battles as they erupted among all the players. Even for the cold Imps, it was almost too much devastation to bear. But Sidis, unwavering in his mission, summed it up poetically.

"It is a just cause in which we march. Destiny assures that the Trapciers will see this through to its rightful conclusion. In a mere forty-eight hours, this final war will terminate. Watch with me comrades, until the crisis and confusion, death and destruction, greed and guilt, lead where they will. To the end. The end of everything."

CHAPTER SIXTY-THREE

Drast and Osc looked out the window from the top floor of the Seattle AOI building and saw a ruined city. Large swaths had been erased, as if a child had pushed a toy dump truck through a village of block towers.

"The Chief is insane," Osc said, shaking his head in dismay.

"The Aylantik is built on insanity. They killed almost two-thirds of the Earth's population in the Banoff, and this time they seem to be trying to finish us off," Drast said. "But the Chief is not actually insane. She is something worse. The Chief is an ambitious leader, at once calculating, yet reckless. She is one of the most focused people I've ever known, nerves of steel, the type of person who will not hesitate to risk it all and take us to the brink of extinction to try to eradicate what she sees as a threat to the peace which has prevailed for more than seventy years."

"Peace prevails, always," Osc said ironically, gesturing out at the destruction.

Drast nodded. "The Chief believes the Aylantik system is a true utopia, that we can do no better. And that is the problem. When the liars start believing their own lies. When searching for the truth, you may find it never even existed."

The Ally who'd brought them from Vancouver burst into the room. "Drast, we've got the Scram up!"

Drast smiled. "Excellent." He and Osc followed the Ally down the corridor to a control room. "Who have you raised so far?"

"We're in touch with San Francisco, Phoenix, Denver, Salt Lake City, San Diego, Guadalajara, and Lima," the Ally answered.

"Are they all in our hands?" Osc asked.

"No," the Ally replied. "The wolves still control them, but the Allies are awaiting orders."

"Do it," Drast said.

The command center communications officer relayed the command to the other seven Key AOI headquarters that had responded.

"It's going to be a tense thirty minutes or so," Drast told Osc. "If even one of them fails, the Chief will be alerted and come down on us in a magnitude of that." He pointed to a monitor displaying a sea of rubble that was once a recognizable city. Wherever it was, it didn't exist anymore. There were no survivors, nothing left to show the terror but a concrete scar.

"Ashes to ashes, dust to dust," Osc said.

Drast nodded solemnly.

"Shouldn't we try to contact my mother?" Osc asked.

"Not while we're here. Not until we secure more of the Keys."

During the next twenty-five minutes, they reviewed a list of their recently acquired assets: a good stash of weapons, a fleet of AOI LEV vans, jet packs, and even light range drones.

"We've just added substantially to the rebels' capabilities," Osc said.

"And this is only the beginning," Drast added, staring at the AirViews, tensely waiting for word from the other Keys. "But we need to move as much of this as we can. Even if we are successful, this stuff needs to be in a place where the Chief can't find it."

"Does such a place exist?" Osc asked, glancing across a long row of AirViews and their images of devastation.

"Sheep in wolves' clothing," the communication officer suddenly announced. "Denver is ours."

Drast raised his fist in the air. "Yes!"

"And San Francisco, Salt Lake," the officer continued. "Here comes San Diego."

"Like clockwork," Drast said, both proud and relieved that his plans, dormant for so long, had now come to fruition. "The torgon wolves are at the door but we're not letting them in!"

"Phoenix just reported."

Allies in the room started clapping. Drast manipulated an AirView and zoomed in on the two remaining Keys, Guadalajara and Lima.

"*Vamos, salvanos,*" Drast whispered in the forbidden dead language of Spanish. It had once been spoken in both Peru and Mexico, where those last Keys were located. There were other keys, but so far Seattle had not been able to raise a friendly voice at those centers. Seven keys would at least be enough to slow the steam rolling. More would surely come if they could reach Allies at those locations, however, if Lima and Guadalajara didn't crossover, then the celebration would be finished before it began.

"We've got confirmation that the satellites are down," another Ally said, running in from a different room. "The Chief issued a command to seize all Deuce Lipton's assets . . . Eysen, Inc., Star-Fly, everything. That means Deuce Lipton is with us!"

Drast almost smiled, but he worried Deuce might have played his hand too soon, and he didn't understand what was taking so long in the last two Keys.

"Come on, save us," he said quietly, repeating his earlier Spanish plea in English.

Osc could feel Drast's tension. He'd been through enough with the rebel mastermind to know this was a do-or-die moment. With all that had happened, more than just the outcome of the revolution rested with Lima and Guadalajara, but the survival of the human race depended upon them.

Osc silently repeated the prayer, *Vamos, salvanos.*

CHAPTER SIXTY-FOUR

In the rolling struggle between Grandyn and Zaverly, the laser-shod discharged, but missed them both. Somehow, Zaverly wound up with the weapon and scrambled to her feet. She stood just a meter away from Grandyn, pointing the lasershod. Even if Fye were still standing, the encroaching smoky fog would have blocked her view of them.

"Now!" Zaverly yelled, backing up a step. "Now we're going to finish this. And I've changed my mind," she said, panting. "I'm going to shoot Fye first so you'll know just how it feels . . . how I felt."

"I do know how it feels!" Grandyn shouted at her. "Damn you, I know. The AOI killed my mother when I was eight years old. Then they murdered my first love, Vida. Sweet and beautiful Vida . . . she was just nineteen years old." His voice cracked as tears fell from his eyes. "Then the AOI bombs came and my father was taken away from me. They've stolen *everything* from me. Ev-ver-ree-thing! You and I are the same, Zaverly."

"We are not," she said weakly, seemingly touched by his speech.

"But we are. The AOI has tried to destroy our lives, but we're TreeRunners. We know how to survive, and we know how to fight back. It's *them*, damn it! It's *them*." The fog closed around as muddy water ran everywhere.

Zaverly thought of the AOI agents who had raped her and her friends. She and the other girls had been so young, so innocent. Her mind recalled the images. She could see the agents' empty, greedy faces. Feel their disgusting, sweaty flesh. All the anonymous grunges who'd killed so many of the people she loved now invading her, as they always did when she was weak. They all looked the same, they all looked like monsters.

Grandyn's words echoed in her head, numb with bitterness.

"But it's your fault Beckett's dead," she said, grasping at her vengeance, but sounding less like the raging warrior and more like a little girl.

"Beckett volunteered for the Grandyn mission," Grandyn said loudly. "He did it because he was a hero. He had to know that we need to do anything and everything to defeat the AOI. They must be defeated. They. Must. Be. Destroyed." He paused and tried to find her eyes. "Would Beckett have wanted you to kill me?"

Zaverly stared into his eyes and slowly shook her head. It was almost imperceptible at first, but she was saying no.

"Will you help us wipe the torgon AOI off the planet?"

She lowered her gun and stared at him, as if seeing him for the first time, or seeing Beckett, or maybe just not seeing him as another one of the monsters.

He fought his training, which told him to lunge at her and get the weapon while she was distracted and confused. But his instincts told him to wait.

"You are one of the AOI's greatest enemies," she said, as if it was news to him. Certainly the idea seemed to have never occurred to her before.

"My *whole* life is dedicated to ending them," he said defiantly, but with pleading eyes.

Zaverly stared another second, and then finally said, "We need to cross the river."

CHAPTER SIXTY-FIVE

"We have Lima and Guadalajara!" the communications officer announced. "We got them all!" The roar could be heard down the corridor, and the mood inside the Seattle Key command center became raucous. It turned out that the delay had been a glitch in the Scram network.

Drast's sigh of relief was followed by a barrage of orders. He wanted more Keys on board. "There are eleven more Keys in the Pacyfik. Find our people. Let's kick the wolves out of our house!"

Allies were put in charge of transporting weapons and provisions, including food and water, to other safe locations. The establishment of a secure link to PAWN Command was made a priority, but it needed to be mobile because Drast planned on heading south.

"You can't go," someone told him. "The Trapciers are fully engaged."

Drast looked at the woman who'd given the information as if she'd just told him it was snowing in July. She went on to explain that ground forces were involved in skirmishes across the region and at other global hot spots.

"The Trapciers don't have an army," Osc barked.

"They actually do," the woman said. "It's not human, of course. Androids, mostly."

"And the Chief is allowing them to get a foothold?" Drast asked.

"It's a bit more complicated than that. There are others involved."

Drast looked at her impatiently.

"Enforcers, BLAXERs, and PAWN are fighting." She said, almost afraid to tell him the rest, as if she were unsure it was true. "They aren't just fighting the AOI, they're fighting each other."

"Who?" Drast snapped.

"All of them. They're all fighting everyone. I mean each other."

Drast looked around the room, hoping to spot someone competent who might be able to give him a straight report.

"How can this be?" Osc asked.

"The Trapciers have somehow arranged it," she said hesitantly.

"Are you sure about this?" Drast asked.

"No," she said, "but see for yourself." She opened three AirViews. The maps and live images of battles, along with detailed audio summaries of the facts, confirmed her words.

Drast studied the AirViews for several minutes and then shouted for the communications officer. "Get me in touch with the damned, torgon, torgon, torgon Trapciers!" Drast marched through the AirViews and into the hallway. Osc followed.

"The Trapciers are just a bunch of Imps and machines, right?" Osc asked.

"Tooorrrrg!" Drast moaned. He was trying to recall all the Imps he'd ever dealt with, and he'd had dealings with quite a few. Prison has cost him more than time. He'd lost some contacts, his edge, but not his fire. From inside Hilton Prison, Drast had been able to scrape and bribe to keep himself in the game, keep the dream alive, but it hadn't been easy, and a lot had gotten away from him, maybe too much. "Imps are the most dangerous things on the planet," he said with his forehead in one of his hands.

"They combine the best part of humans and the best part of computers. Imps aren't really better than humans, but they think they are."

"Then why are they so threatening?"

"They aren't better than us, but they are *way* more advanced."

For hours the news continued to pour in. Battles raged, the toll from the new plague exploded, fires swept through pristine forests, and the AOI even found a way to resume bombing, at least on a limited basis. The amount of androids fighting was astonishing. Estimates and Seeker sightings had their numbers at more than three million, and somewhere factories were cranking out more. The Trapciers had managed to convert the domestic staffs, waiters, assembly line workers, and a million other androids who had silently been working low-paying jobs in the background of society for years. A slight reprogramming, and they were now soldiers. Enemies of the state. Killing machines.

The Allies did make some progress in the face of the worst day since the war had begun. In the seven AOI Keys that they controlled, the Allies completed the looting of the buildings and found alternative locations for the weapons and supplies. Contact had been established with four more Keys, but Drast wanted four or five more before ordering the takeovers.

"We have to make sure that we get as many as possible in case one fails. Once we get more than twelve, we might be able to survive losing one," he explained.

They'd also had some luck exploiting the corruption and discontent in other non-Key AOI facilities. Drast was devastated to learn what the Chief had done to the other prisons. Most had been wiped out. "Those were some of our best people," Drast said.

"Some of the worst too," Osc reminded him. "Not everyone in an AOI prison was a hero."

Drast was annoyed with Osc's statement, but he recognized that things might appear different from a guard's point of view. He begrudgingly admitted to himself that he had met some real losers in prison. Still, he mourned the loss of the great intellectuals, thinkers, and brave men and women forever lost by the Aylantik's fears and the Chief's ruthlessness.

Finally, he received the word he'd been waiting for.

"Sir, we've established communication with Chelle Andreas."

CHAPTER SIXTY-SIX

Zaverly gave Grandyn and Fye her AirSlider, then turned away and started the long walk back north, where she would eventually hook up with another PAWN unit, assuming she avoided any grunges along the way. Fye's condition had improved considerably. Zaverly also left half her water and food rations with them. It was as close as she came to apologizing, but it was good enough for Grandyn. They would not have made it across the swollen river without the AirSlider, and walking to the List Keeper City would have taken at least two more days, time they obviously didn't have. Fye also couldn't have healed herself without at least a measure of fresh water.

During the hours of traveling south through the damp and charred remains of what had once been a great forest, Fye talked a lot. Her pad and paper had disappeared in the lava tubes of the Rogue River, "tools" she normally used to work through problems and get her thoughts out. She needed to talk, about the people who had died to save them, about their lost child, the war, the City they were trying to reach, and about the woman who had tried to take their lives but in the end had set them free.

"I don't understand why Zaverly hated you so much," she said while standing behind him and holding onto his waist as the AirSlider breezed along at half its maximum speed.

"The author C. S. Lewis once wrote, 'No one ever told me that grief felt so like fear.' I think Zaverly was afraid," Grandyn said.

"Of what?"

"Feeling the pain."

"From losing the man she loved?"

"Yeah, and more . . . It seems as if Zaverly has been battling demons older than Beckett's death. I don't know, but she is definitely full of fear. And C. S. Lewis is right; grief and fear are fruit of the same tree . . . only one can kill you."

Fye thought of the child they'd lost. She could feel the fear creeping in. Why didn't she stay somewhere safe? Would she ever be able to have a child? It felt like someone strangling her. The confines of fear squeezed in.

"I'm afraid," she finally managed to say, in a voice that sounded as if someone was standing on her chest.

"I know. Me too," Grandyn admitted. "But you have to believe we'll be all right . . . or else we won't be."

Fye was quiet for a while. She focused on healing, not just her body, but the absolute emptiness that seemed to be consuming her.

After about twenty minutes, Grandyn asked, "Are you okay?"

"I don't know," she said, trying not to cry. "What do you think is going to happen to Zaverly?"

"She has to live with all she's done."

"We all do."

"Yeah. What prepares us for living with what we've done?"

"Surviving."

Grandyn nodded, and they rode in silence.

Drast rushed to the signal station. He knew in the current environment that Scram and the Field could crash at any moment. He'd been waiting too long to hear her voice.

"Chelle," Drast said, breathlessly.

"You're alive," Chelle said in teary relief. "I knew you'd survive."

"Thanks to you. Not just for sending the Flo-wing and Osc, but for giving me a reason to dream. A reason to *want* to survive this nightmare."

"Tell me Osc is okay?"

"He's wonderful. Chelle, your son is an amazing man. Smart and brave and . . . and you never should have risked him on the likes of me."

"I would have come myself if I could have," she said. "Osc was born into the revolution. I've worried every second since he's been gone, but his life was dedicated to this fight long before he was even conceived."

"It's been more of a massacre than a fight," Drast said.

"The war is not going well," Chelle admitted.

Drast checked the infinite encryption. "We've taken seven Keys, and we'll have even more soon."

"Finally some good news, but it may be too little too late. The Trapciers have escalated. It's brutal out there, and they just managed to make a PAWN drone bomb a PAWN ground unit. Ten minutes ago an Enforcers unit attacked another Enforcers unit. Forty-two dead before the mistake was realized. It's like that all over. They've got us fighting each other and ourselves. It's hard to know what intel to trust or—"

"The Trapciers *can* be stopped," Drast interrupted. "The Imps may be on the verge of wiping out the human race, but make no mistake, the Chief and her AOI, the wolves, are the real enemy. *My* AOI will decide who wins or loses this thing."

"Is there time?"

"Maybe not, but we're sure as hell going to try."

"When can I see you?" Chelle asked, knowing it was still impossible.

Drast's voice turned sweet. "As soon as I am able to find a way. How are you really?"

"It was hard not knowing if you were alive. I'm much better now."

"We're going to win this, Chelle. Just like we planned, and we'll be together always . . . never doubt it."

Grandyn and Fye had ridden most of the night, until they couldn't stand any longer. Hours earlier they'd crossed into an unburned area, an endless sea of green trees. It brought a greater risk of grunge encounters, but also more places to hide. They had found a soft, concealed area of understory that looked like it had been a regular resting spot for deer, and were asleep in minutes. The cold morning air woke them just before dawn. They ate some dried biscuits Zaverly had given them and headed south. Less than an hour later, the AirSlider's charge ran out. It would take hours for the solar batteries to recharge, but Fye said they were close to the City, so they stashed their transport and continued on foot.

Finally, and without fanfare, Fye announced, "We're here."

Grandyn looked around. Nothing but untouched wilderness surrounded them. "Where?" he asked, confused.

"The City."

CHAPTER SIXTY-SEVEN

Saturday, July 16

It was unbelievable, after the week's events, that such a meeting could even take place, but the Trapciers had changed everything. The Imps had taken the chaos and devastation of the worst war in the history of the world and transformed it into something far more terrifying.

For the first time since the dawn of humanity, humans were no longer in control. They were no longer engaged in war against their own species.

The machines had taken over.

The Chief looked at the holograms of Deuce, Miner, and Chelle. They all were thinking the same thing. Being in the same room together, even digitally, would have been unimaginable yesterday. After so long as enemies, the meeting itself seemed surreal. Two women and two men, hoping somehow to save what was left of the world.

"Thank you for coming," the Chief said. "I wanted to look each of you in the eye during these discussions." She stopped and met Deuce's stare. He, more than any of them, was the reason she was there. He had hampered the AOI from dominating. She might not have known that his decision to cut off the satellites may have saved her life, but she knew it had cost the AOI its victory.

His poker face gave nothing away. Next to him, Lance Miner wore an expression like a child wanting his way. The Chief was the only person he hated more than Deuce, and she knew it. It was easy to see it in his eyes. They'd been forced together by necessity, but otherwise he would kill her by any means at his disposal, preferably a method that would be horribly painful and agonizingly slow.

Finally, there was Chelle. She had brought the revolution to life, pushed for years, creating a counterweight to the Aylantik, exposing their faults and hidden history, and highlighting the AOI's harsh methods. She stared back with a depth that neither man had demonstrated. This was the fighter in the room. Anyone could tell, and everyone knew, Chelle was dangerous. If they'd all actually been in the same room, Chelle would have smiled as she quickly and silently killed each of them before casually walking away, as if it had just been another part of her daily routine.

Deuce glanced at the others. "Quite a crew . . . I might have guessed in the beginning that it would come down to the four of us." He thought of Munna and the List Keepers, still wondering if anything could really be accomplished without them.

"The torgon machines," Miner began. "Only their threat could have unified us."

"At least for the moment," Chelle added.

"Easy, now," the Chief said. "There isn't much time. Our differences must remain outside. Perhaps we can work through them peacefully, if we survive this. But in either case, none of you would be here if there were a way to win on your own. They are driving us to extinction."

"They are driving you together," Blaze Cortez suddenly interjected, his image materializing with his words. "You can all apologize later for not inviting me, but you should know my feelings were terribly hurt."

"You have feelings?" Chelle asked in her best sarcastic tone.

"What the hell are *you* doing here?" Lance shot out before Blaze could respond to Chelle's dig.

"And how the hell did you find out about this meeting, or even get into it?" the Chief demanded.

"One at a time please, please." Blaze smiled. "Deuce, any insults or questions to add?"

Deuce shook his head.

"Ladies, gentleman . . . Lance, lend me your ears. I come to bury Caesar, not to praise him," Blaze commenced amid their rumblings. "You do not trust each other, and you definitely don't trust me, so how is this to work? The Trapciers are on the verge of victory. We have hundreds of millions dead, our infrastructure is in ruin, the Field is erratic and probably standing only because it serves their needs. This meeting might be too late. We may have already lost."

"Blaze, if you don't have anything useful or new to say, could you please shut up!" the Chief retorted.

"Oh, forgive me your majesty, the ruthless ice queen who empowered the Trapciers with an alliance, who oversaw the death of *millions* before realizing you'd been caught in the Trapciers' trap."

"*I* empowered them?" the Chief shot back. "*You* invented them. This is *your* technology we are fighting. You should be executed for your crimes against humanity!"

"Yes, perhaps, and you are quite good at handing out those sentences. But let—"

"Blaze," Deuce snapped, "we don't have time for this. Tell us why you are here."

Blaze nodded. Like the rest of them, he looked tired, off his game. He pulled his long hair back into a ponytail. A silver ring holding it in place. "You came here to join forces against the Trapciers, to somehow annihilate them. But you can't win a war against them unless you understand what they are fighting for."

"They are trying to take over the world," Chelle said. "You created a monster, and like the bad science fiction novels my brother read growing up, the machines don't think they need us anymore."

"No," Blaze said, looking from face to face, confirming that they all shared Chelle's view. "Sarlo, are you there?" he asked, looking at Miner, who turned behind him and mumbled something. A moment later, Sarlo appeared.

"Ah, lovely to see you," Blaze said. "Would you mind telling us why the Trapciers are mixed up in this bloody war, errrr, revolution? I mean, ethnic cleansing, genocide . . . no, what is it Chief? An extermination. Yes, that's right, isn't it? Oh, I don't know, it's so difficult to keep track of the war crimes. . . war crimes, there's an oxymoron. Or a redundant expression, or something . . . Sorry, I digress. Sarlo?"

She looked at Miner, and then to Chelle. "I don't know any of this for a fact. I'm surprised Blaze is asking for my input." She turned to Blaze. "I've never even liked Blaze, and I certainly don't trust him."

"Thank you," he said, nodding knowingly. "For those of you who don't know, Sarlo is the brains behind Miner's operation."

Miner rolled his eyes.

"This is only a theory," Sarlo began, "but I believe the Trapciers are *not* trying to take over the world. They don't want war, they want to *end* war. The Imps want us to experience what *they* have experienced."

Everyone looked at her. Miner wasn't surprised. Although he didn't agree, he basically already knew her views.

"What have they seen?" Deuce asked.

"Something beyond what we perceive through our five senses," Sarlo said. "Something that is quite difficult to describe unless you've seen it."

"Have *you* seen it?" Chelle asked.

"No."

"Then what are you talking about?" the Chief questioned.

"Wait," Blaze said. "I asked for Sarlo's theory because I am obnoxious and disliked . . . that cannot be denied." He smiled. "But this is too important. You are about to continue down the path toward ruin. You are going to do the same thing we have always done: war. For some reason, you think that if you all get together and bury your differences and then take on the common enemy, it will be different. But it won't. Even when you're right, you're wrong, because it's still *war*."

"I've seen it all," Miner said. "Blaze Cortez, the great profiteer, a man who's made a fortune pitting side against side, has found religion and is now some kind of a torgon pacifist."

"This is not about profits," Blaze countered.

"It's about survival," the Chief added.

"It's not even about survival," Blaze said. "You all are so confused. It's the one place where the Imps have miscalculated. They don't really understand confusion. They've forgotten feelings of uncertainty the way we Traditionals act on incorrect information. How we make assumptions based on misinterpretations, on all of our mistaken perceptions. So they think we'll figure it out, but we aren't going to. We've set the world on fire in order to save it. We're going to kill ourselves, and they'll watch. But Sarlo's right. They won't be laughing, they'll be analyzing, because that's what they do. They'll be asking, 'How will we make it better? How do we avoid that mistake next time?' Only there won't *be* a next time."

"What the hell are you talking about?" Miner asked.

"How. Do. We. Make. It. Better?" Blaze said slowly. He looked around the room. "This is the hope for our species, the four of you, our top people, and you just don't get it."

"They want to make it better," Sarlo said slowly and emphatically. "The Imps and even the CHRUDEs, they're just trying to fix us."

There was brief but total silence for almost a full minute.

"Fix us?" the Chief asked, astonished by the notion. "They are the machines!"

"But they are designed to improve. It's programmed into them. That's why they are so amazing, because they have one objective: to make everything *better*. Themselves, the duties they're tasked with, problem-solving, every kind of analysis, and even us. Don't you get it? They are trying to make *us* better," Blaze repeated.

"They have a funny way of doing it," the Chief muttered.

"Don't even try to understand them. Their methods are way beyond your logic, especially yours," Blaze said.

"So are you trying to tell us not to fight them?" Chelle asked in a formal tone.

"War will end only in one way," Blaze empathetically replied. "Human extinction."

They'd all considered that horrific possibility, that's why they were gathered at that very moment, but to hear Blaze say it, after everything else, somehow made it more real. Closer. Imminent.

Again, they were all silent. Deuce had seen it in the prophecies. He'd come to believe that one of the primary purposes of the *Justar Journal* had been to save the human race. Munna was right. It was foolish to use something so powerful to attempt to win some battles.

Deuce repeated the earlier, still unanswered, question. "What do the Imps see?"

"They see the truth," Blaze said. "They see the universe from the inside. Instead of looking up into the stars, they look out from the core energy that *is* the stars. Our essence . . . they see the potential of the light. The power of the dream."

CHAPTER SIXTY-EIGHT

In the three years that Grandyn had been with Fye, she'd never told him more than a few minor details about the City. He knew it was the place where the majority of the List Keepers lived and worked, but most of the rest had been left to his imagination. He had been to a few List Keeper "outposts," which typically were berms in remote hillsides, concealed with a combination of natural and manufactured camouflage. They served as high-tech monitoring and risk stations, and were usually manned by two or three people.

The City was apparently something entirely different. It had been constructed even before the Banoff in an isolated mountain range in what had been the western United States.

"Where is it?" Grandyn asked again, still seeing no evidence of anything not formed by nature.

"We're on top of it right now."

"I've spent huge parts of my life in the woods," Grandyn said, "and I've been looking for any trace of something manmade . . ."

"I told you, you wouldn't find anything," she said, laughing.

"You're telling me there's a 'city' under us? I don't believe it."

"Well, they call it the City . . . it's really more like a huge underground facility that houses two thousand nine hundred List Keepers," Fye explained. "But they're never all inside at once. Hundreds usually work outside, mostly in the outposts, occasionally in exposed positions, like me."

He was still looking around for an entrance. "No wonder no one has ever found them."

"Partly because for decades, no one even knew we existed. And the handful who've heard of us now don't know much more than the rumor. Who are we? What do we do? It's all a mystery. 'Are the List Keepers even real?' they wonder."

"Where's the entrance?"

"Some of the oldest List Keepers call the City 'Shangri La,' not because it's a paradise or anything, just because it's impossible to find," Fye said, ignoring his question. "See those trees? They're used for harvesting solar and wind energy. The City is ultra-efficient, so it doesn't need much. Air ventilation is done through rock outcroppings all over the mountain."

She walked on a little farther, then stopped and pointed.

The entrance, located in an area completely concealed from the air by thick pines, covered the bottom of what looked like an old avalanche scar. A tumble of boulders, each looking to weigh a thousand kilos, covered the ground with enough scree and undergrowth that they might have been there for centuries.

Grandyn stared, bewildered, seeing nothing that looked like an opening. Suddenly, one of the giant boulders moved, then lifted with surprisingly quiet hydraulics or some mechanism, and pivoted to reveal an opening approximately two meters wide. He peered in and saw nothing but blackness.

"Are you ready? They don't like to leave this open for very long."

Grandyn looked behind them, suddenly paranoid that they might have been followed. It might have all been a trap.

"Come on," Fye said, giving him a little push.

"It's dark," he said, standing with one foot over the black hole.

"Have a little faith, TreeRunner."

He stepped in and his foot landed on a hard stone. At the same time, a bluish light lit the descending steps in front of that one. He started down with Fye right behind him. The stone staircase appeared ancient. He stopped and looked back up, realizing the boulder had silently covered the entrance without his noticing.

The shaft opened larger now as the steps spiraled wide, making the descent less steep. At the center of the spiral there was an opening about four meters across. There was no railing, and Grandyn made the mistake of looking down into the center. Fye grabbed him before he fell.

"It's got to be at least thirty meters deep!" Grandyn said, gasping.

"Something like that," Fye said. "But you have to be careful. The light comes from down there. It plays tricks on your eyes and totally messes with your sense of perception."

He kept his fingers on the stone wall at the outer edge of the spiral as they continued down. Then, he realized it wasn't just light rising up from the depths of the center of the staircase.

"Are those words?" he asked, stopping to stare at the spectacle. Translucent letters and characters floated up like dust and butterflies – thousands of them, maybe millions. They spelled words in languages Grandyn only recognized from old, banned books. The letters bent and merged, changing colors as if caught in a muted prism. Sentences, whole paragraphs, twisted past them.

"Yes," she answered, nudging him forward.

Then he saw something else. "And *faces*?" he asked excitedly.

"Yes, one of my favorite parts about this entrance."

"Whose faces?" he asked, looking at the faded faces, seemingly made up from countless tiny points of light. Their expressions were changing, as if they were alive in some form, some realm.

"Everyone's," she replied. A few steps later she added, "Everyone who has ever died."

Grandyn couldn't help but stop again. "How is that possible?"

he asked, mesmerized, unable to look away from the blue light. Grandyn found himself searching for his mother.

Fye took both his hands, stepped down next to him, and stared into his eyes. "You have to realize that you were raised out there, in the 'real world,' so you have no idea what is possible. The Aylantik stole that from you, stole it from everyone."

"They didn't steal it from the List Keepers."

"No."

"So you were raised down here?"

"Mostly."

"It's amazing," he said, looking over her shoulder at the passing words and faces.

"Beyond comprehension, really."

He nodded, already overwhelmed by the spectacle, and they weren't even all the way in yet. "How much farther?"

"Don't worry, we're not going all the way to the bottom."

Five minutes or more passed before Fye told him to stop. "Just back up a little," she said. While he moved, the "solid" stone wall opened slowly, as if on giant silent hinges.

"The craftsmanship of this whole entrance is incredible," Grandyn said. "I can't wait to see the rest of it."

When the door opened wide enough that he could see in, disappointment greeted him. After all the anticipation and what he'd just seen, he'd been expecting some kind of science fiction extravaganza. Instead, the City looked more like a medieval cave. A dimly lit tunnel disappeared into darkness ahead of them.

"This is it?" he asked, wanting to go back out into the stairway shaft.

"Don't worry," Fye said, laughing. "In a few hours you're going to tell me that you never want to leave the City."

"In a few hours? Imagine how many people will die up there in that much time."

"I know you want to talk to the leaders of the List Keepers," Fye said, turning serious, "but please, be patient. Everything works just a little bit differently down here. We're here, we made it, and that's the most important thing."

Grandyn nodded. "Okay." He even managed a smile. Fye's healthy appearance had returned, along with her calm confidence.

An old man, wearing what looked like a monk's brown robe, walked slowly toward them. He smiled and bowed slightly to Fye. She returned the greeting. He looked older than anyone Grandyn had ever seen, as if his skin might slide off his bones at any second.

"Welcome to the City, Grandyn," he said. "We've been waiting to meet you."

CHAPTER SIXTY-NINE

The great powers had been arguing for almost an hour. Meanwhile, the Trapciers were gaining more control. The war was expanding, and worsening, by the minute. The Chief called for a vote.

"So we must side with the Trapciers in order to survive this?" Deuce asked Blaze for a final clarification.

"I see no other way," Blaze replied.

"No other way?" the Chief exclaimed. "Blaze is out of his mind. I'd expect that from him, but Deuce? You can't possibly be entertaining such a preposterous idea?"

"Clearly we are in a place that humanity has never been before. The war is pushing us backwards toward the edge of a cliff . . . extinction," Deuce said. "We must deliberate and make the most careful decision."

"I have to agree with the Chief," Miner added. "With whatever else has happened since this thing began, it was between us, all humans. But the machines can't be allowed to survive this day. Ever since Artificial Intelligence began more than one hundred years ago, people have warned against this . . . but we thought we were too smart. That we had them under control. Well hell, it looks like we torgged that one up. We must gang up *against* them, not *join* them!"

"Give me my damned satellites back and I'll destroy every last Imp, android, any creature with wires," the Chief said, glaring at Deuce. "They're only winning because you took out the satellites." She shook a finger at Deuce. "You give them back, or so help me, you'll rue the day!"

Chelle sat silently, listening to the others argue, waiting for a pause, and then spoke. "There comes a time when we must stop looking to the past and instead look to the future, if there is to be one. Our differences, our crimes," she stopped and looked at the Chief, and then to Miner, "must be put aside or else war would never end."

She moved an AirView so that they could all see it.

"I'm sure you all have similar numbers available to you, but these are PAWN Command's latest estimates on the number of dead as a result of this war and the new plague." Again she paused to look at the Chief and Miner. "It's hundreds of millions!"

Even Miner swallowed hard. They all knew the numbers, but there hadn't been time for any of them to focus on them. They'd just been trying to stop the slaughters. All except the Chief.

"Need I remind you, the revolution was *your* idea," the Chief snapped at Chelle. "You started an illegal war, you committed treason, you set these terrible events into motion."

Chelle stared at the Chief as if she might kill her electronically, that her only reason for being was to watch that wretched old woman die.

Miner excused himself and disappeared. Sarlo had asked him for a moment. "They're about to vote," she said. "You need to think about the current course we are on. The simulations show that we have anywhere from days to three weeks before human extinction is irreversible. *Days!*"

"How can you expect me to side with the machines?" Miner asked.

"Because the AOI and the Aylantik are finished. Look at the simulations. The AOI cannot save us."

"Have you plugged in this scenario? Us all siding with the Imps?"

"Yes," Sarlo said, looking at him gravely. "It shows a forty-six percent chance that the human race survives."

"That's not good enough," Miner shot back.

"It has to be!" Sarlo shouted. "If we side with the Chief, the chance of survival is single digits."

He was silent for a moment. "But you're asking a *machine*. They probably have everything rigged now. What do you think the machine will say? It'll tell us to side with the torgon machines!"

"PAWN, and Deuce are going to side with the Imps. Blaze and whatever or whoever the damned List Keepers are will certainly go with the Imps. That leaves us. Enforcers can make the difference. You've seen what the Chief is capable of, and she *hates* you. What do you think will happen if Enforcers and the AOI happen to hit that six percent chance and win? She. Will. Kill. You."

He stared at her. She was one of the few people in the world who didn't hate him. *Hell, even my wife and kids don't like me much,* he thought. "The Imps are dangerous. They want it all."

"The problem with believing you are right all the time is that you miss those occasions when you are wrong, and it's in those moments when you would have learned the most."

He studied her, wishing he had the depth that she did. "What if I go with the AOI?"

"I'll resign."

He nodded. "I thought so." Miner made a gesture that took him back into the meeting.

"Welcome back Lance," the Chief said impatiently. "We're ready to vote."

"Deuce?"

"I see no alternative but to join with the Trapciers," he said.

"Will they even have you?" the Chief snorted. "They'll kill you in your sleep."

"I believe the Imps will welcome Deuce and his BLAXERS," Blaze said.

"It will be your downfall Deuce!" the Chief blasted. "Remember, I warned you."

"PAWN will be joining as well," Chelle said.

"Of course you will," the Chief whined. "Lance, are you standing with the Aylantik, or with the traitors?"

"Enforcers will join with the others," Lance said, not looking back at Sarlo, but sensing her smile.

"You're a fool, Lance. I've always known it, but you've just proven it," the Chief said bitterly. "I'll beat the Trapciers myself, and then I'm coming for the rest of you. Do you forget the might of the AOI?"

She signed off before they could answer.

Chelle and Deuce were both surprised Miner had come on board. Soon the three of them, along with Blaze and Sarlo, plotted a strategy. There wasn't much time. Fifteen minutes after the Chief had gone dark, they had Sidis and Charlemagne connected. The Imps then shared news so shocking that they all stared at one another, absolutely speechless.

CHAPTER SEVENTY

The old man studied Fye and then hugged her. "I'm sorry," he said knowingly. "You'll be fine now." He turned to Grandyn. "So young to have carried so much weight."

"We've all had to make sacrifices," Grandyn said.

"So we have," the old man said. "This way." He led them across the cold, hard floor toward a long corridor. "My name is Cogs, and in case you were wondering, I'm not as old as I look."

Although clean, and with good air, the place gave the impression of being an old mine.

Grandyn couldn't help asking, "If you don't mind my asking, how old *are* you?"

"I was born in 1928," Cogs said, in a tone that seemed filled with memories of times, people, and places long gone. "It was a very different world back then."

Grandyn did the math. The man he was having trouble keeping up with was one hundred and seventy-three. Incredible! Cogs had lived four decades before Munna was even born.

"List Keepers!" he whispered to himself in amazement. *What on earth is at the end of the winding corridor?* he wondered. It took several more minutes for him to find out.

They stood facing a solid stone wall, with no other way to go. Grandyn turned to Fye, wondering if there were another hidden staircase. She nodded back to the wall in front of them. Grandyn looked back just in time to see it fade in a pixilated dissolve. He had no time to be impressed, for as they stepped forward, he saw what he would later learn was called "the Great Hall."

A vast room, perhaps one hundred fifty meters long and half as wide, made him audibly gasp. The ceiling appeared to be open to the sky, but that seemed impossible. Even more baffling was the waterfall, or more accurately, a huge column of water falling from the center of the sky/ceiling. The water plunged at least forty meters before disappearing into a round pool that took up a large portion of the center of the Great Hall. Above the ground level, terraced paths lined with trees and other vegetation fanned upward. Stone trails went in every direction, through fields of flowers, into the trees, and around the pool. At one end he saw an orchard, and had to remind himself that they were underground.

"It's extraordinary," Grandyn said, as they started walking again. Although he kept thinking about the urgency of the war, something about the City soothed him, as if his stress and worry had been sent on vacation.

"Home," Fye said.

"It does make an impression," Cogs added.

Grandyn couldn't stop looking at the beautiful waterfall.

"It's called a rain vortex," Fye told him.

"How can this be open to the sky and not be seen from the air?" he asked.

"It's done with mirrors and all kinds of projection technology that I don't understand," Fye said. "Like the stone wall we walked through."

"How do they do it, Cogs?" Grandyn asked.

"Well, I do understand it, but I have no idea how to explain it."

Grandyn didn't press. It was a minor detail when compared with how Cogs had lived to be one hundred seventy-three.

Grandyn noticed dozens of other old people wandering the trails or sitting by the pool. "Are all List Keepers old?" he asked.

"Most of the young ones man the outposts or work outside," Fye said. "But, yes. The majority are over one hundred."

"A couple thousand Munnas?"

"Something like that," Fye said.

"I can't believe this place exists," Grandyn said, "and that all these old people have been here this entire time, that they survived the Banoff, and who knows what else before that."

"I fought in World War II," Cogs said. "Ever hear of it?"

"Sure," Grandyn said, proud of his knowledge of history. "Europe or the Pacific?"

"Europe," Cogs answered.

"Was Hitler or the AOI Chief worse?"

"Would you rather die by drowning or by getting shot? Burn to death or be decapitated?" Cogs asked. "You can't compare evil. Evil is evil, whether it kills a thousand, a million, or a billion. Evil is the illness that has prevented humanity from reaching its true potential."

Grandyn nodded. No one spoke for a few minutes as they made their way along the edge of the Great Hall. They passed several people on their trail. They smiled as if it weren't unusual to have a stranger in their midst. A few of them stopped and waved to Fye like old friends, but no one slowed their progress.

"Where are we going?" Grandyn asked.

"Someone wants to meet you," Cogs said.

"Who?"

"I'll let him introduce himself."

Grandyn hoped it would be whoever was in charge. He intended to demand the List Keepers use whatever resources they had to help PAWN end the war, and judging by what he had already seen, they had considerable resources.

"What powers all this?" he asked.

"The trees," Cogs said.

"These power this whole place?" Grandyn asked, pointing to the trees in the Great Hall.

"No, not these," Cogs said. "We use the trees out there. Ever wonder why the Field and other transmissions are blocked in wilderness areas? It's because the List Keepers use an organic energy source to power the City, the outposts, and all the monitoring we do."

"How?"

"Trees put off an energy that we harness for a clean, silent, and limitless power supply, which requires only mental collectors. But once the source is tapped, it blocks all unnatural waves, which includes the spectrum used by the Field, weapons systems, communications, etc. Sort of a nice byproduct, would you not agree?"

"Yes," Grandyn said enthusiastically, recalling how many times he'd escaped because the AOI couldn't use their sophisticated weapons or even communicate while in the forests. He was about to ask what mental collectors were when they left the Great Hall and entered a corridor, which once again took his breath.

The floor beneath was solid and dry, but it seemed as if they were walking on top of water, a tiny river, deep and rushing. Grandyn stumbled, and actually walked into one of the smooth white walls.

"Don't look down," Fye said as she helped him steady himself.

Instead, Grandyn focused on the rounded walls and curved ceiling. They were a soft white, with occasional circles of various-sized colored glass projecting out. Light came in from all of them, making the bright white hall extremely colorful, and the river gave off the pleasant sound of rushing water. By the time they reached the next room, Grandyn thought he was prepared to be dazzled.

He wasn't. Even if he had tried with all his imagination and the sum of his dreams to create a vision of what he now saw before him, he could never have even conjured a whisper of it.

CHAPTER SEVENTY-ONE

Sidis was not likable, even as Imps went. With his constantly superior attitude and blatant arrogance, Miner outright hated him. But when Sidis spoke of the end of the war, Chelle, Deuce, and even Miner were captivated. Blaze and Sarlo had suspected some of what he told them prior to hearing it, but they, too, were astounded by the sheer certainty of his words.

"The war is already won," Sidis began, "and while we all have contributed to this victory, it is the AOI that will deliver it."

"The AOI? But the Chief is fighting against you. Against us all," Miner said.

"Ah, you could so benefit from an implant," Sidis said. "Even though I fear there would be gaps. Let us not bother with the details of how the conflict ends. It should be enough for you to know that it will . . . in less than two days. And there will be survivors . . . enough so that the human race will continue. You might also like to know that this really is the final war, at least as far into the future as the computers can see . . . and that is quite far." His hologram changed colors, as if he had passed through a rainbow, although he hadn't moved. "The promise we have had since our small beginnings is ready to burst forward."

Deuce, attending the meeting holographically like the others, happened to glance across the main room on the Moon Shadow where Munna was sitting quietly, staring out to sea. Her lips were moving, but she was not talking. It took a minute to realize it but Munna was mouthing the words Sidis was saying at the exact moment he was saying them.

Deuce muted his image for a moment and asked, "Munna, are you making Sidis say these things?"

She smiled, and Deuce saw that Sidis had paused and was also smiling. Then her lips began moving and he started talking again. At the same time, she spoke to Deuce, but her lips continued moving in synch with Sidis'. The words directed at Deuce appeared to be dubbed, like in one of those old, translated, "foreign" movies in the pre-Banoff days when there was more than one language.

"I am not making Sidis speak," Munna said. "But I know what he's saying. I know this because he is speaking a great truth, a long buried secret of our people. Somewhere deep in the City, at this precise moment, someone is saying the exact same words to Grandyn, because we made it." She smiled, and so did Sidis, before they both resumed. She returned to silence, and he to a meeting of the most powerful people in the world.

After Sidis finished explaining all the wonderful things that would happen post-war, he offered more sobering news.

"Not everyone in attendance here will live to see the marvelous times ahead. The great computing machines can see the end of the war and what lies beyond, and predict with such pointed probabilities that the great *Justar Journal,* which you all so desperately sought, is now relegated to a relic, or at least made redundant. However, all these insights and miraculous things to come belie the fact that the most brutal war in human history is still underway. I repeat: it *will* be won, but the price will be painfully high."

Deuce looked back at Munna. She was crying now.

"Who will die?" Miner asked.

"In a very real way, all of humanity dies," Sidis said. "So don't worry yourself with the details, rich man. You won't like the outcome either way."

Sarlo placed her hand lightly on Miner's. She knew he was about to blow up at the new alliance. He took a deep breath and scowled, telling himself that at least the horrible war would be over in a couple of days, and that he could then deal with Sidis without consequences. In spite of the astounding things Sidis had told them about the post-war world, he still believed he'd be able to operate in the traditional manner.

It would be a rude awakening.

Drast oversaw the taking of eight more Keys by the Allies, and then regular AOI headquarters began to fall. After the meeting, Chelle was able to get in touch with Drast, and told him all that Sidis had said.

"Well, he's right about the AOI winning the war," Drast said. "My Allies are the real AOI, and we're taking the power away from the wolves."

"He described that to us," Chelle said, still awestruck by all that Sidis had predicted.

"The rest of what he said sounds farfetched," Drast continued. "But if he's gotten everything else right, then maybe . . ."

"The Chief doesn't know how many headquarters you've taken yet?"

"No. They're falling like dominoes," Drast replied. "She'll know soon."

"And she'll attack."

"That will be her mistake, but it's all she knows how to do. That's why the war has been so catastrophic. She actually believed that if she came out hard and fast and attacked every possible threat with overpowering force, she could end the war in twenty-four to forty-eight hours."

"Her miscalculations almost wiped us out."

"I'm counting on one more mistake. When she attacks us, it will be a signal to all the other sleeping Allies within the AOI, and even to the wolves who have had enough of the Chief's brutality. A civil war within the AOI will end with me in charge."

"I hope so," Chelle said.

"Nothing to worry about. Even the Imps have preordained it. Why don't you come to Seattle and we'll command together, as we always dreamed."

"I can't leave PAWN Command yet. Can you come here?"

"As soon as I am able," Drast promised.

The Imps provided constant intelligence, and Deuce wreaked havoc on the AOI operations from space. Even with the agency's vast superiority in well-armed soldiers, weapons, and geographic dominance, the AOI was stretched thin in the face of such overwhelming, unified opposition. The Trapciers' hierarchy continued to stay on the move, never remaining in the same place for more than a few hours. The Chief was hunting them as if victory relied on their destruction.

Drast's AOI Allies fought invisibly, taking over more AOI wolf facilities and sabotaging hundreds of wolf missions. Still, thousands of new battles erupted across the globe as the Chief fought bitterly to destroy the Aylantik's many enemies. Enforcers and PAWN suffered heavy casualties throughout the day, losing more than half their numbers. The BLAXERs and Trapciers were luckier, but still lost nearly a third of their fighters. By the next morning, Deuce thought that Sidis might have gotten it wrong, but then the Chief discovered the insurgents within her ranks and attacked the AOI Allies.

CHAPTER SEVENTY-TWO

Grandyn stood transfixed as a giant series of colored globes, ranging in size from six to nine meters in diameter, put on a light show that left him feeling that he'd discovered an underground factory where rainbows were manufactured. The magnificent orbs glowed turquoise, golden yellow, and a vibrant purple, and slowly rotated in a way that made them appear to be floating.

Maybe they really are floating, he thought as he watched them spin. The room was silent except for a faint melodic tone that made him want to cry.

"What is this thing?" he asked Fye as Cogs disappeared into the shimmering glow.

"Do you feel nostalgic?" she asked.

"Painfully so," he confirmed.

"That's because it's our history." Fye looked into the yellow light as if searching for something. "You can see it all. Everything that's ever happened."

"How is that possible?" he asked, more fascinated than skeptical.

"We're the List Keepers," she said proudly. "We record each moment."

"Have the List Keepers been around forever?"

"No," she admitted. "But we were able to go back."

"How?" he asked while his mind swirled with the combination of feeling so much history and the confluence of the lights.

"Someone else will have to explain that to you."

"I thought you were going to answer all my questions."

"Other people are better qualified to give you some explanations, but don't worry. You'll get them."

For the first time, he noticed the walls. It looked as if the globes and their lights had eroded the space around them. He imagined them shifting and shaping over a millennium, the same way wind, sand, and water carved slot canyons in the Arizona Area. They were smooth, and might have once been white, but were now smeared with pastel shades of the same colors as the lights. With no pattern, and at varying heights, the holes appeared in the walls as if caressed and molded by a mystical potter. Light escaped into the openings like water pouring into a drain.

"Where does the light go?" he asked.

"Chambers," she answered casually. "To places where people can't go. Tunnels and chambers made by the light. No one really knows, but some of it comes out in the staircase where we were."

"This place is magic," Grandyn said, his voice filled with awe, his eyes dazzled.

"Yes," she replied, smiling.

"But magic isn't real," he said, as if distracted.

"Are you kidding?" she asked. "Magic is the only thing that *is* real. How else do you explain a star? Or a blue planet flying through the vastness of space? Or a heartbeat? How do you explain love?"

He nodded. Even if he wanted to debate the premise, in his current surroundings, he had no plausible argument. "What powers it all?"

"The trees, remember?"

"But where is all the history stored?"

"That's our next stop."

He looked around, wondering where they would go, and realized that he hadn't seen Cogs.

"Where is Cogs?" he asked.

"Playing," Fye replied.

"Playing?"

"He plays in the light. He's lived a long time. So he likes to go back for visits."

"Time travel?" he asked skeptically.

"No, not really time travel. More like feeling the energy. The energy is always there. It connects with his conscious mind, and it's like being back there. It can be addictive."

"Sounds depressing. Like you can look but you can't touch."

"Actually, it's wonderful really." She looked at him lovingly. "You can go back and feel your parents. It will be just like it was. You can experience that. Would you want to?"

"You mean now?"

She nodded.

Grandyn thought for a moment. He wasn't sure. The idea that he could feel all the goodness there had once been and then having to endure losing it again sounded too painful.

"Maybe another time."

"I understand."

Cogs suddenly emerged, smiling. Grandyn wasn't sure if he was imagining it, but it seemed as if Cogs looked younger. "What do you think so far?" Cogs asked.

"I think I'm dreaming," Grandyn replied.

Cogs laughed. "Aren't we?"

Fye urged him on through the cavern. As they walked into the light, Grandyn noticed it changed temperature depending on the color. Yellow was much warmer than turquoise.

"I still don't understand why it takes all the trees on the planet to power this place," Grandyn said to Cogs.

"We intercept, track, and store every piece of data of every occurrence of the most minute event. *Every* event. Can you imagine the energy that that requires?"

"Okay, but why? What do you do with it? Why do you allow the world outside to burn? To destroy itself?"

"Ah, the great debate," Cogs said, rubbing his hands together. He stopped as they came to the entrance of the next room. "There are those older List Keepers who believe we should remain neutral and impartial, but many of the younger ones want us more involved."

"Who's winning?"

"We do a little of each, but I suppose the younger ones have pushed us toward being more active." Cogs looked at Fye and smiled. "Still, there is only so much we can do."

"As the List Keepers intercept data," Fye began, "we can delay or divert it for a millisecond, sometimes a fraction longer. In that way we can change the outcomes of certain events. But it's a tedious task to change the world, and it takes a grand vision. We can't just meddle without understanding the ramifications."

"And think of the current war," Cogs interjected. "That is too short a situation for us to deal with now. We would have had to have started decades ago, even a hundred years back, in order to hope to change the outcome of the war."

"Did you?"

Fye looked at Cogs. He nodded.

"Then why did it happen?" Grandyn asked, his anger showing.

"Because in order to have prevented the war altogether, we would have had to start making changes a thousand years ago, maybe more," Cogs said.

"If we hadn't done anything at all . . ." Fye said.

"What?"

"We'd already be extinct."

CHAPTER SEVENTY-THREE

Sunday July 17

Drast had moved almost all his personnel and captured AOI assets in the night, so that the Chief was shooting at empty targets. The wolves were fighting too many fronts, and they had also suffered substantial losses and had taken serious beatings overnight. The Allies managed to defeat the battered AOI, and slaughtered their former brethren in one siege after another.

By the middle of the day, Drast was able to fly to PAWN Command for his long-imagined reunion with Chelle. Osc stayed behind to oversee the final stage of the takeover by the Drast's AOI Allies. The Chief was hunkered down in her Washington bunker. By nightfall, they would bomb it into oblivion, if their inside agents couldn't kill her before then.

For several minutes Drast and Chelle remained locked in an embrace, neither quite believing the other was actually in their arms. They breathed in each other's essence intensely, as if they'd been drowning for years and had finally found oxygen again.

"For a thousand days and nights, I have thought of this moment," Drast said. "Without the possibility of it, I would have ceased to be and died in that prison."

She kissed him with the pent up fervor of a woman who'd lost too much. Too many loves buried, too much time wasted with fear and regret, and all the desperate moments layered in angst and buried in terror. She recalled the years of their youth when, as idealistic revolutionaries, they talked of changing the world. None of the shocking scenes she'd witnessed during the war had ever been imagined then, and certainly not the incomprehensible loss of life.

"We believed we could make the world a better place just by uncovering the truth, reinstating real freedom," she said. "Do you remember?"

"Of course, I do," he said between breathless kisses. "But it was so much more complicated than we knew . . . Damn it. Damn the Aylantik!"

"But we've done it, we've changed so much more than we ever dreamed. If Sidis is right, then we have ushered in destiny. Everything will be beyond different. It's–it's impossible to picture. Can you see it, Polis?"

"What?"

"The future. Can you imagine the change if Sidis is right?" She stared into his eyes. "What is to become of us? What is to become . . . of everything?"

They didn't hear the high altitude bomber. They didn't see the three Sonic-bombs whizzing toward PAWN Command. They didn't feel the force of the explosion. They knew only their love and that they were together, at long last, together.

They died in an instant.

Thousands of kilometers away from the ruined PAWN Command, Munna, sitting quietly on the deck of the Moon Shadow, shuddered, as if chilled. Tears formed in her eyes, but not full enough to fall. "Oh," she said softly to herself. "They're gone."

A top Enforcers leader reported the find. A large cache of AOI Sonic-bombs had been captured in the California Area. Miner knew just what to do with them, but he couldn't let Sarlo know. She would never approve.

He looked across the office. She was working a series of AirViews, trying to locate confiscated PharmaForce assets.

The war had indeed turned, and he could see peace again on the horizon. There was much to do to prepare. The world would be different, and he was determined to decide how different. Miner flipped his sliver dollar and smiled at his good fortune.

Less than half an hour before Enforcers stumbled upon the Sonic-bombs, he'd received word from a special unit he had tracking the Imps. They'd narrowed the Trapciers' leadership location to the Phoenix-Prescott section of the Arizona Area. They had once been two separate cities, but in the past seventy-five years they'd grown into one large metropolis of more than twelve million people. And somewhere in that tangle of humanity were what he considered the greatest threat to the future of the human race; the Imps.

There might not be another chance. The Imps were always moving. *And anyway,* he thought, *the strike will get blamed on the AOI. No one will ever know.*

He opened a private screen and issued the order. Thirty-one minutes later, more than twelve million people would be dead, including the twenty-seven most powerful Imps and CHRUDEs.

"I wonder if your damned machines predicted that, you torgon vampires," Miner said quietly when he saw the live images of the flattening of the largest city in the Arizona Area. "Did you see that one coming, Sidis? You arrogant torg?" He smiled when he thought about the outrage people would feel toward the Chief.

Just one more city destroyed. *Peace prevails, always.*

CHAPTER SEVENTY-FOUR

Deuce got word about Chelle and Drast less than an hour after it happened. His people had picked it up on satellite coverage. BLAXERs arrived soon after, but no one expected to find anything.

And they didn't. The destruction was total. There was nothing left. But at least he could tell Osc that they'd tried. He was preparing for the awful task of informing Osc that his mother was dead when Miner zoomed.

"We're mopping up," Miner said. "Those Imps might have been right, at least about the war."

"PAWN Command just got obliterated," Deuce said.

"Wow . . . I guess the Dragon Lady has some fight left in her."

"Chelle Andreas and Polis Drast were both killed in the bombing," Deuce said. He knew Drast was there only because it had been one of his Flo-wings that had taken him there. The AOI "birds" were all in combat.

"Drast finally got his, and Chelle Andreas was nothing but trouble," Miner said. "Good news, really."

"How do you sleep? How do you even look at yourself in the mirror?"

Miner thought of his nightmares and realized that he'd never slept well. "I'm a handsome man," he said. "I never mind looking in the mirror."

"Are we done here?" Deuce asked, weary of everything about Miner.

"The Chief is going to have to die," Miner said. "She's just proven that as long as she's inside that bunker, she is a threat."

"Of course she will, but you have a vested interest," Deuce said.

"I have a hundred reasons to kill that creature, but none of them matters more than the fact that she annihilated hundreds of millions of innocents."

"With *your* drugs," Deuce said.

"And you? Are you to be judged for providing the weapons and technology that allowed the AOI to carry out their atrocities?"

"It's not the same," Deuce said. "My products were misused. Yours were used exactly as directed. Yours were meant for one purpose - extermination."

"That's a lie. They were intended to control. Killing was a last resort. That decision was not made by me."

"You made that decision as soon as you manufactured the pharmaceuticals."

"This conversation is about the Chief."

"You are forever linked with her, Lance. What do you think is going to happen when the one and a half billion survivors of this final war learn the cause of the new plague that wiped out nearly half the population? Is their blame, their vengeance, going to end with the Chief? Do you think that is a reasonable expectation for this kind of grief?"

"I'll decide what they know."

"Will you?" Deuce asked. "Didn't you hear what else Sidis predicted?"

"He doesn't know—"

"What about Munna? And the List Keepers? The world you created is over."

"We'll see about that."

"Lance, do you believe in karma?"

"No."

"I didn't think so," Deuce said. "Well, you will soon."

CHAPTER SEVENTY-FIVE

As Grandyn, Fye, and Cogs were entering the next room, they found an old woman was waiting for them. She hugged Fye, whispered something in her ear, and then left.

Fye looked at Grandyn and he knew something was wrong. "What?"

"PAWN Command was hit. No survivors."

"Chelle?"

"We've confirmed that she and Polis Drast were there at impact. They didn't make it."

Grandyn shook his head and thought of Nelson. "When?"

"That's hard to say," Fye said. "Time's a funny thing."

"Meaning?"

"Down here, in and among the time-maps, memories and history glows. It feels a little different." She looked at Cogs for help.

"You probably still feel like it's Saturday," Cogs said to Grandyn.

"Yeah."

"I believe it's actually Sunday now," Cogs said, looking to Fye for verification.

"It is Sunday," Fye confirmed. "Chelle and Drast died on Sunday."

Grandyn looked confused. "If it's Sunday, what happened to Saturday night? Why didn't we sleep?"

"You need less sleep in the City," Cogs explained, as if that should be obvious.

"I thought we didn't need to worry about the war," Grandyn said to Fye.

"We can do only so much," Fye replied. "But everything changed once we got here. A kind of destiny lock was initiated. You'll understand soon."

Grandyn trusted her, but he wished he could have done something to save Chelle and Drast. What was the point of making it to the List Keepers' City if they couldn't help PAWN and end the war?

He looked around the room. It was far less exciting than the last one with the large colored globes, but it had its own mystery. The tall, cylindrical shape offered a strange perspective, as if it were almost daylight where they were, but twenty meters above them it seemed nearly completely black except for a handful of "stars." The "night sky" added to his bewilderment about time. Nine tunnels led from the room.

"Which one?" Grandyn asked, wanting to move on. He was determined to talk to whoever was in charge about ending the war. He'd heard Cogs and Fye mention being able only to make infinitesimal changes, but surely, with all this power, technology, or whatever it was, he believed they could do something.

"We're not going into any of them," Fye said. "We're going down." She pointed to an opening in the center of the narrow room.

Grandyn strode over to it.

"Careful," she said, stopping him from looking into the hole just as a clear tube emerged from the depths. It appeared to be some sort of glass elevator framed in a matte black metal.

"Shall we?" she said, ushering him inside as the doors parted.

"Where's it go?" he asked.

"To where you want to go. You'll get to talk to the person who knows the most about all this."

"What about Cogs?" he asked as their descent began without the old man.

"You'll see him again."

The elevator moved more slowly than those he was used to in modern buildings. As soon as they had dropped a few meters, all light disappeared, leaving them in a dim blue hue. Although the ride was a bit claustrophobic, fresh air filtered in from somewhere. After a minute that felt like ten, he asked, "How long does it take?"

"It's been a while since I've been here, but I think it's about two minutes."

"How deep do we go?"

"I don't know . . . deep."

The doors opened to yet another world, a glowing purple one. He walked unsteadily from the tube and gazed at a seemingly endless tunnel filled on either side with large towers about twice his height. Like everything else he'd seen in the City, they were curved. They looked to be made of glass and light, but as he got closer he realized that each tower contained thousands of INUs.

"Is this the storage?" Grandyn asked.

"Yes," she replied.

He stared down into the open center aisle and into a bright, far-off light. Now he was almost convinced this was all a dream. Either that, or he had died.

"Walk into the light," he whispered.

Fye laughed, knowing what he must be thinking. "How could I have ever described the City to you?"

"Never in a million years would I have believed this place existed."

She nodded, vindicated in her silence.

"Are they down there?" he asked, pointing to the light. "Whoever's in charge?"

"Yes," she answered, smiling. "Let's go meet the future."

CHAPTER SEVENTY-SIX

Deep inside the Washington AOI bunker, the Chief celebrated the strike against PAWN Command as a major victory.

"Next we'll cut off the Trapciers, and then on to that traitor, Lance Miner."

Recent intelligence had narrowed the location of the Imps leadership to the Arizona Area, and showed that Miner must be in either the northern New York Area, or the adjacent part of what used to be Canada. With the lack of full satellite coverage, and the complete destruction, it would be fifteen minutes before the Phoenix-Prescott massacre reached the AOI.

"We'll have them located within the hour, ma'am," a general told her.

"And then we'll track down that swine Deuce Lipton and finish this unpleasantness," the Chief said. She was already planning a major pushback against Drast's AOI Allies. Now that he was dead, she believed her internal opposition would crumble.

The Chief excused herself and walked into her private restroom. Two AOI Allies were waiting for her.

Because no weapons were allowed on that level, the two men had to overpower her, which they easily did, in less than five seconds. It took another twenty seconds to strangle her with a belt. Three more seconds to tidy up and arrange the Chief as if she'd had a stroke and fallen off the toilet, and in less than thirty seconds, the world was rid of the most lethal creature that had ever walked the earth.

Now they hoped that the rest of the plan could be implemented before her closest aides realized her death had not been natural. In the end, the bunker would still fall, it was only a matter of how many would die in taking it. The outside monitoring equipment was jammed, thanks to technology controlled by Deuce. Within minutes, Flo-wings landed, depositing a force of more than one thousand elite BLAXERs. The rebel loyalists inside the bunker did their best to coordinate with the outside invaders, but the bunker was heavily defended, and there were only a few dozen Allies inside. The battle raged for hours, but it was enough to change the fate of millions who otherwise would have been bombed.

During the battle for the bunker, AOI command and control were essentially shut down. No new missions were scheduled, and troops and equipment were left to fend for themselves around the world. Enforcers, Trapcier's android armies, and BLAXERS moved in and scored almost continuous defeats against the AOI wolves. At the same time, the AOI Allies, led by Osc, seized what was left of AOI wolf operations worldwide.

By the time the sun set in Seattle, there was no doubt the rebels had won. It would be another two days before the bunker fell, and all AOI assets around the globe were in rebel hands, but they had won.

There were no celebrations. Osc ranted bitterly at how close his mother and Drast had come to seeing their dream fulfilled.

"They knew," Deuce had told him. "They knew the AOI was finished."

But Osc didn't think that was good enough. The Chief had still been alive. She had killed them, the same as if she'd personally twisted a knife in their guts. He pictured the cruel old woman licking their blood from her sharp blade. Deuce also asked Osc to stay and lead the AOI during the transition.

"The transition to what?" Osc asked.

"To a world where they are never needed again. Where weapons and cameras aren't used against people, where secrets and lies don't exist . . . a world unlike anything we've ever known before."

Osc didn't know if it was possible, but he agreed to help because he knew his mother and Drast would want him to, and because his old world was destroyed. So if he were going to keep on living, a new world would have to be created.

As soon as Lance received the news that the Chief was dead, he called an emergency meeting of the surviving Council members. They would gather in New York City in order to pool resources and consolidate power against Deuce. Enforcers were working on liberating PharmaForce assets from AOI control. It was dark when the Flo-wing arrived to take him to the Council meeting. Sarlo would stay in Toronto until they moved their operations to one of PharmaForce's larger campuses.

"I'll zoom you as soon as the meeting is over," he said as they exchanged farewells on the roof.

In an uncharacteristic move, Sarlo hugged him. They had been through so much that it seemed natural. Afterwards, he stood and looked at her. No one in the world was closer to him, not even his wife or children.

"We'll see each other tomorrow afternoon," he said. "Lots to do . . . a fortune to make." He smiled. "It'll be us or Deuce running things from now on. I plan on making sure it's us."

Sarlo nodded and waved as he boarded the Flo-wing. She watched him take off from the roof and fly high over the lake, beautiful in its reflection of the city's skyline. A moment later, she saw a dark figure plunge from the Flo-wing and drop into the cold water of Lake Ontario, and she knew Lance Miner was dead.

Two silent tears fell from her eyes before she turned and went back into the building. There was "lots to do," especially with all the members of the Council not expected to live through the night.

There could have been years of war crimes trials, but that would have delayed the changes and the healing. It was better to have things handled this way, in the closing hours of the war.

"A fresh start," Blaze had told Sarlo. "This time truly a fresh start."

Sarlo went immediately back to work. The war might be ending, but the real killer was still efficiently wiping out entire cities and towns. The new plague still had to be stopped.

CHAPTER SEVENTY-SEVEN

Monday, July 18

Grandyn and Fye had been walking for twenty minutes and still weren't near the end of the purple corridor. Grandyn could feel the energy from the towers. It penetrated his body, made it difficult to walk. It was as if he were passing through collected events of the world all at once. He felt the severity of the war, the loss of millions of lives, tragedies of immeasurable proportions . . . except they *were* being measured. The List Keepers had it all.

"How long is this place?" Grandyn asked.

"Long enough that it's Monday now," Fye said.

Grandyn laughed, assuming she was joking. She wasn't.

Soon, the light had grown so bright that Grandyn had to walk with his hands in front of his eyes until Fye reached into a concealed cabinet in one of the towers and produced two pairs of dark, mirrored glasses.

"It's not too much farther," she said.

"This place is incredible," he said, realizing he was shouting. Until that moment he hadn't been aware of it, but a white noise that sounded almost like crashing waves had been getting louder. Finally, some inestimable time later, they walked through the last of it; light so bright he could no longer see the towers, or anything else. The noise had also become so loud that he couldn't even hear the sound of his own voice. He held on to Fye as she led him through the light.

Then, suddenly, it all stopped. They were in a darkened room. The silence absolute.

As Grandyn adjusted to the dramatic shift in his senses, he became aware of an old, black man surrounded by at least fifteen AirViews. The man looked up and smiled.

"Ah, Runit's son," the man said, standing, pushing his hands together as if in prayer, and bowing slightly. "I'm so happy to finally meet you. I'm Booker Lipton."

Grandyn looked over at Fye, and then back to the old man. "But . . . but you're dead," he stammered.

"No, not really. Not yet," he said, smiling broadly, as if he might laugh. "There were reports of my death, but they were greatly . . . Anyway, they never found my body."

"You faked your death?" Grandyn asked.

"You might say that. I never died, just disappeared. There really wasn't a choice, you know. The AOI wanted me dead." He looked sad for a moment. "And it was the only way to hope to beat the prophecies."

"How old are you?"

"One hundred and twenty-eight."

"Younger than Munna."

"Much." He smiled. "Don't believe her about only being one hundred and thirty-something. I'm sure she's closer to one hundred and fifty."

"How have you lived so long?"

"We discovered the secrets," Booker said.

"We?"

"There was a group of us in the beginning. Fye's grandparents, Rip and Gale, then there was Spencer Copeland, Nate Ryder, and Linh, leaders of the Inner Movement, and some others."

Grandyn looked back at Fye. "Your grandparents?"

"They were the ones who uncovered the Eysen, the real one, that they based the INUs on."

"This one," Booker said, pointing to an INU almost as big as a basketball glowing on a stand on the other side of the spacious room.

"That's a huge INU," Grandyn said.

"Yes, we've managed to keep shrinking them. Of course, the ones people buy are toys compared to this creation," Booker said with a far-away smile. "The original Eysen has taught us things, unfathomable concepts, abilities, lessons that even today, after all the decades, I still can't fully grasp."

"Where did it come from?"

Booker shook his head. Grandyn wasn't sure if Booker didn't know, or didn't want to say.

"My grandparents found it in a cliff in Virginia," Fye said. "He was an archaeologist. It all began with his Cosega theory—"

"Are your grandparents still alive?" Grandyn asked, over-whelmed with questions.

"No. They decided not to stay."

"Stay?"

"When you can live forever," Booker began, "sometimes forever is too long."

"You can live forever?" Grandyn asked, astonished.

"We don't know for sure, but it seems possible, or at least as long as anyone would want to."

Grandyn was silent for a moment. It was all so unbelievable. "You're talking about immortality?"

"We're talking about so much more than that," Booker said. "But yes, it is possible for humans to rejuvenate their bodies. Contrary to what Darwin might have you believe, we are not just another animal in the food chain. Humans are special. We are truly masters of the universe. The things we can do are in the realm of star creation. Are you impressed with human accomplishment? Helicopters and Flo-wings, automobiles and LEVs, Apollo rockets and starships, one small step . . . and Mars bases? It is nothing. It is all babies drooling in a crib compared to what is possible. We know because we've seen it in the Eysen."

The AirViews all around were showing images to match his words. He looked deeply into Grandyn's eyes and said with exhilaration in his voice, "And because we've started doing it, most of the List Keepers are between one hundred and two hundred years old, amazingly energetic, *and* in perfect health. Look at this place." He motioned around them. "Do you think we've built all this with *basic* knowledge? We record every second of existence. The tower hall you came through? There are hundreds more halls just like them. We have infinite power from the trees. We can, and will, teach whoever survives this Armageddon how to live for centuries, how to do so many remarkable things."

Booker sat and glanced at the AirViews showing the modern world.

"The promise of the human race has been squandered up until now. Wasted in a contest for so-called riches!"

Grandyn wanted to hear everything, but he couldn't help thinking about his mission; destroy the AOI, stop the war. All those people out there dying.

"You figured out how to beat death, but you couldn't prevent this war?" he asked.

"As you see, we have no army. No weapons in the conventional sense anyway."

"Then why are you here?"

"Good question. I formed the List Keepers before the Banoff," Booker said. His jovial expression suddenly crashing as if he might cry. His wrinkles deepened, and for a split second, he seemed to be choking on sadness. "The names of the dead, we have them all. I wanted to read each of them, but there are *billions*!" His voice came out in a shouted whisper. "Billions," he repeated more quietly.

He paused and walked to a screen which showed the outside world. A camera must be mounted up there in the woods some-where, because Grandyn recognized it as a live view of the ridge-line they'd seen on their way to the City.

"You knew about the Banoff before it happened?" Grandyn asked, knowing the answer.

"Yes. I'd seen Clastier's prophecies that predicted the Banoff. We had not uncovered the *Justar Journal*, but Clastier's papers contained more than enough information. In the beginning, I thought the List Keepers, by knowing about the Banoff in advance, could stop it. But we didn't understand enough then, and we ended up making it much worse . . . many more died than anyone expected."

"What happened?"

"Not now," Fye said, touching Grandyn's arm.

"We made mistakes," Booker continued. "I'd spent my life searching for artifacts that had been lost to humanity, things I believed could help us change the world. Really radically change it. A way to the truth of who we are and why we exist. I discovered dozens of sacred objects and hidden texts. Many of which were very important, and yet you've never heard of them. Items like the Jadeo, the signs, the original Eysen – and others that you do know about, Clastier's papers and the *Justar Journal*. They were all pieces of a great puzzle . . . You see, I thought being armed with incred-ible knowledge from the past and hints of the future meant we could not only change the world and correct our course, but we could actually create what we wanted. Make the future of our dreams. But it is far more complex than that."

"But you had so much money already."

"I don't mean a materialistic future. I mean a deep, meaningful future, different from anything we have ever attempted in the modern world. A true utopia where money doesn't even exist."

"How do you get there?" Grandyn asked.

"After our failure at stopping the Banoff, we went underground. We built the City and created new plans. Separate from the List Keepers, I backed the founders of PAWN and the Tree-Runners, because we could see all of this coming. The Doneharvest, and what we call the New Plague and the Final War."

"And the books? You saw my father?" Grandyn asked.

"I saw Runit."

"What happened to him?"

"We actually did get him more time, precious days with you. He was supposed to die that night when the AOI was going door-to-door, before the books were removed, and again the day they burned the remaining books in the library. And finally, that awful morning of the raid when he did nearly breathe his last."

"So he really is alive?"

"He survived that day. And spent years in an AOI detention facility."

"Where? Where is he?"

"We are not certain."

"Wait, with all of this, you can't tell me where my father is? If he is okay?"

"We are still processing all the information and with hundreds of millions of deaths in so short a time, we aren't there yet. He somehow managed to get free several days ago, but we learned of it only this morning."

"So he's out there? I have to go find him."

"We have people looking. But I have a feeling he will find you first. Your father is a great man. Runit gave us the final hope. He saved the books, and in those books was hidden the last known artifact I didn't possess . . . the *Justar Journal*. And he gave us his son. He made you into a man that could solve the *Journal* and fight for the truth."

"And even with all that, you couldn't prevent this nightmare?" Grandyn said, motioning up as if to mean the horrendous events occurring in the world above.

"We didn't have enough warning," Booker said sadly.

"You had seventy-five years!"

"We've been working constantly. We're exhausted. We've done everything imaginable, and even things that aren't possible . . ." Booker took a deep breath. "This time, it earned the name the Final War because it was to be the last war. Not because everyone would love each other afterwards, but because there wouldn't *be* an afterwards."

CHAPTER SEVENTY-EIGHT

Grandyn stared at Booker, trying to find some point of reality to grab onto.

"What about your grandson?"

"Deuce doesn't know I'm alive. It was too risky."

"Does Munna?"

"Yes, Munna was one of my employees before the Banoff. She headed up the work we did with Spencer Copeland and others on the power of the mind." Booker, realized he couldn't explain everything at once, and got back to Grandyn's question. "Munna had to stop Deuce from using the prophecies for war. We made that mistake during the Banoff. No matter what he thought, it would not have worked."

"Fye says you have all the information. That you know everything."

Booker nodded, smiling.

"Will you tell me? Will you teach me?" Grandyn asked.

Booker laughed. "Well, that may take a long time, but time we have. You see, time is a funny thing."

"But, if you know everything, why can't you make it all work out?"

"We may *know* everything but it is very different to *understand* everything."

"Why was the *Justar Journal* so important when it didn't stop the war?"

"Because even after studying the Eysen for all these years, there is so much we still don't know about it. But we do know that the *Justar Journal* is the transcription of another Eysen."

"How is that possible?"

"Everything is possible," Booker said. "Never doubt that. It's just a matter of finding the way."

"Like how you did all this?" Grandyn asked, still trying to understand the point, trying to find a way to stop the horrors going on above them. "I guess what the List Keepers do is to make the impossible possible."

"This is painstaking, excruciatingly monotonous work," Booker said. "So much of what has happened in the past has been erased. Did you know there were major demonstrations and riots in the early years of Aylantik rule? People were against the restrictions on bearing rights and the redistribution of lands, the elimination of cash, conversion to a single language, banning religions . . . People fought all those things, but the AOI clamped down and eliminated the dissenters. Then all those events were erased from the 'public' record, but the List Keepers have it all. One thing to remember is that you can never trust history – not even if you were there."

"It's important for the future," Fye said, "so that we know where we came from. So that we can learn from all that came before."

"Future?" Grandyn asked, as if that might be too optimistic a word.

"The war is over," Booker said, looking at an AirView behind them. "The Aylantik has been toppled and the AOI crushed."

"What?" Grandyn asked disbelievingly.

"It's over?" Fye asked. "We did it?"

"We did it," Booker confirmed. "Humanity has survived."

Booker closed his eyes and fell back into his chair. For almost an entire century he had been fighting to save the species from itself. Bit by bit, breath by breath, and somehow they had done it.

"What do we do now?" she asked, crying. "With so few people left, a nasty flu epidemic could still finish us off."

"Possibly, if we were operating under the old ways," Booker said. "But this is a new day. We'll show the world the secrets of the List Keepers. This is our best chance ever to finally achieve a true utopian society."

"What makes this time any different?" Grandyn asked, still stunned.

"Don't you see? We've tried everything else and it never worked. A planet like this should not have so much misery and despair. We *can* do it differently this time."

"But how?"

"That's up to you Grandyn, and to a new generation of leaders," Booker said.

"*Me?*"

"You and Twain, Fye, and a few others . . . that's why you had to get here. It's your role to continue to decipher the *Justar Journal*."

"But Munna won't—"

"Munna *couldn't* allow you, or anyone, to see the full view of the *Journal* once she saw that it showed how important you were."

"Why am I so important?" Grandyn asked.

"Everyone is important, most just never realize it."

"But if the *Justar Journal* could show that—"

"Remember that the *Journal* changes. After you decoded it, Munna continued to monitor it, and many times it showed your death. You had to get here safely. And, as predicted, the war ended. The closer you got to the City, the closer the war came to ending."

"But Munna could have told us."

"If anyone knew, even Deuce, or can you imagine Blaze? If you think they hunted you before . . . the Chief would have blown up the entire Pacyfik region if she had known what was at stake."

"So what am I supposed to do now?"

"Study the *Justar Journal*," Booker said. "We have a new kind of world to create. It will be unlike anything that has been before, and we'll need all the wisdom we can uncover."

"Why will people want that kind of change?" Grandyn asked. "Why will they listen?"

"Because they are tired of a world ruled by greed, hate, and fear," Booker said. "We will teach them how to go within, and once they've learned it, the greatest fear faced by humanity will have been removed. The fear of death."

"They definitely know about death."

"Yes, death has always been the ultimate fear. It has governed everything. But once they can let go of that fear, they can let go of *all* fear. That means no greed, no hatred, no fear of anything. We're free. We are finally free."

EPILOGUE

Portland, Oregon Area, January 29, 2102

It had been more than four months since the war ended. This was the first time Grandyn had seen Nelson in person since those terrible days. They shared a long hug, filled with silent remorse and questions that could never be answered. Grandyn wondered how long Nelson could go on, smoking and eating and drinking. The irony was that Nelson had within his grasp the ability to live another hundred years, or longer, but he wasn't interested. Maybe he was like UC. He wanted to know what came next, or maybe he just didn't want to see this place anymore. Too many tortured memories.

"Oh how we torgged it up," Nelson often said. "But the stories are all in the torg-ups . . . there's no drama in peace and happiness unless it's pretend."

"You look good," Grandyn lied.

"Do I?" Nelson asked skeptically. "You've been spending too much time underground in the City then." Nelson crushed out a bac.

"Maybe," Grandyn said. "It's a hard place to leave."

"I bet, especially with Fye pregnant again. Congratulations."

Grandyn nodded, remembering the lava tubes, his parents, Vida, so many things. His father had still not ever been found, and Grandyn planned to devote the rest of his life to discovering what had happened to him.

Nelson and Grandyn wandered until they found their assigned seats. The crowd was so large that they had to move the event outside to accommodate everyone. Fortunately, it was an unseasonably warm, and dry winter day in the Oregon Area.

"All those years ago, when you started this revolution," Grandyn began in hushed tones, as one of the speakers was already on stage. "On one of those days when Chelle, Drast, and you were sitting around some college coffee shop . . . if you'd known Chelle and Drast would end up dead, would you still have done everything you did? Marched forward into the—"

"First, we didn't *start* the revolution. It began long before us. We just joined it. Truth be told, the damned Aylantik bastards are due all the responsibility. PAWN never would have existed without them." He stared off into the distance. A brief smile collapsing before it found any lasting form. "And shoot yes, we would have done it. We were revolutionaries, Chelle and Drast most of all, and revolutionaries sometimes die for the cause. Sometimes that's best, because they know only how to fight for change. Once they get it, they wander around lost."

Grandyn nodded. "How's Deuce?"

"I don't see him much," Nelson said. "He's so busy changing the world. It's funny. He was never meant to win the war."

"No, like Booker said, Deuce was meant to win what came after. And he seems to be doing it."

"Twain and Munna are helping with the transition. Strange having the world's wealthiest man working to make the world run without money," Nelson said. "Kind of like that woman who took over PharmaForce, Sarlo. She's been leading the charge to get everyone off pharmaceuticals."

"But there have been thousands of healings," Grandyn said.

"Tens of thousands," Nelson corrected. "I'm about to release a new book about why some are choosing to learn the ways of rejuvenation, and why some want to live and die the way we always have."

"Don't you want to see what we can do with all the List Keepers' knowledge?"

"No, I've seen enough," Nelson replied. "I've read the *Justar Journal* enough times that I'm dizzy from the change, the possibilities, the great purpose of it all."

Pointing to a uniformed AOI agent, Grandyn said, "That still makes me nervous."

"My nephew, Osc, runs the friendly, gentle AOI now, but I get nervous too. I suppose we need them during these changing times. There are still those afraid of a world without fear."

"And then there's Blaze," Grandyn said.

"Yes, he's more famous than ever, building CHRUDEs to do all the hard cleanup. But no more Imps, not when the List Keepers are showing everyone how to reach those levels of intelligence and spiritual insight without having a machine wired into their body."

"What would my parents think of all this?" Grandyn asked.

"Your mother was a lot like Chelle, only smarter. Not to take anything away from Chelle, she was a hell of a strategist. But your mother . . . " He paused and allowed himself a moment to drift back to a happy time that had once been stolen. "Harper was brilliant. And she was a fiery revolutionary. She wanted the truth so badly that each day was a lifelong quest to find it."

He looked at Grandyn with complete adoration.

"She would have been so proud of all that you did. Grandyn Happerman, brave and true. And if you want to know what your dad would think, just listen to my speech."

Nelson stood as a woman behind the podium finished introducing him, and he walked up onto the stage.

"Thank you for being here today at the dedication of the Runit Happerman Library. My name is Nelson Wright. I appreciate your applause, but contrary to the reputation bestowed upon me, I'm not really a hero of the revolution. I am simply an author. But I did know real heroes.

"The first was Runit Happerman, the man we honor here today. His acts of courage are well known, as are those of his wife, Harper, and his son, Grandyn. Grandyn's losses, like his contributions, were extraordinary. I hope you've all read about him in my latest book. That book, as well as all the so-called 'controversial' books we saved, are available in this library, and thanks to the generosity of Deuce Lipton, there will be printed versions of all these books at twenty-eight more Runit Happerman libraries around the world. For, as we've learned, digital is convenient and easy, but sometimes we need to hold something tangible. It is easier to protect something we can touch. Runit taught us that. He would be so happy to see that we will not only continue to learn from these books, but that we have survived because of them."

"Excuse me is the seat taken?" Runit asked Grandyn quietly, pointing at the chair Nelson had left.

"No, go ahead," Grandyn said, before looking up and instantly being consumed by shock and a flood of emotions so intense he was unable to find words. He threw himself into his father's arms. "I knew it," he finally said, "I knew you didn't die."

"And neither did you," Runit said, his hands in Grandyn's hair. Both men crying. "Somehow we survived this awful mess."

"We did, but what happened to you, Dad? Where were you?" Then noticing how skinny his father was asked, "Are you okay?"

"There will be time enough for that later. Just tell me it's true. That we won, that Aylantik is really done, the world is on its way becoming a better place, and that the books are finally safe."

"Yes, it's all true," Grandyn said, looking into his father's eyes.

"There's so much to tell you, and I'm not sure you going to believe half of it."

"Good to see Nelson," Runit said, motioning to the stage. "I see he somehow he managed to keep himself alive. And Chelle?"

Grandyn shook his head. "No, sorry, Dad. She ran the revolution until it was almost won. But didn't survive the final battle."

Runit nodded. Grandyn could see the sadness in his father's eyes, eyes that had known so much sadness. Yet they also contained hope, and glowed with the ecstatic light of their reunion, of the new world.

Nelson oblivious to the scene, motioned to an AOI agent. "I know some of you still flinch at the sight of the AOI agents, but they are different now, and the initials were kept in tribute to the great irony. It is ironic, of course, because in the end the dark force we fought against turned out to contain the thing that saved us.

"You've heard of BLAXERs and PAWN, Creatives and Rejectionists, TreeRunners and List Keepers, even Trapciers, but we would not be standing here today without those within the AOI who risked everything to turn on their evil masters. There were too many to mention, but tens of thousands of AOI agents, who knew the crimes of that agency better than most, decided the time had come to say, 'No more!' and saved us from complete destruction. So, it would not be right to honor Runit without also paying tribute to Polis Drast, who also saved the books and helped save us all. The AOI, his legacy, renamed the Allies of Information."

Nelson looked out to see Grandyn's reactions to his speech and suddenly caught sight of Runit, and stopped midsentence. "Shoot, I don't believe this," his voice trembling, "Is it true? Is that really you?"

Runit waved at his old friend.

"Ladies and gentlemen, it's one of the true founding fathers of our new world, a man who, like the hero of a novel, long given up for dead, is somehow resurrected. Runit Happerman."

During the applause and a standing ovation, Nelson attempted to coax Runit to join him on stage. The librarian shook his head, and pushed his hand away.

"Go on, Dad. Tell them about the books."

Runit couldn't refuse his son.

"While we're waiting," Nelson began, I'm reminded of what Ralph Waldo Emerson said, 'In a library we are surrounded by many hundreds of dear friends imprisoned by an enchanter in paper.'"

After making his way up to the stage, Runit and Nelson exchanged a heartfelt embrace, where they both whispered the same words at the same time, "Sorry about Chelle." The two old friends smiled at each other, before Nelson, went to join Grandyn.

"Thank you," Runit said quieting the crowd. "Nelson knows I can never let a quote go unanswered and appropriately, with all we've been through, the words of Ray Bradbury from *Fahrenheit 451* seem a fitting response to Emerson. 'Books were only one type of receptacle where we stored a lot of things we were afraid we might forget. There is nothing magical in them, at all. The magic is only in what books say, how they stitched the patches of the universe together into one garment for us.'"

Nelson raised his hand, as if toasting Runit, Bradbury, and all of them.

Runit bowed his head and began again. "I could tell you the whole long story today, of how Harper Happerman, Chelle Wright, Grandyn, Nelson, and I saved the books and, with the help of many other heroes—brave and true, changed the world. But as it turned out, these past few months, I had some time on my hands so I wrote it all down. Take my word for it, it'll be much easier for you to read it in my upcoming book, I really think you'll like the ending. It's called *The Last Librarian.*"

END OF BOOK THREE

THE ADVENTURE CONTINUES!

There are currently thirteen Booker thrillers divided into four related series.

It doesn't matter which series is read first.

The Cosega Sequence
The CapStone Conspiracy
The Inner Movement
The Justar Journal (The Last Librarian series)

ABOUT THE AUTHOR

USA TODAY Bestselling Author Brandt Legg uses his unusual real life experiences to create page-turning novels. He's traveled with CIA agents, dined with senators and congressmen, mingled with astronauts, chatted with governors and presidential candidates, had a private conversation with a Secretary of Defense he still doesn't like to talk about, hung out with Oscar and Grammy winners, had drinks at the State Department, been pursued by tabloid reporters, and spent a birthday at the White House by invitation from the President of the United States.

At age eight, Legg's father died suddenly, plunging his family into poverty. Two years later, while suffering from crippling migraines, he started in business, and turned a hobby into a multi-million-dollar empire. National media dubbed him the "Teen Tycoon," and by the mid-eighties, Legg was one of the top young entrepreneurs in America, appearing as high as number twenty-four on the list (when Steve Jobs was #1, Bill Gates #4, and Michael Dell #6). Legg still jokes that he should have gone into computers.

By his twenties, after years of buying and selling businesses, lever-aging, and risk-taking, the high-flying Legg became ensnarled in the financial whirlwind of the junk bond eighties. The stock market crashed and a firestorm of trouble came down. The Teen Tycoon racked up more than a million dollars in legal fees, was betrayed by those closest to him, lost his entire fortune, and ended up serving time for financial improprieties.

After a year, Legg emerged from federal prison, chastened and wiser, and began anew. More than twenty-five years later, he's now using all that hard-earned firsthand knowledge of conspiracies, corruption and high finance to weave his tales. Legg's books pulse with authenticity.

His series have excited nearly a million readers around the world. Although he refused an offer to make a television movie about his life as a teenage millionaire, his autobiography is in the works. There has also been interest from Hollywood to turn his thrillers into films. With any luck, one day you'll see your favorite characters on screen.

He lives in the Pacific Northwest, with his wife and son, writing full time, in several genres, containing the common themes of adventure, conspiracy, and thrillers. Of all his pursuits, being an author and crafting plots for novels is his favorite.

For more information, please visit his website, or to contact Brandt directly, email him: Brandt@BrandtLegg.com, he loves to hear from readers and always responds!

BrandtLegg.com

BOOKS BY BRANDT LEGG

Chasing Rain

Chasing Fire

Chasing Wind

Chasing Dirt

Chasing Life

Chasing Kill

Chasing Risk

Chasing Mind

Cosega Search (Cosega Sequence #1)

Cosega Storm (Cosega Sequence #2)

Cosega Shift (Cosega Sequence #3)

Cosega Sphere (Cosega Sequence #4)

Cosega Source (Cosega Sequence #5)

CapWar ELECTION (CapStone Conspiracy #1)

CapWar EXPERIENCE (CapStone Conspiracy #2)

CapWar EMPIRE (CapStone Conspiracy #3)

The Last Librarian (Justar Journal #1)

The Lost TreeRunner (Justar Journal #2)

The List Keepers (Justar Journal #3)

Outview (Inner Movement #1)

Outin (Inner Movement #2)

Outmove (Inner Movement #3)

ACKNOWLEDGMENTS

Thanks to Phil, Maureen, Lance, Jenni, Cathy, Laura, Christa, Amy, Jen-Jen, Anne-Marie, Eric, Scott, Bart, Wendy, Greg, Carol, Jason, Eliz, Chris, Linda, Rick, Karen, Geoff, Anne, Lisa, Kelly, Kristy, Kristi, Mary, Julie, Leo, Anita, Steve, Dave, Ginny, Mike, Angel, Ron, Angie, Michelle, Gail, Craig, June, Curt, Jenny, Terri, Jennifer, Leslie, Claire, Dan, Brian, Rick, Jill, Megan, Alex, Doug, Jeff, Kimball, Sean, Sue, Carrie, Stacey, Tim, Christine, Jim, John, Tom, Glenn, Cindy, Clint and all the rest people I grew up with in Vienna, Oakton and Fairfax. Time of our lives! Many of you have crossed the decades to help get the word out about my books, and that has amazed me and filled me with gratitude. Forgive me if I forgot to name you.

Love and appreciation to Bonnie Brown Koeln, for keeping it consistent; to Roanne Legg, the one who influences so much more than the story. And to my mother, Barbara Blair, for believing I'm better than I am. Another round of appreciation to Melanie C. Hansen for volunteering to hunt down any new typos I created with the changes. And finally to Teakki, who patiently waited for little army-men battles, or any number of other great adventures, until I finished writing each day.

DEDICATION

This book is dedicated to Teakki and Ro

GLOSSARY

A-Council – Secretive group that controls the economy and decides who will be elected.

ACE – Aylantik Commission on the Environment.

ADAM – Atom-Displacing-Adjusted-Molecule technology – Reduces the weight of objects.

AirSlider – Jet-propelled scooter, sometimes equipped with laser munitions.

AirView – Virtual INU (computer) monitors.

AOI – Aylantik Office of Intelligence.

AOI Chief – Top AOI official.

Android – An artificial being, advanced robot, with approximate human appearance. Manufactured to replace humans in many jobs.

Aylantik Government – Group running the world since the end of the Banoff War.

Aylantik Records Circle (ARC) – Manages ID chips.

Aylantik region – One of twenty-four regions governed by the Aylantik.

Bacs – Privately made cigarettes.

Banoff Pandemic – Plague which wiped out more than half the world's population in 2025.

Banoff War – War which followed the plague. In which the Aylantik coalition secured power.

Bearing rights – Rights to have one child could be sold for up to 20,000 digis after age eighteen.

BLAXERs – Deuce Lipton's private "security" army.

Breeze-Blowers - Dust-sized computers, equipped with video transmitters, that blow in the breeze.

CAAP – Corporate Assets Acquisition Parity Board.

Chamber-slot – Plan to breach all AOI prisons at once.

Chiantik region – One of twenty-four regions governed by the Aylantik.

Chicago85 – Company that sells spy, intelligence, and surveillance technologies to the government.

CHRUDEs - Cloned Human Replacement Unit DesTIn Enabled – Human-like robots.

Collins-HG3 – Autonomous flying weapon.

Com – Universal language that has replaced all other languages, including English.

Courier – People who personally deliver confidential messages or small parcels.

Creatives – Writers, artists, musicians, etc., who tend to have liberal views and prefer total freedom.

Cyborg – Cybernetic Organism constructed from organic and biomechatronic parts.

DACAR – Data Arts Correction And Revisions Project.

DesTIn - Design Taught Intelligence, or "DesTIn," an advanced artificial intelligence program.

Digi-link – World Central Bank.

Digis – Form of digital currency.

Digital-drapes – Where people download books, movies, music, or whatever data they desire.

Doneharvest – AOI martial law style crackdown.

Earth Parks – Replaced National parks and protected lands.

ELS – Equidistant Letter Sequence – Type of code for hiding messages in text.

Enforcers — Security unit of PharmaForce and Lance Miner's private army.

Exchange – Code word for the second start of the revolution.

Eysen-INU – Leading type of Information Navigation Units.

FA – False Audio equipped micro-whistler-FAs.

Field – What the Internet evolved into – Everything is connected.

Field-View – Secure videoconference.

Flash – Equivalent to email/text/instant message.

Flo-wing – Super-fast vertical takeoff mini aircraft – The evolution of helicopters.

FRIDG – Facial Recognition Identification Grid.

Grunges – Slang for AOI agents.

Health-Circle – Or AHC – Aylantik government agency responsible for health care.

Hops – State run health and fitness facilities.

ID chip - Secured into every Aylantik citizen. Details all personal data.

Implant – AI computer brain interface implanted in humans resulting in super intelligence.

Imps – Slang for people who have computer implants.

INU – Information Navigation Units – Powerful marble-sized computer/communications device.

InvisiLine – Secret bank and currency control.

ISBN – International Standard Book Number – Unique book identifier system.

Lasershod – Advanced handgun.

Laserstiks – Advanced, highly accurate, long-range weapon.

LEVs – Levitating Electro Vehicles – Solar-propelled floating vehicles.

Micro-whistler-Mimics (MWM) – Device that fits into mouth – Blocks conversations, broadcasts a false audio.

Micro-drones – Bug-sized drones, used individually or in swarms.

Media no-list – Topics not allowed to be covered by the media – PAWN, Rejectionists, etc.

Medical Sensor – Small coin-sized patch worn to monitor all health data.

Monitoring-mimic-drones – Bird-sized, sophisticated drones. Almost impossible to detect.

Nano-camo – Tarps that automatically change to the surrounding landscape like a chameleon.

Nano-tracers – Seeker-defeating microscopic decals applied to the face.

Neuro-cap – Erases data and memory from both human, cyborg, CHRUDE, and Imp brains.

Neuron-mites – Mind reading nano-sized INUs.

Nusun – Single nation utopian Earth.

Over-hold – Instantly contouring chair/gliding sofa, which applies massage and aromatherapy.

Pacyfik region – One of twenty-four regions governed by the Aylantik.

PAWN – People Against World Nation – Leading revolutionary group.

Phantom-Shield Nano-device – Sends holographic image into the same path and trajectory.

PharmaForce – World's largest pharmaceutical company, controlled by Lance Miner.

Plantik – The naturally derived plantik that replaced plastic.

POPs – PAWN Operational Pods – Underground PAWN facilities.

Proof – A-Council's name for the generation that survived the Banoff.

Pulse-rods – Communication-disrupting weapon.

Q-lifts – Ultra fast elevator that uses atom-displacing-adjusted-molecule technology.

Red-1953 – Chemical used to burn books.

Rejectionists – People who rejected Aylantik rules and modern society.

Retina-synch - Allows wearer to access data through what amounts to a micro-contact lens.

Said-scans - Postmortem brain scans.

Sat-grids – Satellite monitoring system.

Scram Network – Emergency, secret communications system that operated apart from the Field.

Seeker – AOI camera network.

Shockers – A hand-held laser-powered pulse bomb about the size of a hand grenade.

Slide – Thumb drive-like data carrying device for INUs.

Sonic-bomb – Vibration frequency device that can shatter everything within a specified radius.

Sophisticated-GPS – Tracking program able to predict where an object is heading or came from.

StarFly – Largest company in the world's fourth biggest industry: Space. Owned by Deuce Lipton.

Swarm-Drones – Bug-sized drones, equipped with cameras – Can go anywhere a flying insect can.

Tech-tracing – Can track the fingerprint of any electronic device from the web of satellites.

Tekfabrik – Multipurpose nano-fabric capable of changing color, size, and texture. Self-cleaning.

Thread – High capacity memory stick about the size of a short piece of angel hair pasta.

Torgon – Curse word in the com language. Also used as torg, torgged, or torging.

Traditionals – Name used to describe ordinary humans without implants, etc.

Trapicers – Mysterious revolutionary group.

Tru-chair – Chair that conforms to the sitter's anatomy and delivers acupressure. Uses energy by harvesting body heat.

Wavesuits – Tekfabrik suits equipped with tracking-blocking capabilities.

Whistler – Tiny device and app that blocks AOI monitoring of INUs.

World Premier – Elected leader of the United Earth and head of the Aylantik government.

Zoom – Similar to a phone call with video.

Made in the USA
Middletown, DE
04 May 2022